THE
FARM

Hell Hath No Bounds...

(The Ranger Poltergeist)

By

Albert A. Ernst

"" —

THE FARM.

By Albert A. Ernst.

ONE.

May 29, 1994.

When Mike Aurora turned off from the #3 highway toward the small hamlet of Ranger, fifteen miles southwest of Leoville, Saskatchewan, he was reminiscing over the freak inheritance which had brought him out here to the boondocks and the strange but wonderful farmstead which he had inherited from his uncle Joe. One could hardly call the old hamlet of Ranger a village anymore (though it had once been such) where the derelict farm sat untended, uncared for. Uncle Joe's acreage was one of the few not to be grabbed up by the land-hungry, big-time local farmers who had turned the northern grain-belt into a kind of Communistic gulag where the rich prosper and the small shareholder like uncle Joe – well – sort of lapsed into a senile memory of better days. Most of the smaller farmsteads had either long-since ceased to exist or been bullied by the Government to "Go Big." Most had "Gone Big" and grown a Big Fat Debt. Unpayable, of course. Except for old uncle Joe. Joe Aurora had had a knack for keeping his head above water.

His nephew, Mike, pondered this as he swung his old but reliable Chev Impala station wagon onto the gravel road which passed as a main road out here in east-central Saskatchewan (one of the Great White North's most impoverished provinces, where there were more cows than people!). There were more trees here than down south: tamarack, birch, poplar, spruce, black willow. Further north, muskeg. Black Sabbath's *"Wasp"* droned quietly from the station wagon's cassette player, mirroring Aurora's own morbid personality. At twenty-three years old, he had grand plans for the summer (let's not even think of winter). He'd quit his crummy mechanic's job two weeks ago, began packing his meagre belongings inside his shabby $300 basement suite in Shellbrook and discontinued his telephone and electricity service (the absentée owner was having the place condemned!).

He'd bought himself a stack of second-hand, outdoor

survival guides, studied them with the raptness of a monastic pupil for a few days, then decided his career move. Not only had uncle Joe (his only living relative) bequeathed him ten thousand dollars but a decent farmhouse and a small but charming homestead. Mike wanted to be a writer. He would organize his material here, plan an outline for his first full-length horror novel.

In the meantime, he'd consider doing odd jobs; there were plenty of farmers hereabouts, some good friends of his, who could use an extra hand during harvest, and he wasn't averse to hard labour.

Mike Aurora, unmarried, single, had much going for him this hot, sultry, blue day. He was no city-slicker off to the great blue yonder, plunging unheeding into unknown wilderness like some 19th-century pioneer. He knew what he was doing. He'd lived on a farm near Prince Albert as a youth, at eighteen moved to Shellbrook, landed himself a job in a local garage. He had few friends. A loner by nature.

The rough, gravel road was flanked on either side by towering Jack pines, brooding brutes spreading their dark green canopy over the murky forest floor. The grid road – a scarcely maintained logging road – dipped sickeningly into breathtaking ravines, irksome pebbles and grapefruit-size rocks posing a perilous juggernaut for tires as Aurora's slate-gray station wagon sped along at a barely legal fifty-five m.p.h. *Oh, so sorry, 80 k.p.h now, innit?* thought Mike cynically to himself. No fan of metric. Not Mister Politically Correct. He cranked up the cassette player's volume. In the back of his overstuffed '77 Impala, all of Mike's worldly possessions–which wasn't much–filled the rear up to its long side windows.

What he really needed out here was a WOMAN, Mike thought to himself.

Unfortunately, the few sexy broads in Shellbrook and surrounding districts thought Mike a bit strange. No–loony. He didn't drink a lot, that was his problem. Hadn't attended any parties lately, either. Stayed away from nose candy, wacky weed, etc. Loved gothic horror novels a tad too much. Didn't socialize a lot. Tacked horror movie posters onto his bedroom walls. Aurora digged morbid, historical things: WW I and II; ancient history; criminology. Heavy metal music. Well, that was okay amongst Mike's crowd, but those kind of girls were – what's a pleasant word – whores. (Rings in the nose, lips, eyebrows, he grumbled to himself, ought to be restricted to *RED-LIGHT DISTRICTS AND ZOOS!)*

The rutted grid road created havoc with the station wagon's suspension. A blazing-hot sun seeped through the car's windshield, turning its upholstery into sticky, hardened red lava against bare skin. The orangey scent of pine lingered in the pure country air. Mike flinched whenever his bare arm touched the seat. He clicked off the stereo volume, pulled out the little black cassette and tossed it into an open glove compartment. He couldn't wait to reach the farm, to explore the numerous shacks which he hadn't had keys for when he'd first visited the place almost four weeks ago. That he'd found odd. Of all the ancillary buildings on the farm, only the large, two-storey house had locks which the executor's keys fit. The rickety outbuildings had defied scrutiny through their dusty, grimy windows. Most were locked, however. Mike would find out soon enough what junk they held. Probably antiquated farm machinery.

Mike had heard that old Joe had been a connoisseur of trashed antiques and various bric-à-brac, or as Joe's friends would have it – junk.

The Impala purred along almost noiselessly save for the snap of twigs and constant thump of small rocks under its large tires. The narrow, rutted grid road rose sharply, plunging downwards once more into a gully resonating with the urgent sound of a swift-moving culvert stream; pine cones scattered hereabouts dotted the grid thoroughfare a rusty red. Aurora breathed deep, inhaling the sweet, pungent odor of conifer and grasslands growing in rampant profusion along the semi-abandoned roadside. Seldom did traffic frequent this old backwoods country road anymore except for the occasional, leviathan tractor. Here was boreal wilderness tract, untouched, rife with marshland. It was a welcome change from the urban environs of P.A. (Prince Albert) and Shellbrook where Mike had often shuttled back and forth during his high-school Bantam hockey tournaments (he'd been a high-flying scorer). Or from his downtown Shellbrook apartment and garage-job site, for that matter. Mike was glad he'd quit his piss-ant job at Macy's Texaco gas station. Four years he'd worked at that oily grease-monkey's hellhole, pumping gas for three years before working his way up as an apprentice mechanic. He learned fast. He'd learnt well. Mike loved motors, engines of all kinds, gas, diesel, two-cycle, four-cycle, V-8, you name it. He just had a knack for greasy things. Like his old man (who'd been dead for fifteen years). After his old man croaked Mike had been sent to an orphanage in North Battleford, then to various foster-homes.

Twenty yards ahead, an overgrown, sorry excuse for a road branched off from the main route, snaking its way through a high meadow brimming with alfalfa and prairie thistle. It hadn't been harvested for over two years. Mike turned off sharply to his left, almost missing the obscured turn-off, cranking the station wagon's power steering hard to angle the car deftly onto a dirt trail. The big, clumsy vehicle scythed its way through the uncut meadow noisily, occasionally rising suddenly over a low knoll then zooming downwards with an exciting lurch which left one feeling giddy. The old road to Joe's place hadn't been tended to in years. Knobbly, sprawling elm (Dutch elm disease seemingly having left this acreage alone) stood sentinel along the waving, blue/yellow meadow. Purple bellflowers grew everywhere. The trail itself, though potholed, wasn't too badly overgrown, but hemmed in tightly by overzealous three-foot-tall thistles. (Aurora wondered what kind of fertilizers the farmers used, for he'd never seen weeds so run amok this time of year!) Dinner-plate-size rocks jolted the car's big tires mercilessly, grass winding sonorously around the Impala's axles.

The station wagon rolled effortlessly over the terrain, only minding occasional rocks which it climbed turtlishly over. The stench of exhaust fumes fouled the air, masking the aroma of dog-rose and spruce, alfalfa and buttercup. Big, bright yellow flag iris poked their somehow sinister heads over purple-blue alfalfa fronds, as if watching the long, gray automobile as it passed, turning their eyeless faces slowly toward this leviathan invading their field.

A strong west wind rippled the meadow, giving Mike the unsettling feeling that the local plantlife was somehow *sentient*.

Jesus, I've just arrived, and already I'm going stir crazy!, Aurora thought to himself humourlessly.

Unripened alfalfa expanses showed ruddily in the distance; wildflowers and the scent of herbs lingered on the midday airstream. A flock of Canada geese flew by overhead in a V formation, squawking their heads off.

The farm lay a quarter of a mile ahead, one of the few areas not bulldozed to make way for new farmland. Mike was no farmer. He hated the bastards. (With a few exceptions.) He'd turn the old farmstead into an acreage. Large stands of aspen intermixed with birch and spruce practically surrounded the bucolic, decaying homestead, whose environs come autumn would turn a glorious shade of yellow. A few tamarack, nearby, would drop their needles come autumn. Blurry, gray shapes of derelict farm buildings showed up hazily in the distance. Concentric rings of rotten, collapsed wooden fencing bound the large clearing, the remnants of a previous generation's corrals and stockades. The place had once been a pig farm. Uncle Joe had kept a few cattle for his own use. Nothing else except for some chickens and ducks. All this Mike had learned from his uncle's executor, a local man (a bozo) from nearby Spiritwood who hadn't had a lot good to say about his dear, long-lost uncle, bane of the district by all accounts. For the last twenty-five years the old man had been a recluse, only occasionally straying away from his own backyard to replenish his supplies at the local general store (no longer in existence). Mike, ironically, had never met the man, or even known of his existence. Indeed, it seemed a miracle that he should inherit the old man's dough, for it was well known that Joe had no love for his fellow men. Other than that and what a few burn-out acquaintances had told him, Mike knew nothing about him.

The old farmhouse's steeply sloped, shingled roof rose slightly over the trees, having a rather somber attic loft with louvres for windows. It was a simple, gabled roof, backwoods type of architecture. Mike had loved the old house at first sight; even if it *was* a terrible mess. A typical, bachelor's house. Perhaps worse. Mike figured it would take him all summer to clean the filthy, run-down shack. Although structurally sound, it looked as if it hadn't been swept, washed, or painted in decades. And old Joe had been clearly senile, having draped uncured bearskins up in the attic. Mike had nearly freaked when he came upon one! Thousands of empty cans had been stacked inside the kitchen entrance. Perhaps in hope of a premature recycling movement?

The Chevy Impala coasted quickly down an incline, and he was there. The rustic scenery was like a Little House on the Prairie episode, with perhaps a few more trees. Mike flicked the ignition off, then stretched lazily, sighing with a happy smile.

Contented, Mike opened the driver's door, stepping

out onto the pathway's gloriously warm sunshine, shutting the car door and leisurely drawing a pack of Craven "A" menthols from his shirt pocket. One of his goals this summer was to quit smoking, something he wouldn't be able to achieve in a smoke-filled garage. All of his pals smoked.

Out here he could concentrate on just that. First make the place livable.   Fix any leaks. The immediate future excited him. (He was going to be a writer, or so he hoped!) He'd bought a brand-new Smith Corona typewriter a few months back, and now it seemed that opportunity was at hand. He'd begin his novel here, a vampire epic set in upstate New York and a fiend-infested cemetery. Aurora's grade ten education would suffice. He'd been writing short stories for a good many years, had even had one published in a local, small-press fiction magazine. He had the general outline figured out in his head already. Now all he needed was time and solitude. The old house would provide just that. As for his funds, Mike had withdrawn five hundred bucks from Shellbrook Credit Union, not a lot for a year, perhaps, but then $10,000 really wasn't a lot of cash nowadays. Aurora often wondered where his uncle had gotten such a wad. Maybe he'd sold some cattle?, Mike thought. It certainly wouldn't last forever. But living out here could be cheap; Mike fully intended to clear the thorns and shrubs from the garden area, grow himself a vegetable garden beside the house.

Sunlight glinted with a glare off the derelict house's windowpanes as Mike drew his Bic lighter from his shirt pocket and lit himself a cigarette. He glanced around pleasedly, noting the tumbledown, pioneer-era barn behind the house leaning drunkenly to the left and vulnerable to the next prairie wind which might come along. Green moss festooned the decaying barn's sagging, saddle roof. Opposite it some distance away stood another, somewhat newer, construct; another barn by the looks of it. It had a quaint, gambrel roof. Mike glanced up at his uncle's farmhouse, wondering how much repair-work those aged wooden shingles needed. The house had no plumbing. A sturdily-built outdoor toilet sixty paces distant, weathered by years of prairie storms, stood unobtrusively within the shelter of three looming, black poplar.

Mike sauntered down the uncared-for dirt path toward the house then down a flagstone pathway, whipping out his wallet from his back pocket and retrieving the house-keys from its side compartment. The smell of rotted manure wafted across the yard, a not unpleasant scent. Faded, brownish paint on the verandah looked flaked and severely weathered, the western-style, bulbous balustrade lending the humble farmhouse an unexpectedly grand look to its front deck. An addition had been built against the building's east side, a possibly later introduction. Nonetheless, its sloping roof sagged.

Aurora mounted the steps carefully, cautious of the verandah's creaking, sagging timbers. He jiggled a skeleton key into the door's rusty, old-fashioned lock, twisting the metal doorknob open with a "clack." Hmmph. Some anti-burglary device. *"Remind me to replace this with a new lock,"* Mike muttered to himself.

The foyer's musty odor of neglect assailed Mike immediately. Plenty of Lysol and T.S.P (tri-sodium phosphate) would be needed to freshen the air, clean mildew off the walls, floor, ceiling.

He stepped inside the kitchen, glancing about indifferently to the grime and general squalor of the place. Aurora had never seen such a mess. Mike closed the door, and then, to remedy the sudden, disconcerting lack of light, opened it wide – airing the place out. He went over to the white porcelain kitchen sink (now rusted), peering into its empty basin. Last fall's dead spiders, flies, and red ants crouched permanently in its deep, twin sink. Grime smeared the windowpanes directly above, blocking light. Shreds of cobweb hung from warped window-frames. A lone spider scurried up one of the strands, disappearing into the woodwork. Colorless, gashed (flowered?) linoleum lay on part of the kitchen floor; the rest was white tiles. The faded linoleum had to go. The white tiles could be cleaned, and would be more useful than linoleum. Mike wandered aimlessly about the house, assessing its potential, noting in his mind what needed serious repair: But he was no carpenter; mechanic only by circumstance. The place would need scouring, endless toil. He'd figured out where he would put his Hi-Fi equipment. Upstairs, the three bedrooms were empty, devoid of beds and furniture. Where the hell did old Joe sleep?, Mike wondered. Attic? Mike doubted that. No windowpanes up there. The farmhouse had no electricity (it once had, though, by all accounts), only a monolithic Blaze King oven/stove, a beautiful white porcelain-fronted antique hulking in the living room, a monstrosity used for baking, country-style, and for heating water inside its reservoir. Its tap still turned. Not corroded. Outside the building stood an old-fashioned, hand-pump-operated well – not a pleasant sight.

Everywhere lay empty cans, tin cans in the kitchen, living room, pantry; big ones, small ones, a lifetime's worth of discarded debris making it hard to even maneuver around.

Mike found most of the furniture up in the back of the attic: bedsheets, blankets, bedsprings, mattresses tattered and rotted, dressers, an armchair – which confirmed his earlier suspicion – old man Aurora was senile beyond the umpteenth degree.

His nephew stood amongst the jumbled furniture up in the attic in befuddlement, looking about wildly, frowning. The old rat had basically lived up here, alone in the dark, eating crackers and bonbons. Mike was amazed anew that the old codger hadn't frozen to death. Crumbs littered the tatty red carpet, along with various candies and candy-bar wrappers. Mike laughed aloud to himself, saying he'd burn most of this shit.   From what little he'd heard from the bonehead executor, old Joe Aurora had been loopy for several years before the old bastard kicked the bucket. Mike was sure the world was not grieving.

Although he'd never met him, common gossip implied Aurora's uncle was crazy as a shit-house rat. In other words, detested by virtually everyone hereabouts. Mike had heard he'd been one unpleasant old coot.

He trudged back down the attic steps, finding himself in the spacious kitchen once more. (Spacious but for the hundreds of tin cans, that is.) He slumped contentedly onto a chair beside the big, sturdy, oakwood table, just resting. Now that he was here, he knew not where to start. So many things to do. Should he flip a coin? Sweep, wash floor, clean windows, wash out cupboards, haul down some of the furniture? How about neither.

This was getting him nowhere. Mike stood up,

stretched, then marched toward the   open door. He dashed down the verandah's steps and bounded off toward the various outbuildings, ramshackle sheds, granaries, and derelict barns out back. A dozen round, rotting hay bales sat inside the big red barn, their pungent alfalfa fumes scenting the barnyard's pure, country air. Uncle Joe had sold off all of his Jerseys a few months before his untimely death – to cover unpaid arrears, apparently (as if foretelling his demise?), conveniently solving that little dilemma. (He must've axed his chickens and ducks as well, Aurora thought to himself.) The last thing on earth Mike needed was a dozen or so cows lowing out in the pasture. He seriously considered getting a couple of goats however, maybe some chickens. Beyond the dark, sorry-looking corrals, a hay meadow lay peacefully soaking up sunshine, where little blue butterflies fluttered amongst the flowers.

A few derelict and totally wrecked old vehicles sat about, probably abandoned for decades, but no sign of a pickup truck, or car, in any way, shape, or form one could consider driveable. Probably sold, or stolen by some opportunistic person or persons unknown.

Big heaps of decade-old manure near the derelict, saddle-roof barn would provide a veritable gold mine for one's garden. Impressive stands of dead timber nearby, with a little hard work, would supply a cold winter's firewood. Plenty of good, seasoned poplar. He'd have to buy himself a chainsaw. He could probably drag the deadfalls from the bushes, avoid having to get a truck. And, a real bright idea this, he'd purchased (through a Canadian mail-order company) recently a state-of-the-art wind charger, a 20lb. mini for small cottages and R.V.s. Mike planned to buy an AC inverter and avoid the cost of purchasing expensive 12-volt appliances. Maybe in the future add a solar panel or two, as well. The past year and a half he'd been trying to learn how to play acoustic and electric guitar, something Mike planned to continue out here, though it was proving a tough grind. He knew he'd certainly never be no Eddy Van Halen. His best friend, Nick Tremaine, had been dabbling with drums for a few years but with no luck (and not much talent). Anyhow, living out here on the farm would be a lonely proposition, so Mike Aurora fully intended to find himself a worthwhile hobby. Several worthwhile hobbies. Aurora suspected however that maintenance and repairs would be a full-time occupation. He was absolutely determined somehow to install an electric well-pump and some plumbing. He'd need to redo the wiring. Apparently, there'd been hydro here, once, but for reasons unknown old Joe had allowed his payments to lapse; eventually, Sask Power had disconnected his service and had recently removed the transformer from its power pole.

Upon inquiring the cost of reconnection, Mike had been quoted a figure of anywhere from six to ten thousand. For twelve hundred bucks (including G.S.T) he'd acquired a wind turbine and two 12-volt, deep-cycle Davidson marine batteries. And he wouldn't have to feel guilty about the environment.

He had a gasoline generator (though grossly undersized), as well, in the back of his station wagon. Because there was *NO WAY* Mike was staying out here, alone, without some form of electricity, during the bleakest of winters.

He meandered back to the faded, flaking farmhouse, in no hurry to begin spring clean-up. Nonetheless he fetched a broom, dustpan, and detergents from the back of his station wagon. Studied the potential of kitchen and living room; he'd soon have the squalid, old house cleaned-up and tidy. Given a year or two. Mike guessed the building's age to be in the sixty-seventy year range. Possibly one of the older homesteads at the time of the province's inception in 1905. He wouldn't bet on that, though. Warped cedar siding, obviously ancient, masked the front of the house; the rest consisted of fieldstone, plywood, and red brick, even a patch of ancient log cabin incorporated into it. An old log cabin originally, later enlarged and rebuilt. The place was severely weathered, splotched with moss. A cock-eyed, iron weathervane/rooster stood on one leg atop the farmhouse's high peak. Low, three-tiered windows harkened back to pioneer days.

Through careful scrutiny Mike discerned the original, mud-patched, log-built cabin buried amongst later refurbishments at the rear of the big, A-frame, two-story dwelling. Tattered, yellowed newspapers still clung to the partially ripped-away siding; another of uncle Joe's idiosyncrasies? Somebody'd been vandalizing the place, ripping away much of the planks at the rear of the old farmhouse. Its flaking three-layer paint had faded to a sickly, bleached, denim blue. The missing planks would have to be replaced, along with some exposed insulation. House repainted, if its decaying wood wished to see another fifty years. Remnants of obsolete electrical fixtures dangled lifelessly from planks or posts; scattered about the backyard lay hundreds of antique glass power-line insulators: these were collectibles, worth money. Glass shards littered the rotten, mossy back steps and yard for a fifty-foot radius. Pine cones snapped underfoot as Aurora wandered along the woods' perimeter, occasionally kicking at a rusty tin can. Speaking of cans, Mike had yet to consider what to do with the humongous piles inside the house. Maybe bury them.

Back inside the farmhouse, Mike busied himself sweeping decades of dust, dirt, and grime into a dustpan and flinging it out the door. (He'd rummage around in the back of his Impala for a garbage can later.) It took him half an hour to sweep the filthy kitchen. He tossed hundreds of rusty, empty cans, jugs, and plastic bottles into a large cardboard box, hauling it out to uncle Joe's garbage pit out back where he chucked the lot. He scoured the worn tiles with Spic-'n'-Span, then the dirty yellow arborite countertop till his knuckles hurt. When he'd finished he no longer recognized the kitchen.

The old house's most redeeming feature, thought Mike, was the foyer's spiked plaster ceiling, and adjoining living room's elaborate, scallop-molded stucco overhead. Fortunately neither had yet begun to flake, obviously a late introduction to the building. But by whom? Mike gazed, head tilted back, at the marvelous plaster designs, an incongruous, civilized addition to such rustic surroundings.

By six o'clock, Mike had hauled his sleeping bag, food hamper, clothes and various odds 'n ends into the house, plonking them down on the living room floor. He brought an armload of dry poplar firewood into the foyer, stacking it in a corner, then lit the mammoth black/white woodstove in the living room. The fire flared up immediately, soon giving the musty farmhouse a warm, cozy feel. Inside the kitchen, windows, table, countertop, walls, floor, cupboards had all been scrubbed clean and disinfected. Mike fried bacon and eggs for supper on the heater's jet black, cast-iron stovetop. He'd washed the old man's faded Tupperware and china, proud of his new, white sink as he dried the dishes, still wondering whether or not to chuck them and use his own. The old man's gas range, a tiny, yucky green antique, wasn't working (or out of propane?, or both).

Mike sat pleased at the big, polished table, savoring greasy bacon and soft-cooked eggs, washed down with a generous draught of orange juice. Twilight settled lethargically over the rustic Saskatchewan countryside, casting a mauve pall over the prairie wilderness. A small clock above the gas range (which he'd wound earlier) ticked away lullingly as Aurora, mouth full of food, pondered tomorrow's agenda. The cluttered living room would be next. Mike thought about cleaning up the old grandfather clock by the banisters and seeing if it still worked. Since his nut of an uncle had dragged most of the house's meagre furnishings up to the attic, Mike would have to haul it all down again. Down the attic's steep, narrow stairs. He'd been surprised there hadn't been a decent bed anywhere. What a drag. He'd noticed an armchair and loveseat up there which would be a chore and a half dragging down. Empty jars, tin cans, wrappers, assorted junk would need to be cleared out of the living room first. But he looked forward to it.

He lit himself his second cigarette of the day, leisurely relaxing after a scrumptious supper (to him, at least), the grease somehow seeming to make a smoke more enjoyable. Aurora sat back, listening to crickets and bullfrogs clicking and ribbiting outside in the dusk, competing for territory somewhere in the mosquito-riddled sloughs and mud holes of north-central Saskatchewan. Barnes' Lake beyond the aspen and spruce wilderness provided much of the cacophony.

A faint, curious, tinkling noise trickled teasingly down from upstairs: a sound of chimes or possibly bells, a high-pitched resonance alien to the hubbub of nature.

Mike, his mouth stuffed with one last slab of bacon, frowned in bewilderment. He listened hard; the faintest of chime-like, fairyish tinkles drifted about from the upper story. Wind chimes? He tried to recall whether he'd seen any upstairs or outside the house.

Slowly, he rose from the table, the kitchen darkening as a crimson sun settled below the tree-fringed western azimuth. Mike stood up, instinctively heading for the decrepit stairs to his left.

On the landing, darkness swallowed the banisters as Mike dashed up the steps, two at a time, halting disorientedly as the queer, musical chiming faded away then renewed itself. He glanced quickly into the desolate trio of bedrooms, darkening by the minute, before being tugged almost magnetically toward the haphazardly narrow attic stairs. The chiming began anew, leading him upwards like a Pied Piper leading rats.

He reached out, pushing open the squeaking attic door at the top step, peering inside into the graying, dusk gloom. Jumbled furniture leaned tipsily against one another, having been crammed haphazardly years ago up in the two, long, intersecting attic bays.

The tinkling stopped. The faintest echo of xylophone-like noises still lingered in the close, musty, attic air. A hint of mouse droppings with decayed insulation clung to the air. Mike stepped shakily into the low attic, crouching, cautious with his steps on the old floorboards as he crept forward into the attic bay, cursing himself for not scrounging a flashlight from his overstuffed duffel bag. The attic was growing dark now, its tin louvres allowing only the slightest glimmer of blood red light from a westward-dying sunset. Slipping around an overturned armchair, Mike glanced up suddenly at a silvery glint of metal high up in a corner of the attic bay.

Wind chimes.

Heart in his mouth, Mike slowly expelled his breath, heart beating wildly.

The gaudy metal chimes dangled motionlessly as Aurora peered up at them, gently touching one of the multicolored crescents with the tip of his finger. Crescents, triangles, squares, circles. A resonating iron alloy which tinkled ever so softly with the slightest breeze. Mike chuckled to himself, his tattooing heart slowing down to a normal pace.

He stepped into the tiny, uncluttered niche near the doorway, gazing about at the ramshackle attic space crowded with boxes, scattered papers, moldy open suitcases. Cat hair clung to the faded, worn furniture. But where was the cat?

"Almost thought you'd come back, you senile old bastard," Mike said aloud, laughing cynically to himself. "No room for ya, old man. This is my house now, not yours. Finders' keepers, losers' weepers."

He laughed aloud again, spinning out of the despondent attic.

No wind stirred up in that dark, cramped attic space, nor, especially, near the rousing chimes.

Yet the air wavered.

TWO.

Flickering flames cast a red glow from the woodstove's firebox as Mike lifted one of the stovetop-rings and slid a slender stick of wood inside, leaving the cast-iron lid off momentarily as he spread his sleeping bag and numerous blankets on the hardwood floor. The room was dark, though his big, six-volt flashlight shone brightly from the kitchen table a few paces away. Springtime nights were still cold, too cool to sleep upstairs, for sure, without central heating – and, certainly, without a bed. A steady chorus of frogs' chatter out in the swampy wilderness filled the unnerving night silence. The house was quiet. Mike unpacked his duffel bag, sorting his toothbrush, toothpaste, deodorant, etc. and piling them atop an ancient dresser. He slid a stack of old Penthouse back-issues into an empty drawer, moving about the room with an attentive crouch, moving this, repositioning that, ever fussy. He stood his brand-new, midnight black Yamaha guitar (still inside its burgundy leather case) in a corner. Earlier he'd unpacked his small, aluminum, unused 300-watt wind charger from its cardboard box; he intended to set it up soon, maybe tomorrow or the next day, on a tall spruce or pine pole next to the house. However, being no electrician, he was certain the high-tech gadget's instruction manual would be confusing in the extreme. He had all the wiring necessary to do the job. Mike planned on driving the seventy-odd miles to North Battleford, the nearest city, the day after tomorrow, check out Canadian Tire or Macleod's for either an inexpensive AC 110-volt inverter or a gas generator if need be. He didn't relish spending a thousand bucks on one.

Mike had one already, but it was grossly undersized; bought at a garage sale, he'd never been able to start it. Wasn't sure it would ever run.

His sleeping area ready, Mike replaced the iron plate back on the hulking, black/white heater, not yet ready to retire. He crouched on the floor, leaning across the bedspreads for his pack of Craven A's. In one month's time, Mike promised himself, he'd quit smoking. His funds were disappearing rapidly due to his expensive habit: at a rate of $100 big ones a month. And he wasn't a heavy smoker. He sat on his sleeping bag, leaning back as he exhaled blue-gray smoke from his mouth, anticipating tomorrow but half dreading it.

That damned chiming again. Mike perked his ears,

listening distractedly to the haunting, melancholy, melodious tinkle of glass-like metal. The slightest breeze blew from the west.

The wind picked up tempo, in ten minutes, blowing hard, lifting the corrugated tin from the barn's roof some distance behind the house. Mike could hear wooden shingles clacking together up on the peaked rooftop of the old house. Finishing his smoke, he butted out in a jar lid, then stripped down to his underwear. Vicious "whooshes" of wind batted at the windows, searching for entry like malevolent phantoms. He slid beneath the covers, curling up beneath as the springtime storm unleashed its fury. A tigerish roar of thunder from the east split the night silence during a temporary lull, rolling all the way to Regina. Patters of rain hit the blackened cedar shingles, soon building up to a steady pat-pat-patter on the attic roof. Another thunder-blast split the night asunder, shaking the ancient farmhouse to its foundations. Mike smiled, thinking up a bizarre scenario for his horror novel's prelude. He loved a good, wicked thunderstorm. It was all part of his dark, primitive, gothic nature. He lay there thinking, head above the blankets, daydreaming (night dreaming?).

And he slept.

****

Thirteen black-robed men chanted above the open grave as Mike stared up at them, his mind screaming, body paralyzed. He tried to move his frozen limbs, his muscles unresponsive. Tall, black, Dominican-style pointed hoods hid their faces from view. They resembled a more sinister version of the Ku Klux Klan. As Mike stared, unblinking, one of the monks began to scoop up wet dirt in his hands, throwing it into Aurora's bogland grave.

Suddenly he stood beside them, incorporeal, watching helplessly as the body that was him was slowly covered with sopping-wet bog soil, obliterating first his head, then his shoulders. The other twelve attendants continued to chant. It sounded like Latin. He drifted fog-like betwixt them, attempting to tweak their long, black, linen robes yet unable. His misty fingers passed through the fabric, through flesh and bone, unheeded. He screamed soundlessly at their absurd, pointed hoods.

Birch and aspen saplings hemmed in the clearing, chillingly familiar as Aurora floated about with nerveless feet not quite touching the ground. The merest breeze jerked him here and there, separating his foggish form momentarily. The trees' leaves were crisp and yellow, suggesting autumn. If Mike had been able to feel anything, he might've smelt the tang of fir boughs jutting out from mixed deciduous trees.

Withdrawing a brilliant, gold box encrusted with precious gems from his robe, one of the men said a short charm, a limerick of some kind, beckoning Mike slyly toward the small, red-velvet-lined, open vessel. Deep brown eyes twinkled cunningly behind the pointed hood's round eyeholes; small, sunken, pig-eyes.

Against his will, Mike's misty body began to gather in on itself, coalescing into a tight, compact, blue-gray mist. His legs began to stretch like moist chewing gum, seeping toward the strangely alluring gold bogey-box in the stranger's gnarled, wrinkled hands. Old, bony, claw-like hands: withered, as if mummified. At once, the mock mourners removed their gruesome hoods as one, revealing horrifically grotesque swine's faces. Sharp bristles stuck out from their long snouts and leathery, deeply-wrinkled faces, tusks curving up from protruding chins. Malevolent eyes glinted with hatred as the Klan members pushed and prodded the Mike essence into the tiny chest, forcing its precious metal lid down onto the valiantly struggling, shrinking, little puff of cigar smoke named Mike Aurora. His gaseous essence pressed hard against the surprisingly firm, gilded lid closing down upon him, exerting an amazing pressure against the wobbling, glowing box. A magic box, realized Mike too late to his mounting horror! And he knew now what they meant to do with that box.

At last, with a terrible click sounding like a gloomy, doom-spelling cathedral bell to his ears, the cask's charmed hasp clamped down against the miniature treasure chest followed by an iron combination lock to help hold in Mr. Mike. The thirteen quasi-human swine laughed with a distant, chortling, snuffling disgusting noise offending his sanity. He pounded ineffectually at the box's lid, causing the tiny coffer to jump and jerk in the Custodian's skeletal hands. Snorting, the Satanic assembly carried Mike, wobbling wildly now in their hands, toward the ancient farm beyond the trembling, reverberating, laughingly-knocking aspen, paper birch, Jack pine, tamarack, and black spruce.

The Dark Assembly reached a pyramid-topped well cover in front of the old farmhouse after what seemed an eternity of jostling, shaking, and gleefully deliberate bouncing of the enchanted capsule. They chanted before the stone well's curb, saying a prayer to the Dark One residing below.

Then dropped the immensely, unnaturally heavy vessel of Mike essence down the well, grunting and snorting with piggish satisfaction as the gold-laminated magic cask plunged down the yawning, circular shaft.

Mike felt himself plummeting at rocket speed, terrified, sensing rather than seeing the ribbed, iron-banded well shaft slamming against and denting the gold box as it hurtled through space. He felt claustrophobic, surrounded by cold, cold iron. And as he zoomed downwards at impossible speed, he felt the vessel's bottom melting away as if it were a comet entering earth's atmosphere. He was burning up! Burning up in a space-black void. The Mike essence dropped through the bottom screaming, his scalp tingling, suddenly aware of every sensation as he whizzed downwards at lightning speed; a 1/100,000 scale spiritual shaft of bluish light hurtling through a lightless cylinder toward the earth's center. Had he been mortal he would've died of fright, his heart exploding, brain hemorrhaging.

An enormous, orange-red, glowing, molten sphere of sulphurous liquid below awaited the plunging Mike essence, a gigantic, tideless sea alight with a phosphorescent red glow as Mike screamed aloud in eternal darkness.

It was a lake of fire.

****

Mike awoke screaming!

Darkness shrouded him in the midnight silence, the only sound the intermittent drip of raindrops from the house's dangling, worn eaves. The thunderstorm had passed. A phosphorus blue-yellow glow from a corner of the living room caught Mike's wide-open eye, just glimpsing it from the edge of his vision as it blinked out. A strange shaft of eerie, transparent light. Mike imagined it had a vaguely human form.

"Jesus Christ," he whispered, rubbing his sore, tired eyes as he blinked at the thick, cloying darkness. For a terrifying moment he'd wondered where he was. He lay back in his blankets once more, breathing heavy, sweating profusely, heart beating like a bass drum. Only a dream. How reassuring. Mike smiled, chuckling, wiping sweat-droplets from his slick forehead. The house's mildewy odor jogged his memory. Ah yes, the farm. The sour smell of dried crackers and moldy nectarine pits tossed in a corner permeated the house. Mike had plenty to do to clean up the filthy, old farmhouse. Plenty of junk to throw out, burn, or refurbish. The place would require airing out and a liberal dose of disinfectant all over. The house stank. Old man Aurora must've been literally loony in his last years, letting the place go to pot like that. Apparently the old bastard had died on his tractor, the small, dull-red, Massey Ferguson still hunkered down tread-deep in the soft garden mud. Nobody'd bothered to replace it inside the rusty little shed behind the barn. It and the house (not including the old barn) had been the only other buildings on the property left unlocked. The executor of Joe's will had searched the house high and low for extra sets of keys (no doubt also looking for the old crony's supposed thousands hidden in the house somewhere).   Didn't every recluse have a stash?

Mike rolled over, smiling cynically to himself. Yeah, right! Would that he could find another wad of the old man's stash. Probably an ex-whiskey runner, the old crow. Mike knew very little of old Joe's past, except that he'd been in trouble with the Mounties back in the Dirty 30's for some unspecified misdemeanor. An orphan at eight, Mike had lived with his foster-parents in the tiny hamlet of Belbutte, near Spiritwood, for six years until, pop!, one by one, they both died – she of heart disease at 65, he of a stroke at 60. Mike had never had much affection for the two old goats. Money-hungry sycophants of the foster-care bureau, he'd always suspected. They hadn't much affection for him either with his long hair, wild music, and rowdy school days as a self-proclaimed tough. Mike hated school, but had pushed on anyway, finishing grade ten. The half dozen friends and acquaintances had made classes a little more bearable. Aurora fondly remembered smuggling whiskey to school in little glass jars, stolen from his foster parents' stash; his buddies Nick, Steve, Tom, and Mick the Mouth helping him down his contraband at noon hour at the school's empty bleachers in Spiritwood. All the same, he wasn't a particularly popular guy at Spiritwood, Medstead, or P.A. elementary schools. He had been shuffled off to another pair of yahoos who owned a farm near Prince Albert when he was fifteen. They'd tried to make a good little farmer out of him. Didn't work. Aurora went through the motions but his mind was elsewhere. Carpathian castles. Haunted, Olde English manor houses, crawling with bogeys, bats, and barn owls. Gothic, fog-bound cemeteries. Medieval dungeons. Dungeons and sorcerers. Dungeons and Dragons (the board game). Maidens and sword-masters. Conan, the Barbarian. Anywhere but the present. Not the typical, Teenage-Mutant Ninja Turtle perhaps (nor, for that matter, the average goon). Just plain weird; an inveterate occult dabbler.

His friends were as far out on left field as he was. Tinseltown Terror. Hallowe'en nightmares, come to knock on yo' door, sucka', so doon' mess wi' us, funky white boy.

Mike's inner ramblings turned weirder and weirder as he drifted off to sleep. An uneasy slumber. Misty, sinister figures danced behind his eyelids, through gothick railings, baroque buildings, terror-inspired alpine vistas of some vampire-infested East European country like Hungary, Serbia, Slovenia, Romania. Count Dracula's castle on its crag high above the Argeş river in Transylvania rose in his mind like a black, arms-outstretched phantom, a ruined, brick/stone fortress on limestone cliffs, site of horrible mass-murder of thousands. How'd that be for a psychic medium channeling thoughts and emotions on a moon-filled All Hallow's Eve?

Mike slipped off into sleep, his mind emptying like a ship's bilge pumps.

****

He wandered about the North Battleford mall almost mindlessly, stopping here and there to browse, compare prices, marvel at the latest technological gadgets. He weaved among the department stores, unfamiliar with the large North Battleford shopping mall on Railway Avenue, just outside of town. Oddly enough, Mike hadn't been as far north as this, or not that he recalled, one of the province's oldest, smallest, and seediest metropolises. He browsed avidly among the cassette department at Woolco, checking out its impressive CD, tape, and record selection for his favourite rock bands' latest albums, then moved on. He planned to stop at Sam the Record Man on the way out of town. Aurora meandered about the household department looking over kettles, AC appliances, cooking utensils, ornaments, bedding, etc. He bought a couple of pairs of cheap Levis on sale at half-price for $9.99, regular $18.99. Mike was a wily shopper, a habit quickly learned while on a shoestring budget. Next he explored the Met department store at the other end of the mall, buying a bargain-price set of bath towels, a spade, candles, one case of 10W30 engine oil and a pair of Bushnell binoculars for outdoor jaunts. Next to the Met, at Safeway, he purchased eggs, spareribs, chicken, three bags of sale-price flour, two ten kilo. bags of likewise white sugar, baking necessities, sealers, typing paper.

On the way out of town, Mike stopped at KFC for a bucket of fried chicken, vowing he wouldn't do so again for at least another six months. One only lived once, so, okay, occasionally he splurged. What of it? His Kentucky Fried would last Mike, a single bachelor, at least four days. If he didn't pig out.

He'd bought the two deep-cycle marine batteries, groceries, HM cassettes, "AA" batteries, second-hand clothing, jeans, 125-watt AC/DC inverter to complement his not-yet-installed wind charger, engine oil, fuses, water dispenser, stationery, wiring, Panasonic personal cassette player and binoculars he'd had marked on his list.

However, he realized half way home that he'd forgot to mark down kerosene. Idiot. It was now 9:15 p.m., getting dark as Mike left the suburban traffic behind along with N. Battleford's infuriating traffic lights and uncontrolled intersections. The blacktop seemed in fair condition as Aurora's barely rusted four-door Impala sped along at a sedate fifty-five miles per hour toward Cochin, and, beyond, the small, lumber town of Glaslyn. From North Battleford to Medstead (a dying village) the drive would take approximately one hour. Another thirty minutes on lousy gravel roads to the non-village (ha, ha) of Ranger. (With such a catchy name Mike somehow expected a U.S. marshal-style R.C.M.P. detachment nearby, bear cops, Smokies sporting Southern-style, gallon cowboy hats and six-shooters.)

He passed slowly through the sleepy village of Deadstead (oh, sorry, Medstead), a vaguely familiar assemblage of non-descript, pastel-colored houses, a hockey rink, Credit Union, elementary school and swamps beyond. (He'd attended school here for one semester when he was eleven years old; His only recollections were of beating up some kids he didn't like.)

Aurora disliked yet longed for the small village: population 148. Why would anyone yearn for this place, he wondered? He left it behind, feeling better because feeling watched.

Nuts.

Mike felt totally lagged-out when he finally reached the farm at 10:15 p.m. The sky was dark, overcast, pitch black. No house lights, yard lights to greet him to his new, uninviting homestead. Only an abandoned, overgrown group of shacks arrived at after a bone-jarring, rutted, turtle's crawl over a series of knolls and disused roadway leading into rustic wilderness. A landscape of aspen, pastures, and tall grasses reclaiming the sordid farmyard. Nothing but an old, picturesque, junk-strewn farmstead. Mike loved it, had loved it at first sight. Loved its balsam poplar, spruce, fir, tamarack, and trembling aspen which come autumn would turn a lovely pastel yellow. Nearby were stony meadows full of Indian paintbrush, ox-eye daisies, wild strawberries, ladies' slipper. Had he been a poet he would've written a bard's eulogy.

The route crossed an abandoned railroad track, the rails and ties removed years ago.

Mike carried his groceries by flashlight into the electricity-less house, rushing back in the light of his car's rectangular, quartz-halogen beams to collect the remainder from the station wagon's rear.

In the mood for a more balanced meal, Aurora stuck his barely touched bucket of KFC in his hamper under the cupboard – the coolest place in the house (have to remember to put that meat and shit in the root cellar tomorrow, he reminded himself).

He heated himself a late meal (using the pathetic, wood-fired monstrosity called a woodstove) of baked potato, sour cream, raw carrots, sweet 'n sour spareribs, Southern fried chicken, Green Giant whole-kernel corn. A rich feast (for him). Mike wished at times like this that he had a wife or girlfriend to cook his meals, but, fortunately, he was an accomplished chef. He could fend for himself. Mike thought most young women his age were sluts, out to milk rich guys for all they could (and never surprised to see the prettiest girls sitting in the passenger seat of their boyfriend's sportiest, sixty grand, hot-rod envy of town). And most men degenerate, amoral monsters unworthy of the light of day. Mike Aurora, Antisocialist. His theme song, "Antisocial", by Anthrax.

By lamplight he wolfed down his meal, assorted red candles arranged about the foyer, kitchen, and living room adding an archaic ambience to the place. Mike, fool, had forgot to write down one of the most important items on his list. Another coal-oil lantern, perhaps two. Blockhead. He'd kick his ass if he were able. A mellow, golden glow radiated throughout the ground floor rooms.

He grabbed another piece of greasy KFC chicken, still warm, from his hamper, making a thorough pig of himself.

Tomorrow, maybe, he would tackle the wind generator project again. He'd experienced a snag when the twenty-foot pine pole he'd prepared yesterday had proven too slender and, therefore, unstable, for the apparatus. He would need a stouter, stronger tree trunk to ensure ability to withstand strong gusts of prairie wind. (He'd begun to wonder if he shouldn't fork out the money to buy steel pipes for a tower instead.) Aurora was an amateur at this, after all, not knowing what he was dealing with, what sort of facts and figures were needed for successful operation of a wind- charger out here in often windless rural Saskatchewan. The machine's warranty promised a working start-up windspeed of eight m.p.h for the small generator and rotor-blades, but Mike had reservations about this. Just how heavy a wind was eight m.p.h?

He sat at the table reading an Archie comic till eleven, still enjoying the old farces and their far-out adventures. He especially enjoyed the excellent artists' renderings of sexy, bikini-clad beach bunnies. Veronica (Ronnie), Midge, Betty. Not Ethel. Jughead was a real clown. What a food-bill that crowned Pinocchio's pop must have!

Mike poured himself a shot of lemon gin in a crystal

glass, occasionally enjoying getting, if not stinking drunk, then feeling mighty good. He hadn't partied much since his high-school days in P.A. (Prince Albert). His friends were all working in Regina: one a bar bouncer (seriously), the other a Canadian Tire mechanic, the other a bum.

Suddenly his cobalt-blue gas lantern dimmed, a bluish glow illuminating the old kitchen, a fifties' style room which showed its age. Mike glanced up from his tattered comic book, his eyes straying about the Lysol-smelling kitchen with its dark, inky shadows in plain, drywalled corners. Much of the building needed painting or wallpaper. Aurora's scalp tingled uncomfortably, hairs on the back of his neck raising like hackles.

He sensed eyes at the back of his head.

Mike glanced cautiously over his shoulder, expecting to see the bogeyman crouching in a corner. Or a bogle, a brownie, or several other types of occult phenomenon which regularly appeared in the books and horror movies he'd read or watched.

But not even a puff of smoke showed in the murky kitchen shadows. Only a dull green Coleman propane oven, a small, paint-flecked apparatus with four rusty burners sitting in a corner beside a chipped porcelain sink and faded, veneer-paneled wall above. Mike peered into the candlelit living room, a mellow, yellowish glow cast from candles set atop an old dresser. His bedspreads sprawled awkwardly on the timber floor looking vaguely…different. And as Mike watched, heart beating loudly, he could've sworn he'd seen movement beneath the covers.

Slowly Mike rose from his high-backed wooden chair, deftly picking up a butcher knife from the countertop as he slid silently, carefully, toward the quiet living-room visible through the open doorway.

He yanked back the bedding, knife raised in anticipation.

Nothing. His bedding was as it had always been, yellow sheet, blue cotton bedspread, gray-beige cotton blanket, two more blankets plus a shiny, sable sleeping bag spread over a large, thick, foam mattress. (From up in the attic.) Mike peeked about the corners of the room, feeling somewhat foolish.

Must be tired, he told himself. Eyes playing tricks.

He turned back to the kitchen; frowning, then cursing.

The coal-oil lamp had been snuffed out.

Aurora snatched a flashlight from the dresser, tiptoeing cautiously, butcher-knife in hand, toward the darkened kitchen and foyer. One of the candles, too, had been blown out, he noticed. A draft somewhere, maybe? Mike stumbled against the big, decrepit, trestle-size table, barking his shin on a bulbous leg. No one was about. The wicks must've burnt short (both of them?). He studied the colored glass lantern, then lit its perfect wick. It flared up healthily, no gripes nor other creepy idiosyncrasies.

"Fuck off, old man," Mike said aloud to the four, unresponsive walls. "Yo' place in hell, remember? Nobody wants you here, you old fart."

There, that exorcised the spirit of the moment, thought Mike to himself. He chuckled quietly, sweeping back his dark hair from his sweating forehead; a rich mane of long, straight hair. He doubted the old man was listening. Rest in peace, amen.

Old fart.

Mike washed the last of his dishes in tepid water, stacking the wet plates, pots, and pans in the porcelain sink. He was glad it wasn't a single basin. That would be a drag.   He smoked another cigarette while perusing the latest issue of Cheri, Mike's favourite sex mag. Then he jotted down tomorrow's agenda: sweep rooms, wash floors, work on wind-charger's pole again. Explore the farm's locked sheds and numerous other interesting old buildings. Maybe even begin his horror novel.

One o'clock, Mike slid underneath the covers, snuggling beneath the mountain of blankets while dreaming of a nightie-clad fuck bunny of his choice. A buxom, dark-haired, bodacious siren straight out of the centerfold pages of Cheri magazine. He didn't consider himself a perv, just a straight, hot-blooded, nineties' male who sometimes fancied he lived in the Bronze Age. He was partial to dark-eyed sex goddesses with long, black, chestnut, red, or platinum hair. Didn't relish blondes much. Now, perhaps, with a little *mula* stashed away, he could consider looking for some good-lookin' Pet to share his humble abode, somebody with brains preferably. And a bod straight from heaven (or hell, depending on one's ideological sympathies). A succubis, they called it, wasn't it? Mike wondered on the brink of sleep whether there really were, as the Good Book (good book, ha, ha) says, succubi, demons in human form who frequently copulated with human males, bore children. Perhaps, Mike ol' boy, you should hold a groovy séance, contact the spirit world and ask 'em to send one down. Gettin' awful lonely down here, Mikey, Mike, Michael. Just close your eyes, see what happens.

Mike shut his eyes.

****

"Mike."

"Michael."

Aurora opened his eyes groggily, confronting darkness

as he jerked awake suddenly from a deep slumber. The house was dark; a faint, cock-eyed sliver of a moon scarcely illuminating the living room. Loons trilled from a nearby slough, their haunting melody sending chills down Mike's spine.

"Michael."

A soft, feminine voice floated across the room, rousing the befuddled Aurora as he lay in his blankets, still half-asleep. "Wha -? Who's there?" murmured Mike peevishly. As if in a trance, he slipped from beneath the bedcovers, standing up in his long-johns and following the captivating, feline summons which echoed softly across the living room from some unknown source. He didn't even question his actions, unsure whether sleepwalking or dreaming. The cold, hardwood floor, though, felt real enough beneath his bare feet. Mike bumbled forward blindly, steered by Providence as he entered the empty kitchen and strayed toward the brick alcove at the entrance beneath a rickety staircase. He stood a moment, staring at cloying darkness, then mindlessly reached out his hand to touch the cold, rough wall.

A white, phosphorescent hand passed through the crumbling masonry, clasping Aurora's with a gentle, sensuous grip; an icy, slender, luminous hand with long, colorless, manicured fingernails. A woman's hand. Or a goddess's. Mike stared spellbound, not at all surprised.

He'd summoned her.

As he watched, his blue eyes widening in surprise, color seeped into the pale, cream-white, insubstantial flesh, the lovely, surreal appendage seeming to pass partly through Mike's own with an exciting tingling deep within his bones. Aurora gasped aloud, still incredulous as the spectral, female hand turned a lively, fleshy pink and

warmed astonishingly in his own. It gripped the back of his hand gently, eye-level to the wall.

An angelic, gorgeous face appeared through the brickwork, smiling coyly at him as it turned a rosy-cheeked, fleshy hue to match its suddenly corporeal hand. Dark, liquid eyes gazed back questioningly from a squarish, misty, but attractive face half materialized through the old, brick alcove's wall. A young girl's face, yet curiously ageless, blinking rapidly as if trying to recall past eras. And then, Venus-like, she stepped out from the alcove.

A flowing, diaphanous, scintillant white gown boldly exposed the spectre's nakedness beneath, her grip solid and demanding now as she stood brazenly before him, smiling quizzically. Mike drank in the details with wary eyes, travelling the length of this girl/woman's incandescent, voluptuous body. He knew she was not real. Couldn't be. Her breasts jutted out prettily from dainty lace/silk fabric, mouthwatering in their fullness, her bodice seeming to shimmer and heave as if breathing. Long, chestnut, buttock-length hair with oceanic waves tumbed forth down the phantom's back, tempting Mike to reach out and take a fistful of its silken delights in his hand.   Yet he did not.

"Who….*what*, the fuck are you?" The question sounded stupid in his ears. The spectre cocked an eyebrow comically, as if reading Aurora's mind. She didn't answer. Rather, she asked a question of her own.

"You like?"

Mike blinked rapidly.

"You desire?" She had a vaguely Spanish accent, her raven tresses reinforcing the impression of a Spanish doll. "I would be your…fuck bunny, as you would call it." She tittered, then continued.

"Am I not…what you would say in your language…sexy?" She turned around slowly, showing Aurora her wide hips, hourglass figure, delectable buttocks tantalizingly showing through the clinging, silk material. She giggled. "I be your secret, Mike," she breathed. "You may be my Master tonight. And for as many nights as you like."   She grinned conspiratorially.

Mike seized her arm.

"Who are you? What are you doing here? What…the fuck are you? A dream?

Mirage? Huh??"

The sultry phantasm's eyes darkened, frowning at Mike's hand on her arm.

"No one important."

"I'll break your arm, wench. Is this some sort of gag? Who put you up to this…this…" Mike's voice trailed off. Nubile, young women don't usually materialize through walls. Not even the best sleight-of-hand artists could do this, he reasoned. Mike gaped, speechless.

The spectre sighed. "I'm what you among the living call a 'brownie'," she volunteered. "A living phantasm, yet undead. I'm the astro-projected spirit of a woman you shall meet soon, her alter-ego. A wanderer. She sleeps, I wander. I can go anywhere. You can call me Wanda."

Mike frowned. "I'm dreaming. Or sleepwalking."

The seductress placed a warm, comforting hand on Mike's arm. "I assure you, you're not dreaming." She glanced down at his bare chest, eyes filling with longing. "Come. We have only four hours till daylight."

"Huh - ? Four hours for what? Where?"

She smiled deliciously, dark eyes lighting up. She had the virtual body of an exotic dancer, Aurora noticed, sculpted to lure the unwitting into troubled waters. And, oh man, was *he in deep over his head!* The brazen vixen ran her forefinger down Mike's bulging bicep alluringly. "I have certain…freedoms, which only the living, and not the dead, have." She wrapped her arm around his neck, kissing Mike's lips demandingly, groaning passionately from deep within. Her dainty left hand dropped to his waist, slowly slipping his thermal underwear down over his buttocks. Mike, finally relenting, moaned aloud, clutching *"Wanda's"* nubile body close, his hands wandering over her backside as she sighed and met his tongue with her own. They kissed again, lips smacking.

"Please come." She led Mike out of the dark alcove, toward his makeshift bed on the living-room floor. She held his hand like a coquettish schoolgirl.

She pushed Mike back onto the bedsheets, kissing him urgently as her uncanny breath quickened. She tugged off his underwear, straddling him, then kissed him again; seeking his neck like a vamp. Then she rolled over onto her back, pulling Mike on top, moaning deliriously as he kissed her sweaty neck. 'Wanda' sighed aloud, scissoring her legs around him; clutching him close as he cleaved into her, matching his rhythm as Aurora's pulse quickened. She licked his neck, kissing his shoulders, then biting.

Jesus, she's a vampire! Mike thought crazily. She moaned in ecstasy, whispering, sighing in rapture as Mike pinned her hips and licked her nipples.

He knew he was dreaming when he climaxed with an unbelievable, roaring-wet rush.

THREE.

Mike awoke at a quarter past eight. He stretched, stifled a yawn, then sat up in his bedcovers, mind still foggy with sleep. A strange, oddly-disturbing nightmare danced elusively from his memory. He remembered something about a woman, a beautiful, nubile woman about whom *something* didn't seem right, but not much else. Aurora, exasperated, struggled in vain to recall what the dream was about, so damnably realistic but now faded with the coming daylight. Sunlight drifted lazily into the living room window, a warm, spring ray of life-giving energy. He could feel his body pulsing with life. Mike snatched up his neatly folded clothes, tugging them on, his mind already on the day's agenda.

He cracked two large eggs into a cast-iron frying pan, six slices of bacon already sizzling inside the big black fryer. He set a carton of orange juice on the scarred ancient table, his plate, and a glass. The outdoor propane tank had still been half full when Mike checked three days ago. Aurora was rather surprised that its rusty nozzle still turned. He'd solved the burners' complaint; a plugged jet, that's all.

The oven, though, he could've lit an acetylene torch to for all the good it would've done.

A bacon and eggs breakfast with toast (toasted over a wire burner) washed down with cold, refreshing orange juice perked Mike's senses, preparing him for the tasks ahead. Agenda #1: Install wind generator pole beside the house, strap securely to chimney. #2: Begin digging up the weed-choked, neglected garden area. #3: B 'n' E locked sheds in yard. #4: Sweep cobwebs from shithouse.

Aurora started with the easiest: he swept out the derelict outhouse sitting by a thicket of sprawling raspberry bushes. After that, he took up his new spade, pick, and axe in earnest, marched toward the fenced garden enclosure to the west of the house and began the day's labour there for a promised three hours, no more, no less. He hacked at thick roots with his axe, broke the weedy, sapling-infested, rock-strewn soil with his rock pick, and when he'd finished had achieved an impressive 20' ft. square patch of cleared, double-dug, black soil. Earthy, pungent, loamy garden soil. Obviously the old man had manured or composted the wooden-fenced plot well over the years. It would make a fine vegetable patch, Mike guessed.

By noon, he'd finished in the mucky garden. (A week's rain had made the ground soft, but easy to dig.) Aurora spent an hour or so attaching his shiny, new wind charger – an ingenious luxury in these backwoods – onto a twenty-foot spruce pole (a temporary measure, until he could burgle a tower somehow) scrounged from behind a decaying tool shed. With some difficulty he raised the pole, securing it with guy ropes, nestling it beside the east corner of the house in an angle of the building, where he strapped it tight with chains and strong bungy cords to the stone chimney (the house was a hodge-podge of different styles and building materials). A long, sturdy ladder had come with the property. Mike felt quite pleased with himself.

The electrical hookup could wait. Mike wasn't yet ready for that big job. It would take some brainstorming. The sheds out in the distant yards beckoned. By four thirty, anxiety was killing him. He was itching to know what was inside those buildings. Probably nothing. Just junk. Mike hefted a hammer in his hand, trudging out to the farmyard and its three clapboard sheds which sat forlornly some distance away on the overgrown, reclaimed acreage. The old homestead was small, five acres at best. (There was more, he'd soon discover.) Aspen, birch, white spruce closed in on three sides of the derelict acreage. Tall, yellowed grass and tiny, stunted saplings surrounded the various ramshackle outbuildings crowded around the two-story, peaked farmhouse too large for one person. The house was now a faded blue/gray.

Mike walked leisurely around the side of one of the big, long sheds, inhaling a deep, satisfying breath of pure country air, the fragrance of honeysuckle, decayed manure and ancient, heating lumber wafting across the yard. Spring thistles with a healthy head start on the season nudged against the dilapidated outbuilding's south wall, seeming to reach out at Aurora with spiny, prickly branches. Last autumn's burrs were in profusion along with a random assortment of dandelions, bluebell, and buttercup. Big anthills had been constructed along the length of the wall. Red ants. Grrr. Mike hated those little bastards (didn't everybody?), those little pincer-heads. He planned to do some ethnic cleansing of a very special kind this year, for they were everywhere. You can run…but you can't hide…

A bulky, corroded padlock secured the big building's double, loading-bay doors, looking as if it hadn't experienced a key in its slot for donkey's years. Mike rapped the ancient lock with his claw hammer, expecting it to pop open. It did not. He jolted it again. Again. The iron was much stronger than he'd expected.

On the tenth try, the great padlock snapped off from

the latch. Mike swung the squealing iron latch back, hauling open the loading-bay doors with an effort. Musty decay assailed his senses, mixed with the smell of spilt oil and grease. A grungy cement floor stained by countless years of oil and gasoline met Aurora's slowly adjusting vision. The old, spacious outbuilding was dark; little light shone through the begrimed, multiple, west-facing windows. Mike detected the faint outlines of antiquated machinery at the rear of the building.

He entered, sauntering toward the decrepit machinery in the back. Some of it was old lawnmowers, minus motors, blades, handles. Various dismantled engines lay scattered about the shed. Or should he call it a workshop? A cluttered mixture of nuts and bolts, engine parts, appliances, wiring, broken toys, empty, greasy boxes. Countless coffee cans brimming with nails, screws, nuts, bolts, miscellaneous odds 'n ends lined the grimy walls on sagging shelves. Dust and grime coated everything.

It was the plastic-wrapped factory boxes stacked behind sheets of plywood which captured Mike's rapt attention.

Hitachi, Mitsubishi, Yamaha, Panasonic, Sony...televisions, radios, stereos, marine equipment, surveying equipment.

What the - ?

He rattled the boxes, bug-eyed.

Hundreds of factory-fresh appliances, never opened,

never even inspected…with dates ranging from 1936 to 1983. Some were antiques obviously, having never seen the light of day. (He checked inside, tearing off wrappers, making sure it was what he thought they were.) Hunting rifles, still in their original cases. Slowly Mike began to realize with astonishment that the entire shed was crammed with stolen (?) goods tucked away behind innocent-looking junk. For over fifty years uncle Joe, that sly old fox, had been running a racket, part of a big-time crime syndicate perhaps. Mafia, Hell's Angels, who knew? The old man must've had important connections, influential contacts. And never had a major criminal record!

Or maybe he'd bought a lifetime's supply of warehouse freebies for a song, heh, heh…

There were dozens of cases of pirated whiskey, vintage wine, foreign beers, cartons of unopened cigars. (The old man was either a thief, or had spent one hell of a pile of money stockpiling this stuff, Mike reasoned.) A stack of cigarette cartons from various famous American brands stood literally stacked to the ceiling in one corner. Over everything sheets had been thrown, though some had been torn off, as if searching for something in a hurry. Every imaginable type of gadget was represented here, brand names lined up neatly atop the other as if in some rustic, abandoned warehouse. Cases of Rolex, Casio,

Timex watches. Swiss watches. Clocks. Home appliances. Stereo equipment, expensive toys, silverware, crystal, heaps of exquisite jewellery inside waxed boxes. A millionaire's expensive hoard.

What the hell...??

Aurora began to babble with joy, dropping to his knees to thank his new god and benefactor. No more bills to pay…no more used furniture and appliances. No more guilt-trips over wasteful spending sprees. He'd just take out an extended loan, from here, his new bank and very own warehouse. Mike started to laugh aloud, shouting with delight as he rose and hugged the monolithic boxes of illicit goods. No one would ever know. He kissed the boxes with joy and reverence, rubbing his cheek against the cool, plastic wrappers.

"Oh, my god!" Mike dashed toward a nearby corner, tossing aside expensive

items to reveal cases of syndicated porno magazines, many which had long-since gone out of circulation. Old Penthouse, Playboy, Swank, Hustler…boxes upon boxes of dirty magazines, and below, by God, unopened cases of "blue" movies. XXX-rated. Many ancient. He ripped the decaying cardboard cartons open with his bare hands to reveal the outdated contraband.

Mike sat down on the chilly cement floor, exhausted. He suddenly had a humongous headache. He began to rationalize. Was this only a dream? Perhaps he was dreaming. The thought was sobering. Aurora began to worry. If this was syndicate, big time, Mafia…Mike's excitement rapidly began to dissipate. Biker gangs. Mafia. Gang warfare. And they would know about the place. Would know where he lived.   One missing thing, one stolen iota…and they'd fry him for supper. Make him a pair of cement shoes. Break his kneecaps, at best.

Go to the police?

Go to the police???

No way, José!

What should he do, what should he do?

Sit tight. Wait. See what happens. He considered it strange that whoever owned this stash hadn't moved it someplace safer. A warehouse in Chicago or L.A. Montreal. Edmonton. Or dumped it on the black market. Sitting out here in a prairie shack like so much refuse seemed ludicrous to him. Surely whatever crime racket was responsible for this knew it was just a matter of time before somebody squealed on uncle Joe.   And how did uncle Joe fit in? Somebody could peep through a smashed window, crawl inside, even, and discover Aurora's "secret." Five to ten, they'd get, these big-time (surely?) extortionists and money launderers if they were lucky. There must be *tens of thousands* of dollars tied up in this great, ramshackle tool shed! Perhaps middlemen occasionally hauled away loads of it to prospective buyers.

But then what the hell did he know about the black market?

Possibly the prime runners had already been busted, doing time right now?

Maybe.

Maybe.

Oh, what a load of hooey!, Mike thought to himself disgustedly. The old man probably just bought all this stuff 'cause he's a compulsive spender. A real nutball if ever he envisaged one.

The sun began to set. A brilliant, fiery, lilac sunset lit up the horizon. Shadows darkened the big, ancient shed. Owls hooted mournfully from the Saskatchewan wilderness, occasionally uttering a spine-chilling screech from their hidden, twilit roosts. Bullfrogs lullabied a croaking chorus from a nearby lagoon. Whispering north winds stirred the rustling aspen leaves, the distant house's eavestroughes, decayed shutters. Cedar shakes up on the old, barn-like shed's roof clacked together; many of them loose or missing.

Finally, Mike stood up, sobered, closing the big bay doors behind him and walking morosely across the eerie, darkening farmyard toward his deceased uncle's unlit farmhouse. It looked a sorry state in the fading, dusk light. An amber hue now lit up the horizon; the sun having vanished.

He lay in bed and waited for the mysterious woman he now remembered as Wanda.

FOUR.

She came at a quarter past eleven.

Mike felt a whisper of a kiss against his cheek, then his lips, and knew he was dreaming when she took his flaccid member into her mouth. Next he felt her exposed breasts against his groin. He didn't bother opening his eyes, repeating "you don't exist" inside his mind.

When he opened them she was there. Radiant.

Beaming with satisfaction, a luminous, yellowish glow which lit the benighted living room like some oversized firefly. The seductress smiled satedly, beautiful yet forbidden, kissing Aurora's lips again. She was real, he was now certain. So warm, solid, yet yielding like a genuine flesh-and-blood woman. She wore a cherry-red blouse, openly revealing her perfect, braless breasts. Helpless, Mike's hands roamed the girl's back, for part of him did not wish to partake of this unnatural, unholy act, blasphemously crossing the veil of death. But she wasn't really dead, was she? Yet his lips sought her cleavage with a will of their own, licking the gorgeous stranger's astonishingly salty, lifelike skin. She moaned in pleasure, guiding a full breast to his mouth.

They embraced awhile, exploring each other randomly, languorously. And suddenly Mike realized he wasn't dreaming. Couldn't be. "Wanda" felt too real. Her perfume too overpowering for an illusion. He did not fear for his soul, did not fear she was uncle Joe in spirit disguise.

For she loved him. With her pliant, willing body she brought Mike to the brink of climax - another dimension, another existence entirely; caressing, licking, kissing, sucking. Crooning, moaning, sighing, groaning. Panting in heat. She laughed playfully in Mike's ear, sliding a long, raspy, feline tongue into his earlobe.

She came like a real woman, this time not vanishing into nothingness but savoring the exquisite pleasure, crying out and begging him as Aurora filled her with his essence whilst she held his neck to hers. They kissed hungrily, sweating oilily, locked together. Wanda performed fellatio like a pro, no insubstantial ghost here. Again they smooched, mouths smacking noisily in the light of the moon. And he reciprocated the favour until she was screaming. They lay together, exhausted, happy, caressing like familiar lovers.

"Soon, my love," she whispered, kissing his cheek, "We'll be together, I promise you." Her own cheek glowed a fleshy, lively pink. Her skin slightly paler than ought to have been, and hot, feverish; Mike kissed her neck, inhaling Wanda's intoxicating smell, enjoying her flavour.

"Is that a threat?" he whispered playfully.

Wanda laughed huskily, kissing him again. "No. I'm not dead, remember? But undead, *nosferatu* – though I don't suck blood. Nor," she continued, wiping goo from her chest, "would I prefer your death, I assure you. We couldn't share what we just had if you were dead. Most souls have little or no power in the Hereafter. Am I boring you?"

"No. But tell me one thing. Am I dreaming?"

"Perhaps we both are. In our sleep. Here. Pinch me."

Mike pinched her arm.

"Oww!" Wanda rubbed the area, smiling sheepishly. "Now let me. No. Better yet, a hickey."

She kissed Mike's strong, muscular bicep, sucking hard until the pressure caused a red swell on his upper arm. "In the morning, you'll know if I'm real."

"But who are you? Who are you really? I don't believe you're a ghost, nor a vampire." Mike patted her fleshy derrière reassuringly.

"In a way, *Miguel*," began Wanda smilingly, misty-eyed, "I'm not real. I am alive, a genuine living woman, unknown to you – a horny woman. But I'm not really here, except in spirit. What you believe you feel – i.e. my tits! – are only a very pleasant simulation, a diversion, for we have connected...within our dreams."

"You've lost me."

"I can't tell you my real name," Wanda said evasively. " Not yet. It just isn't done....it's part of the game. I, the girl you've melded with, am psychic, so are you, and for whatever reason, we've made a lasting contact. But, I feel somehow that we were lovers before, in some prehistoric age, and will be again. We were once, I recall, separated by tragedy."

She began to cry.

And vanished into mist.

****

Mike woke in the morning feeling totally burnt-out. He lay a long while, his mind foggy as spring sunlight sprayed through the three-tier living room window in a prism of lemon yellow. He sighed with melancholy as the dream faded. Last night, after "Wanda", or whatever the hell it was had vanished, he'd dreamt of her in another place, another era. Mike hazily remembered vaguely shifting shapes of stone, of monolithic pillars and chanting wise-men dressed in flowing white togas. Dimly he recalled their sacrifices, of horses, chickens, rams. He recalled that they were dubbed *Goidels*, a term he didn't recognize. They were outlanders, he remembered, barbarians from some oriental land, newcomers. He'd thought the great, monumental standing stones resembled those of Carnac, in Brittany, France, which he'd often seen in photographs.

Mike had been tied to a stake, he remembered with a shudder. A burning stake. Not the usual wicker fireworks, or wicker men, which the invaders generally used.

He lay recalling the dream. Or nightmare. He remembered somehow the name *Gwyddels* (somehow related to Goidels?), another unfamiliar appellation, that they also called themselves Scotti, Scythii, Scythians, and that Mike himself had been a Cumbrian, a Cimmerian, whoever the fuck they were, some powerful race of long-extinct barbarians vying for control of Europe's lucrative salt, gold, tin, jade and amber trades, and the mountain passes controlling them. He was a renowned warrior Mike recalled (!), a blue-eyed, tattooed giant, a berserker, captured in a lightning raid from whence he remembered not. His name was something like *Conigcatylati*, an unpronounceable jumble now that Mike thought of it. It looked, and sounded, Celtic.

A beautiful young maiden, his betrothed, had been roped to the top of a table-like group of monstrous stones as tall as a house. Fires all around burned on the dewy ground, the fair-haired savages howling and yelping ecstatically as they leaped through the roaring, soaring Beltaine flames. Many, however, were red haired. A robed priest stood atop the altar-stone beside the girl, preparing for the sacrifice, his sacred knives at the ready. It was midnight. A full moon lit the black sky like a hollowed-out gourd, for it was All Hallow's Eve. Samhaín. Conig and his queen were to be married on this day. Mike's 'fiancée' had been a warrioress, a mercenary from Armenia who'd travelled west with a roving band of *Sarmatii*. As far as he remembered, the Romans and Greeks hadn't even existed yet.

Toward dream's end, Mike remembered hosts of screaming, banshee-like barbarians bearing various steel, copper, or bronze weapons pouring over the dikes. Gold and silver, plates of armour, torcs, buckles, shields twinkled and flashed in firelight. Then he'd been slashed free, remembered the thrill and exalted furor as he snatched a steel broadsword from one of the slain and cleaved a Scythian in two, felt the delicious bloodlust as he dashed toward the dolmen, sword in hand…

Then the druid had raised the bloodied knife, holding

high the warrioress's dripping heart in his left hand.

And Mike had awoke screaming.

****

He spent the afternoon working in the garden. The reality of last night's dream had gradually worn off. And the other episode, whether dream or reality he knew not. Didn't want to know. Only anticipated "Wanda's" return once more, for he remembered now. Her name wasn't Wanda. It was Melissa. Or some pagan equivalent. Some barbarian queen of humble birth whom he'd loved and vowed to marry. Mike cleared some more earth, happy as a child, hands working automatically, at one with the soil; his mind elsewhere.

The sheds. What to do about the sheds? Were they safe from intruders? A great liability? (Where the fuck did that shit come from?, he asked himself for the gazillionth time. Was it really stolen, or had he dropped both oars in the water?) Mike intended to explore the others, soon. He relished the thought. At the very least, he'd move some of the outbuilding's expensive gadgets and stolen electronic equipment into the house, as soon as he'd charged the wind generator's twin marine batteries. Its little propeller-like rotor was spinning madly even now, charging the household's 12-volt, deep-cycle batteries. He mustn't tell a soul about the shed, not even his untrustworthy, pseudo-friends. They'd rat for a Crimestopper's reward, or clean him out when he's away, he was certain. Trust only me, myself, and I, he'd always said.

A chilly nor'wester blew across the meadow as Mike sat upon a log smoking a big, Cuban cigar. He felt tired and bleary-eyed. He'd have to drive to nearby Spiritwood soon to buy more groceries. Nearby, yellow daffodils fluttered in the breeze, bloomed just days ago. Deep purple violets clustered around the decaying log. Mike sat forward, elbows on his knees, scheming.

Four o'clock he stood at the single door of one of the bigger outbuildings, eyeing its rusty combination lock dispassionately. He hated to break it. But it had to be done. The ancient building, sited beside a rust-streaked, Rosco steel silo, hadn't a single window, so breaking one to crawl inside was not an option. Not that he'd do that. Mike thought it might've been a hay loft once; the smell of silage hung about the place. Collapsing, leaning timber fences strangled by rose briars stood nearby in a sorry state, a relic of harder, simpler times. Aurora liked its mossy, rustic air of aged permanence, as if saying *"We'll never die."*

There were loading-bay doors as well, but he opted to enter through the small side door; it looked flimsier.

He brought the 4-lb. ball-peen hammer down with a vicious crack, snapping the lock from its stuck, corroded latch. A second blow broke the unhinged clasp from the rotted doorframe. Aurora ripped the door open, nearly tearing the cheap, veneered thing from its rusted hinges. The old toolshed hadn't been entered in untold years. It looked it. Moss and mould had accumulated over the decades into a thick mat up on the sagging roof. Though marginally smaller than the first outbuilding he had entered, it was still a behemoth of a building with its pioneer-era, saddlebow roof. (He figured it was a smaller, albeit much later, clone of that behind the house.) No light penetrated the stale, wooden building. Boxes upon boxes lay tossed randomly about the 20′ x 40' ft. edifice. On closer inspection they proved thankfully empty, save for spiders' and mice nests.

However, two feet down amidst the jumble appeared a gleaming pair of handlebars.

Oh shit.

An hour later Aurora had uncovered the machine – plus a score of others. They were used, obviously rich kids' toys. Others seemed brand-spanking new. Like a '77 Yamaha IT 250 on/off-road motorcycle, still gleaming, would you believe it! A 1984 Honda Shadow. Kawasaki KX 125, well-used obviously.

But what caught Mike's eye was an ancient, battered Harley.

A '58 Sportster, 750 cc's, single saddle. Teardrop, Fat Bob gas tank. A beauty. Antique (collector's item!, if he wasn't mistaken). Full of integrity, sex appeal, meanness. Faded metal, leather, studs, chrome. Several hundred pounds heavy, Mike guessed. A monster. It was badly scuffed, dirty, grimy, showing its years; he doubted it would ever run. It had a huge V-Twin engine beneath its chassis, plus a chromed, oval oil filter.

Alongside it to his shock stood a well-used Harley Davidson Electra Glide. Metallic blue. Fat Bob tank, balloon tires, panniers, windjammer, the works. Loaded. Still worth a wad of money.

Jesus H, I've stumbled onto a goddamn biker's haul out here, Mike thought feverishly.

All of the bikes were dusty, draped with cobwebs. One could see they hadn't been touched in years.

So far today unearthed bright green Kawasaki dirtbike, blue Ducati trail bike, white Harley Electra Glide (the type used by state troopers in California), faded maroon Sportster…bright blue fibreglass IT Yamaha…

There were more beneath the stupendous pile of filthy boxes.

Mike rushed back to the house, grabbing a flashlight.

By midnight he'd uncovered fifteen motorcycles buried under various dirty debris. Dirtbikes, minibikes, derelicts, street racers, recent models, collectors' editions, massive Moto Guzzis, Harleys *(three of them, for Chrissakes!)*, Indians, feisty Suzukis, Hondas, Husquvarnas, Yamahas, Bultacos, Kawasakis.

But why?

Why here?

Why not unloaded right away? Surely a thriving black market in the States, eastern Canada, overseas…

No use wracking his brain over it. It didn't make sense. Mike raced over to the other, opened shed thirty feet away and hefted back a box of Penthouse to his place.

FIVE.

Wanda (Melissa) didn't appear.

Mike waited. And waited. And waited. He fell asleep at sunrise.

And catapulted out of bed at eight when the farmhouse started to shake, rock, vibrate.

Then it stopped.

At first Mike thought "Somebody's brought an effin' bulldozer. A wrecking ball."

Outside all was still.

Nobody, outside, at all.

He explored the old building from attic to basement. Finding nothing broken, dislodged, or out of place.

No damage at all.

Mike sat at the table for over an hour, perplexed. He hadn't thought tremors occurred in Saskatchewan, this far north. An earthquake? He rushed outside in a panic to verify if his wind turbine still stood. Amazingly, it did. He puzzled over why the windows hadn't shattered or cracked, as was often the case with a tremor of this magnitude. The morning sun angled over the trees, sliced in half by their crowded treetops. In the farmyard, fragrant apple blossoms were blooming, white flowers imparting a pretty vista to the ancient homestead. (Mike thought it a small miracle they'd matured this far north.) He'd noticed the four fruit trees were both crab and regular apple. The fruit would be delicious come fall, and ripened and available for canning come winter. He looked forward to home-baked apple pie. Perhaps he'd ask Wanda…

Wanda. She didn't exist, you idiot. Just the sign that he was cracking up. Loony tunes. He'd already signed a lifelong commitment to his very own, exclusive, funny farm. Which wasn't funny. He ought to contact *National Enquirer* (or some other tabloid) and explain how he'd had sexual relations with a demon girl. Wicked Wanda, vampire; first Mike's semen, then his soul...

But Mike knew that he was now, at least, technically wealthy. Or so it seemed. And if the mob knew of his location (which they did), in mortal peril. (Or not.) What to do? Sell the farm, move to Arizona? Call the R.C.M.P.? Go on extended – permanent – vacation? Blow his brains out?

Fuck 'em all, and fuckin' no regret…

Hell no, I won't go…

Mike moped about the farm all afternoon. He explored the old, slowly collapsing barn behind the house, the chicken yard and coop (minus chickens), empty pig pens, decayed cattle stalls. Aurora enjoyed the earthy, fragrant barnyard smell, its myriad range of odors, of well-rotted manure, flowers galore, fresh lumber, rotted logs, conifers and stagnant backwaters nearby. He wandered over to the slough behind a wooden granary, peering thoughtfully into its murky, green depths and endless variety of vegetation within and around. It would make an ideal lagoon, an outdoor sewer, if it weren't so far away .

As he entered the garden enclosure he made a wide berth around the old man's little red tractor. It seemed oddly sinister today, a mean snarl to its rusted, bug-eyed grill. Twin headlamps, both broken, stared back as if with ill-intent. As if contemplating rolling forward on its fat, treaded tires to crush him with its heavy back wheels. A nasty thought. Why do you think up these things, Mike?

Stubbornly resisting a feeling of unease, Mike climbed onto the old tractor, shifting its stiff gearstick playfully. It smelt appealingly of grease and heavy farm oil, old rubber, heated, decaying upholstery on the hard seat.

But the tractor didn't like him.

Climbing off, Mike repressed a shudder as he touched the warm, metal rear fender. He felt extreme distaste for this lump of metal cluttering his garden. Must sell the damn thing, or put it back inside the barn.

It was then that he remembered his uncle had died on the machine. The thought gave Mike the creeps.

He spent the next two hours till suppertime rummaging through the "appliances, gadgets, and what not" shed, searching hopefully for a compact garden tiller. Nope. No such equipment here. (He'd noticed, mildly surprised, that there were no personal computers or the like: maybe they'd sold out on Day One, a regular black marketeer's auction, thought Mike with a wry smile.) Plenty of other interesting things, however. Like a factory-fresh Hitachi VCR; an expensive one at that. Mike didn't own a VCR. The device's coaxial cable was present, too. Too short though, if he wanted to set it on the dresser next to his TV – no problem. He had a cable he'd stolen in P.A., a long one perfect for his – *repeat that, his* – house. He decided he'd watch some blue movies tonight, see if anything caught his fancy. Aurora worried if several seasons of cold, prairie winters had ruined some of this stuff; appliances, books, microchips. Yet the boxes were obviously airtight, and most were sealed, from what he could detect. Mould had gotten at much that wasn't. And it was all his. For now. Mike felt a delicious, forbidden thrill at the knowledge, immensely jubilant at his secret stash which nobody (he hoped) knew about. Except the Mafia, unless they was doin' time. For *l-i-f-e*, hopefully.

Aurora began formulating desperate plans to protect

the farm from hoods who might conceivably drop in one night to pay him a visit. (At some point, he'd have to realise that he was being paranoid, delusional, beyond the umpteenth degree! But for now, caution was paramount.) The various assorted handguns, illegal automatic weapons, high-powered rifles and twenty-gauge shotguns might come in handy, thought Mike. Yet he knew he was in no position to survive a shootout with hired hitmen. Or bikers. But the sight of these big-boys' toys arrayed before him inside this shed made him feel safer, a false bravado.

Mike carried a .45 Magnum in a holster, strapped to his chest, a Remington pump-action 12-gauge shotgun, and U.S. army issue M16 high-powered automatic rifle back to the house.

And barricaded himself for the night.

****

The ancient Harley balked at starting.

That was *no* surprise; after countless years buried under greasy cardboard boxes within the old outbuilding, neglected, no wonder it wouldn't fire when Mike jumped down on its tough, high-compression kickstarter. Machines had a way of mysteriously ceasing to function over so-and-so number of years of disuse, considered Aurora.

A quirk of Mike's nature led him to try and coax the big Harley into running. He tinkered with its starter decompressor a bit. The day was hot, the early June leaves unfurled like little green flags. Heat waves blurred the pasture. Swallows flocked across the barnyard like hordes of oversized purple butterflies, flitting about and finally landing on rooftops in lieu of power lines or telephone poles. That's right, there wasn't even a telephone out here. Mike fiddled with the bike's choke, its gas flow, checked the oil filter. It wasn't great, but passable. Its tiny leather saddle was cracked and brittle with age, definitely needed replacing. The venerable old hog exerted a fascination over Mike far out of proportion to its value in terms of beauty, cleanliness, newness. In fact it was a horrendously ugly bike, but bore an irresistible air of timeless decrepitude and indestructibility. Aurora naturally gravitated toward antiques. He'd like, someday, to become an antique dealer.

Several of the motorcycles Mike had already had running and taken for trial runs around the farm. The thrill of riding each machine (including one mini-bike) almost stilled his heart as Mike sped through the pasture, up and down its rolling hills, carefully keeping well away from the road and out of sight of nosy neighbours. He loved the exotic motorbikes, the roaring power beneath his thighs. The big ones were scary, for he was afraid of taking a spill, having a bike fall on top of him, break his leg, or involve an ambulance or neighbours somehow. No police needed out here, thank you. The leggy dirtbikes were fun, racy, ripping around the barnyard with their knobby tires, chewing up the sod, their bleaty, whiny exhaust pipes spewing nostalgic-smelling two-stroke fumes into the air. Their engines emitted a loud, nasty, high-pitched noise which screamed across the pasture. The Suzuki was his favourite, an older model, used, yellow motocross lacking decals, taillight, headlight, or signals. It had a square, black racing plate where a headlight ought to have been. The big racer was a lanky 450, of nondescript model (Mike suspected by the shape, however, that it was the characteristic 1981 RM 450, one incredibly fast bike, by all accounts). Which was the funniest thing. Virtually everything inside the sheds had had its serial numbers filed off. No need to worry too much about police.

But why do that? If uncle Joe had bought, or acquired, these bikes legit, why file off the serial numbers?

It wasn't police Mike was worried about. He'd been here almost a month now, yet no mysterious vans, bikes,

Cadillacs or new sports cars – Lamborghinis, Trans-Ams, or Porsches, for instance – had been seen skulking about nearby. There were few enough $60,000 dollar vehicles this far north of P.A., Saskatoon, Regina, North Battleford. Yet he knew…he knew…just a matter of time before some goon spoils Mike's year. Head blown off, face down.

So why not go to the cops, turn it all over for a reward?

No way.

He had a rabid paranoia of police officers, wondered how the hell he would explain all this shit in his yard without sounding like a con…

Keep what interests you then, let the R.C.M.P. haul away the rest?

Mike wanted it all. He was greedy.

Upon closer inspection, he'd discovered earlier that virtually everything had been opened, serial numbers filed off, and then boxes professionally resealed with a glue gun. Any names or addresses had been scotched as well. Still he failed to understand how his uncle Joe had managed to get involved, nor from whence the pilfered goods came from. And how it had been stolen, especially that which had been new. Nor how uncle Joe had gotten away with it all these years. Why hadn't it been offloaded eons ago? Perhaps this was the remainder from one or more major, unsolved warehouse heists somewhere? An endless plethora of questions besieged Mike's brain.

Wanda had not returned for over two weeks since her last visitation/materialization.

He missed her sorely. Their scintillating sex. Except for occasional jaunts to the nearest grocery store, town, or city, he'd socialized with nobody. Was becoming paranoid, deranged, unhinged. When not cultivating his newly-sprouted garden, Mike spent most of his time drooling over porno movies on his purloined 19-inch RCA color console TV (powered by gas generator) and illicit VCR. What a misfit he was becoming. Single, lonely, moderately wealthy (it seemed to him) through an inheritance. An outcast.

Days he spent staring vacantly at his electric typewriter's keys, writer's block after his novel's first chapter. The Smith-Corona's keyboard eluded him of interesting things to write. The manuscript "Return of the Vampire…1993" was going nowhere. No big advance for Mike's mass-market bestseller would be forthcoming this summer. Or winter. Who cares?

Tuesday, June 28, 1994, Mike dreamt of Melissa.

Conan (Conigcad) was leading a cohort south through the treacherous Caucasus massifs of Armenia (or whatever the hell gibberish they called it at the time), having marched at a brisk pace across the Russian steppes, straying over the Parthian border into Moldavia, beyond the Carpathian mountain-passes and jagged peaks and then eastwards into Caucasia once more, in search of ravaging brigands; his fleet, mounted prey ever elusive. He'd been chosen by the High King Dristan to lead a crack troop of gladiators against the massing hordes of the eastern steppes. Far to the east, in Central Asia and southern Siberia, Mongols and Huns had overthrown the venerated *Uchel-Ri*, Trostig, High King of the East, bringing catastrophe and plunder to the feuding, mercantile folk of western *Rhos Land* (Tir Rhosieg). All this had occurred abruptly, just over a year ago. Now a new generation of interlopers had flooded in from Mother Russia's steppe lands, reaching western Europe in isolated bands of opportunistic marauders. They'd pillaged as far west as Gaul and Ysbäenia, settling in insular, self-contained communities on scarped hilltops commanding estuaries and headlands, facing the hostile natives across fortified hills. Soon to be outdone concerning the magnificence and ingenuity of their hillforts. At first it had seemed they were renegade compatriots, expelled for tyranny from some distant land.

But it had soon become apparent, although the newcomers called themselves *Gaedhels*, like the Caledonians of Macedonia and northern Greece, that these freebooters whose language sounded oddly familiar were Outsiders. Great Gods, some said. But they were not gods. Nor even particularly bright. They quarreled amongst themselves for the ungodliest reasons. And they died like mortals, their blood flowing like any slain foes'.

Their weapons however were steel, more than a match for the putty-like bronze swords and shields of the *Armäenii* whom they'd annihilated.

Fortunately, blacksmiths had been teaching the behind-the-times Westerners the novel art of smelting iron for several decades. This marvelous, godly new alloy had come from the mysterious East, from the ultra-warlike Sarmatians along the shores of the Black and Caspian seas who were thoroughly drubbing the south Chechnians and distantly related Medians, or Farsi, barbaric fireworshippers. It was rumoured of the distant Sarms how, for want of manpower, their tallest, bravest women had for centuries trained in the forbidden arts of war, learning swordsmanship, cavalry, composite bow on horseback, or longbow infantry. To Conan this seemed hilarious.

He'd thought so until he'd met Felissa.

She'd captured his awe and respect from the first he'd lain eyes on the Belgic queen at her modest capital of Dinas Aur, City of Gold, which would someday be called Leningrad, as the prophets knew. Queen Felissa had impressed the humbled Conigcat (his warrior name) with her forthright nature, stunning beauty, and shockingly bawdy remarks. She had inherited her uncle's throne, surprising the populace of Bel with her rapacious desire to conquer, to extend the old man's domains into a pan-Belgae empire. Few clans had dared resist. She had taken the whole of the Germanies and Gaul, crowning herself *Ymheraduress*, Empress of the West.

Conan had been smitten by her. (Literally.)

He in turn had earned a fearsome reputation as a courageous and mighty swordsman, master-at-arms, familiar with the superior, new iron weapons, and the even more devastating swords of steel. Conigcat had fought bravely, for he knew these savages would give no quarter. Nor would his seasoned unit. The Scolots were headhunters, bloodthirsty barbarians who would drink their foes' blood, or impale them on horses.

The battle raged on till dusk.

Hundreds of well-armed *Gaédheltacht* leapt from overhanging boulders, or rained deadly arrows from their bows onto Conan's Etruscan and Minoan infantry. The Mediterraneans' long, heavy, oval, eagle-emblazoned shields protected them from much of the Goidels' merciless barrage. The battle-crazed Scythians (named after their scythe-outfitted chariots which had displaced the wandering Cimmerians from the steppes), screamed in rage and bloodlust, yelling to the great god *Dághda*, the All-Father, to ensure victory. If triumphant the Scotti would cut off the vanquished men's noses, ears, penises. And take home their scalps and skulls.

The path had proven deadly treacherous to the outnumbered Cymräe.

By nightfall, the majority of Conigcad's warriors lay slain, wounded, or dying. Many had fled out of sheer cowardice, only to be cut down and scalped whilst still alive. Their screams, moans, and pitiful cries filled the mountain pass as dusk descended onto the rocky valley gorge. Mt. Elbrüz loomed in the distance, its glacial cap, moraines, effluvial channels and sandy, gravelly, former-glacial ravines and glens safe havens against hostile invaders. The Chechnians, Parthians, Georgians and Armenians were insidiously advancing, year by year, like a slow-grinding glacial mass down the valleys. And there'd be no escape.

Disarmed, trussed-up after being outnumbered, outfoxed, outfought, Conigcad and his troops were marched eastward up the glens, pushed viciously and stumbling as night fell like a funeral pall. Several hundred stormtroopers of the Empress's finest and most loyal legion had been reduced to two hundred seventy-three bloodied, wounded wretches. Maniacal Gaels lashed their backs with leather thongs as the subdued prisoners-of-war were transported higher and higher into the lofty pass. Some of the weaker, more timid would be taken as bedwarmers for the savages' warrior elite, as was the homosexual warrior-caste's wont, a custom as yet restricted to the Scytti and their Oriental, Negroid, and Australasian neighbours. Conan vowed he'd not be one of these, vowed he would kill a thousand-score of the barbars, these usurpers, as he and his sorry remnant of a contingent were marched toward the Gauls' fortified encampment high up in the frigid Caucasus pass. They'd stolen not only his people's technology, priesthood, and mangled language, but enslaved their women and children as well. The wrath of the Belgae and their giant, blondish allies, the Cimbri of Scandinavia, would be a terrible retribution. The Goidels' blood would fill the Cimbris' sacred cauldrons.

Immediately the Gaulish fort came into view, a concentric, drystone ring of ramparts looming over the prisoners from a spur in the pass. Hundreds of defleshed human skulls grinned macabrely from twenty-foot walls. A bright, crescent moon balanced on the upper rampart. Below the crest, several earthen embankments protected the Gauls' citadel.

Once inside the rath's impressive, rough-hewn walls, Conan's bedraggled, dispirited cohort were gathered around a sacred well.

And one by one were thrown in as a sacrifice to *Teüfel*,

or *Teutates*, God of War, as an offering; to be buried alive.

Three thousand years distant, another place, another time, Mike Aurora awoke screaming!

****

He woke in a sweat, his pulse thumping, heart in his throat and drumming loud. Goidels? Scythians? Cimbri? Who were these assholes? As Mike sat trembling on his mattress on the living-room floor, his mind clicked. Goidels. Gauls. He remembered now. In his high-school textbooks on social studies Mike recalled a particularly boring class taught by an excruciatingly boring teacher, old Mr. Rattlesbottom. It was about the Celts, jerks who painted themselves blue and scalped each other. They'd sacrificed people and cattle (and whatever else was handy) in wicker men. Nice guys. They'd also invented Hallowe'en. The Celts, remembered Mike (berating himself for not catching on earlier) were Gaelic speakers. Irish yokels. St. Patrick, another asshole, had converted the pagan Irish who previously enjoyed jumping about like salmon, challenging friends and family to duels and racing around in chariots for no known reason. But who the hell were the Cimmerians?

Britons.

The other side of the Celtic branch.

Mike had been a Briton. Named Conigcat.

He smiled nostalgically.

****

Mike smashed the third, but largest, outbuilding's single door in with an axe.

For weeks he'd put off entering this, the last of the farm's sheds. Its rusted lock had resisted repeated blows with his axehead. So Mike bashed the door in.

He'd feared what he might conceivably find. Couple of Russian tanks? More M16 assault rifles? Hey Sticky Fingers, throw in a couple of 'dem grenade launchers and bazookas, will ya?

No Patriot missiles here. The long, low, near-hangar-sized shed was well supplied with windows, six per side. Plenty of sunlight illuminated the colossal building. More junk tossed about. A heavy layer of dust, cobwebs, and grime coated the shop's interior. Dead flies lay everywhere. Birds had roosted yearly up in its rafters.

Toys, wrecked furniture, glass from a broken window, machinery, parts, tobacco cans of nuts and bolts, rotting, stinking vegetables, tattered blankets, nutshells and yellowed newspapers lay scattered about. Over here a child's spinning top. Over here an antique phonograph, its funnel-horn still intact. Worth big bucks. Over here a battered trombone. Several wrecked acoustic guitars, including an electric, fifties'-style, Buddy Holly Fender. Mike intended to salvage the quaint, old musical instrument. Seventies' pin-ups from girlie mags still tacked to the woodframe walls, askew and faded but alluringly sexy. Penthouse Pets, Playboy Playmates, Swank…

He wasn't surprised to find the hoards of silverware under tarpaulins at the rear of the building.

He *was* surprised, however, to discover a human skeleton's finger-joints protruding through the dirt below some decayed boxes.

Mike shouted aloud in fright.

At first he thought he was dreaming; then he pinched himself, realizing he was not.

The finger bones were real. The genuine McCoy. A primate's hand, or human, carelessly buried here in the garage's (?) dirt floor. Mike pulled it from the earth in disgust, expecting maggots. It was surprisingly clean. He scratched beneath the surface, searching for the missing forearm.

Mike's heart pounded wildly. The grisly bone was but a single, solitary fragment. He wondered maniacally if it had pushed up through the soil from the earth's own, underground pressure, as rocks often were. Or perhaps some unknown agency? He began to tremble. Jinx farm! Skeletons in the closet, I guess! Mike dug around with his axehead, then raced back to the garden for a shovel.

Three feet down, and nothing. No sign of a burial. (He scratched his head, thinking "Okay, where's the rest of it?") The old outbuilding lacked a floor, as if unfinished. The ancient hand-bone was yellowed, perhaps a relic of an Indian burial ground. Creeps! A large mound of earth beside him kept sliding back down into the shallow hole. Six hours later, at twilight, Aurora quit, speedily refilling the empty 'grave'. An ancient burial ground. Nothing to have a hairy about. Happened all the time. Just be thankful no poltergeists plagued the farm.

Yet.

Really ought to contact some archaeologists about this, Mike thought.

He turned his attention to the hoard before him, delving deeper into the treasure trove, astonishment growing with each discovery.

Sixteen indigo-blue plastic crates held an eccentric's hoard of silverware, expensive china, wedding and anniversary commemoratives, gold centenaries, more jewellery, bronze statues of seeming antiquity, heirlooms, precious gems. Mike leapt up and down in the uncomfortably cramped space for ten seconds, whooping with joy over his astounding, unbelievable find. A cashe! A friggin' stash! The day Who came to Who village, the Grinch who stole Christmas! Aeeeeeeeeeeee!

Okay, buddy boy, calm down, get a grip on yourself!

Mike tenderly placed the old tarps over his stolen find, looking about furtively and rubbing his hands together, smiling schemingly. (Suddenly the pistol-holster on his shoulder didn't seem like such a barmy idea after all, he reflected.) A bloated, full moon hung high in the south-eastern sky, a huge, crater-pocked, white orb so luminous and deceptively near one felt one could almost climb there on a celestial ladder and touch it. It reminded Aurora of Swiss cheese (okay, so he was hungry), which also reminded him that he had a chunk of it in his hamper. And fresh homemade bread.

10:00, gotta rock. Gotta rock n' roll on out of here, get some nourishment in my belly, Mike berated himself. Can't be caught in here. Ever. Never mind his nearest neighbour lived four miles away. A cautious rat is a live rat. And dead men tell no tales.

Mike closed the big shed's shattered door, stepping furtively out of the shadows and into the light of the moon. Feeling watched. Grotesque birch and aspen shadows seemed to shift menacingly, as if darting away from his stalking form.

"Hey you, what the fuck are you doing here?!!"

Mike nearly jumped out of his skin, deafened as a blinding, white-red blast cracked the night silence. An automatic pistol-shot rang out from the grounds dead ahead! He rolled to his right, landing heavily on his shoulder and tumbling several feet into a rose briar bristling with thorns.

Another shot exploded from the yard, followed by a flickering flashlight beam. Mike winced, expecting a bullet to slam into his prone body. He'd been damned lucky already not to have his head blown off.

"Come out of the rosebush, punk, or I'll blow yer friggin' head off. You 'yere me? Punk? Hey?! You know what I mean, man!?" A gruff voice snarled an oath, a loud, low, bowser-type growl with a most definite Yankee twang. Mike, quivering, could barely discern the trespasser's craggy features from his prickly hiding spot. He watched, terrified, as the thug cocked his snub-nosed revolver again.

"That's it. I'm gonna put a bullet in you, boy. Say bye-bye, kid."

Mike, panicked, yanked the suddenly-remembered Magnum from his shoulder holster, frantically aiming its long barrel through a rose briar.

An ear-shattering *"ca-boom!"* split the night silence. Mike's wrist jerked up, knocking his forehead with the big revolver's butt. The intruder - a mere, dark silhouette - jerked back suddenly, pitching backward as Mike's bullet slammed into his chest with brutal impact, throwing his foe five feet before sprawling the interloper flat on his back before the warped, collapsing, moss-dotted cattle corrals. Mike leapt up screaming from the thorny, clinging rosebush, rushing forward to pursue his attacker.

The assailant lay in a crimson pool of blood, a gaping softball-size hole in his chest. Mike grimaced nastily, cocking his .45 Magnum and pointed it dispassionately at the intruder's head.

The dying man's gray eyes had already begun to glaze.

Mike blew his head off, shattering it like a pumpkin.

****

Aurora spent the last hour before midnight rubbing salve on bleeding scratches caused by sharp rose-thorns. Fortunately, his bomber jacket had taken much of the thicket's brunt except where the sleeves had pushed up, exposing Mike's plaid-shirted forearms. Briars had gashed his collar bone nastily.

Mike worried not at all about the body left out in the farmyard. What were the chances of somebody else walking onto the property on a night like this. It had begun to rain about an hour ago. Nor did he think it likely the assailant's corpse would rise up and walk off, or be commandeered by someone else. He'd blown its head off. And had felt no remorse afterwards. As if he'd done it before, killed countless scores without compassion.

By midnight it was raining cats and dogs.

Mike stood in the dark kitchen, revolver in hand. He stared out the old-fashioned sash window, waiting for an ominous beam of headlights or a flashlight's flicker from the driveway. His eyes flicked nervously from corner to corner, expecting an attacker, human or otherwise. A solitary candle in makeshift candleholder stood to his left atop a cupboard. All windows and doors locked and braced from within.

He awoke in Wanda's arms just before dawn.

At first he couldn't believe it. He'd come to convince himself over the past few weeks that she had never existed. A figment of his imagination. Nor could he comprehend how this ghostly woman had materialized under his bedcovers without his waking, reaching in a panic for his pistol. She hadn't announced her coming. Mike patted her solid upper back skeptically, her flesh firm and somehow warm. Impossible. She smelled of clover.

"After this night we'll not meet again."

Mike was astonished to hear the revenant speak. He had so thoroughly convinced himself that he'd only heard Wanda's lush voice inside his head, those exquisite nights past.

Mike did not respond. Instead, he rolled her over onto her back.

"I killed a man tonight."

"I know."

"Doesn't that surprise you?"

"No," replied Wanda, smiling languidly. "I'm aware of everything you do, *Miguel.* Day or night. I know your every thought....You can't hide from my all-knowing eyes."

"Everyth..."

"I know what movies you watch, what magazines you read. And what you do to sate your desires." She rolled over, then smiled. "In 1500 B.C., I was High Priestess, remember?" Wanda had begun to speak in Celtic, a veritable shock, for Mike recognized it as such immediately, and understood.

To Mike's astonishment he answered her back in fluent, archaic Brythonic.

"Yes, I remember now."

"Did you think I'd abandoned you?"

"Yes. I'd thought you were but a dream. Where did you go?" Mike nuzzled Wanda's neck, kissing her throat tenderly.

She sighed, smiling with pleasure.   "Ummm. I had business elsewhere."

"Where elsewhere?"

"None of your business."

"Where?"

"Oh, Michael! Stop." She chuckled sexily, pecking his cheek, then thrusting her tongue into his mouth. He entered Wanda with ease, licking, caressing, kissing and sucking on her ponderous breasts as she matched his rhythm, caressing his arms, back, and buttocks as her breath quickened.

"Where?"

"Oh, baby, please… I met with the Druids."

Mike halted, stunned as Wanda thrust toward his hips.

"Druids…"

"Uh hm. The *Gorsedd Ddu*. The Black Circle. Judges who persecute those who stray from the Path…Oh, *Miguel*, keep it going, it feels so good baby, mmm…"

∎∎∎

He silenced her with a long, urgent kiss, oblivious of time, space, reality as Mike exploded five minutes later like a Saturn rocket to Wanda's orgasmic moans, cries, and heavy breathing. She clutched him close, squeezing him like scissors and kissing his chest as she climaxed with a scream.

"Was it good for you?"

Mike jerked awake from a pleasant doze, body slick with sweat as "Wanda" lay sprawled atop of him, her lovely, raven-haired head upon his chest. She was absolutely scintillating, sinfully beautiful and smiling coyly. Her cheeks, Mike noticed, were flushed and rosy. He kissed her forehead, eyelids, lips, cheeks, ears, neck. So in love. So out of his head. In love with a ghost, a "guest", or *geist,* as the Germans called it. Sex guest. She stretched luxuriously, naked on top of him, blankets thrown off during their heated, delicious lovemaking. A forbidden love. Blasphemy.

"It always is. You're my first, and you're not even real, but a friggin' ghost."

"Perhaps."

"So why are you here? To keep me company? Get your jollies in the spirit world?"

"To finish unfinished business."

"With whom? Or what."

"The barbarians. To destroy mine enemies, fill the

world with the bodies of the dead." Wanda sat up slowly, a manic gleam in her eyes. "I was sent by God to annihilate the unbelievers, our ancient foes who hath returned from the grave to pervert and subvert my planet. You and I shall turn their hallowed lands into a cemetery, my love, and will rule for a thousand-year reign. Shall resurrect the great standing-stones, usher in a millenium of peace and prosperity for our own. Civilizations will bow to us as gods, do our very bidding, kill our enemies, enslave the survivors."

Mike sat up, stunned.

"Yowsa, yowsa, yowsa! You are a madwoman, Wanda. You sound like an Aryan Supremist. Like Adolf Hitler. I like you." Mike paused, frowning. "Just how do you plan to do all this?"

"You'll see."

Surprisingly, Mike didn't for a moment question her sincerity.

As he dozed, she whispered in his ear, *"my Dark Lord of the Sith..."*

He drifted off to sleep, exhausted.

****

Mike buried the body in the forest, careful to extract several hundred dollars in crisp bills from the hooligan's wallet and burning his I.D. card after copying down its info. Bill Wallace, from Tacoma, Washington, a man with dual citizenship, aged 35, crew-cut brown hair, was rolled over unceremoniously into a six-foot-deep hole in the ground. Songbirds and squabbling magpies twittered and chattered restlessly as Aurora shoveled spadefuls of rich, black forest soil smelling of pungent humus into the grave. He said no prayers, no special words when he finished the grisly job. He knew he should next locate the criminal's (for Mike was sure the man was Mafia) vehicle, which must be somewhere nearby. Hidden in a lane nearby, probably. (The trespasser couldn't have come by bus, because no Greyhound service operated out here.) Mike had dragged the body two hundred yards into the broad-leaf forest, at the most open spot he could find. He'd brought a pick to loosen the soil and rocks. The corpse – by now stiffened with rigor mortis – had been heavy as a sack of dirt as Mike dragged it through wild strawberries, raspberry brambles, Saskatoon bushes, and clumps of violets on the forest floor. The now-rank cadaver Mike guessed approached 6' 4", weighing over 200 lbs., a genuine tough monkey if ever he saw one.

Wide, lantern jaw. Ivory white, false teeth. (He'd discovered his dentures only after stepping on the damned things while dragging the stiff away from the stockade.) Tailor-made clothes by the looks, expensive cuff links. Unscuffed, shiny, black leather Gucci shoes.

Mike thought not at all of whether some busybody, relative, or R.C.M.P. might track the stranger here in this leafy, gloomy, mixed aspen/birch forest. He'd tucked the trespasser's snub-nosed pistol into his belt, carefully washing down the spot where his assailant had been shot. He'd poured two five-gallon buckets of steaming water onto the ground, cleansing the patch of trampled, blood-soaked grass.

No one must ever know.

Mike was at least relieved to know the man wasn't a plain-clothes police officer...

Afterwards he scattered leaves, twigs, forest debris over the tell-tale, freshly dug earth.

And stalked off to find the intruder's vehicle.

Mike found the car, just as he'd predicted, parked in a nearby field approach. It was a nineties' model black Mercedes-Benz, sparkling, immaculate, hidden behind a big thicket of pussy willow. With the deceased's keys he unlocked the car, checked the gravel road for traffic, then calmly started the sporty sedan and backed out of the field, easing the beautiful Mercedes off the main road and down his narrow driveway. Mike drove the turbo-charged 190E into the barn, heaping piles of rotten alfalfa onto 'his' new car. He intended to put his own plates on the vehicle and use it. Someday. When he's old and gray. The snazzy-looking Mercedes, well concealed now beneath a ton of hay, would tell no tales.

Until discovered.

The vehicle had been rented at a Tilden agency in North Battleford, which worried him. They'd turn over every stone in the province looking for the swanky mid-size car. Mike burnt the car's registration and identity papers, buried its plates.

He patched the chicken-wire fence surrounding his garden enclosure, mending it with bailer-twine to keep out deer and raccoons. Next he puttered-around in the toolshed beside the outdoor toilet, killing the rest of the day trying to fix an old kerosene lamp's broken wick mechanism.

Next he wheeled out the defunct Harley from one of the sheds, rolling it with an effort toward the distant barn, where he could fiddle with it to his heart's content without some yokel catching him with the illicit, old bike. Mike feared some nosy neighbour might walk into his yard unannounced, ask vexing questions or wander about the buildings unnoticed. People were wont to do that at the most inconvenient of times, he rationalized.

The sun had begun to set as Aurora rolled the bike into the tin-roofed barn, pushing the big machine with difficulty up a slight incline and over several knolls and ruts, grunting with effort as he forced the wide tires over each bump, rock, stick. (It was a chopper, so, rather awkward to steer.) At least the tires were solid, he reflected. The Harley smelt good, familiar, its oily engine and ancient metal wonderful to the ex-mechanic's senses. Especially if one were to restore it. Mike had no intention of sprucing it up, adding new chrome, paint, etc. He merely liked the challenge of getting the old monster running.

Which he meant to do even if it killed him.

<u>SIX.</u>

Mike stared entranced out the living room's sash window as the freak snowstorm raged outside. Freak because it was July 31, rather early (!) in the year for snow. However, he had witnessed, once, a white-out as late in the summer as August here in Sask. This wasn't totally unheard of.

But a drag.

Twenty minutes later, it was over.

His property was down in a hollow, a micro-climate, you might say – where temperatures frequently dropped below the norm, compared to other locales nearby. Nonetheless, such abnormal extremes were unusual, even for the Lakes district of central Saskatchewan.

Aurora cussed as he thought about his tender, flourishing plants out in the garden freezing. But maybe, with a little luck, he could replant. Since the temperature was hovering just above 0° C, he was sure that hardier, larger vegetables, like cabbage or potatoes, would survive. (But then again, he wasn't about to start emptying his piggy bank to lay a wager on it.) Mike stood at the window, smoking idly as he watched gusting snowflakes outside the drafty farmhouse. Inside his living-room the big woodstove radiated a glorious, toasty warmth to combat the old house's numerous drafts. He had twice baked bread in the big black-and-white woodstove's oven, a trying, exasperating experience, indeed, for one unaccustomed to life without electricity in this loon-haunted, prairie wilderness (the propane range's little oven never had worked, by all accounts). All the same, Mike loved the silence, the tranquility; the only noises that of frogs, owls, loons, and crickets. Coyotes' *cai-aaiing* sometimes kept him awake at night.

Ululating, spine-chilling wolves' howls often set his hair on end.

Mike's novel, after weeks of writer's block, had kicked into motion again. He was currently on page 105; a chapter involving a vampire-plagued cemetery in upstate New York, exorcism, vampire hunters from Kindersley, Sask. It was going well. Plenty of nights of research (encyclopedias, guidebooks, what-not) had gone into the book. It was his first real attempt at writing a novel.

Mike's Smith Corona office typewriter sat on a dresser beside him, plugged-in and ready for another two hours' work. It was a superb machine, cream white, slim, state of the art. A vastly superior machine to his old, stiff, tiny

Brother model – an ancient mechanical typewriter. It boasted a built-in 75,000 word memory, auto erase, auto recall. The ribbons cost a whopping $12.95 each (compared to $3.95 for a manual's ink ribbon). Effin' rip-off.

The leaden sky was darkening quickly, sun descending. Supper was cooking on the kitchen range and living room's woodstove: sweet 'n sour ribs, boiled carrots, pasta, baked potatoes in the woody.

Mike had yet to drag down some of the old man's furniture from up in the attic. He'd brought his own furnishings, coffee table, and stereo equipment in the back of his Impala from Sherbrook. He didn't relish crawling around up in the creepy attic. (He was severely allergic to dust.) Mike kept the house clean, though not spotless.

Aurora sat in his high-backed rocking chair, flipping through a recent Sears catalogue for a cheap, small gas burner. He'd found the old propane kitchen range, even the three top burners that did work, highly unpredictable. It often blew out for no reason, as if some playful sprite were blowing on it.

Ghosties.

No ghosties here.

I'm sure.

Except Mike swore he often felt eyes on the back of

his head. Like now. He glanced over his shoulder, relaxing, then tossing the plastic-smelling catalogue onto the floor and pushing the "on" button of his c.d./cassette deck nearby with a plasticky "click."

He sat listening to Mercyful Fate's latest, "In The Shadows" (no wonder he was so jumpy), bobbing his head to "Return of the Vampire…1993", a title he'd stolen for his horror novel. King Diamond, lead singer, was purported to be a genuine Satanist. Mike could care less. If he wanted to be the man's disciple he would've joined the band's fan club, pasted the ugly bastard's mug on his walls with posters from Hit Parade. He liked their music, what of it?

Mike had been doing some research into the occult, witches, possession, vampirism. He'd learnt that Stonehenge in the sixties had been a gathering place for modern-day druids before the British government cordoned-off the place – they'd been gettin' the fear. Fear of the devil. Ha!

He'd discovered what Saxons in the Middle Ages did to suspected witches. (Hung upside-down and roasted slowly.) He hadn't known this. Nor what the Gauls did to defeated enemies. An Indo-Iranian or possibly Hunnish tribe called Scythians used to impale their most-loyal warriors on horses, leaving them atop their king's burial mound, or bury them with their deceased chief and numerous strangled concubines (this was an honour for them!). He'd learnt of the Son of Sam murders in New York state.

Morbid stuff.

No wonder he was loony.

The murdered man's body, buried discreetly in the forest, had stayed put and untampered with, he'd made sure of that. Over two weeks now, and nobody suspicious had shown their faces. No Mounties. No Al Capone look-alikes. Paranoid, jumpy as a dog-mauled kitten, Mike had rigged-up a burglar alarm in the house (for what good he wasn't sure). Then regretted it. Nearest police were over twenty miles away. They wouldn't hear it. Nor, really, did he want them to. "Excuse me, Mr. Aurora, but there seems to be a dead man buried on your property. You wouldn't happen to know anything about this, would you?"

"Honest John, officer, I had no idea."

Yeah, right.

Mind you, it (the burglar alarm) might frighten the bejesus out of anyone trying to break-in, so a little extra security was always comforting, he reasoned.

But there were definite limits to what appliances one could run on DC, or even a gas generator-powered Mickey Mouse operation like Mike was powering out here in the sticks.

At seven-thirty Mike sat down for supper, ate in silence, smoked a cigarette before preparing for bed. (His purloined generator was out of fuel; no television tonight.) A single night-lamp on a countertop lit the kitchen. A boisterous Great Horned owl hooted outside somewhere nearby, possibly roosting in one of the old-growth aspen or spruce. Aurora washed a few dishes and left them in the sink before retiring. Three kerosene lamps illuminated the foyer, scullery, and living room along with an electric reading-light powered by Mike's twirling, whirring wind turbine outside. (A quasi-sine-wave inverter supplied the recommended house current.) Aurora meant to rummage through his uncle's 'hot' sheds tomorrow for another nightlight. Possibly two. Yet Mike had reservations about openly using these pilfered goods. In case an officer or a hit-man shows up on his doorstep to "account" for the missing things. Ah, gee, officer, I had no idea the stereo, guitar amp, heater, VCR, TV, books, typewriter, bikes and jewellery were stolen. Honest!

He sat in the living room reading Funk and Wagnall's "D" encyclopedia volume under kerosene lamp till ten. The old farmhouse's silence was unnerving. (Once again, his deep-cycle batteries were low on voltage, a constant irritant and the reason for the place's disquieting silence; a vast gulf of quietude without the mind-dulling but comforting drone of television, radio, or pre-recorded music.) A ghostly, moaning wind outdoors whispered at the old farmstead's stone/clapboard walls. Spruce boughs tapped annoyingly on a window at the back where the scullery was.

"GIVE – ME – BACK – MY – PENTHOUSE!!!!!!"

Mike nearly leapt a foot out of his chair, hair standing on end! A terrifying, horrific bellow seemingly emanating from all four walls shook the house like a hammer-blow. An angry, gruff, rage-shaking (elderly?) man's voice shattered the peaceful silence.

"MIKE AURORA, YOU FUCKING SON OF A BITCH!!! GET OUT OF MY HOUSE!! GET OUT OF MY HOUSE!!! OUT OF MY H-O-O-U-S-E!!!!!!"

Aurora snatched up his .45 from the dresser bearing his word processor, dashing into a corner and hunkering behind the woodstove as if expecting a fusillade of machine-gun fire.

Kitchen utensils began to sail about in the dining room, whizzing wildly about the place. A night lamp started to blink madly. Mike stared about crazily with disbelief, recalling *having turned-off the inverter two hours ago!* A vicious gust of polar wind assailed the living room, scattering Mike's sheaf of typed pages in an ever-increasing tornado, buffeting Aurora hostilely as he knelt behind the old stove.

"OUT – OF – MY – HOUSE!!!"

At once the whirlwind abated. A melancholy sigh seeped through the first-floor rooms, followed by a patter of feet sneaking up the creaking staircase.

Mike hopped up from his hiding place, waving his pistol maniacally and yelling as he raced after the contentious spook. Or whatever it was. He dashed up the stairs two at a time, wielding a hastily snatched six-volt flashlight in his hand as he stormed after the invisible intruder.

He banged doors open noisily, searching each room for the culprit. Mike peeked under piles of linen, ransacked closets, then, bracing himself, raced up the attic stairs to the old man's former lair. It was empty.

The mischievous spook had vanished.

Perhaps not. The old man's armchair was gently rocking...

Mike toppled it over in a fury.

Soon he was struggling with an invisible entity!

His unseen aggressor seized Mike's wrist in a glacial grip, battling for control of the handgun. An icy, undetected arm wrapped itself around his neck, choking.

Mike felt for all the world he was wrestling with a genuine, flesh-and-blood antagonist. A rather weak little ghost. (He nearly went into hysteria when he realized he could feel, *but not see*, his opponent's hairy arms in a death embrace!) Aurora flipped his invisible attacker over by using his right leg while jerking hard on his assailant's neck. Or what he assumed was a neck. Miraculously his six-volt lantern (having landed heavily on the attic floor) had remained alight. A powerful beam showed the vaguest shadow of Mike's overpowered, scrappy uncle's ghost (or whoever's) smelling disgustingly of rotting flesh. And grave mold.

He beat the shadow's curiously realistic, nondescript head in until the amorphous figure vanished. Then he pummeled wood.

■■■

3:00 a.m.

Mike Aurora sat jumpily in his rocking chair. The ticking grandfather clock filled the house's eerie silence with its sonorous "tic-toc, tic-toc, tic-toc." Aurora, bleary-eyed, searched the living room's dark corners for cunningly creeping shadows.

He held his revolver, not sure what harm the big handgun would do to a ghost. How to kill that which was already dead? Mike felt cosy, warm, sitting with his back to the woodstove. He had all corners of the room in view except that behind him. He felt no overwhelming, debilitating fear, only exhaustion.

■■■

A ball rolled from the darkened kitchen toward his feet.

Mike gazed down at it in shock. A street-hockey-sized red plastic ball lay motionless at his shoe. Aurora nudged it with his foot.

It leapt up, smacking him in the face.

Enraged, Mike grabbed the ball as it tried to scuttle away, chucking the ice-cold object into the roaring woodstove.

And swore he'd heard screams from inside.

From the glass door-panel an old man's face, contorted with rage, glared from within.

Mike turned away. Then fitfully dozed.

He awoke at four in the morning with a jolt, certain he'd been tapped in the chest with a finger. He shone his lamp around the room, about to click it off when, from the corner of his eye, Mike caught sight of his Panasonic stereo's cassette-deck button pushing inward. Obviously someone invisible wanted to hear Megadeth. So let him. Or her. Or it.

The mischievous spook would not let it rest. Mike frowned, perplexed, as he watched the stereo's big, round volume knob slowly crank upwards in the beam of his six-volt flashlamp, the tape player roaring suddenly with thrash metal as Mike's pesky "friend" pushed the volume indicator to ten. Dave Mustaine's wailing guitar solo

("Holy Wars...The Punishment Due") almost blew Mike's eardrums as well as his speaker towers before he leapt up and unplugged the ghost in the machine.

Which continued to play, undaunted.

It went silent almost as quickly as it had arrived.

Mike growled at his uninvited guest to eff off and leave him alone.

Sulking, the entity ceased its antics.

Soon the sun had arisen.

■■

SEVEN

A hot August sun scorched Mike's back as he knelt before the big Harley beside a low, peaked-roof shed. An hour ago he'd started trying to pushstart the monster bike from the barn toward the outbuildings, hoping the downhill slope might start the old machine. He'd cleaned the plugs, replaced its oil filter, cleaned the fuel lines. Still no go. Mike at least had the bike firing now. Compression fine. Why wouldn't the X!@¢$%&*¥@¢* start?

An overly-warm black leather vest on Aurora's back had him sweating. His muscular arms were bare and scorching. Droplets of salty, stinging sweat fell from his brow like warm rain.

All week he'd been working on the bike. He had cleaned out its rusted, faded teardrop gas tank with solvent, wiped grime from the engine, put in new sparkplugs, engine oil, and repaired two of the sparkplug wires. He'd even replaced broken or burnt-out bulbs. To top it all off, he'd even cleaned the carburetor. And what reward?   Nothing!

■■

Mike loved the old bike for all that. Its fat tires, 750 cc V-Twin engine, resplendent (though lusterless) chrome, rubber front shock absorbers, chopper-like front end. Its oval, chrome oil-filter cover. The bike was nearly an antique. Custom built, he presumed; parts of it looked completely non-standard.

White potato blossoms had bloomed in the old man's rickety greenhouse this week. (He'd had them covered with blankets; after six hours the freak snow had melted, the weather turned baumy again, and the schizoid God of storms had stomped off in a huff.) Though no green thumb, Mike was sure he could grow a few turnips, beets, tomatoes, beans, peas, carrots, maybe even a few pumpkin in his well-manured plot. Much had been reseeded after the fiasco of only a couple of weeks ago, including innumerable transplants. Twice a month he added a few gallons of diluted fish fertilizer to his growing menagérie to ensure a healthy harvest this autumn, unless hail wiped them out. Bloody hail. Unpredictable.

Mike's sunburnt upper arms were peeling. Later he intended to have himself a hot, outdoor shower. He'd rigged an ice-cream pail beneath the house's eaves, out of sight of anyone who might enter the yard. Later he would watch a few porno movies, flip through the hundreds of Penthouse and other assorted back-issues he'd stashed away. Type another chapter for his novel. Maybe. Unless the resident poltergeist had other plans. Mike knew it was his feisty, old uncle who'd accosted him last night. Who else could it have been? An alien? An elemental?

He wasn't afraid of the old man. Why should he be? Concerned maybe, but not frightened. (Shit, no.) The old bastard was dead. Buried in nearby Medstead cemetery. Poltergeist antics weren't going to force Mike away from the farm. It was his now. And the thousands of dollars' worth of stolen merchandise (?) which the old man had hidden as part of some highly lucrative black-market racket. Essentially, the problem in turning over the goods to the R.C.M.P., Mike felt, would be proving that he'd had no part in criminal actions involving innumerable stolen wares. Plus there was the murder he'd have to account for, albeit in self-defense, and the victim's rented Mercedes-Benz hidden on the property.

What a botch he'd made of it. Why hadn't he notified the police, while he'd still had the chance? At least collect some sort of reward. Mike was certain he'd soon end up at the bottom of a lake somewhere. He had already killed what he assumed to be a gangster, taken the dead man's gun.

Did he really think he could get away with all this?

On the other hand, maybe there were no gangsters; he'd simply had a minor mental breakdown which necessitated a short and comfy stay at the nearest rubber room? He was certain the local sanitarium in Battleford would be happy to accomodate him!

An ominous crunch of tires and rumble of an approaching vehicle caught Aurora's rapt attention, causing his adrenaline to rush. *This could be it!* He frantically grasped the Harley's high handlebars, and, with a titanic effort, pushed the bike behind the big work shed. Mike grabbed up his shotgun sitting nearby, making a mad dash for the nearest bushes. The house was unlocked, Mike berated himself as he fled through the underbrush. Hunkering down on his haunches, heart thumping, he waited tensely for the approaching vehicle to round a bend of the dirt road winding its way through the meadow. Mike clutched his pump-action rifle tightly, staring wild-eyed through the foliage as a red '72 Ford Gran Torino sports car rolled into the farmyard.

Jesus Christ. It was his buddies from Prince Albert! They'd hinted they might drop by a few weeks back to check out his inheritance, maybe throw a housewarming party, bring a few girls. Bad timing, guys. Mike crouched in the broad-leaf forest with his shotgun aimed at the sporty '70's model Ford as it stopped in front of his deceased uncle's dark, brooding farmhouse. The two-door was packed. It was Nick's, he could tell. Nick

Tremaine rarely washed the car, allowing it to get streaked with mud as it was now. Bonehead.

No less than eight youths, including four girls, climbed out of the sports car, clearly well pickled as they waved their beer cans about and laughed. They were yelling obscenely, generally making a nuisance of themselves. If they hadn't been acquaintances of his Mike might've peppered them with both barrels, he was that far gone.

No. Four men, six women. Two more clambered from the dull red Torino's back seat. He didn't recognize any of the girls. Three of the youths Mike recognized as his old high school buddies, Nick, Tom, and Steve, the other dude he'd once had the pleasure of punching his lights out. Typical grease-haired, leather-jacketed punk. A skinny, dirty-blond geek at that. Nick and Tom each carried two cases of Molsen Canadian and Labatts Blue, respectively.

The geek kicked Mike's door in, laughing.

Setting his pump-action rifle against a peeling paper birch, Mike raced out from the trees, furious, running full-out toward the derelict farmhouse.

Nick and Tom caught him before he thrashed the leather-jacketed punk who was now rifling through Aurora's cupboards for something to munch on.

"What's yer' problem, dude?" The grease-haired senior high laughed in Mike's flushed face as he stood before him, while Nick shoved a can of beer into Mike's hand and clapped his back jovially. "Have a beer." Nick laughed.

"Oh, wow, man, you looked like a goddamn red Indian come runnin' after us from the bushes," laughed Nick Tremaine, sitting himself down at Mike's behemoth table. "Great place ya' got here, Aurora. House, farm, shitloads o' property. I like it. You gonna farm the place, raise a few cattle or sumpin'?" Tremaine took a giant swallow from his beer can, glancing about the room with ill-concealed curiosity. Outside, the six girls wandered around the farmyard, giggling, making Mike uneasy as hell.

"No," he replied eyeing the unfamiliar girls nervously through his kitchen window.

"Oh, you're not, eh?" Tremaine pursed his lips, nodding.

Dirk Simpson, the tow-headed, opportunistic twelfth-grader (who's hair looked like it had been combed back with vegetable oil) whom Mike had always instinctively disliked tossed Steve Colter a box of Paulins' crackers from Mike's cupboard.

"Hey, guy, what's that stupid thing ya got twirlin' up on yer roof? A weathervane?" Simpson asked whinily.

"A windmill, asshole."

Colter interrupted. "A windmill! What you want

something like that for? You gonna start a flour mill?" He laughed aloud, a regular comedian.

"It's a wind charger," Mike informed him tiredly. "There are no powerlines out here."

They'd laid his bread, margarine, jam and cinnamon spread on the table, helping themselves uninvited. Nick lit up a joint, offering it to Mike who accepted it with alacrity and inhaled a few token tokes. Although he rarely turned down narcotics, he was no drug hound. Mike wished they'd go away.

The blond ruffian wandered into the living room while Mike was distracted, turning on his stereo. Steve Colter shut the door, slumping down in a wooden chair with his feet up on the table, laughing. Mike got along all right with Colter, a half-breed (Meti?, who gives a shit) Indian who prided himself more white man than Native. Steve had earned himself a tough-guy reputation at elementary school. He, too, had been a foster child.

Dirk sat down at the table, burping loudly, propping his black cowboy boots on Mike's tabletop. (Recently, it seemed, he had begun to emulate a certain Happy Days' character, with predictable results.) Rush's "Permanent Waves" E.P blared from Mike's cassette deck. Which was surprising, because Mike knew Dirk liked rap. Everyone but Aurora were talking all at once. The music not too obnoxious.

Mike secretly wanted everyone to leave. He didn't feel in the partying spirit, nor was he up for socializing. The lingo circulating about his kitchen table was like this: "eff off, eff that, up your a**, man, f*** off, A-hole, c***." It got tiring after a while.

Sometimes he questioned the company he kept.

Dirk Simpson, crude jerk that he was, had found one of Mike's Penthouse issues and was now burning a hole in the unfortunate centerfold's crotch with his cigarette. Aurora, pissed-off, snatched the glossy magazine away, threatening to beat Dirk's face in. The sophomore, shit-faced, merely laughed hysterically.

An hour later, Mike had drank three beer and was starting to relax, an embarrassing, silly smile seeping across his face.

Half an hour earlier, around five o'clock, the kitchen door opened and a bevy of foxy ladies entered the house. Some giggled sillily, intoxicated, whilst others were more restrained.

"Hey Mike, meet Cassandra, my new babe. My main squeeze," Tremaine announced with slurred voice. A plain, but buxom blond with long, straight hair went around Nick's chair, wrapping her arms about his neck and giving the dark-haired, wide-jawed youth a squelching hickey. Mike felt he was intruding. Heh, heh, in his own house.

"And this is my sex machine, Debby," squealed Steve Colter, laughing hysterically as a rather cute, short-haired sophomore slapped his dark head. Dirk Simpson, an obvious, lewd pervert, was still actively pursuing the other four, apparently unattached, girls. He farted aloud to catch their attention. Steve Colter punched him in the head.

Mike retained a dignified composure, secretly applauding his Meti friend for punching Simpson in the noggin. Dirk dared not challenge Colter to a scrap, merely exchanging foul names with the big buck, as he tauntingly called him.

Two of the women looked distinctly ill at ease. They seemed out of place (or at least, it was plain *they* thought they were in the wrong place). Mike's shrewd, oceanic eyes noticed that one of them was a veritable knockout. Her glossy, auburn hair was lustrous as a model's in a photo shoot, way past shoulder length, nearly down to her butt. Her eyes were gray-green; lovely eyes. She was introduced as Jodi Andersen, had toasted him with a disarming, stunning smile. He guessed (correctly) that she and her darker-haired girlfriend didn't relish the company they'd chosen today, either. Steve and Nick held a short contest at the table to see who could burp the loudest. Mike reckoned they'd drunk eight to ten beer each, by the flush of their faces. They were already blitzed when they'd arrived. His mind began to wander as their shenanigans continued.

He worried about his shotgun left out in the bushes. Would somebody find it? Or the sheds. What had those girls been doing outside for over half an hour?? Mike recalled with sickening horror that he'd busted the sheds' locks. Had he covered everything thoroughly? He hadn't expected his former school chums to show up. Should have.

He snapped back to reality, catching the gorgeous Jodi staring at him quizzically across the table. She looked away quickly, staring off into space as Dirk and Steve sloshed beer in each other's face. They were harmless blokes, however, wouldn't likely start a fisticuff. A couple of good ol' boys. Farmboys, like Nick and Mike. Oh, and Tom Bent. Tom Bent who lay on the living room floor since the rowdy gang's arrival at 2:45 p.m., passed out after a three-day liquor binge. He'd hit hard on Canadian Club.

Mike also noticed that Jodi (was that her name?) sipped her beer bottle slowly, glancing from the corner of her huge, flashing eyes, as if expecting a misdirected blow from one of the two males horsing around nearby, their piercing laughter and shouts of derision drowning out all coherent thought. She, Jenny (her gal pal), and Mike seemed to be the only ones not already plastered.

He wished he could remember her last name.

He began to feel famished around six o'clock. Nick and Cassandra were busy necking in a corner. Her sweater was off. Dirk Simpson and Steve Colter were arguing heatedly over which Major League baseball team deserved to win the World Series this year. Mike could care less about baseball. He'd tried it in high school and hated it. That tiny ball was too hard to hit, and pitched way too fast.

The zany idea of cooking spaghetti and meatballs for supper entered his head and, once stuck in his craw, could not be dislodged. (He'd canned several jars of hamburger this summer, seeing as he didn't own a refrigerator.) As Aurora mulled the idea over, Tom Bent stumbled into the cigarette-smoke-clouded kitchen, slumping himself down wearily in a chair after his three hour snooze on the living-room floor. He looked pale, blinking rapidly because the pot smoke stung his pale blue eyes. "How ya' doin'?" he asked Mike with a slurred voice.

"Fine. You?"

The blondish, long-haired youth merely nodded, raising a hand but unable to respond. He smelt like he'd bathed in whiskey.

Except for occasional raised voices the kitchen was quiet, or as near as could be with a party in progress.

(The 'party dudes' infested Aurora's home with a noise which made the resident poltergeist seem tame by comparison!) The sun was still fairly high in the sky, although heavy, ominous rainclouds were scudding relentlessly northward. Thunderheads rumbled threateningly from a distance. Mike was glad the old farmhouse had no serious leaks.

Aurora dreaded trying to cook supper with these drunken yahoos stumbling about. As he glanced around the room he noticed the nice-looking honey sitting across the table from him was still nursing her fourth beer. The others had drunk in excess of a dozen, Mike guessed. Or more. He'd had six, and wasn't sure he could stand up straight, let alone walk a straight line. He hadn't drank beer for almost a year and was unprepared for its potency. Mike was glad the revellers hadn't discovered his half-full bottle of gin he kept under the kitchen sink, which he occasionally tippled from.

Putting off supper for a while, Mike furtively studied the sensational co-ed sitting at his table. She had enormous, gray-green, sensuous eyes, full lips, and a well-developed figure. An air of fresh-faced school girl innocence hovered about her. Her silken hair was magnificent, tucked behind one ear, parted to one side over her left shoulder. Intricately interwoven tresses alongside her face he found especially exquisite. Very long, her hair was, a style Mike had thought had gone out of fashion and replaced by the ubiquitous tomboy/business-woman style. The sexy stranger's eyebrows were thin; arched high over eyes which registered slight unease. He realized now that it was her natural expression. Her face was rather square, but in an un-masculine way, cheeks flushed as if caught in a lie or verbally challenged. (He thought she reminded him of Zena, Warrior Princess, from the popular TV series.) She was tall, for a woman. Mike knew nothing at all about her, only that she hailed from nearby Medstead, the dingy little town he'd passed through (his old haunt) on the way to the Battlefords some weeks ago. He didn't recall her from grade school. Mike wondered if she were a student there, or graduate, or whether going steady with some athletic hunk (hunk of shit).

He prudently looked away when she caught him staring, quickly dropping his eyes to scratch grime from the tabletop, a natural faker. Mike Aurora, unlike practically everyone else in that house, was a virgin (unless one counted nocturnal encounters with a ghost as natural coitus).

He stood up, downed the last dregs of his beer, then announced his intention of cooking supper. The guys laughed, hooting, throwing jibes as Aurora searched a lower cupboard for suitable pots and pans. Sexist pigs all, they naturally thought his ability to cook *hilarious!* If he'd had more backbone, less geniality, he would've expelled the whole lot from his house. Even Jodi, the fresh-faced angel over there. Well, perhaps she could stay. Though why she would, he hadn't a clue.

Mike almost added baking soda instead of salt to his meatballs, so flustered and inebriated as the distracting revellers moved as one, guffawing, into the empty living room. He hoped the inquisitive girls wouldn't peek into his box of dirty magazines and think him a pervert. Mike stalked into the adjoining room, hiding his unfinished manuscript lest somebody decide to use the clean, neatly-typed pages for a convenient ashtray, or toilet paper. Drunks were notorious for doing such, Mike figured.

■■■

Glancing about the room, detecting no spooks (he shuddered), noting everything in order and out of harm's way, for, basically, the bare living room was empty save for an electric typewriter, bedding, cassette deck, electric guitar/amplifier, boxes of books and odds 'n ends (much of it crammed into a closet, or an alcove under the stairs).

Mike ventured back to the kitchen to add some onions to the frying meatballs. He was still tipsy however, not exactly sure what he'd put in the concoction. The kitchen was a safe haven from the noise. His stereo had been silent for over an hour. Mike hoped the revellers wouldn't screw around with his tapes, spill beer on the cassette cases.

"Need any help?"

A gloriously feminine, seductive voice startled Aurora as he stirred the night's macabre creation.

He turned around, face to face with the stunning creature he'd been studying obliquely for the past three hours. He did, indeed, have his hands full at the moment, at a loss over what veggies to cook. Or should he make baked potatoes? He'd yet to dash outside and fetch the vegetables from the handy, locker-cool root cellar his uncle had built, decades ago, abutting the antiquated house. (Or somebody had.)

"Uh…"

"We're not just having meatballs for supper, are we?" She gave a cute, amusing grimace. Mike could almost read her mind, and it went like this…*eww, straight meatballs, without pasta, no vegetables; bachelors are so-oo incompetent!   Talk about poor diet!*

"Don't you have any vegetables?" she inquired nosily.

"Well, yeah,…but they're in the root cellar. I have to nip outside and grab some. Mind watching this so it doesn't scorch?"

"Sure. No problem," she said, smiling.

Mike rushed outside, heart fluttering as he ducked into the dirt storehouse to track down some red potatoes, broccoli, and four cans of whole-kernel corn. He somehow felt guilty knowing about 'Wanda,' whom he hadn't seen in almost three weeks. Had she really existed? No doubt somebody'd put him in a rubber room if they found out he'd been bonking an imaginary girlfriend!

Jodi was busy stirring the nearly-scorched meatballs when Mike returned. He plonked a paper bag of vegetables onto the recently varnished tabletop.

"I'll cut up the broccoli and start it, if you like," she offered.

"Sure. Thanks. As you can see, I'm kinda' like a chicken running around with its head cut off," slurred Mike apologetically. "I'm still a bit woozy." He chuckled. "Actually, I'm staggerin' drunk."

Jodi laughed aloud, a heaven-sent peal of mirth strumming Mike's heart strings. He liked the sound of her deep, sexy, womanly laughter.

"How many potatoes should I peel, Mike?" asked Jo familiarly, sitting down at the big table with a small paring knife.

"About thirty. Probably the whole bag. I'll help with that."

They sat peeling potatoes like a model, married couple in contented silence. Neither, in reality, knew the other.

Yet they felt amazingly at ease, as if having known each other for years. Getting to know one another, however, was like jumping a major hurdle.

Mike hunched over his bowl of potato water, completely at a loss over what to say.

(He had his mind on a certain cadaver out in the forest.)

His stereo blared to life in the living room. Dirk Simpson seemed to think it was his toy to play with, even though Aurora had expressly forbid anybody to mess with his expensive cassette deck and receiver. Nick Tremaine stood in the foyer with a Penthouse magazine wide open, ogling and laughing over some poor girl's anatomy along with his companions. The girls, too, were laughing.

"What's your book about, Mike?," asked Jo. "Can I call you Mike? Or do you prefer Michael?" Her fawn-like, sensuous eyes seemed to sparkle in the lamplight like greyish green beryls, precious gems.

"It's about a journalist who stumbles upon a lair of modern-day vampires in a cemetery, due for demolition, in upstate New York. Kind of a horror novel, lots of chills and gore."

"Oooh…sounds scary," Jodi exclaimed dramatically. "Don't you get the willies writing in this old house all by yourself?"

"Actually, I'm not alone," Mike answered casually. He paused. "This place is haunted."

Jodi gasped, sensuous mouth dropping in mock suspense. "Really? Oh, are you putting me on?"

Mike glanced about the kitchen. "Well, just between you and me," he slurred, "there are two resident ghosts here. One's a beautiful woman of unknown origin, the other's my dead uncle. Don't tell the others – they'll think I'm loony tunes."

Jodi laughed conspiratorially.

"What does this 'lady' look like?"

Mike peered across the table at her seriously. "A bit like you, but darker…sorry, I've forgot your name again."

"Jodi."

"Well, uh," he stammered, "her hair's a bit longer than yours; almost down to her backside. Her eyes are darker. Spanish, I think. And her nose is a little bigger, with a slight bridge. Kinda' strange the way it starts just above the eyeline; she has dimples, too, did I tell you that? She only wears a nightie."

Jodi laughed sexily, almost purring, Mike thought. She nodded knowingly, playing along.

"Have you slept with her?" She glanced away, mildly flustered.

"No," he lied with an uneasy chuckle, discomfited,

"but I'd like to. But she's dead."

"I think you're making all this up," retorted Jodi, feigning indignation.

"You're right. I am," Mike lied. But his face was serious.

They peeled in silence for another ten minutes, the only sounds that of the party proceeding in the next room, the music, and a rising storm wind outside.

Andersen stood up with feline grace, setting her pot of broccoli on the range to boil, fiddling with the burner's knob.

"You have to light the burner, it's propane," said Mike aloud.

"Oh. Where's your matches?" Andersen wasn't a smoker.

Mike stood up, patted his shirt-pocket for a lighter, then reached over the range's hood into a high cupboard and withdrew a box of strike matches. He stood alluringly close to her.

The scent of her fragrant, rose-scented perfume made him dizzy with yearning. She smelt like Wanda.

She took the pack from his lingering hand, aware of his eyes on her flushed face as she lit the burner.

Mike glanced up at the clock hanging on the kitchen wall, realizing it was almost ten o'clock, time to light another lantern. He proceeded to do so. Although the midsummer sun had set only minutes ago, little light penetrated the house once the sun arced to the west. The farmyard was hemmed in by full-size, prickly spruce and a few ancient, leafy deciduous trees.

Jodi sipped her fifth beer, standing by the range, reluctant to enter the noisy, boisterous living room. The kitchen was a safe – albeit temporary – refuge. She stood near the sink, watching Mike prepare supper for his ten unexpected guests, no easy quest. She realized he was a competent cook, unusual for a guy his age.

She remarked that he liked weird music when Colter put an Exorcist tape into the cassette deck. Mike chuckled sardonically, nodding. "I'm a strange man," he said cryptically.

"Oh, hey, I'm not criticizing," exclaimed Jodi apologetically. "I like metal myself, though I'm not a regular. But it's cool."

Mike was suddenly at a loss for words.

"Have we met before?" asked Jodi suddenly with a puzzled, suspicious expression. "I – I seem to recall your face from somewhere..."

Mike shook his head slowly, pursing his lips. "I used to attend school here (near Spiritwood) for a few years – can't say I recognize you, though. Only time I've been to Medstead, since then, was five weeks ago. But I only passed through." Mike's blue eyes held a mixture of fear and awe.

"Hm. Maybe it's déjà-vu," she said lightly. "Maybe we knew each other in a past age." Andersen giggled, crinkling her eyes becomingly. Her voice was slightly slurred, Mike noticed. As was his. An easy seduction possibly, if only he knew how. Surprisingly, he felt she would not surrender so easily to a date rape. Nor was he inclined to try it. Even a subtle seduction at the moment was beyond his ken. He was well into his eighth beer.

They simply stood and sipped their Labatts, comfortable next to one another. Ironically, Mike did not feel nervous in the least in this sexy, bombshell's presence. He wondered fidgetingly for the umpteenth time if she had a boyfriend, but knew not how to tactfully ask.

A deliciously scary crack of thunder rolled across the sky from the east like a cannon ball. Jo shivered with delight and anticipation of a rip-roaring summer storm. She mulled over Aurora's talk of ghosts. Mike, too, loved the thrill of a thunderstorm; the electric static in the air. He wished he had the balls to ask her for a walk outside. But supper was sizzling on the kitchen range, potatoes boiling lovelily. Perhaps afterwards...

"I think your farm is really neat," remarked Jodi at last. "You're so lucky. Not many people inherit farms nowadays, in this age of repossession and debt. Are you going to raise some livestock?"

Mike considered this for a moment. "I might. I'd like to raise a few milk goats." He smiled sheepishly.

Jodi's eyes gleamed, smiling attractively; a surreal china doll with endearing dimples. Mike had an image flash across his mind of him and her coupling languorously on the living room floor.

"Goats are cute. They make great pets. I had a pet nanny called Martha when I was a girl."

"Aren't you still a girl?" jested Mike drunkenly.

She eyed him with disdainful amusement, playfully poking Mike's chest. "I'm a ...*w-o-m-a-n*, not a girl," she drawled, jutting out her fabulous tits in mock humility, then laughing. Her breath smelt overpoweringly of liquor.

Mike laughed along, eyes clinging – no – *glued*, to her sweater-bound, Wonderbra breasts, toasting her with his beer can. "Here's to yer' womanhood, then, and may ye keep it fer' as long, or as short, or as...never mind," he slurred with a crooked, silly grin. He was quite drunk, and emotionally overwhelmed.

Jodi merely smiled, a slight, wry, embarrassed quirk of her lips as she sipped her Labbats Blue.

Mike had begun the spaghetti over half an hour ago, now turned to prepare the pasta sauce.

Andersen's eyes lingered on his back, hardly thinking as she placed a hand on his back and gently rubbed. Mike didn't react, was too surprised. The girl's unbidden reflex action seemed so natural, so...*familiar*, that he couldn't respond. She leaned against him coquettishly, drunk, breathing warmly in his ear with her breasts pressed against his back. Mike's erection grew with agonizing intensity, straining against his jeans.

"Perhaps," she said with a pause, "we could go for a walk, get away from these jerks," whispered Jodi in Mike's ear. "Would you like that?"

Mike nodded.

Tonight's my lucky night!, he thought.

Jodi disengaged then, kissing Aurora's cheek before stepping out the door and into the rumbling night.

****

Nick, Steve, and Tom were playing cards. Blackjack. Everybody else sat conversing on the living room floor in lieu of recliners or a sofa (although three chairs from the kitchen were in use). Each held a beer in his or her hand. They'd eaten supper a few minutes ago, were now drowsy and content. No more arguments filled the silent farmhouse. Jodi sat between two other girls, quiet, waiting for Mike to finish cleaning off the kitchen table and countertop. Little pools of yellowish-blue light emanated from the twin gas lamps, one on top a dresser, another on the floor.

He entered the living room tipsily, half-expecting the bogeyman to leap out from the shadows and spoil his party. He'd come to expect this of his dear, dead uncle.

Jodi looked Mike's way, green eyes shining and expectant. He jerked his head sideways, unnoticed by the others, motioning for her to join him outside. Wordlessly the pretty co-ed got up and headed toward the candle-lit dining room and adjacent foyer. Outside, it was raining heavily. Thunder boomed deafeningly across the boreal forest like jet sonic. Aurora, uncertain what the vivacious brunette had in mind, waited a few minutes before joining Jo under the eaves. He guessed he'd screw her silly inside his deceased uncle's barn.

They kissed heatedly, like reunited, long-lost lovers. Raindrops dripped lullingly from the antiquated farmhouse's sagging, galvanized eavestroughs, gathering in a large puddle near Aurora's wind turbine's tower. He was thoroughly surprised by Andersen's horniness, grinding his lips against hers. She held him tight, moaning deep within her throat.

A cataclysmic thunder roar shook the night. Mike swore he felt the entire Canadian Shield shift beneath his feet. Jodi disengaged from his lips, embracing him tightly. Her arms locked about his neck. Aurora, spellbound with the scent of this woman's fragrant, freshly washed hair and captivating, lust-igniting perfume, merely stroked Jo's damp tresses. She molded perfectly against his body.

Though he did find it odd to be whispering to her in a foreign language utterly unfamiliar to him.

A searing lightning flash split the darkness twain. Jodi shivered deliciously in Mike's arms, feeling soft and vulnerable and totally desirable.

They turned away from the house, strolling in the pouring rain without any particular direction in mind. Jo's arm encircled Mike's waist, his draped about her shoulder.

The rain abated considerably. They strolled for about five minutes, not talking, nor needful yet of further sexual contact. It was as if they'd known each other for ages, yet separated for an indeterminate period of time. An excruciatingly long time. Reunited. She seemed to him more than a recent acquaintance, an easy lay in the hay. In fact he somehow doubted this seemingly fragile woman could be taken against her will. A distant memory in the dim recesses of his mind dredged up the image of a high-spirited warrioress. A warrior queen.

They soon became soaked. Fortunately, both wore weatherproof jackets. Jodi wore a tight pair of hot pink jeans, accenting her lovely, tightly clad rear. Mike anticipated stripping them off of her legs and ducking his head between Jo's thighs, pleasuring her.

Somehow they ended back at the house once more, inexplicably not screwing in the barn as Mike thought they ought to have been. He wanted to savor this moment however, savor this irresistable woman's delectable aroma. Perhaps she was leading him on, he didn't know.

"Later, Mike," breathed Jodi in his ear. "I have this dreaded feeling something weird is about to happen."

He nodded, feeling her up, kissing her rosebud cheeks, ears, neck while Jodi moaned encouragingly.

Somebody shouted in bewilderment from the house. A terrifying thumping suddenly shook the walls, galloping over the structure at impossible speed. Up and down the two floors of the derelict farmhouse a series of heavy, quick knocks pounded the fabric. Screams issued from inside.

One of the girls was levitating when Mike and Jodi ran inside! She spun in a dizzying circle, wailing, limbs flailing wildly as she was propelled across the living room. Dirk Simpson was yelling incoherently, bug-eyed.

Other objects whizzed about the house, forcing the inebriated spectators to duck. Mike's ballpoint pens were dancing two by two in mid-air. An outraged, palsy-shaking, elderly voice hollered from out of nowhere.

"*GET OUT OF MY HOUSE!!!!!!*"

Phosphorescent lights flashed unnaturally in the pandemonium, multi-colored spectrums of a disembodied rainbow which floated about the farmhouse. Down the staircase they came, an ethereal collage of horror, of half-formed shapes writhing in a green mist…all at once the twin gas lamps' unhealthy flames turned a sickly blue, then died.

Except for the wildly-blinking, dancing orbs, no light now lit the house.

Everybody fled upstairs in a stampede panic.

The front door wouldn't open.

Crowded into an empty bedroom on the second floor, Mike and his companions awaited the next unholy assault. The whole house suddenly felt as if it were −10°C. They huddled in a corner, shuddering as monstrously loud footsteps pounded their way up the staircase. In utter darkness, the partygoers stood stock-still.

The bedroom door burst open, crashing against the wall with a jarring thud.

In floated the surreal, firefly twinkling lights, descending on the screaming, cowering guests like silent bees. In absolute, Stygian blackness arms jostled against each other in a blind panic. Curiously, the motley array of macabre, pulsing lights shed little illumination.

Ghost lights.

Dirk Simpson was levitated into the air by unseen hands, flailing in horror as he sailed helplessly out of the bedroom and down the banisters.

"Help me, goddamm it!" Dirk wailed.

Nick and Mike dashed down the stairs after the floating youth held aloft by flashing lights. Tremaine seized Dirk's jacket sleeve, hauling desperately as the wide-eyed freshman floated slowly toward him.

From the top stair leapt a grotesque, glowing, pulsating, half-human, many-tentacled Sci-Fi spectre straight into Mike's open arms!

His frozen face of fear would've done a horror movie's actor proud.

Whether gigantic spider or octopus he wrestled with Mike was never sure.   It stunk of rotten, week-old meat, yet also vaguely like algae or putrid seaweed, or sea urchins, gone bad, he'd once seen on the wharfs of northern Vancouver Island during a holiday. Mike, Steve, Nick, Tom and a couple of girls fought tenaciously with the horrible 'thing' as it flailed its half dozen rubbery tentacles about the banisters, its life-like suckers suctioning horribly against skin and clothing, its appendages akimbo. Clearly the bloated body resembled an octopus, although hairy as a tarantula! Its head, however, was unmistakably that of an old man with long, shimmering, white hair.

It also possessed monstrous fangs and diabolical strength!

Suddenly the seven grown adults were grappling with air. They sprawled outlandishly atop each other, feeling rather foolish. From the top landing, four astonished girls stared, uncomprehending. The dancing Will-o'-the-Wisp lights rapidly began to diminish, leaving the banisters in virtual darkness. Then the old house was dark and silent once more. An ominous silence. And a choking stench of sulphur.

And outside the unmistakable roar of Nick's '79 Gran Torino gunned to life.

Its headlights flashed demonically when the mortified onlookers peered out of a kitchen window, or crowded in horror around the now-open door.

Suddenly the sporty Ford with its jacked-up rear end leapt forward into gear, unbelievably *doing a wheelie!* outside in the darkness in front of Aurora's house. The terrified revelers looked on in shock as Nick's empty sports car, its interior light glowing, rip-roared with mag wheels squealing and flinging sod around the unlit farmstead, swerving wildly with racing engine like a couple of punks joy-riding someone's lawn.

Then it disappeared into the night, flying recklessly out of the farmyard and into the nearby fields.

Where it stalled.

Even Nick Tremaine, jabbering and incoherent, was too terrified to chase after his berserk, self-animated Torino.

✳✳✳✳✳✳✳✳✳✳✳✳✳✳✳✳✳✳✳✳

A horrifying silence settled over the house. Bleary-eyed, teeth chattering, the eleven revelers waited in darkness for *"it"* to return. (Their unseen antagonist had, evidently, dematerialized the kerosene lamps!) Finally, after what seemed an eternity of agonizing suspense, Mike ventured bravely into the kitchen once more, searching for candles.

They, too, were inexplicably missing.

However, he did find one half-burnt stub in an empty drawer. Mike's dim flashlight barely lit the frosty kitchen. He could see his breath in the air. Bizarre, gothic lightning-flashes off to the south accompanied by a rumble of thunder briefly lit the old-fashioned, sash window.

Mike crept back into the living room, settling down on his haunches while lighting the candle set in a beer can.

The partygoers had been shocked into near-sobriety by the insane entity's antics. Nick worried aloud about his car. Two girls sobbed in fear, crying *"Poltergeist!"* Jodi clutched Mike's icy hand beyond the circle of candlelight, resting her head on his shoulder. Nobody seemed to notice the two strangers' over-familiarity with each other. None of the women had chosen the bawling Dirk as their companion. At last the scared youths drifted off into an uneasy slumber.

The spook returned at three o'clock.

Steve Colter was the first to jerk awake. He nudged his girlfriend, Debby Lawson, now became spine-tinglingly aware of a sinister scratching, crawling noise from the old, wallpapered walls. He kicked Mike in the shin, jolting him awake.

"Somethin's crawlin' inside the walls," Steve hissed alarmedly. "You got rats here?"

"Not that I'm aware of," murmured Mike cryptically.

Suddenly an alarming cacophony upstairs jolted everyone wide awake.

A tumbling, slamming, jarring, hell's bells racket vibrated throughout the old building. As if somebody – or *something* – were rolling rocks down the stairs!

Nick's girlfriend screamed when a heavy recliner bounced down the stairs and settled lethargically against the balustrade, wedged upside-down against a wall.

Moments later a bulky, wooden rocking-chair came hurtling down the dark stairwell to splinter into several pieces followed by what looked to be a couple of bowling balls (!) and numerous shot-glasses which exploded against the banisters like rapid-fire gunshots.

Steve shot up from his spot in a corner, yelling wildly and fleeing the house.

Various debris and projectiles hurtled down the stairs' landing to the foot of the staircase, shattering glass and wood alike.

Mike shone his candle up the stairs, ducking just in time to avoid decapitation by a gently spinning butcher-knife which thudded into the wall behind him! Ancient toys were being flung haphazardly down the stairs by an unseen agency, crashing with finality against the hardwood steps.

An armless doll promptly jumped up, biting Betsy Andersen on the knee.

Nick tore the crazed, plastic thing away from the hysterically screaming sophomore's thigh, flinging the gnashing, somehow-animated doll across the room. It ceased to move.

Derelict furniture banged and thudded down the banisters, bumping drunkenly against one another. Nick Tremaine grabbed his girlfriend's wrist and fled the house hollering blue murder, followed by two others. As if part of some bizarre puppet show, furniture began to dance, rockers and armchairs swerving dizzyingly, bowing ludicrously, controlled by some super-normal, unknown agency devoid of strings or electronics. Tom Bent leapt up, wide-eyed, fleeing the farmhouse with two rocking chairs in hot pursuit sailing demonically after him.   Dirk Simpson seized a chair from mid-air, flinging it crashing against the banisters, only to be knocked down by a heavy, antique bureau floating about crazily, dipping dangerously as if about to keel over from its precarious, gravitational buoyancy. Mike, powerless, battled in vain against swirling debris, the foyer and kitchen oddly intact.

Finally, hand in hand, he and Jodi vacated the house.

Outside in the darkness and rain everybody was talking at once. Many were hysterical. Steve Colter madly announced his intention of walking home, though home be over fifty miles away! Frustratedly Mike tried to unlock his station wagon, its door-lock stubbornly and mysteriously resisting his car key. Nick suggested breaking the Impala's passenger window, which Mike balked at.

The pandemonium seemed to be confined to the house, or more precisely, upstairs. The furniture Mike now realized was being thrown from the attic. The old man's furniture. All over a box of stupid Penthouse magazines.

What kind of motives drove this nightmarish poltergeist? Why didn't it just take the damn things back which Mike had, unwittingly, brought from one of the sheds? Jodi Andersen clutched his bomber jacket's sleeve. Her hair was wild. As was Nick's.   His stood on end!

Steve Colter looked up in fright as the bedroom window above began jerking up and down, open and close, open and close, jarring the dark windowpanes. Nonsensical, chattering, beastly noises emitted from the ghastly, unlit attic. A deafening crash of thunder overhead shook the earth.

When Nick's maniacal car rolled into the driveway silently, headlights suddenly flashing on, the nine scared-out-of-their-wits youths dashed heedlessly onto the farmhouse's verandah, turning to see if the deranged vehicle approached, its motor idling cunningly, red and orange taillights and hazard lights, blinking, lighting the night.

The Torino advanced, its grill somehow sinister, a gleaming row of grinning, chrome teeth. Like a shark.

The ten terrorized youngsters bolted into the cacophonous house, harboring in its relative security from the unholy machine revving angrily out in Mike's yard. The black night offered no escape from the farm's demonic antics.

Mike alone stood firm out on the derelict verandah,

defying the machine to roll forward. If the homicidal sports car felt so inclined, murder on its mind (or engine, fuck he didn't know), Mike knew he and his guests would be safer inside, for neither doors nor windows were large enough to allow Nick's possessed, deranged muscle-car into the house. It might batter itself to pieces trying, though.

Suddenly the car died.

Its flashing emergency lights blinked out, the Torino's motor ceasing to idle. Black, rain-sodden night enveloped the silent vehicle like a wet blanket.

Inside the house all was quiet. Possessed furniture which only moments ago had been dancing crazily about the big farmhouse now sat scattered where they fall. Toys, wrappers, glass had been flung recklessly about the besieged dwelling. Dangerous shards of glass littered the floor, the coffee table, even Mike's word processor atop a dresser. Yet surprisingly, none of his other personal possessions had been moved or tampered with. Childish antics had tossed inestimable amounts of junk throughout the house.

Tom Bent lit up the carnaged scene before him in a ghastly, bluish light thrown from his cigarette lighter. His flaxen hair looked white in the foyer's cluttered chaos.

Suddenly an infuriated, masculine, and *utterly mad!*, palsied bellow echoed boomingly through the house.

"MIKE AURORA!!! ***YOU FUCKER!!*** *I WARN YOU, ONE FINAL TIME: GET – OUT – OF – MY – H-O-U-S-E!!!!!!!!!!!"*

The walls reverberated with the Incarnate's fury.

Everyone cringed in a corner. Not a single pin-prick of light (Bent's lighter had gone out) illuminated the cataclysm-struck building.

Then suddenly out of the air materialized a phosphorescent host of screaming, rushing, disincarnate entities, poking, prodding, and jabbing the yelling, fear-stricken victims who slammed into each other mindlessly like milling cattle. Nick Tremaine tried the exit's door handle, unable to turn its knob, then was thrust away from the door. A silvery, glowing, shapeless form threw him screaming to the floor!

Four college girls dashed about the kitchen, wailing, crying hysterically as the demonically grinning spectres poked and jabbed with mitten-like hands at their twisting bodies.

Mike struggled with a blobbish, translucent, sheet-like entity grinning with crocodile's teeth and cat's eyes. It glowed a sickly, greenish vapor smelling like *burnt rubber.* The monstrous apparitions seemed to lack substance, as if not quite corporeal enough to seize a firm grip. Wrestling with them was like handling Jello. Mike overcame the insubstantial forms easily, tossing the leering, amorphous blobs aside.

Panicking, Aurora's guests began to separate, running in opposite directions as the hellishly persistent phantoms pursued the shrieking, wailing, cursing targets throughout the spacious, two-story farmhouse.

Punching the floating, grinning, cock-eyed spectres was quite useless; the youths' fists seemed to pass straight through the oozing blobs' elastic forms! Suspiciously resembling painted, three-dimensional globs of melted rubber, gooey, inarticulate blobs of weirdness, the nightmarish, darting entities were nonetheless imbued with a life of their own. Doggedly pursuing their distraught victims, the unholy, rank-smelling, chittering banshees chased the disorganized revelers throughout the old house.

Seeing some of the more determined combatants overwhelm their bubble-gummish attackers however heartened their angered, tiring prey.

Soon the jabbering phantasms were being tossed about the house, strangely impervious to blows but nonetheless solid enough to be momentarily gripped and tossed aside, becoming more dense, as if their wallowing, invertebrate forms allowed just enough leverage to clamp one's fingers onto. Very much like some buoyant, spineless hell-spawn, jellyfish, Mike thought crazily as he threw his chittering, luminous aggressors against a wall, ridiculously seeming to stun the hellish phantoms!

Lacking legs or feet, the phosphorous, shrieking 'things' were ludicrously being thrown flailing against cupboards, or sent gently sailing through the air from the banisters, landing skiddingly on the floor and trailing a disgusting, snail-like slime. The snarl-haired, screeching, party-colored blobs lit the farmhouse with their own bright, pulsating, internal glow. To Mike they seemed like king-sized glow worms. The gnashing of their insubstantial, deadly-looking but seemingly harmless, dagger-like fangs looked almost comical (or would have seemed so to the disorganized rabble, at least, had they not been nearly in the clutches of madness), for the spooks' bark was indeed worse than their phantasmagoric bite!

Without warning, the thwarted beings quickly vanished like puffs of smoke. They smelt like the interior of electronics' equipment, voiced Mike distractedly. Reminiscent of rubber, like a department store's unopened wares.

The chittering fiends had nevertheless managed to separate the now-sobered youths. Party-dudes and dudettes in twos and threes sat shivering in various bedrooms, or several to a room, marooned in cloying darkness. Even their lighters failed to illuminate the old dwelling's unnatural, inky gloom.

When Mike glanced at his watch, he found to his

astonishment that it read only 4:30 a.m. Surely this was impossible! Yet his watch was still ticking.

He sat sprawled against someone's hip, wedged into a corner of an unused bedroom closet on the second floor. The room was empty, completely devoid of furniture.

Mike's companion shifted, sitting up. He flicked his silver flint lighter, revealing Jodi's shocked face as she peered about with open mouth. Her big, olive-green, long-lashed eyes registered unmitigated fear. Yet he was glad to see her.

"All right?" Mike murmured.

Jo nodded, distraught. "Yeah. Where is everybody?"

Mike shrugged.

The sun wouldn't rise for another hour yet. Jodi and Mike stood up and exited (he'd burnt his thumb, cursing aloud, using his lighter) the musty closet, fumbling about in the unrelenting dark like sonar-less bats. They found the bedroom door locked, as they'd left it, though Mike suspected a wooden barrier would not bar the ungodly assailants. He immediately knew he must sell the farm, and quick.

Two small, bisected windows bordered the stuffy bedroom; one facing north, another east. The faintest suggestion of dawn emanated from the horizon. Which meant the sun would soon rise, rescuing the cowering party-animals from their individual, barricaded rooms.

Jodi held tight onto Mike's arm, pressed securely against him as they peered out the window. Below, the dewey grass, pebbled footpath, and sadly neglected patio plants were suddenly lit by a reassuring half-moon as scudding clouds raced northwards on a cool, brisk wind.   A scattering of twinkling stars were revealed to the purpling southeast. Beyond the farm's rough, gravel drive Mike could make out the three large outbuildings to the northeast, the source of all his misery, their silhouettes spread ominously over the old farmyard. Tiny birch saplings and quaking aspen became gradually visible from welcome moon-rays revealing a silvery, overgrown homestead where new trees had begun to regenerate after a disastrous fire had cleared the old growth.

Mike knew then that he could never sell the farm, would do anything possible to thwart and eventually exorcise whatever malign, time-warped spooks haunted the old homestead. Even if it meant calling in an exorcist, a Spiritualist, or priest if need be. However Mike's faith in either's genuineness was about as solid as an impending avalanche.

Heavy footsteps neared the bedroom, followed by a sharp rap on the door. Mike opened it cautiously, confronting darkness; demanding who's there.

Ice-cold water splashed into Mike's face, giving him a momentary shock as he spluttered indignantly.

Andersen raced to his side, scared, eyes darting about fruitlessly. She slammed the door and panickingly slid the dead-bolt back in its slot. The doorframe shook violently as the unseen intruder pounded the door, rattled the doorknob. Jodi and Mike stood on the defensive, heart in mouth, awaiting the revenant's materialization inside the room. They stood near the door in frightening, horror-inducing darkness. Without lamp, flashlight, or candle, they were sorely, dangerously vulnerable.

The invisible assailant's antics ceased.

Bravely Mike opened the door, peering fearfully down the hall. Jodi clung to his arm, petrified. The hallway, too, was unlit, and, to his knowledge (he shuddered), empty. A mysterious whiff of pine needles and pungent, flowering Coltsfoot hung in the air. Stubbornly, like Daniel entering the proverbial lion's den, they ventured out into the hall, creeping cautiously down the cluttered passage toward the stairwell. They carefully tread down the squeaking steps, avoiding scattered litter and debris as they descended. The air still felt unnaturally cold.

Ectoplasmic slime oozed from the walls.

Jo snatched her hand away from the grotesque wall with a startled cry, wiping the gross, freezing-cold, clinging slime against a banister rail.

Mike cursed aloud, ordering at the top of his lungs for the disgusting, ghostly manifestations to vacate his home.

He told the old man and whatever else haunted Mike's farm in no uncertain terms to eff off and leave him and his companions alone, consigning the cranky sprites to Hell.

Downstairs it looked like a tornado had hit. Everything was in a shambles.   Aurora's unfinished manuscript had been strewn carelessly about the ground floor of the house. His electric typewriter lay upside-down on the living room floor. Excrement (who…?) lay in fresh piles upon the floorboards. Mike groaned aloud, cursing. His speakers, stereo, guitar, amplifier, everything had been toppled over or tossed about randomly during the last hour or so.

The back door stood open, hanging on one hinge. Glass lay everywhere, including the steps. Sheets and blankets lay strewn about the back yard, wet.. Books and magazines lay soaked in the dewy grass.

The front door leading into the kitchen was open, but unharmed. More of Mike's possessions lay scattered upon the verandah.

Scudding clouds overhead obscured the moon once more, the horizon tinged by an imminent sunrise. Nick's car had disappeared.

He and his girlfriend Cassandra appeared out on the verandah deck, each wielding a large spanner. Several others joined the shell-shocked group.

The sun arose at 5:15 a.m.

Aurora's ten horrified guests sat in the living room, discussing the night's uncanny events with undisguised trepidation, as if expecting the phenomena's return. They spoke in whispers. (He held a baseball bat; others wielding various makeshift weapons.) Mike brooded as the others chattered breathlessly, sitting morosely on the paper-strewn floor after the youths cleared aside much of the debris. He dare not tell his hyperventilating, overexcited guests what had caused the poltergeist's manifestations, nor of what his dead uncle had stored in the clapboard sheds. They really needn't know. Yet he felt some explanation was in order.

He was totally caught off guard when Steve Colter threateningly demanded that explanation.

Mike's claim of ignorance on the whole matter wasn't taken well. Colter, a tall, husky, bluff half-breed Indian started playing the tough guy, boxing his ears. The swarthy youth had him by his shirt front at one point. Even Aurora, ordinarily an easy-going fellow, began to lose his cool. His 'friends' grew rabidly hostile toward him as the morning light chased away the shadows.

Voices were raised, tempers flared as the quarreling rabble attempted to swarm the not-easily-intimidated ex-minor hockey league enforcer; they backed off hastily when Mike, cursing like a pirate, began throwing haymakers and rabbit punches like a pro: shadowboxing with suddenly shy opponents.

Mike had had enough of his so-called friends' rantings. He told them to get the Hell off his land. They wouldn't budge; Nick Tremaine demanded financial compensation for his car. The Meti Indian whom he'd thought his friend violently started punching Mike's shoulder, demanding answers and threatening a knuckle sandwich if not forthcoming. The big youth was well beyond his wits, having already ripped Mike's T-shirt. The two grown men were evenly matched should a scrap break out, though Mike knew Colter to be one tough customer, one who liked fighting dirty.

Nick rushed outdoors, fruitlessly trying to unlock Mike's station wagon. Aurora dashed out the door when Tremaine threatened to break the driver's window with a rake. Tom Bent seized a pick-axe and began hammering at one of the car's passenger windows.

To everyone's astonishment, the glass refused to shatter.

Steve grabbed the rock-pick from the skinny, smaller Bent's hands, ruthlessly bashing at the stubborn driver's-side window.

Yet despite the muscular youth's best efforts, the window refused to break! The gathering onlookers gaped in awe, some frightened, others openly accusing Mike of an elaborate, nightlong hoax. Obviously they were not thinking straight. Angry now, he told them to shut their faces. Dirk Simpson and Mike began to wrestle.

Mike soon had the tall, but scrawny, freshman pinned face-down on the gravel. He jerked on the leather-jacketed punk's arm, pinned behind his back, the youth crying out angrily. He'd given the blondish smartass a bloody nose and fat lip with a solid right cross and a sucker-punch uppercut. He'd always detested this pompous asshole. (The fact that he was always calling him *"dude"* didn't help Simpson's cause either.) Colter's hostility toward Mike temporarily vanished, openly cheering him on as he gave the macho high school student a sleeper hold. It seemed everybody was unanimous in their vehemence toward Dirk, who was a several-times-failed grade twelve bully from Shell Lake. They'd had run-ins numerous times with the jerk during various Midget hockey tournaments.

Nothing could induce the station wagon to open.

By noon Mike, Nick, Steve and Tom decided to track Tremaine's Torino down. It surely couldn't have gone far, they reasoned. They were a bit afraid of the sports car, still. Dirk Simpson marched off, swearing, towards the road, preferring to hitch-hike home rather than stay another hour at this Amityville Horror house. Nobody protested or bemoaned his going. Everyone jeered as he stalked out of the farmyard. He'd left at 11:25.

Fifteen minutes later, four of the girls also departed, on foot, including Colter's, Tremaine's, and Bent's girlfriends. Clearly pissed-off, frightened, the young co-eds angrily declared they'd never speak to them again! Somehow, after all they'd witnessed, they still believed the five grown men had planned, rigged, and executed the previous evening's entire charade. No amount of cajoling could convince them otherwise, skepticism taking over in the light of day.

Mike suspected the three high-school dropouts and two Andersen girls accompanying him still thought he was setting them up for another nasty surprise. They gave him annoying, speculative, side-long looks. The six youths trekked through the field, searching nervously for Nick's Ford Torino. Gravel crunched underfoot as they walked down the lane, the heady scent of spruce boughs and peppermint-like milfoil leaves lingering in the morning air. It was a bright, blue, summer's day, clear skies. No wind. A dirt road meandered through the wild alfalfa field, rising steeply over sudden knolls.

Meadows and one small, disused pasture dotted with horse mushroom enclosed the farm's lonely environs. One could almost believe last evening's ordeal had never happened, thought Mike unhappily.

The car wasn't in the fields. Nor was it to be found on

the main through-road. The six pedestrians probed the area in trepidation, fearing the strangely-animated sports car. They explored half a dozen field entrances, following erratic tire tracks in the mud. Hot, noon sunshine had already dried up much of the dirt road's surface.

Oddly they found the stationary vehicle in the same field approach where Mike had discovered the mobster's (?) rented Mercedes.

The bright red Torino seemed okay save for fresh streaks of mud and some unexplainable scratches on its souped-up hood.

Nick unlocked his sporty-looking car without difficulty, slouching into the bucket seat and starting the Torino's four-barrel 350 engine without mishap. The car idled fine; a low, throaty, sexy rumble.

On closer inspection, however, he found his cassette tapes and vehicle registration papers were missing from the glove compartment.

Nick swore ceaselessly as he checked beneath and behind its black leather bucket seats. Somebody (or something) had stolen his insurance papers and tapes!

Tremaine, stubborn cuss that he was, declared he'd not be leaving the farm until he regained his possessions. He accused the absent Dirk of somehow jimmying open his car and stealing his favourite hard-rock albums when the youth had set out almost two hours earlier. Dirk had apparently eyed Nick's cassettes covetously on the way down. The idea of things vanishing into thin air didn't seem plausible to Tremaine at the time, even after all he'd been through.

He drove the five youths back to the farm while discussing the previous night's events in a more logical, level-headed state of mind. Clearly, they unanimously agreed, they hadn't been the victim of some amateurish gag designed to scare their pants off. Nick and Tom were inclined to believe they'd witnessed genuine, paranormal manifestations, as did the two girls. Steve Colter still believed it had been a hoax, and that Mike was at the bottom of it all. They'd almost had another altercation a while earlier while hunting for Nick's Ford Gran Torino; when Mike had asked him a question, the big, good-looking, gregarious buck had told him to eff off, smirking, then shoving him when Mike suggested he do the same. Push had come to shove, the two youths ready to fight. (Colter knew full well though that Mike could and probably would beat the crap out of him, for Aurora had been their team's highest scorer as well as premier tough guy in minor-league hockey.) Mike had almost gone wild, challenging the big Metí right there and then on the trail. Trying to make light of it (and humiliate Mike in the process), the half-breed Indian backed off, cajoling, strangely unwilling to commit himself to a scrap.

Jodi and her younger cousin, Beth, had little comment as the sports car sped roller-coasterishly back to the farm. They contrasted sharply, for Beth's hair was black, cut short. Her makeup was too heavy; tear streaked. The two girls sat in the back seat with Mike and Tom. Aurora couldn't help sneaking covert glances at Andersen's charming face, entranced by her big, bedroom eyes and long, endearingly cleft, high bridged nose. Her smile made him drool, his heart experiencing nuclear meltdown.

The farm was as they'd left it. Beyond the house, sunlight bounced off of the huge, modern barn's rusted, sheet-metal roof. The troublesome outdoor sheds crouched back in a clearing, opposite the two barns, some hundred or so yards from the house near an old, rotten corral. The corral where he'd shot the intruder. Mike felt nervous just thinking about the derelict outbuildings.

He certainly felt uneasy about having these snoopy yahoos traipsing around the farmyard.

Inside the house, Mike brewed a pot of coffee while his guests sat smoking in the ramshackle living room, unheeding of the mess around them. None lifted a finger to help tidy the room. Mike felt he best wait until they were gone. He desperately wanted them to leave. Except Jodi. He wanted her under his bedspreads tonight.

Spread.

Pity he had no phone, Nick called from the foyer. Yeah, responded Mike. Pity.

Pity. He didn't miss one.

Nobody bothered to stand his stereo console upright, which lay face-down on the hardwood floor. Mike worried it might be busted. Cheap plastic buttons, dials, etc. The glass doors on the stand were shattered. Miraculously, his precious $500 speakers were still standing upright and unharmed.

One of the plastic keys on Mike's word-processor's keyboard had been busted. Glass fragments littered the varnished floorboards. Cutlery and dishware from up in the attic had been smashed or thrown indiscriminately about the house. Girlie magazines lay strewn around the living room. Leftover spaghetti smeared the foyer, dining room, and pantry. Thankfully Mike's own dishes, up in the cupboard, had been miraculously left untouched. The rest were smashed. His console television also stood undamaged in a corner. He cringed at the thought of gathering up all of his scattered manuscript pages.

No sign, oddly, of the piles of excrement he (and others) had trodden on earlier...

Steve Colter and Tom Bent drank the last five beer remaining in their Pilsner box. Mike never had cared for beer (he was a whiskey man). He thought the only people who drank beer were cranky farmers with beer-bellies, red faces, and nothing much better to do than sit around in some grungy bar listening to honky-tonk music. He mused wickedly that they ought to be ethnically cleansed, "for the good of all."

Yessiree.

Why, the very first day he'd moved into his uncle's claptrap old house, a couple of farmer neighbours had dropped by and threatened to beat his sorry ass if he didn't get the hell off of "their" property (obviously thinking he was some delinquent squatter from the city, a street rat, looking for a place to shack up for the winter!). They'd been quick to skedaddle, though, after, explaining the situation, he'd introduced Mr. Axe into the conversation...

At the stroke of four, Nick Tremaine decided he wouldn't stick around for the evening's festivities, after all. He'd begun to question his previous bravado ideas. Steve Colter had tossed his empty beer bottles in a corner, smashing them carelessly, laughingly adding that a few more broken bottles wouldn't hurt! Mike realized then for the first time that these guys really weren't his friends after all. All these years they'd siphoned money, booze, dope, and cigarettes off of him, never paying him back. He no longer wanted to know these jerks, these users. They'd always left him in the lurch when Aurora got into trouble. This was one of the few times that Mike hadn't had to pay for the beer, drugs, smokes. Yeah, they were users.

In the debris-littered foyer Jodi got Mike alone for a few minutes, apologizing for their not getting together to make sparks fly. She really wanted to get it on with him, she confided. Tremaine's '79 Torino roared to life out in the yard, blaring its bugle horn. The gorgeous, leather-jacketed bombshell Jodi (he had no idea her age) jotted her phone-number and address on a slip of pink paper, pressing it into Mike's hand then surprisingly kissing him hard on the lips; then smiled. Maybe another time, she suggested. His legs felt weak.

And the five frightened visitors left with a screech of tires and Colter's middle finger thrust out the window in Mike's direction.

Eff you, Beavis and Butthead, Mike thought sourly.

He felt a buoyant sense of relief.

EIGHT.

Mike cleaned the corrosion from the Harley's battery connectors, basking in the warm summer sun as he knelt beside the aged Sportster. He hadnt a clue what to do with the other bikes. He wanted to take each for a spin but feared somebody might drive into the yard (at this point, he was beyond paranoid). Some of the machines he'd yet to coax into starting. Today he'd finally managed to get the Harley Davidson's V-Twin engine running – albeit briefly – knowing it was just a matter of time, now, to get the derelict, old bike to turn over a new leaf. It was a veritable biker's gift-horse, reflected Mike, with high, ape-hanger handlebars, the bike's custom paint sadly faded. He'd already taken one of the other hogs for a ride, last night when all was dark, cruising the big, white Electra Glide with oversized tires around the farm and down the main through-road for a couple of miles.

He'd enjoyed the brief ride immensely, the enormous 1300's dual-halogen fog lamps more than adequate for night driving.

He adjusted the bike's carburetor now as he prepared to kickstart the drab, old motorcycle to life, straddling the V-Twin's tiny saddle while leaning over the engine. He'd cleaned and polished the big hard-tail's tarnished chrome, feeling like a Hell's Angels biker as he slammed down upon its kickstarter with his right foot, loving the bulky motorcycle's lean-and-mean looks, its cool, chopper-like forks extending from high handlebars. The bike lacked luggage racks, windjammer, or any other modish frills or accessories save for a tatty pair of leather side panniers. It still had its original mirrors. He especially liked the old-fashioned, round speedometer and tach with their outmoded r.p.m and m.p.h dial faces.

The wide, cumbersome monstrosity had strong compression. Which was a good sign. Mike feared the machine tipping over on him. He noticed its ancient kickstarter was gibbled; strong as he was, Mike wasn't sure he could get the bike upright, should it keel over, or be dropped while riding.

Repeatedly Mike kicked the kickstarter down, swearing aloud as the old pig sputtered, then died. Its greasy, iron kickstarter hit the crankshaft case with a dull clank each time, perhaps bent from some previous mishap.

Finally, after his fifteenth downstroke, the big bike's engine turned over with a cough, rumbling satisfyingly though misfiring as Mike revved the relic's engine softly. A deep, throaty growl emitted from the Harley's dual exhaust system, echoing off of a nearby shed. A throbbing, thrilling power reverberated beneath him. The motorcycle's big headlight wasn't working. After all these years, he oughtn't be surprised. Its bright, round, red taillight was, however. Loud pops farted from its bleating exhaust. The motorcycle was idling lousily. Without revving it Mike was sure the derelict would stall and never start again. He guessed a bike such as this would be worth several grand, once restored.

The stink of exhaust surrounded him as he sat on the motorbike revving it juvenilely, a cloud of blue-gray gas fumes wafting out toward the driveway.

As he revved the rusty '58 Sportster (or was it a Softtail?, XLH?; he wasn't sure), Mike considered next trying the snazzy, bright-red '84 Moto Guzzi EL tourer which sat concealed inside the padlocked wooden shed at his side. It, too, was a monster. He hadn't been able to start it when last he'd ogled the assorted motorcycles, feeling like a naughty delinquent eyeing a peep show on a red-light district's city street. *Pinch me, I'm dreaming!*, Mike screamed inside his head, grinning from ear to ear as he glanced pleasedly around the old farmyard and the various relics cluttered about. Near an empty steel granary fifty yards or so away sat a rusting, red, New Holland hay baler; beyond the distant barns, several old junked cars or trucks now screened by cascara bushes and tall, prairie grasses.

He was just about to pull in the clutch and click the bike into first gear when a small, fire-engine red, unfamiliar Datsun rolled into the yard, in plain sight of Mike's contraband idling in front of the shed.

Mike swore under his breath, heart beating like a prairie chicken's wings as he switched off the engine. No place to hide. Caught with his pants down, in a sense. No chance to conceal the bike. His fight or flight impulse kicked in like the Starship Enterprise's™ warp-drive engines. Nearby leaned his Remington semi-automatic high-powered rifle propped against the ancient, sunbathed, nostalgic-smelling shed. Mike thought he was going to piss his pants.

To his heart-stopping relief and sudden arousal he saw it was the stunning Ms. Andersen, driving a modest early eighties' Datsun hatchback. What the devil did she want? Sex? Mike, smirking, got off the Harley, his long, sweat-dripping hair over his face and shoulders as he swaggered toward the knockout honey who was now (wow!) climbing out of the dusty, red hatchback. She wore a dynamite purple-silk miniskirt leaving nothing to the imagination and a maroon satin blouse stretched tightly over tent-like, drool-inspiring breasts. Jodi's black -silk-suspendered thighs would entice a chaplain to give up his vows as she stepped out from the small hatchback. Mike hadn't seen her since their lusty encounter almost a month previous. He hoped she wasn't after his money, his 'grand' inheritance. He forgot about his rifle by the shed.

She met him three-quarters of the way to the disastrous sheds. Jodi Andersen, sashaying like a street-wise hooker with high-heels, purse slung over her shoulder; expressionless beneath sunglasses as she walked across the yard, her Datsun parked discreetly behind his house.

She lowered her sunglasses in appreciation.

"Excuse me for drooling," said Mike casually, "but you've either come from a hot date, or you've come for my body." He tried to leer but managed only a goofy Ernie from Sesame Street look.

Andersen, a quirky expression on her face, laughed aloud, punching his shoulder playfully; then she smiled, blushing. "It's a gruellingly hot day. A girl's gotta dress for the nineties." She paused. "And I'm a nineties' girl, Mike. A real swinger."

Mike sensed she was only joking. (She *was* only joking, right?)

"Actually, I was visiting my girlfriend in Leoville," Jodi continued, "so I stopped by to see if you were still alive."

She eyed him with concern, their ghastly, shared experience not forgotten.

"So, how are you, Mike? Any more 'things that go bump in the night'? Seen any hundred-foot Michelin men lately?" She took his arm casually, as if strolling with a long-time lover toward his house. Then she stopped.

"What's with the rifle? Were you out hunting?"

"Uh…yeah. Hunting."

"Hey, *c-o-o-l,*" Jodi gasped, "where'd you get that neat old bike," breaking away to admire Aurora's '58 Harley. "It's a chopper, isn't it?"

"Yup. Found it in the shed." Mike felt like clamping his hand over his mouth.

"Really?"

"Yes, indeed. Let's go back to the house and have some coffee."

Jodi balked suddenly, clutching at him with a motherly scowl on her face – demanding why he hadn't phoned her these past three weeks.

"Well, uh, it's like this…" He searched for a savvy way to tell her without sounding like a complete moron, or a liar at worst. "My, uh," clearing his throat, "my uncle – or whatever – kinda 'absconded' with the phone one night." (He wasn't sure she knew he'd never had one.)

(Truth was he'd lost her friggin' phone number!)

Andersen put her arm around Mike's waist proprietarily, smiling. "Good one, Mike."

Inside the refreshingly cool kitchen he set a pot of water on the range to boil, artfully dodging Jodi's questions about the bike.

"This place looks nice and tidy now," observed Jo, glancing nervously about the kitchen and foyer. "Have you experienced any more, um, visitations, since that night? I –" she turned to him with a look of concern, "I was worried about you, Mike. You shouldn't stay here. Something's dreadfully awful about this house." Andersen paused, twisting her fingers. "Something bad could happen to you."

"Is that a threat?" remarked Mike, tongue in cheek.

Jo laughed along, vivaciously jutting out her chest. "I didn't mean it to come out that way!"

Mike chuckled for a moment. "No, this place's been fine. It took me a couple of days to clean up the mess. I still don't know what the hell's goin' on. I've been thinking it's my senile old uncle who's come back to reclaim his property." He drummed his fingers nervously on the countertop. "That doesn't sound very plausible, does it?"

"Did he die here?"

"Yeah. Out in the yard. On his tractor."

Jodi shuddered noticeably.

"I've never believed in ghosts," confided Jodi seriously. "I still don't. Could it have been," she hinted, "a hoax?"

"You mean did I set it up?" Mike asked. "Nope. Several real weird things have occurred here recently. I'm beginning to think I'm losing my marbles."

"Sorry. Okay. What I meant is, perhaps someone wants you outta here?" Jodi got up from the table, idly joining Mike by the olive-green propane range which rarely worked properly.

Mike considered her words a moment. They had a certain plausibility. But why should someone wish to fake a haunting, rather than simply knock him off? No one would ever miss him.

"How?" he asked. "Puppets? Hidden mirrors? Cheesecloth? Film projectors?"

"I don't know. What do you know about this place, Mike?" Jodi paused. "About your uncle, I mean."

"Not a lot," Mike lied. "I never met the old bastard. He was apparently a crank. A recluse."

He placed a ceramic mug steaming with black coffee down on the table, then another. "Sugar and cream?"

"Yes, please."

Mike set a saucer of chocolate-chip cookies and

Goody Rings atop the polished tabletop, then sat down.

"Smoke?" Aurora lit a Rothman's.

"No, thank you."

"As I say," remarked Mike, exhaling a blue-gray cloud of smoke, "the farm's been surprisingly quiet. Maybe the old man doesn't like visitors."

Jodi grimaced; shaking her head wryly. "Is that a hint?"

"No," Mike chuckled. "I like you. I want you to stay."

They sipped their coffee in a lengthy moment's silence.

Jodi sat there with distinct unease, chewing her fingernails and eyeing the room nervously. She felt more at ease outside.

After what she'd experienced last time, she was amazed she'd returned at all.

"Was anything damaged that night?" asked Jodi. She peered nosily over Mike's shoulder into his re-arranged living room, as if expecting a bogeyman.

Mike nodded grimly.

"Broke one of the dials on my tape-deck, and busted one of the tab keys on my typewriter. Other than a lot of broken dishes and junk everything else seems okay."

"Why would you want to stay here in this…this…charnel house," Jodi remarked distastefully.

"Got nowhere else to go. It's my farm," Mike said

testily. "Damned if I'm gonna let some ghost scare me off."

"So you're gonna play the tough guy, huh?"

"One tough customer, honey. One tough hombre. I ain't afraid of no ghosts. Ooops." Mike clamped his hand over his mouth, becoming serious. "Sorry uncle Joe. Didn't mean to offend you and your lively friends."

Jodi laughed out loud. Mike surmised, then, that she was the prettiest woman he'd ever seen. Her warm, inviting smile, those big, long lashed, starlet's eyes, made his mouth water. She had a curvaceous bod that just wouldn't quit. He wondered if she was a good lay.

To Mike the house felt suddenly steamy. He stood up, suggesting they go outside, he'd show her his garden (the sheds), the barn – no, not the barn!, walk around his deceased uncle's pleasantly rustic farmyard awhile. Perhaps go for a walk in the meadow. Jodi said she'd like that, baiting him with her eyes. Mike suspected she was as "overheated" as he was.

"Did I ever tell you have nice tits," Mike remarked as they strolled toward his vegetable patch. He immediately felt as awkward as a twelve-year-old. Jodi blushed, grinning, shoving him away.

"No, you hadn't," she teased breathlessly, "but I'm glad you noticed. By the way, you're a pervert."

"Runs in the family. You know I dreamt last night that

I was a Celtic barbarian, and I'd abducted you after you'd bested me in a sword duel?"

Jodi halted. "You're weird, Mike." She barked a laugh, grimaced becomingly, then dashed toward his garden enclosure.

"Oh, neat! A real, down-home vegetable garden. Did you, like, grow this yourself?" Jodi stood admiring the assorted raised beds; hand on her hips.

Mike, poker-faced, replied in the negative. He said he'd been aided by fairies.

They walked into the broad-leaf forest, hand in hand, keeping well away from the dead man's lonely, forested grave (the presence of which, Jodi hadn't a clue). Mike pointed out various trees and wildflowers, who's identities he'd been brushing-up on. He picked an orange tiger lily from the forest floor and stuck it in Andersen's hair. She laughed sexily.

They wandered into the flower-scented meadow, where he picked wild rose, ladies' slipper, monk's hood, purple lupine, babies' breath and bluebells, bedecking Jo's exquisite, gold-burnished hair with a dazzling sprig of glorious-smelling wildflowers as she stood there smiling with misty, bedroom eyes. Toward the road they strolled, arm in arm, breathless in each other's company, inexplicably infatuated yet shy.

Mike told her his aspirations, his research for his

horror novel, his latest foray into Celtic mythology which he'd never found interesting but now thought fascinating. The latest book he was reading, he explained, was a controversial hardcover (borrowed from the local Lakeland library) about the various prehistoric invasions of Ireland, T.F, O'Rahilly's "Early Irish History and Mythology," written in the thirties, which proposed that there were two Celtic invasions of Ireland: P-Celtic Brittonic, followed by Goidelic, who'd gained control over the country by genocide. Jodi was mildly surprised and stimulated by this tall, dark, handsome stranger's eclectic personality. She felt no fear out here alone with him, no sense that he might ravish her in the meadow. Her experience of men extended to her ex-classmates' buffoonery and two brothers' burping and farting contests at home when her mom and dad weren't around. They were gross. Most guys her age were swine, she'd discovered.

"How old are you, by the way," inquired Mike. "You're not, like, jailbait, are you?"

"No," exclaimed Jodi with a laugh. "No. I'm twenty. How old are you?"

"Twenty-two."

They halted at the edge of a barley field, sitting down, exhausted, on a rotted log. Fat, purpling clouds were beginning to scud across the late-afternoon sun. The pair soaked up the heat, and not just the sun's heat. An old, broken hay bale yards away gave off a rich, pungent odor of rotting alfalfa and deers' urine; marble-sized droppings littering the ground.

Mike inquired where she lived, what she did for a living, what her future aspirations were. She was a waitress in a restaurant in nearby Glaslyn, responded Jo unhappily. She wanted to be a pop singer, confided that she had been singing privately for seven years (had even had a tutor in school), and had learned to play piano. She had no idea how to achieve her goal. Mike was impressed.

"Oh my God! Six o'clock already, getting late," exclaimed Jodi, glancing at her watch.

Mike put a hand on her warm, suspendered thigh, leaning forward suggestively. "I'd love for you to stay the night. I....might not be safe alone."

Jodi considered this for an agonizingly long moment, her breath quickening. "Mike…" He ran his hand up her thigh. "I don't think…"

Her resolve melted when she gazed into his hypnotic, blue eyes.

"God, I like you," she exhaled. She felt dizzy; her breasts heavy, aching to be touched. His breath breezed against her cheek, smelling of Chiclets. She nodded her assent. "Okay. But I warn you, any weird occurrences and I'm gone."

He smiled, taking Andersen's chin in his hand and kissing her tenderly; then rose from the log.

"Mike…" Jodi took his hand. "I'm not on the pill." Her big, expressive eyes flooded with uncertainty, gauging his reaction.

"That's okay," he reassured her. "We'll be careful."

They strolled back to the house, arms about each other's waist.

And made supper.

<u>NINE.</u>

"What did you do with all the furniture from upstairs, Mike?" inquired Jodi as she helped him prepare supper.

"It's sitting in various rooms, incognito. The stuff's hardly recognizable after I cleaned it up a bit," volunteered Mike as he peeled a turnip. "There's an armchair and recliner in the living room, and a chest of drawers, which I repaired, in the foyer."

"Aren't you worried about the phenomena happening again?" Jodi asked in surprise.

"Nah. I put everything back in -"

Jodi looked at him, puzzled.

"Back in the attic. I think the old coot's jealous of his belongings. As long as they stay up there, he's fine."

"You mean, like, he – it – was being sarcastic by throwing stuff down the stairs, as if he were saying *"Here, you want my things? Take this!"*

"I think so, yeah."

"I hope so," Jodi breathed aloud. "Listen, Mike. Why don't we go back to my place. I have a basement-suite in

Glaslyn."

"To yourself?"

She paused.   "Well – no. I have a roommate."

Mike rejected the idea offhand. "No. I don't like to leave the place alone."

"Why not?"

Mike hedged. "Never know who could drive in, break into the place." He swivelled his eyes toward the panelled kitchen wall. Jodi sensed he was holding something back.

"Maybe the old man won't return," Mike said reassuringly.

She gave him an odd look, highly dubious of that.

For supper, Jodi'd made spicy beef stroganoff, which bubbled appealingly now in a big, cast-iron frying pan. Turnips and cabbage were also on the boil. Mike just loved turnips.

He slipped into the living-room darkening from the sun's dying rays sinking in a western sky, switching on his record player. He knew Jodi liked Iron Maiden's "The Number of the Beast" LP, so he played that at a modest volume.

Jodi called from the kitchen, asking whether he'd learned to play that guitar she'd noticed over in a corner. Mike answered that he'd tried, but had never taken guitar lessons; he'd had the electric Yamaha for less than two years. Why, did she wanna start a band?, he jokingly remarked – to a resounding *"No!"*

He was actually a pretty good guitarist, according to people he knew, had gotten the metal style down pat, but was nowhere near ready, he felt, to start a band.

Jo found Aurora's Alice Cooper *"Killer"* LP not at all nice listening; a demonic album full of macabre songs with weird, horrible titles like "Dead Babies", "Halo of Flies", "Under my Wheels", "Desperado." She remarked it was no wonder Mike's house was possessed!

More than once Jodi tried, without success, to convince him to returning with her to her much safer (and *quieter*) Glaslyn apartment suite – roommate or no roommate.

Supper was ready by nine – unusually late for the famished youths.   Mike and Jodi tore into the repast with a gusto neither had experienced for a long, long time. They ate in romantic candlelight, conversing at the big, dark, polished oak table like a couple of academics (taking their mind off of last month's horrific events), discussing ancient Egypt's pyramids, Roman rule, Gaelic lore. Mike poured he and Jodi each a tall glass of expensive white wine (XOXO), which he'd bought in Spiritwood. The sun had set, painting the horizon a lurid, pastel mauve of streaky cirrus clouds. Aurora congratulated his charming, temporary 'maid' for the delicious meal, a recipe he could never make (Mike's cuisine abilities were limited, for the most part, to simple fare: spaghetti and meatballs, eggs and toast, canned soup, vegetables, and fried meats, plus an impressive array of baked goods). Jodi, laughing, remarked that she'd be glad to teach him; Chow Mein, Beef Bourgouignon, Chinese chicken balls, the works. She'd majored in Home Economics at Medstead elementary school.

The fireball, scarlet sun had vanished completely by ten o'clock, leaving the pair sitting in amorous candlelight thrown by three, spiralling, red candles on the tabletop.

Then they slept together.

****

The house was silent. The two star-crossed lovers lay contented in each other's arms, listening with rapt fascination to the breezy "whish" of moving spruce boughs outside and the beating of each other's hearts. A strong wind rustled the aspen leaves beyond Mike's deceased uncle's farmhouse. Through a window he could discern several ghost-white paper birch amidst the northern treeline. A perfectly spherical, crater-pocked moon loomed enormous in the lower-southeast, midnight skies.

Jodi kissed Mike's hairy chest, sliding lower beneath the blankets to experiment with his tantalizing but remarkably unfamiliar organ, doing things she thought she'd never do.

She slid up beside him again, sighing romantically. Mike caressed her silken, burnished hair with his fingers; utterly exhausted. A Great Horned owl (he could see it through a window) hooted eerily from its branch, then flitted off under the light of the moon after some unsuspecting prey. Jodi nestled warmly against Mike's chest, smiling peacefully, thinking idly that those pure-white aspen were likely what caused many ghostly superstitions. She pondered Aurora's haunted house, thinking with a chill up her spine that her and Mike's exquisite lovemaking might have been watched by some disincarnate being. A lewd, voyeurish old man who'd watched the two inexperienced youths practice oral sex, screwing each other silly in romantic candlelight.

She'd never imagined it could be so good. Mike had teased Jodi's nipples with his tongue, then strayed between her lovely, big breasts, finally sucking and licking them before mounting her.

She'd lost consciousness upon her first orgasm.

Mike, for his part, was simply amazed at what'd occurred tonight. Jodi was even more corporeal than 'Wanda' had been, believe it or not! He thought he'd known how soft, how warm, a woman's body would feel. Although her nice, soft tits were somewhat smaller than Wanda's (whom he missed sorely), Jodi's face was, arguably, prettier, her lithe, young body a natural aphrodisiac. He'd taken precautions not to impregnate her, withdrawing just in time. She was so tight he couldn't believe it; he was surprised their yelling hadn't awakened the old man's spirit, for Mike knew his uncle had been a dirty old man. He'd found kiddy porn magazines down in the basement, which he'd thought totally disgusting. (And as things were to turn out, wise to have burnt them.)

"You never did own a telephone, did you, Mike."

"No. Of course not."

Jodi enfolded him with slender, well-toned arms, kissing him hungrily. "Liar." She lay on top, straddling him, enjoying this intimate act like a flustered schoolgirl. He was surely the dark, handsome stranger she'd been making love to in her dreams and fantasies. For months she'd imagined entertaining someone like him in her bed, or in her car, or on some swanky, isolated beach — someplace like Hawaii or the Caribbean. Bermuda. Tonight she'd loved it when Mike had f***** her breasts.

Such a kinky, unpredictable guy he was proving to be!

Mice started gnawing and scratching at the walls, exercising and strengthening their rodent teeth. Aurora hated trapping the innocent-looking thieves.

Jodi propped her chin on her elbow, admiring this virile stranger. *He's such a thrillingly handsome man,* she thought, with a sinuous, muscular body which drove her wild. *She felt like a rabbit!* Bright moonrays as if from some giant, celestial flashlight illuminated the living room through a plain, old-fashioned, three-tier sash window. She found it strange – yet exhilarating – to be sleeping with this guy on the floor of an old, haunted farmhouse. What an adventure. *Wait till she tells her girlfriend, Stace!* Aurora's chest was like something out of a superhero comic strip. She liked that. A slight, pubescent mustache grew above his lip. He seemed almost familiar – painfully familiar. But she couldn't recall where she'd met him before. *What a weird thing, eh?*

The big, black woodstove with its white porcelain front radiated a wonderful heat inside Mike's living room. The breezy night was unpleasantly chilly. Jo realized to her chagrin that she was in love with this strange man. She hardly knew him! It wasn't fair! How dare he steal her heart! (Maybe, if she was extraordinarily lucky, he wouldn't turn out to be an asshole.) Marriage (oh, bliss!)

was too early to consider.

Andersen hardly realized it when she began to levitate!

"Jodi!" Mike cried. "Where the hell are you going?!"

"I don't know!" she cried, laughing. "I'm levitating," yelled Jo in dismay. "Oh my God, Mike, get me down!!" She floated four feet above him now, limbs flailing. She began to scream hysterically. Mike grabbed her wrist, dragging her down without opposition. The disturbance ceased when Mike cursed at the unseen entity, threatening to burn the sheds down. The feeling of oppressive gloom which invariably preceded such manifestations suddenly vanished.

Jodi stared at Mike wild-eyed, bewildered.

"What…what do the sheds have to do with this 'thing'," she demanded crossly. "Tell me, or I leave."

Oooops.

"Uh…the sheds…oh, those…" Mike paused tellingly, ransacking his brain for a quick answer. "The old man – my uncle – had some things in there."

"Like what? And how do you know that's the reason? Did he *'tell'* you?"

Mike raced for an answer.

"Just some junk. He -"

Jodi leapt up, reaching for her underwear. "That's it, I'm leaving. You're fucking full of shit!" She spun around, angry, facing Mike red-faced in the buff as she struggled with her bra straps. "You're lying! Why are you lying to me?! What's in those buildings that has that old bastard so worried –" Her face lit up with an idea. "I'll see for myself."

Mike realized with growing horror that he'd foolishly forgot to lock the   sheds!

He watched helplessly as his buxom girlfriend hurriedly dressed; she slipped her burgundy rayon-silk blouse over her shoulders, quickly tugging on her black mini-skirt, then her blue suede jacket. "Call me when you're ready to tell the truth," she snapped, rushing toward the kitchen door.

"You're not leaving, are you?" Mike called out frantically. "Please, come back. Really, there's nothing in the sheds," cried Mike, panicked.

Jodi, flinging open the front door, yelled back.

"Yeah?! We'll see! I hope those buildings aren't locked, Mike, 'cause I'm gonna break the locks," she threatened angrily. "You've got something in there you're hiding. I'm goin' over to the sheds now, Mike. Bye."

She rushed out the door, flashlight in hand.

Mike scrambled to his feet, dressing himself as if he were trying to win a Guinness World Record for speed dressing. Andersen mustn't go into the sheds, no one must! Even if he had to bodily restrain her! If others were to know what's in there, there'll be hell to pay! Damn that snoopy little slut!

Mike ran a pell-mell 100-yard dash barefoot (he'd misplaced his shoes) toward the trio of sheds, shirtless as he chased Jodi's fleeing figure in blessed moonlight.

He searched the nearest shed frantically, hampered without flashlight.   Jodi couldn't be found.

Mike searched the smaller one next, calling Andersen's name. The building's windows had a decade's worth of grime, and it was pitch-black inside.

By the time he'd located her Andersen had already yanked the four, big, tattered tarpaulins from the awesome hoard.

"Oh, my God," murmured Jodi.

Mike dropped his chin in defeat.

Enough moonlight shone through the grimy, south windows to illuminate assorted brand-names of stolen warehouse merchandise: Panasonic, RCA, Sony, Hitachi…all boxed, all swathed in plastic…

How to explain this.

Mike felt as if he were groping in a nightmare, a ludicrous series of events going by in slow motion; when he moved, it seemed like he was wading in lake water. All this couldn't be happening. None of this is real, Mike told himself. When I awake tomorrow morning all this shit is gonna be gone.

He put his hands on Jodi's arms.

And knew then she had to die...

But that he couldn't do it.

So be damned.

He embraced her from behind, inhaling her cantaloupe-smelling hair.   Some scented shampoo which drove him wild. He remembered the glorious feeling of cleaving into this lovely woman tonight, how she'd licked his ears, his neck, as he climaxed.

"I don't understand," Jodi said aloud, bewildered. "What is all this?"

"You shouldn't've come here," murmured Mike, squeezing her tight. "This complicates everything."

Jodi wrenched away from Mike's grip, spinning around to face him.

"You're some kind of black-market dealer, aren't you? A – a kleptomaniac."

Mike chuckled hopelessly, shaking his head.   "Oh, baby, I wish it were that simple. No, unfortunately, I've no secret penchant for doing warehouse heists or cat burglary. This we can blame on good ol' uncle Joe."

Jodi eyed him up and down, clearly incredulous, suddenly realizing her peril. This stranger she'd slept with tonight could turn out to be a killer!

"I don't know why or how he got ahold of this stuff," Mike explained, "nor who or what we're dealing with. Obviously we're talking mob. Hell's Angels, that sort of thing. There isn't a big enough black market to merit this amount of booty. 'Least not around here."

Jodi turned back to gaze at the assorted boxes of appliances, souvenirs, objét de art. All, apparently, stolen. She swivelled to face him, not daring to turn her back on him for long.

"I think you're lying," she bravely accused with a sarcastic grin.

"You've got to believe me," Mike begged. "I had nothing to do with this. It's the old man. That's why he wants me off the farm. God knows why, but I don't think he knows he's dead."

Andersen's face grew even more incredulous, scornfully amused.

"Oh, I see. Your dead uncle's ghost has returned to reclaim his contraband. Yeah, right! Get a Life, Michael."

"That's exactly how it is! You witnessed the phenomena in the house that night, and tonight's. Could I have stolen all of this?" Mike stepped forward, pointing out various brand names.

"Look at this. Franklin Mint coin collections, worth a fortune. And here, half a dozen Sony disc players, '89 models. And this. A Hitachi microwave, worth four hundred bucks each. Back here." Mike squeezed between the ten-foot stacks of cardboard boxes. "Cartons of cigarettes...Rothmans, Camel, Du Maurier, Players, Export

'A', Macdonald's Menthol, Craven 'A'…"

Jodi squeezed between the plastic-smelling boxes, gaping at the eight x twenty stacks of unopened cigarette cartons, miraculously undamaged by mold, mice, or rats. She noticed with disbelief the many cartons of expensive Cuban cigars.

"This is nothin'," Mike remarked, "come on, wait till you see what's in the *other* buildings!"

Andersen followed, excited but puzzled, as the two marched several paces east toward yet another, slightly larger, outbuilding. Bright moonrays aided them as they crossed the grassy yard. Mike winced and swore as he trod on slivers and pebbles.

Inside the biggest shed, a long, rectangular, barn-like edifice with loading-bay doors and cement floor, Mike showed Jodi the fourteen pristine motorcycles, explaining that some were obviously scuffed, presumably stolen from people's yards, while others seemed brand-spanking new. Jodi marveled at the huge, shiny, crimson-red Moto Guzzi 1300 (Italian make), the two newer-model Harleys (worth several grand, Mike guessed aloud), the classics, antiques, assorted dirtbikes, minibikes and on/off road machines. Surprisingly, no quads, ski-doos, or three-wheelers were present.

Or at least, none that he'd found, yet.

Jo was left speechless.

"I can't believe this!" she squealed. "It's like – it's like a warehouse or a department store, Mike! My God, there must be thousands, *hundreds of thousands* of dollars' worth of stolen merchandise here!"

Mike nodded sagely. "That's right. The only problem is, is that this stuff belongs to some pretty ruthless hoods no doubt. I don't know what to do."

Jodi sobered.

"Mike, go to the police. You'll get killed sooner or later if you don't. You'll get a reward if you turn this stuff in!"

"I'm afraid. They'll nail my ass. They'll frame me, I know it. What alibis have I got? I don't know anybody who can vouch for me," Mike fretted. "This doesn't exactly happen every day."

Andersen squinted, tossing her long, rich, chestnut hair in confusion. She had no immediate answer.

"It'll have serial numbers. All the police need to do is trace this stuff's origin, and you can prove your innocence."

"No. That's where you're wrong. Every single item has had its serial numbers rubbed off."

"How?"

"Dunno. File, I think."

They stood side by side, staring at the various 'hot' goods lit by beclouded moonlight shining through the loading bay doors. Mike put his arm around Jo's narrow shoulders, smelling her hair as she huddled against him. She was several inches shorter than his six-foot height. He began to feel chilled standing out here in this shed in his jeans; bare-chested and barefoot.

"I'm freezing like a snowman. Let's go back to the house. I'll make some coffee."

Jodi, unsure whether to believe Mike's innocence, reluctantly allowed him to lead her back to the sinisterly waiting farmhouse.

They sat on the living room floor sipping steaming Irish cream coffee, lit by a mere. half-burnt candle. Jodi and Mike felt as shy as teenagers who'd just met (which, in a sense, they had), sitting on their haunches so close their knees were touching.

Mike, taking a chance, reached out and touched Jo's burning face. Her breath quickened, her body overly warm. She didn't interfere when he unbuttoned her blouse. She felt like a virgin again, scared, excited, allowing Mike to nuzzle the cleft between her breasts.

She moaned when his left hand slipped beneath her mini skirt, straying between her thighs and gently rubbing her panties.

Mike set their empty mugs aside, then, her face in his hand, kissing Jodi's anticipating mouth.

Jo allowed him to remove her blouse, then was surprised

when suddenly the ice melted and she was laughing coquettishly. Their tongues twirled playfully, darting into each other's mouth.

"Oh, Mike," Jodi whispered. "I need you."

She unzipped his bleached jeans, kneeling subserviently before him.

And gave him fellatio for the second time that evening, her mouth feeling astonishingly wet and familiar – like Wanda's – to Aurora's overexcited senses as he clutched the young woman's breasts. Jodi's body sang with joy as he caressed her; leaning forward on her knees.

She wouldn't let him explode in her mouth. That would be disgusting. Instead she turned around, leaning forward on her elbows, moaning and then smiling as Aurora sank into her while cradling her breasts from behind.   Mike absent-mindedly glanced at his watch, noting the late hour of 3:30 a.m. as he kissed this beautiful nympho's quivering spine. Jo's long, drawn-out sighs filled him with wonder.

They came together, in another position, nestled in each other's arms as if in a bed of down.

Mike woke alone. Warm, late autumn sunrays shone upon his bedcovers, washing the room with a mellow glow as he stretched luxuriously and groaned aloud, smiling. He was naked beneath the blankets. Mike realized with a sudden jolt that Ms. Andersen, that incredible, bodacious, lusty woman, was not by his side. Yet the tantalizing sizzle of frying bacon and the delectable aroma teased Aurora's senses, reminding him of sex. Jodi reminded him of sex. Food reminded him of sex. He recalled last evening's heated lovemaking with a mixture of awe and pleasure. Or could he be only dreaming?

Jodi, hips rolling seductively, sashayed into the living room wearing a pink tank-top and tight white cut-offs *(she brought an extra set of clothes, the minx!,* thought Mike), kneeling down on the floor to give Aurora a lingering, lip-smacking French kiss.

"Love you," she whispered. "How many eggs would you like, baby?"

"Huh? Oh. Three. And be quick about it, wench. Bring me breakfast in bed, little woman."

Andersen giggled, licking Mike's ear with a raspy tongue. "What are you going to do if I don't?"

"Screw the hell outta ya."

"O-kay. Now get dressed. It's almost ten o'clock. Here." She tossed him his macabre, black, Mercyful Fate T-shirt.

He dressed, joined Jodi in the sunlit kitchen and kissed her long, tanned neck from behind.

"I think we've been bonking each other for months, unbeknown to each other," Mike whispered.

"Umm. Maybe." She tittered as he squeezed her from behind, breathless, and not only from Mike's amorous embrace.

They ate breakfast at the table, suddenly bashful as they eyed one another. They sat opposite each other. Without a word Jo stood up and led Mike into the living room after finishing her breakfast of bacon, toast, poached eggs and pineapple juice, wildly making love to him again on their makeshift bed.

She awoke in his bedding an hour later, cradled in Aurora's strong, hairy arms, having momentarily passed-out during intercourse.

"Jo."

"Hm?"

"Would you move-in with me?," he asked. "I know the farm is cursed and all that, but I've got to have you, and I won't take no for an answer."

Andersen thought this over for a long moment.

"God, I don't know, Mike. This place is really weird."

(However, she found herself strangely unable to say what needed saying: *Only a fool's fool would live here.*)

"You're worried some thugs might show up, right? Or maybe, like, you'll be teleported to some never-never land?"

Jo nodded, worried.

"I feel we've known each other in some previous life.

No, *seriously*," he continued, "I know this sounds crazy, but somehow I feel we were meant to be together. Before I met you, I was the living dead."

Jo smiled, turning to face him, her eyes quizzical. "You sure know how to ignite this lady's libido. Why should I trust you? How do I know you're not a jerk just out to use me, or some kind of sex freak? I've never had a lover," she said, pouting, "and am very naive. Maybe you're a womanizer? A – a sado-masochist."

"I'm not, honest!," Mike pleaded. "I'd treat you like a princess... Besides, I've jinxed your car, and now you can't leave. Believe me?"

"Yes," she whispered in Mike's ear, misty-eyed. "You've jinxed me, baby. You've done magic on my ol' heart, you voodoo child."   She smiled a sexy, dimpled grin. "Please, make love to me agin'."

****

They stood inside the smallest shed doing inventory on stolen merchandise. Jodi was astonished. Twelve cases of jewellery, seven ultra-expensive, high-powered binoculars, military issue, three genuine Oriental heirlooms of possibly

Indian or Burmese origin, eight boxes of what looked to be pirated videocassettes, sixteen M16 and eighteen AK-47 Kalashnikov assault rifles (!), forty handguns, two large boxes of dynamite, seven super-expensive Sony Walkmans, one 8000-watt AC-DC inverter and a five hundred-watt wind generator (?!), four crates of German Moselle-valley wine, 1898 vintage, seventeen alligator-leather ladies' purses, four gasoline and/or diesel generators, and one Suzuki quad (entombed in a crate, unassembled).

And a partridge in a pear tree.

Some Christmas gift list, Jodi murmured. Perhaps old Joe's farm was Santa's northern depot? Mike laughed at that. Santa Claus, in fact, was the Grinch who stole Christmas!, he cried aloud.

Afterwards they went for a stroll down the main road, admiring black-eyed Susans, monk's hood, butterfly orchid, tiger lily, cattails along wet streams, also keeping an eye out for suspicious vehicles parked in field approaches or road verges. Mike said nothing of the black Mercedes he'd discovered in a field entrance. Jodi had been with him, now, for ten days. It was a humid, balmy, bright blue September day, not a wisp of cloud in the prairie sky. They'd secured the three explosively dangerous outbuildings with new padlocks. Jodi had no idea she and Mike were doing reconnaissance for sporty-looking vehicles.

On and on they walked, ostensibly searching for rare flora while Mike scanned the environs for suspicious activity (a group of bikers sitting in a field reserved for furlough, say, or a black limousine by the roadside). Nothing so melodramatic was to be seen.

He showed her an old, derelict manor house, a couple of miles away, to the left of the gravel main road, exploring the place with juvenile fascination. Across the road, screened by trees, lay the working farm, Nimchattan's, which owned the dilapidated, three-storey farmhouse. (It was really an anachronism, both thought, some bourgeois wanna-be squire's attempt to raise himself above the peasant masses.) Why it stood abandoned, Jodi and Mike had no clue. *Maybe it was haunted,* said Andersen half-jokingly. Or the abode of a serial killer. Grand, snarly old oaks, not native to the area as far as Mike knew, stood sentinel before the dirt road. A wonderfully picturesque, mossy trail led to the hipped-roof farmhouse. Around the overgrown yard, rusty farm machinery and defunct automobiles sat in roof-high quack grass.

Inside the structurally sound, pioneer-era dwelling, a fabulous stucco ceiling, peeling, but much like Mike's own, but more grandiose, clung yet to the parlour's ceiling. *Fantastic!* He found a complete CB400 motorbike model in a box in one of the ground-floor rooms which he decided to smuggle out. Jumbled about the grand, old edifice were assorted bits of furniture, some of it, likely, antique. A huge brick fireplace inside the leak-damaged parlour caught both youth's attention. Broken asphalt shingles atop the decrepit manor's pyramid- hipped-roof had allowed rainwater to ruin a portion of the room, including an otherwise almost-perfect mosaic in plaster. Much of the house was devoid of furniture but strewn with junk left behind by squatters, or from previous tenants. Mike knew nothing of the building's history, and had prowled the forlorn old house only once, while returning from a leisure-drive to nearby Birch Lake, a large, unstocked freshwater morass surrounded by dense prairie woodland and rich, prime farmland. He remembered his Impala station wagon having had a flat tire on that terrible dirt road.

Andersen mused aloud as to why this once-magnificent prairie manse had been abandoned. It seemed a marvelous abundance of good, usable building timber. The foundation seemed intact. There were *"No Trespassing"* signs posted about the property; maybe the Nimchattans deemed the big house to be of special family pride, Jo suggested.

Upstairs Jodi almost screamed when she bumped into a stiffened bearskin, draped over a railing, up in the attic. (She'd thought it was a spook, or a sasquatch!) Mike laughed aloud at that, studying the dusty, stinking bearskin with morbid fascination.

They ran wildly from the house when what appeared to be *white sheets* (!) arose from the attic floor, pursuing the horrified trespassers down the spruce- and oak-lined drive!

Mike and Jodi ran as fast as their legs could carry them, lungs pumping like bellows. They wailed aloud in fright down the gloomy driveway towards the road, boughs and branches seemingly reaching out to seize their clothes or hair. Across the dirt road, in the opposite farmyard, the Nimchattans' hog farm was unbelievably oblivious to Mike and Jodi's mad flight from the sinisterly enticing farm house.

Out on the grid road Mike halted. He spun around to see if the amorphous, sheet-like spectres trailed behind. He wondered maniacally if the nightmarish *things* hadn't actually been kids in white sheets 'floating' after them, or whether he and Jodi had only imagined them. Admittedly, the attic and ground floor rooms (some of whose windows were boarded up), had been dusky and poorly lit.

Nothing at all stirred on the dusty road.

Yet Mike and Jodi could've sworn, under oath, that they'd seen 'sheets' floating lazily down the abandoned driveway after the two fleeing interlopers.

Jodi began to weep, urging Mike to keep running, cursing him roundly for bringing her to the old, abandoned house. *The region was an effin' psychic's paradise!,* she screamed aloud. Out of breath, the two finally halted in a field approach, doubled over and winded.

What a ghastly, horrifying visit this was turning out to be!, thought Jodi bitterly to herself. Why had she ever come here? Sure, the sex was incredible, but jeez! Her lover's haunted farm (which was scaring the piss out of her and anyone else stupid enough to stay there), and now a neighbour's derelict, haunted farmhouse which chased one with sheeted ghosts! *Give me a break!*

They ran the last 1000 yards to Mike's farm.

And confronted a black Mercedes in his yard.

TEN.

Mike grabbed Andersen's arm, heading frantically for the nearby bushes until noticing the car had no license plates.

What kind of maniac would…

Jesus.

They stalked toward the car in awe, keeping an eye out for trespassers.

Mike recognized with horror the Mercedes 190E immediately, noticed the straw strewn on its hood.

This couldn't be.

Yes, it was! The bloody very Mercedes which over a month ago he'd parked under a round, torn-apart hay bale inside his deceased uncle's barn. *Impossible!* He feigned ignorance of the metallic intruder's previous existence.

The Mercedes had been parked drunkenly, slewed halfway across the driveway, facing the house, as if some stoned driver had sleepily wheeled the vehicle to a lurching stop in front of Mike's diabolical farmhouse. Its headlights were on.

The motor wasn't running.

Mortified, Mike dragged Jodi through the bushes, circumventing the farmyard until sighting one of the sheds in a hollow some distance from the old house, cautioning his befuddled partner to silence.

He crept toward the smallest of the sheds, dashing toward the mossy building in a half-crouch through tangles of thorn and service-berry bushes. Jodi stayed put, watching nervously as this mysterious man who'd become her lover darted down a leafy incline toward the outbuildings below. She felt an overwhelming surge of love yet horrifying fear for him. Too many disjointed events were happening all at once. She crept down the hillside after him, disobeying Mike's orders, wanting to be at his side.

Mike dashed from tree to tree, finally within arm's length of the smaller building which held the caches of weapons and ammunition. Approaching the house, without a weapon, was out of the question. Whoever had discovered the Mercedes-Benz was probably ransacking the place now, Mike realized.

Or had the automobile moved itself?

The silvery, gleaming padlock was still on the door. Mike withdrew a key from his wallet, eyes darting about the clearing for signs of intruders.   Barn swallows, goldfinches, and orioles flitting about the yard caused his hair to stand on end, startling him, anticipating attack.

He grabbed an Uzi sub-machine gun from beneath a tarpaulin, having entered the building wide-eyed and fearful. The automatic weapon would do as well as any, he guessed. Mike clicked a curved clip hard into its cool, black stock. He felt like Rambo. Except this Rambo didn't know how to use the damned thing! Steady gunfire? Spurts? They did it in the movies with short bursts, Mike remembered. Staccato machine-gun fire.

Where the hell was the safety lever?, he wondered feverishly.

Jo clung to his side as the two darted from willow, to birch, to aspen, to fir, inexorably nearing the old, dark homestead. No one, as yet, had exited the house. Aurora's wind turbine, noisy as usual, spun like an airplane's propellor high above, oblivious to any suspense, up on its mast.

He kicked the front door in, yelling *"Pray to me, you mother******!"*

The kitchen was empty.

As were the adjacent living room and foyer.

Aurora dashed upstairs like a Nazi stormtrooper, yelling, machine gun ready for action.

Up in the attic, the only being present was old uncle Joe's invisible, cantankerous shade and his spirit-world buddies.

Jodi clung to the back of Aurora's sweat-stained, black T-shirt.

"Ooops," Mike whispered. "I think maybe our intruders must be out in one of the sheds. Maybe I shouldn't have made so much noise."

"I'll say," Jo remarked with a murmur.

After a hair-raising trek out to the ancillary buildings Mike and Jodi verified that nobody was (and had ever been) in the yard. That left the car to be explained. They searched the premises for over half an hour.

"Listen, Jodi," Mike admitted at last, grabbing her shoulders. "There's something I, heh, heh, haven't told you yet."

She looked at him quizzically, her big, long-lashed, gray/green eyes melting his heart.

"When I said nobody'd been here before, 'bout the sheds," Mike began, "I wasn't exactly telling the truth."

Andersen tilted her head, a strong, expectant feeling of impending disaster quivering in her belly. She stood beside him in the barnyard, hand on his chest. Her surroundings became suddenly, intimately clear; small, faded red Massey Ferguson tractor mired at the edge of Mike's garden; riotously lush vegetable plot; steel "Rosco" grain silo betwixt two of the big, clapboard sheds; outdoor toilet to the side of the house beneath dense, green spruce boughs; yellow-black finches flitting about a bright blue, miniscule, house-shaped bird feeder; big red barn full of moldy hay back of the house; another ramshackle, sagging byre opposite in imminent threat of collapse; muddy farmyard crowded with relics and unsightly, decaying corrals. "Like what," she asked innocently.

Mike sighed, dropping his chin, still cradling the incongruous Uzi in his right arm.

"Nobody was supposed to know this." He hesitated, choked, and then started to cry. He righted quickly.

"I killed a man."

Jo's expression, for a moment, remained immobile. And then her big, almond eyes grew wide.

"I was out in one of the sheds one night when he intercepted me," blurted Mike. "The bastard took a couple of pot-shots at me with a snub-nosed revolver. I had a handgun with me, in a shoulder-holster. So I shot him."

"In self-defense, that is," muttered Mike, as if an afterthought.

Andersen slumped down onto a huge rock, attractive

face ashen. The strong, pungent, musky fragrance of spruce entered Mike's nostrils as if for the first time. Everything seemed unreal: surroundings, conversation, everything. Even the colors seemed freakishly brilliant and unnaturally evocative on this sunny, summer's day.

He tried to explain the events unfolded.

Jodi began to cry, pitifully railing at fate for such a devastating turn of events. Mike felt infinitely sorry for her, yet unable to offer solace, too mired within his own self-pity. *"Oh, Mike, why did I fall in love with you,"* she gasped sobbingly as he clutched her wrists. "You *bastard!!"* She wanted to pummel Mike's chest, his face, but he was too strong. She wailed in misery, blubbering like a little girl. He loved her beyond measure then, but was utterly helpless.

Finally he embraced her and stroked Jodi's hair until her sobs subsided.

****

Mike parked the Mercedes 190-E back inside the cool barn without a word. He piled it with hay and straw once more, hoping to Christ it would stay put. He gazed at the empty stalls, wondering how many cattle had rubbed against those railings; Jodi had tearfully gone to the house to fix supper.

An hour later Mike returned, inquiring of his weekend lover "What's for supper?" as if nothing untoward had happened. As if he wasn't a confessed murderer. What chance would he stand in court? He'd already lied to her. What else was he hiding? Jodi replied in monotone voice that she was making cabbage rolls. Did he like cabbage rolls? Yes, indeed, smells good, remarked Mike.

He set the sub-machine gun on a dresser, then snapped a clip of rounds into the butt of a Luger-like handgun (he had a different one for every day of the week, it seemed) and stuck it in his shoulder-holster, feeling like John Wayne in a cheap Western. He hid the pistol discreetly beneath his oversize T-shirt.

"You're foolish to think you can defend this place," Jodi remarked sourly, standing defiantly in the kitchen passage. "Who do you think you are, Flash Gordon? Grow Up. Go to the authorities, you blockhead. You wanna get your head blown off!?" She stood with her arms crossed beneath tantalizingly protruding breasts. *She's beautiful when angry,* Mike thought, assessing Jo's shapely, suspendered thighs below a scintillant, purple mini-skirt. She wore a dark gray, turtle-neck sweater.

Mike said nothing. Jodi whirled away, stalking into the

uncomfortably warm dining room. Rays of late-evening sunlight angled through the open front door; light splintered and diluted by shadow as refracted sunshine streamed into the white-tiled kitchen from the west. She wanted desperately to strip down to her bra, for the sweltering evening was gruelling in its relentless, slow bake. Her cabbage rolls were in the oven simmering along with baked potatoes. She'd open some sour cream to go along with it.

She hadn't meant to stay the weekend. But she was now reluctant to leave, fearing for this strange, handsome, headstrong man whom she'd been screwing since Friday night. She hoped she hadn't gotten knocked up, for they hadn't practiced safe sex, as promised. However, she felt normal, no symptoms of morning sickness whatsoever; her body alive with mixed emotions.

Andersen felt giddy just thinking about their wild, imaginative lovemaking. Like Mike, she'd been a virgin, having never much trusted men. Only her vibrator, which she kept a secret from everyone (including her girlfriend), which she kept under her pillow. Thinking of this brought to mind the time her dad had found a Playgirl magazine under her bed, when she was fifteen. God, how embarrassing! Jodi was sure Mike masturbated regularly, judging by his stacks of girlie books. But then maybe not. Hadn't he said he'd found those in a shed?

He was a masterful lover, however, taking his time with her. Any girl would be glad to pitch her tepee with Mike, mused Jodi with a smile. That was part of the reason she stayed, terror and all; she enjoyed playing housekeeper for him.

She removed her cashmere sweater, thinking "If he thinks I'm coming on to him, let him!" The farmhouse was sweltering, and Jodi was sweating like a triathlon finalist. Her neck felt greasy and slick. Why shouldn't women go topless, or at least shirtless, as men do in summertime, Jodi reflected.

Mike entered the broiling kitchen, suddenly averting his gaze, as if he'd never seen Jo half dressed before. He peeked into the oven (working now after he'd blown the lines out with an air compressor), then grinned, his face flushed.

"What are you doin', playing with yourself?" he teased, snapping the strap of Jodi's black, see-through Wonderbra from behind. She boasted a fine 36-24-34 figure. A gorgeous, exotic dancer's bod.

"Oww!" she cried, big eyes twinkling merrily as she turned and slugged him in the chest. "Stop that, you…oversized rat," she murmured huskily. Her rouged, pouting lips were full and sensual. "I'm not playing with myself, you pervert. It's just too damned hot in here. Why don't you have an outdoor barbecue-grill or somethin'?" Mike embraced her, gently cradling this delicious-smelling femme. She hugged him back tight with an amorous caress.

Mike released her, peering with a squint out the kitchen window. He heard coyotes howling somewhere in the distance. A soft, rising breeze outside played with the farm's roundish, quaking aspen leaves. Bright, orange/black northern orioles (among the few he'd seen this year), swooped about the farmstead. A particularly magnificent swarm of colorful blue-and-cinnamon butterflies hovered above the mossy footpath like great, tropical birds. Aurora knew little of insects, wanting suddenly to learn more. And of birds. Plants. Animals. He desperately wanted to familiarize himself with the farm's myriad spruce, pine, tamarack, fir, and deciduous flora. Incorporate them into his horror novel if he could.

The novel which since the captivating Jodi's arrival was going nowhere. However, he'd written over two hundred pages of gore, suspense, black humor, gothic backdrop, and steamy sex over these past three months. He kept his second-hand encyclopedia set, dictionary, thesaurus, etc. beside his word processor for easy reference. He'd even carried into the house a brand-new Mac computer and some CD-Rom software (which he was still scratching his head like a monkey over), as well as a Canon dot-matrix copier from one of the bigger sheds, though he'd yet to take it out of its box. The assemblage sat unused in a corner of the room, gathering dust.

He had hauled in plenty. A Sony Walkman. Magnasonic DVD player. Several antique handguns. An Uzi. Porno movies, magazines, CD Rom. Satellite-dish kit, unassembled (which he had NO idea how to set up), which sat stupidly upstairs. A multi-disc, programmable CD player. Four big hunting knives (he collected fancy hunting knives, although, ironically, no hunter). Electric heater (useless, he'd discovered). Train set (seriously). Binoculars, 10 x 40. Various household appliances.

You could say he was becoming spoilt rotten.

Jodi interrupted Mike's jaded thoughts, wrapping her beautiful, bare arms around him from behind while caressing Mike's stomach and crotch at the same time.

"After supper," she cooed enticingly, "I wanna enslave you, you sex machine, put a charm on you so you'll do my bidding for evermore." She licked his earlobe.

He turned and kissed her heatedly, amorously fondling her boobs.

****

Mike awoke from his slumber with a start. He thought he heard a car door slam. Andersen lay on the mattress beside him beneath the bedding; fast asleep.

The front door burst open with a terrific, jarring explosion, literally kicked off its hinges and splintering where the old-fashioned lock gave.

Without hesitating Mike snatched up the submachine-gun at his side in absolute darkness and leapt out of bed, covering the kitchen entrance. Oddly, not a speck of light shone from the dining room.

Jodi murmured sleepily as he dragged her by the arm toward the massive woodstove, complaining crabbily, bewildered, as he pushed her down behind the cold heater. No light lit the house, not even from outside.

He covered Jo's mouth with his hand.

A noisy tramp of heavy boots stomped into the foyer, gruff voices whispering urgently, assigning directions. A great, black, billy-club-size flashlight shone suddenly from the kitchen and into the living room, miraculously missing Mike's blankets (or not?) spread out over a foam mattress on the bare wooden floor. He estimated there were at least three adult males, maybe four.

Even more horrifying because, Mike, reluctantly, had allowed Jodi to convince him to go to the nearest R.C.M.P. detachment tomorrow and confess all. And pray for mercy. He might be acquitted by virtue of self-defense.

He balanced his weapon on the big wood heater's stovetop, finger pressed tensely against the trigger as he peered down the Uzi's short, hole-ventilated barrel: for all its jack-hammerish power, the illegal, Israeli-made weapon was scarcely bigger than an old-fashioned, long barreled handgun. (But with the deadliness of a sawn-off shotgun.) Mike sighted inky darkness amid pools of flashlight-beams beyond the lethal weapon's large sights, strangely calm and cool-headed as he waited for the intruders to enter.

Suddenly four masked men in tweed suits (!) stepped into the kitchen, pointing in different directions in flashlight beam as the brazen housebreakers advanced, completely oblivious to their own peril. Whether they'd come with a large truck to haul away their stolen booty or merely to kill him or the old man (for he presumed they were unaware of uncle's Joe's passing) Mike didn't know. One of the men began to dash upstairs, a huge silencer-pistol held professionally in front of him. Mike waited only long enough to verify they weren't police before opening fire.

Aurora sprayed the dark living-room and foyer with staccato machine-gun fire, a "rat-a-tat-tat" of deadly, deafening, explosive high-power ammunition ripping apart the wallpapered wall. Strangely unmoved he watched the trespassers jerk about like marionettes, painting the walls with gaudy streaks of blood and brains. One interloper creeping stealthily up the banisters (getting off a couple of shots in reply) did a grotesque, jerking dance before he pitched, sprawling, over the heavily-varnished rails which, moments afterwards were, too, ripped to bullet-holed splinters.

For twenty mad seconds Mike peppered the benighted front room of the house with lethal gunfire while Jodi screamed incessantly, hands clamped over her ears from the sawn-off looking Uzi's terrifying, stuttering violence. (A crazed Samurai, bushido-inspired battle lust had come over Aurora like one possessed, she realised afterwards.) Mike's insane spray of submachine-gun bullets shattered the intruders' lone flashlight, deafening he and Jo long after his rampage of death ceased. After nearly half a minute of relentless machine-gun fire, Mike and Jodi knew with horrifying certainty that he'd snuffed the housebreakers' lives, the only other light having emanated from his weapon's jittering barrel: an orange-red volley of vicious, flaming bursts which set one's teeth chattering.

After several minutes of heart-stopping anxiety, Mike cautiously crept forward, assault-rifle cradled in the crook of his arm.

Nobody from outside, thankfully, had rushed toward the house.

He fumbled for a tiny blue penlight beside his bedspreads, its little beam horrendously picking-out the hair-raising results of his carnage.

Bits of hair and globs of unspecified gray matter specked the orange/yellow, flower-papered parlour's wall. The miniature beam lit up a gory scene of blood-spattered plywood, wallpaper, and drywall. Bulbous balustrades had been blown to bits. Bodies lay everywhere. It looked like the Amityville Horror house might've after Ronald DeFeo had wasted his parents, brothers, and sisters as they lay in their beds, thought Mike. Jodi began to retch.

Mike had blown their heads off. His lunatic rattle of machine-gun fire had torn the unsuspecting hoodlums' bodies apart, riddling their clothes and flesh with bloodied holes. Their mangled bodies lay sprawled about the foot of the stairs, thrown five feet in each direction from the force of the several-hundred-rounds-per-minute bullets' impact. The Uzi had created a horror scene on Mike's dining room floor, splashing blood and ammo all over the walls, floor, or creamy kitchen tiles. Jodi continued to puke behind Mike's enormous, Blaze King woodstove, stark naked. Aurora's purloined submachine gun had stitched crisscross, zigzagging patterns of red on the men's pristine gray tweed suits. Mike stared discompassionately at the horrific scene, feeling nothing at all but pride in his novice's marksmanship.

It's just me, against the world.

Lizzy Borden's 1987 heavy metal rock-anthem pounded in his head.

Me against the world...

Me, against the world...

****

Four more bodies were buried in the forest surrounding Mike's house.

Five hoods had been dispatched at the farm by Mike's over-zealous instinct to protect his insane inheritance. Just when he'd decided to confess everything to the police Mike had murderously opened fire on the masked hoodlums, shooting to kill, not to wound. Such were the grim thoughts of Mike Aurora, unestablished writer, that dismally cloudy morning of Friday, September 9, 1994. He buried the bodies alone, for Jodi had gone to the small town of Spiritwood to buy groceries. She'd pledged her word that she wouldn't go to the police. Not yet. It wasn't as if he had killed four unarmed innocents in cold blood. (Surely?) They didn't appear to be undercover police officers, thankfully, judging by the scarcity of I.D.'s. Jodi needed to get away, reorganize her muddled thoughts, her game-plan. She had not intended to stay the entire month, but Fate had pulled the proverbial rug from under her.

No songbirds sang in the broad-leaf forest that grim, overcast morning. A silvery sheen radiated the surroundings from refracted, cloud-fogged sunlight, an imminent thunderstorm brewing. Thunder overhead rumbled as a rare, Indian summer's storm prepared its militaristic, Dorian assault. *'God, let it not bring hail,'* whispered Mike aloud as he heaped dark humus over the communal gravesite. A mass grave. (Just what I need on my criminal record, my next resumé, Mike reflected.) The forest would soon be enriched with the decayed flesh of these dumb bastards, he thought. Nobody takes me by surprise. He was sure the world would be better off without these terrorizing thugs stalking its soil. What judge would convict him for offing these human piranhas? Mike was certain he would be let off for manslaughter.

And Jodi? What of her?

She might squeal, open her big mouth. Or leave the district. She might marry him. Move in with him. She really was the loose end in all this, the unguessable factor. Would Jodi be safe here? Eventually a whole squad of black-marketeers would show up for Mike's day of Reckoning. (Why *had* they chosen this quiet, little prairie backwater for their illicit dealings, their 'hot' goods' depot, Mike wondered for the umpteenth time.) What kind of racket was he dealing with here? He knew of no such large, organised crime syndicate in the province, no such market locally for such a stash. And how and why had his uncle gotten involved?

The questions were unanswerable and, now, irrelevant. In a couple weeks' time he would mosey into the woods and add more soil to the leafy gravesite, thereby ensuring that it was level now, and would stay level in the near future. By God, he had no intention of doing time in P.A. penitentiary.

He was adamant now about keeping silent about the murders and the farm's lethal contents. Maybe it would all blow over soon, and no one need bother about a few missing low-lifes. How many private individuals could be involved in such a scam, what Aurora guessed to be a fairly elaborate, yet amateur operation, like backwoods' moonshiners or those pot-plantations grown in mountainous British Columbia swamps which the Mounties busted every year.

The basalt-black, '95 Suzuki 4 x 4 Sidekick which sat in Mike's yard, however, yet needed consideration. He could drive it into a lake somewhere (which would be a shame) and hope nobody discovered it. Or he could dismantle it. Bury it in a pit. Park it behind the barn and set it on fire. Hide it under some brushwood. He and Jodi had rifled through the immaculate jeep's interior for information on the four-wheel-drive's ownership and place of origin (for none of the victims carried I.D., surprisingly – save for one, and that was in the glove compartment). It was a bona-fide, registered vehicle, its plates mud-smeared. Jodi had found the 4 x 4's insurance papers underneath the front seat along with a small bag of marijuana. So it seemed fairly straight-forward who he and Jo were dealing with: some dude named Jeff Archer who resided on #15 Delacorte Drive, Saskatoon, owned the Suzuki, probably a small-time drug dealer and B. 'n' E. artist. Mike had found a snub-nosed revolver in the glove compartment, registered to same.

Mike sprinted into the bushes with pistol drawn around three o'clock, when he heard a slow-moving vehicle's tires crunching on the pasture's dirt/gravel road, himself having come from the grim wilderness with a rock-pick over his shoulder, shovel in hand. But fortunately it was only Jo returning in her dusty Datsun.

Aurora went to her aid, helping her unload the groceries from her hatchback. Jodi asked nervously if anything untoward had happened while she was away. Nope, he replied. Mike informed her that he'd finished burying the four murdered men, having kept their weapons and ammunition. Unsmiling, Jodi told him he was a psychopath.

"So are you gonna abandon me to the wolves," demanded Mike as he slammed the Datsun's trunk.

Jodi considered for a moment. "I ought to," she reflected bitterly. "But who'll save you from yourself? You're such a jerk, Michael," she remarked. "And not very bright."

Mike shrugged, following her into the house with a bagful of groceries.

"Does this mean I'm not on your Christmas list anymore?"

Jodi turned, eyes blazing, angrily dressing him down for such flippancy at a time like this. Then she set her paper bag of groceries on Mike's tabletop and embraced him, weeping aloud.

"How could you be so stupid, Mike," she whispered. "Why did you have to open fire? We could have run!"

He shrugged, emotionless. "Can I help it if I'm a good marksman? Hey, I'm a great shot! If anybody can survive, I can. We've got the element of surprise."

She turned away, shoving foodstuffs up into the cupboard. Her eyes brimmed with hot tears. Yet nothing she could say would change reality.

Mike stood admiring Jodi's figure, her nice ass and

comely hips,   slender hourglass shape accented by a pair of sinfully tight, fashionable, Calvin Klein's blue jeans and a form-fitting, gold-spun cashmere sweater which blended admirably with her red-highlighted hair. Yet he felt no desire for intimacy with her lithe body just now. Time for love later.

"What are you going to do with the jeep," Jodi demanded, turning to look Mike in the eye. He never ceased to be amazed at how breathtakingly beautiful she was. She ought to be in pictures. Perfect eyebrows on a face as if sculpted in some cosmic china factory. Her sensuous, ocean-storm eyes tinted with a hint of green; big, luminous eyes with long, mascaraed eyelashes which were one of her finest attributes. Much as he enjoyed Jodi's slaver-inspiring breasts, her lovely, rounded ass, it was her small, heart-shaped face which he admired most.

"Hide it under brush," Mike reflected. "I hate to see such a beautiful, new, 4 x 4 put to fire or dumped in a lake. Maybe someday I'll drive it myself. If I'm still alive."

Jodi remained silent.

They prepared supper in an uneasy truce then, two hours later, watched a videotape and then climbed, exhausted, into bed.

****

Mike spent the next few days at his writing while Jodi played homemaker. She enjoyed being his live-in maid and midnight lover. (Whenever she wasn't fretting over their lethal situation, that is.) Jodi hadn't told him yet, but she'd decided to move in with him. Mike wouldn't last a week alone she was certain, for he was too reckless, too cock-sure of himself. Any day someone could come and open fire on him, who did he think he was?

They sat in front of a big RCA console color TV watching a video-recording of *"Love at First Bite,"* laughing at the outrageously hilarious vampire spoof, the TV's volume turned up to drown out the steady throbbing of Mike's misappropriated gasoline generator chugging away outside, the movie almost over. Outside it was dark, the sun having set at 8:47 p.m., over an hour ago. The doors were locked and deadbolted, shades drawn. Mike sat beside Jodi on the bedspreads with his arm around her, their backs to the wall. After days of scrubbing and scouring, they had cleansed the awful kitchen, living room, banisters and foyer of spattered blood, brains, and intestinal fluid, patching submachine-gun bullet holes with wood filler and then repainting over much of the house's grungy, ground-floor rooms with a hastily improvised pastel green. Two sheets of drywall had had to be replaced. (He'd borrowed her brother, Mark's, truck to do it.) The huge, authentic grandfather clock, standing sentinel near the kitchen passage and alcove, had also been riddled with gunfire. How it had survived the barrage of weapons' fire Aurora had no idea, but, amazingly, the laminated tic-toc's wooden body had taken most of the flak (and not much, either) and not its fragile glass dialface, nor inner mechanisms. Ironically, it stood near the devastated staircase. Both Aurora and Andersen felt a horrible, creepy feeling knowing of the stuttering fusillade of gunfire which had taken four men's lives here in this very room. It now seemed a diabolically oppressive, hastily patched up, chamber of horrors. (Some day, someone would dwell on its being the scene of multiple murders, the house a famous landmark of iniquity, thought Jo with a shiver.) Surprisingly, Mike's antique, expensive grandfather clock, over two months previously, had been miraculously undamaged by supernatural assault which now seemed only a far-fetched nightmare to Jodi and Mike. For one terrifying night he and his companions had been unwitting actors in a surrealistic, horrifying movie-set without mortal producers. Rather it had been one of Satan's grander productions of poltergeist phenomena, with uncle Joe playing the starring role. Or so Mike believed. He was still surprised that nobody had heard his sub-machine gun's noisy *"b-r-r-r-r-r-r-r"* of gunfire, not even his neighbours who lived four miles distance.

Somebody was looking out for him.

The spoof over, Mike and Jodi began to neck.

Only to be rudely interrupted by an ominous flickering of the sole, patchwork-patterned, shaded nightlamp. The lovers ceased their antics, noting Mike's VCR blinking a steady green glow of "12:00" on its slim, black face. The TV set had been switched off, now only a dim, phosphorescent haze. An owl's hoot gave the two a start. Aurora got up and lit the large, kerosene lamp on a bureau holding his typewriter, anticipating running out of fuel (though cognizant of having topped-up the like-new generator with gasoline earlier in the evening). Fuel capacity typically lasted six hours; he'd only had the television on for four. As a backup he could always rely on the wind charger for short periods (the gas generator operated his 375 watt, 27-inch television). However, the living room seemed unnaturally dark, no matter what time of day, and Mike's oil lamp shone inadequately beyond the bedding.

The big lamp flickered out.

Then the oil lamp.

On the blank TV screen a myriad of colourfully glowing, shapeless figures danced about wildly, like a chemical reaction witnessed in a laboratory beaker. *The damned television set was shut off!*, thought Mike, incredulous. He was afraid. Afraid of another ungodly manifestation. He couldn't afford another battering of his personal possessions. What he'd inherited was his by birthright. He needed not another rehearsal for the movie *"Poltergeist."*

"Guess I'll have to go to the police tomorrow," said Mike aloud conversationally, "and spill the beans."

The phenomenon ceased. Whether astral lights or genuine pre-manifestation energy Mike didn't know. He had no idea of the workings which prompted these occurrences. All he knew was that someone – or *something* – wanted to keep the sheds' contents a secret.

The two lights flared up again, kerosene lamp flickering into life with a slow, bluish, rising glow, nightlight blinking on instantly. The lamps shed little light beyond a four-foot radius; obviously aggravated by the dark, gloomy staircase and a floor and ceiling which inhibited illumination. Mike thought he ought to paint the untouched, rear portion of the living room a brighter color to facilitate easier reading. Inky shadows seemed to crouch in dark corners, almost as if creeping furtively up on you while you weren't looking; even from the corner of his eye Mike thought he detected a glimmer of motion. For the first time he began to appreciate how sinister his deceased uncle's farmhouse was. The entrance parlour's stucco-plastered ceiling, with its decorative spikes and spiral whorls and strange acorn-crest (more befitting a Hollywood-conjured estate) bestowed upon the prairie house an almost manse-like, ominous atmosphere; an ambience Jodi had remarked upon when noticing the dwelling's plaster mosaic that first, fateful afternoon. The bizarre farmhouse seemed more manor house than pioneer dwelling, especially in the dead of winter, or the slowly awakening, sinister but lively reanimation of a prairie spring. This was typical, aspen country; found throughout much of the hinterlands of Alberta and Saskatchewan. Grim, boreal forests of mixed conifer and deciduous trees added to the wondrous awe yet terrifying silence and decrepitude Mike often experienced. He didn't fear the back-country, or the many predators amidst the boreal and muskeg wilderness, but inhabited a delightful fantasy world of demon-haunted forests, evergreen glades, stony meadows and bird-inhabited groves. One particular larch grove surrounding a squelchy, wet, reedy, muddy bog a couple of miles east of the farm, near Junor hamlet, came to mind, a phantasmagoric paradise which could take one back to Dark Ages' Europe (where they buried victims in peat bogs) or to pre-colonial America.

Mike was relieved the phenomena had stopped. He reminded himself the next time he was in Spiritwood he should order some books on occult matters with that tiny library's microfiche. He glanced about the living room, checking for vaporous signs of impending manifestation. He sniffed the air for hints of lingering, peculiar smells which usually accompanied such materializations. None. No ectoplasmic slime visible anywhere. Jodi lay beneath the bedspreads, wearing only a matching gray bra and undies as she nestled between the covers, yawning sleepily as Mike glanced nervously about the room. Obviously she had more faith that he could control the phenomena than he did, as if a mere threat might render a spook harmless.   In fact Mike knew perfectly well that whatever entity or entities haunted the farm could easily turn the derelict house topsy-turvy, could even seriously injure someone if it had a mind to do so. (Which he wasn't sure of.) A heavy rumble of familiar, far-off thunder grumbled to the north. It had been doing a lot of that, all summer. Outdoors, crickets and frogs sounded like a chorus of creaky bedsprings. A sepulchral-sounding, insomniac owl hooted a double bass note while coyotes wailed somewhere in the night-shrouded distance. Aurora remarked cryptically that on a spooky night such as this, he and Jo could surely expect another unearthly visitation from his dear, dead uncle. Jodi grumbled, hidden beneath the covers from the chilly, autumn evening air. The cold woodstove hadn't been going for some nights now.

Such an evening would be ideal for a séance, a sitting, thought Mike morbidly to himself. Could it be done with two people? (Hell, he didn't know.) How about an ouija board. He sat in his yellow briefs and deep purple T-shirt thinking for a while, pondering the impenetrable mysteries of life after death while smoking a fat Cuban cigar. A true coffin stake, if ever he knew one. Next week, Mike promised himself, he'd quit, cold turkey. Or die in the attempt. Smoke rings like wispy ghosts floated above his head, spewing from his mouth like a dragon's fiery breath. He fancied he could see shifting, misshapen skulls forming in the smoke rings. A full moon, dogged by rainclouds, occasionally shone lethargically through the quiet living room's sash window. Mike stretched his tired limbs, having been as busy as a mole uncovering more stolen goods inside the largest of the sheds. That's right, more embezzled hardware. Beneath literally a ton of ancient boxes of empty beer bottles Mike had discovered, rather astonishingly, another well-protected stash of Hi-Fi equipment, even two fully-assembled quads and three brand-new Bombardier and Arctic Cat ski-doos (still in their packing crates). Very clever. Christ. Uncle Joe and his confederates had gone to great pains, bracing the pirated thefts with new lumber to hold the beer bottles' crushing weight. An ingenious, seemingly natural platform or, more precisely, what Mike assumed to be a huge garage-sized worktable straddling two walls cunningly concealed an extraordinary amount of booty, the contents of which he hadn't even begun to assort. He'd made one hell of a mess in the already impossibly cluttered building, having torn apart much of the greasy, grimy countertop to unveil its hidden booty. (He discovered only afterward the hidden sliding panel giving egress to the framework.) Who would've guessed that this engine-parts-scattered/worktable-cum-bankvault concealed such remarkable finds. Not he. He'd been flabbergasted. Jodi had squealed in amusement. She'd been tickled pink, then afterwards had yelled at him for not calling the police. He was being a stubborn ass, he knew, but Mike couldn't help it. His eyes were, indeed, bigger than his stomach. Always he kept reminding himself…What if?…What if nobody ever harassed him again? Why…he'd…be…Rich! Rich beyond his wildest dreams. He wouldn't sell the stuff, no, no, he'd use it himself! Somewhere in the back of his head a little voice kept singing out… *"You're crazy, Mike Aurora, you Crazy!"*

Mike heeded it not.

He settled back into the blankets, grateful for the foam mattress buoying he and his slumbering girlfriend from the hardwood floor smelling of fresh varnish. Jodi snuggled against him amorously beneath the covers, nudging his briefs playfully. Mike liked the feel of her hand against his bulging erection. Was she a sex maniac or what? He slid under the blankets, sighing aloud as Jodi's mouth planted itself on his chest, then enveloped his member. Mike turned her over deftly and sunk his face between her thighs.

****

They opted to spend Tuesday afternoon at an autumn fair in Spiritwood, a fast-growing town nearby about twenty kilometres to the southeast. The day was unseasonably warm, though the temperature had dipped below zero the previous night. Jodi and Mike enjoyed themselves immensely, sharing cotton candy, kissing heatedly on the ferris wheel or trying their hand at various skills games, Aurora having won her a huge teddy bear. The shooting competitions he was sure were rigged. Up on the whirling, twirling Octopus ride they'd almost puked, feeling as dizzy as drunks afterwards. Later, when much of the parking lot had emptied, they'd made slow, passionate love in the backseat of Mike's '77 Chev Impala, screwing each other silly. She just couldn't get enough, he marveled, wondering at this auburn-haired bombshell's insatiable lust as he lay in Jo's arms, fearful somebody might tap at his window. He needed the time away from the farm or Mike would've gone insane. It was Jodi who'd suggested they go to the fair this sordidly hot Tuesday, September 31. He was glad he'd satisfied her voyeur's fantasies as they lay nude inside his sweltering station-wagon as evening shadows lengthened. He'd discovered she'd learnt her mind-blowing love techniques from various books such as the Kama Sutra, the Kama Houri, Nice Couples Do, etc. The most he'd read was Everything You Ever Wanted To Know About Sex….and assorted mens' magazines.

They dressed in a hurry, smiling sinfully, conspiratorially as the lovers prepared to leave the emptying fairgrounds. Jodi wasn't sure which she'd enjoyed more: the amusement park, or the fantastic sex. She'd initiated it, as she often did, scintillatingly teasing him then climaxing together sweatily.

Thankful she hadn't gotten pregnant that first, delirious night, Jodi had since been practicing safe sex; she'd used a diaphragm most times.

Mike nibbled at her ear as, giggling, she buttoned up her orange, rayon blouse, kissing and fondling her before sobering and starting his ever-reliable station wagon. *Savatage* cranked out a metal ballad from his tape player.

Jodi fancied few of Mike's tapes, finding his headbanging music too depressing, too psychotic. Too much like the farm, come to think of it. *He really is a strange man,* she thought, staring out the passenger window at rye fields now blurring past at a sedate ninety kilometres per hour.

As a sudden whim Mike turned off to his left, driving down a narrow, disused lane away from the blacktop as Jodi asked in puzzled voice where they were going. Mike, coy as ever said "You'll see."

He parked before an ancient, abandoned farmhouse (another one, Oh, my God!), getting out of the car to explore the derelict homestead.

Jodi reluctantly followed, serious and subdued, wondering silently why Mike relished visiting graveyards and old ruins (he'd strong-armed her to three cemeteries, already, this week). Sometimes he scared her. Jodi held his hand, holding her breath lest something weird happened. She wondered if Mike wasn't some sort of paranormal magnet. The old farmhouse was a shambles: an A-frame eyesore barely holding itself together. Most of the shingles were missing, and a good deal of the roof. Parts of it had caved in. Cedar shingles were rare in these parts, Mike informed her, as if she actually took an interest in such arcane bits of useless knowledge. Mike gloried over a disused wringer/washing-machine sitting chest-high in the rank green grass; wrecked automobiles, a moped, and various junk littering the grassy yard which could be plainly seen from the highway between Spiritwood and Belbutte (a tiny hamlet where Mike had lived for a time – he'd even shown Jodi the old house he'd lived in; of course she'd been thrilled [Yeah!]).

Inside the old cabin Aurora marveled at – what? Junk. Andersen had no idea what he found so interesting. Decay? Junk strewn about at random? Sometimes she wondered about him. He was w-e-i-r-d. He was beautiful. Maybe it was that (and not just their fabulous lovemaking) which attracted her to him like a bear to honey. Call it fatal attraction. They matched well, opposites attracting (he the cerebral, albeit muscular, loner, she the gad-about). She stayed close by, clinging near as Mike snooped in cupboards, a bedroom (?), kitchen. She smelt his manly odour and sex (not quite hidden by the pheremone-maddening cologne) and wanted more, chiding herself for her fecklessness.

More derelict antiques could be found inside. Hoover vacuum cleaner. Sears tapedeck, busted. Flashlight buried amidst dust and debris. Coffee percolator, minus cord. Broken eyeglasses. *"Look, human bones,"* whispered Mike dramatically. Various animal bones from some long-dead denizen lay in a corner. Much of the floor had caved-in.

Outdoors, Mike swung Jo round and round, feeling more relaxed than he had in some time, then sat down on a decayed front step to light up a cigarette.   His last one ever. Tomorrow, smokeless, cold turkey, and god help Andersen if she got in his way! She teased him laughingly of this for several minutes.   Jodi, at ease now, lay her head in his lap, reclining lazily, alluringly sexy on her back, the swell of her breasts protruding under a revealing, open-necked blouse. She wore bleached, cut-off denims. Mike resisted the urge to squeeze Jodi's responsive tits. But his mouth watered all the same.

"Game?" she asked with an inviting smile, sensing his adulation.

Mike considered for a moment, then declined, using the evening's lateness as an excuse. In reality he'd had his fill of love for the day, anxious to return to the farm as it was getting dark. He declined with an apology, kneading his fingers through her glossy hair. Jodi smiled sinfully, beaming, her alabaster cheeks shining healthily in the rosy twilight. How he loved her then, considered proposing but hadn't a clue where to begin.

"Tonight, though, I'll get you, Mike," suggested Jodi coyly, licking her full, luscious, ruby-red, cherry-like Desi Arnez lips as she bounced away from his lap. At the moment he did not doubt it. She'd receive his remaining bodily fluids, all right. He felt languorous, giddy, swaggering toward his gray beater of a station wagon with his girl on his arm, feeling like a proud, strutting rooster. In fact, he felt ten feet tall. She made him that. Tonight she would cook his meal, afterwards serving him her excellent body in lieu of dessert. *Oh, what more could a man wish for!* What an honor to screw this randy, drop-dead-gorgeous wench every night. The thought made him hard as granite. Birdsong lingered in the evening air; bluebirds, swallows, warblers galore, skylarks, crows, jays, magpies, scrapping ravens, all of which Mike had come to identify. The heady scent of wildflowers wafted on the breeze. Aurora wondered if the quarrelsome, chittering birdlife felt as randy as he.

Mike drove home, allowing his horny, snuggling girlfriend to unzip his jeans and lovingly perform fellatio. It was a miracle he hadn't crashed.

ELEVEN.

Mike helped Jodi unload her meagre possessions from her Glaslyn apartment from the back of his boat-like car crammed full with kitchen utensils, a love seat, bed rails, appliances, keepsakes, artwork, ornaments etc. etc. Fortunately she had very little in the way of furniture; most of what she'd used had stayed in her former basement suite. (Her Datsun hatchback, however, was packed to the roof.) The morning wind was brisk and cold, a partly cloudy autumn day in the first week of October. Jodi had landed a job several days ago at Mel's Diner, a truckstop café between Medstead and Belbutte. Although her wages were peanuts (hardly worth it if it weren't for the tips), it would give her a feeling of independence and contribution, rather than sitting around the house collecting welfare, Mike reflected. Better she be doing something besides moping around the house. And it would be a huge load off his mind knowing she was providing an income rather than draining his quickly dwindling cash reserves. Having the two loitering about aimlessly would do neither of them any good. While Mike had his maddeningly difficult book to write (which he was sure the whole world wanted to see), Jodi, he felt certain, would be driven mad with boredom. He didn't want that. Especially since, after The Incident, their mutual reliance had steadily grown; they shared the same all-consuming interest in outdoors studies, rambling endlessly through the backwoods which encompassed Mike's property. He had only twenty-five acres, more an acreage than the typical, Saskatchewan farm. A mere hobby farm. Tamarack, Jack pine, spruce, white birch, a smattering of Dutch elm, poplar, aspen and fir Mike and Jodi had come to love as if part of an extended family. Both had always enjoyed the outdoors. Fortunately Jodi was no city girl, and therefore not one inclined to pine for her former, suburban environs. Knowing how crazy she was about flowers, he daily brought her a fresh sprig of fragrant, kaleidoscopically-colored wildflowers in exchange for a peck on the cheek. Some even he had trouble identifying, even with a thick 1000-page field guide titled *"Wildflowers of Western Canada."* Some of them he was sure were orchids of unidentified strain, bog and marsh their habitat.

With acres of good pasturage as incentive, Mike had acquired two Toggenberg goats of *'heintz'* lineage at an auction-mart near Saskatoon. Each had given birth to twins four weeks ago in a large pen he'd improvised from various broken-down cattle corrals and patchwork lumber. Jodi had been delighted, instantly falling in love with the two chestnut brown, gregarious she-goats, little devils, and their wobbly-legged, jumpety offspring. One of them was a buck, the others does. Jodi and Mike took turns milking the graceful-but-mischievous nannies inside a small milk-shed recently hotched together. He decided not to de-horn his little pet goats, nor castrate the buck; instead he'd sell the billy at auction later and in the meantime keep the feisty little varmint in a high-fenced separate pen. Mike had named him Satan.

Already he and Jodi had captured dozens of cute, cuddly, playful baby goats on color film, chewing their cud, munching on grass or just generally making a nuisance of themselves. Their mothers had arrived hornless; one a friendly, docile, naturally hornless nanny whose buck and doe had also inherited their chocolate-brown mother's peculiar trait; the other had had her horns cauterized years earlier. Both had that nasty, mischievous habit of running away and *"b-a-a-i-n-g"* immaturely whenever milking time was at hand, obviously enjoying the game of "Let's see Mike fume." Mike had borrowed Jodi's older brother Mark's Ford Custom E150 pickup-truck for a day to bring the beasts home.

Three weeks earlier she'd taken Mike home to her parents' house near Medstead, a fairly well-off hobby farm, to meet her three brothers and her mom and dad for the weekend. They seemed like nice folks. What they thought of him, Mike hadn't a clue. Her dad was an elementary-school teacher at Medstead High, as was her mom. Just the same, as a first timer at this sort of thing, the experience had scared the hell out of him.

Fall had crept up on them almost without warning and pounced; two days ago Mike had awoken to look out his living-room window and see heavy frost on the ground, dismayed to see his immature, experimental squash plot coated with hoar-frost. His tomatoes out in the greenhouse had also been heavily damaged, though not catastrophically, still capable of ripening, Mike felt. But then what the hell did he know about gardening? All in all his garden-plot had proven a minor success, though by no means a bumper crop. (The freak snow storm in August had made sure of that.) He'd been fortunate to achieve what he had, for, despite loamy, rich soil, the weather had been mostly cloudy and cool much of the summer – a typical, east-central Saskatchewan summer lately. To top it off, Mike was certainly no green thumb, in fact bloody lucky to have grown a modest, down-home vegetable garden. He estimated he could be largely self-sufficient this winter, foodwise.

Jodi carried some of the odds 'n ends from her over-stuffed Datsun into the house, leaving Mike to wrestle some of the bigger boxes from the back of his station wagon. He didn't mind, for she'd already offered to cook supper tonight all by her lonesome, no shared task this evening. He had work to do. Sometimes there really was such a thing as too many chefs in the kitchen. Afterwards they'd planned to watch an old *"Godzilla"* tape on his purloined VCR.

For over a month, he and Jodi had experienced no real, paranormal activity save for the occasional gimmick or missing things – i.e. toothbrush, wallet, cassette tapes, watch and a handful of coins and loonies which had reappeared as quickly and as mysteriously as they'd vanished, give or take a few hours, or sometimes days. (Dire threats usually achieved results.) Jodi had witnessed a fishing-rod reeling wildly on its own in the alcove where cans and other food items were stored on shelves. That had freaked her out, but not overly so.

Yet Mike often wondered why Jodi had committed herself to this derelict, demon-possessed house smack-dab in the middle of nowhere. Certainly the knowledge of an imminent gangland-style hit upon him/her and the inevitable poltergeist phenomena occurring must scare the bejesus out of her! How long could Mike patrol the farm daily toting a machine-gun before someone drives in and rubs him out. A quick salvo of gunfire from a car window. A night assault while he and Jodi lay sleeping (which Mike did little of, lately). And, worst of all, the sure knowledge that he would eventually be arrested on five counts of murder. Sooner, rather than later. For Mike felt sure the authorities would nail his ass with trumped-up first-degree murder charges.

Jodi, for her part, had taken an overly-optimistic view of the stolen hardware (for they still argued over the validity of that presumption), the numerous murders committed (albeit in self-defense), the various poltergeist happenings which often left her and Mike baffled and afraid. Nobody, so far, had investigated him. What evidence did Mike think would lead the local R.C.M.P. here? He'd hidden the two vehicles. They'd heard no news bulletins on the radio describing a missing Mercedes-Benz rental car and a shiny, new, black Suzuki jeep 4 x 4.

She also, erroneously, misguidedly believed that she and Mike could somehow banish whatever malevolent, occult forces infested the old homestead. But Mike had few illusions about that, no faith in some Spiritualist crap solving their problems. He loved a good, gripping ghost story as well as the next guy – more so – but when it came right down to it he really didn't believe in all that paranormal mumbo-jumbo. Paranormalists, indeed. Ghosts yes, but psychics? Huh-uhn.

Jodi gave him a well-deserved "thank you" and a kiss on the cheek when they'd finally finished unloading and unpacking. Simply her breathtaking smile was all the payment Mike needed. They set about rearranging the living room, scullery, kitchen, and foyer to accommodate her numerous household wares, furniture, crockery, knick-knacks and family photos of smiling teenagers and parents on bountiful fishing expeditions at sundry north-Saskatchewan lakes.

Afterwards, while perogies and leftover sweet and sour meatballs simmered on the stovetop, Mike and Jodi re-erected her large, queen-size bed (brought home on the roof of his car) upstairs in one of the disused, unfurnished bedrooms. She asked Mike why he'd never bought himself a decent bed, at the very least a second-hand hide-a-bed or cot at a Salvation Army store. He had no answer (too cheap), finally using thriftiness as an excuse. (Actually he'd grown used to sleeping on the floor, cognizant of the fact of his having plenty of firewood to heat the house.) The long winters, he knew, would be frightfully cold. He disliked the idea of sleeping upstairs. Mike, by nature, was a stubborn cuss through habit. Fortunately, they'd chosen the room with the lone dresser (the one flung from his uncle's attic!) as their love-nest. It also had a wardrobe closet, and a mirror inside the cubby hole's door. The bedroom was big, but filthy. It had but one window. The room was uncarpeted and bare, painted a nondescript dull blue. Really needed a paintjob, including the crumbling, plaster ceiling. Dry rot had begun to form. Rings of damp showed on the ceiling.

Jodi watched Mike read the papers while he ate supper, smiling furtively at her wildly handsome heartthrob as he made funny expressions while unaware of scrutiny. He hadn't had a smoke in almost three weeks, and was slowly forgetting his nasty, old nicotine habit. He now chewed on cinnamon sticks. How she loved this magnificent live-in lover of hers; she couldn't for the life of her understand how any woman could desire another woman when eligible young studs like Mike Aurora were available. Jodi, however, realized to her chagrin that Mike might have been the last, decent guy on earth whom she'd just snatched up (literally!). She found Mike's long, straight hair simply irresistible, for he washed and combed his barbaric mane regularly. To her he was like a throw-back to the Dark Ages. And he was well-built, lean yet muscular, not scrawny, making that special spot between her legs tingle. His eyes were a deep, dark, ocean blue, innocent yet arresting. When he frowned he often turned her on even more (what's that lingo, "Oh, baby, you're beautiful when you're angry"?). Come to think of it, he reminded her of that comic strip character *Conan the Barbarian*, thought Jodi with a private smile. His hands were big and powerful, and infinitely talented. Whether playing guitar, handling a spade, weight-lifting, or fondling her boobs, he never ceased to arouse her. She loved to massage Mike's neck, or give him an all-over body massage whenever his muscles felt sore after a gruelling day's work, a convenient, clever, and sensuous excuse for seduction. He almost always brought her to climax.

Mike glanced up from the table, fork halfway to his mouth, catching Jo's dreamy, appreciative gaze.

"What?"

Jodi blushed, glancing away bashfully like a besotted schoolgirl.

"Nothing. It's…just that I love you, that's all."

Mike returned to his paper, all a-grin. He preferred to tell her he loved her when she was experiencing orgasm, keeping her guessing. What was more, she knew it.

Jodi reflected somberly how her mad infatuation with this soon-to-be outlaw would ultimately bring her to ruin: he was a murderer (self-defense?, or just for kicks, she wasnt' sure), battling human and unseen forces of evil which neither he nor she could fathom. Any girl with a bit of sense would've left him long before now, she intuited.

Mike tried to remember how many times they'd made

love since he and Jodi had met. Almost daily, he was certain. Twice, sometimes three, four times a day. And surprisingly, each time it felt like the first, for Jodi was superlative in bed. He loved to lick her boobs. She loved it when Mike sucked on her toes. Why, he had no idea. Some strange foot fetish. He honestly didn't know why Orientals needed strange aphrodisiacs to get it on, but suspected they were unable to get off otherwise, considering their total lack of compassion (as he perceived) for the fairer sex. Unlike the ancient Celts and earlier Bronze Age cultures (which he'd been doing a lot of research on lately), who allowed women an astonishing amount of freedom, though Mike deeply suspected the Irish with all their legends about polygymous liaisons had been real bastards in reality. It was the British tribes, the *Cymry*, and their continental counterparts, he felt, who were intriguing and mysteriously democratic, as well as some of their later Viking allies, whose barbarous women were so feisty. For reasons even he couldn't fathom he'd begun studying Welsh, a bitch of a language to learn, if you asked him.   Hadn't some bigshot linguist said it was "easy"? Sure. For a Martian. Mike wondered if all languages were this hard. If so, no wonder nobody digged learning new tongues.

No wonder Welsh was a dying language.

He tried to coax Jodi to learn Celtic with him, but so

far she'd stubbornly balked.

After an exotic supper which Mike burpingly congratulated her on, he and Jodi set to work gathering up his bedding from the living room floor, and hauling it up to their new, swept/washed bedroom. He was thankful they had only one bed; that way he'd get to screw her constantly.

They sat on her queen-size bed reading Publisher's Weekly under lamp light, or, in Jodi's case, Family Circle. Andersen, smart girl that she was, had brought three AC nightlights, so it seemed Aurora's Dark Ages' atmosphere of candlelight and gas-lit gloom were over. A part of him would miss it.

Mike didn't much relish the fuel bill he was racking up, though. He could almost feel the loose change in his pockets seeping away.

From the bedroom window they had an unsurpassed view of the moon-lit driveway, plus the three hulking, clapboard sheds far off in the distance. He had erected a chain and "No Trespassing" signs at his field entrance, for what good it would do. He kept an AK47 assault rifle, pistol, even a bowie knife on his person or at his side, handy at all times. Special power-saving devices, including outdoor lamps with motion sensors, had been installed; Mike had rewired the house for off-grid electricity within the last week. He'd had to rig up outlets and wiring of his own for the wind generator and other equipment, including four golf-cart batteries, a voltage regulator, 600-watt AC inverter, and 53-watt photovoltaic charger. He also kept a voltmeter/ammeter with 60-amp integral shunt handy.

Around midnight, gazing longingly into each other's eyes, they climbed beneath the comforters and switched the lights out for the most intense lovemaking yet.

****

When Mike awoke he found himself in another world.

Another era, another place, call it what you will, he thought to himself, realizing both to his surprise and unease that he was barely clothed. He wore a rough, sleeveless, rawhide jerkin, loincloth, and weird latticed boots straight out of some Conan comic strip. Something seemed to bind his hair. Mike raised a hand to his forehead, feeling a band of silver around his head. What the hell is this?! Where am I? A blazing orange, chrysanthemum sun balanced on the verdant foothills. A dazzling, green carpet of turf-like, cropped grass lent the outdoor scenery a romantic pastoral vista not unlike some color photographs of Ireland, the Emerald Isle, he'd seen, or of black-and-white pics of picturesque, rustic, but vaguely sinister mountain scenery of spruce-dotted Yugoslavia or the Carpathian Alps. The heady scent of wildflowers teased Aurora's olfactory senses; wild rose, bluebell, tiger lily, yellow tulip, purple rhododendron filled the montane landscape like a Dutch flower plantation run amok. He had no idea where he was.

A heavy Iron Age broadsword with marvelously incised bronze hilt lay at Mike's side as if a companion during his long slumber. He picked it up in awe, eyes aglow, weighing the monstrous weapon in his meaty hands. He guessed it weighed several pounds. The sword lay sheathed in an ancient, leathern scabbard. Around his bullish neck hung a heavy necklace of silver ingots, an ancient version of the first coin currency. Mike's bronzed body seemed packed with muscle. And when he looked at his reflection in a crystal-clear brook nearby he found to his dismay that his once-dark hair was bleached (with lye, presumably), and impossibly curly.

He stood up feeling ten feet tall, realizing also that he seemed much taller, huskier, than he'd remembered. Ironically, he began to recall certain past-life details while remembering his own 20th-century existence in tandem.   Mike felt like an oversized version of Hulk Hogan.

Thirty or so yards distant a majestic, black steed

grazed on the various grasses, sedges, wildflowers which Mike – or was it Conigcad? – saw growing in profusion beside a bulrush-hidden mountain stream attended by Cattails. Judging by the sun's position he estimated it was early morning, around seven o'clock. His belly growled, for Mike/Conigcad was famished, couldn't recall eating for – over a day?

When Conigcad unsheathed the great sword he found it was coated in wet blood from tip to pommel.

He whistled shrilly, not at all surprised when the small, barrel-bellied Carpathian mountain pony came trotting toward him, its ebony black, lustrous mane billowing wildly in the wind. A cool springtime gust of humid, montane wind, a nor'easter, changed from breeze to bluster as it blew down from the highlands. Elm and water-birch stood scattered about the bottomlands like twisted, gnarled figures, some of them forever leafless and stark, others young and vigorous with blossoming leaves. The wych-elm in particular were sacred to Conig's tribe, having provided life-giving fuel throughout that fateful Long Winter many eons past.

How he'd got here, alone and isolated, he had no clue.

But he was certain a Turkman ambush had been the principle cause. He now identified the country as Macedôn, or Alban (modern-day Slovakia, Macedonia, Albania), heavily-forested montane ranges which corresponded to the boundaries of 20th-century eastern Serbia.

It was the intriguing fires up in the hills which had enticed the High King's moss-troopers to investigate the curious camp flames which had lit up the night for miles around. Hundreds of them, an unusually large – and uninvited – assembly. A horde. When Conigcad's scouts had ventured into the alien camp they'd discovered to their astonishment a large band of nomads, whose disturbingly dark skin and queer turbans invited derision and laughter from the King's liveried soldiers. To their bafflement the newcomers had spoken an utterly unfamiliar tongue; no amount of sign language nor gesturing could break the inexplicable language barrier. All the King's wizards knew that no other tongue was spoken beyond the dreaded Scolots' domains to the east. Why had *Crom*, the Great Instructor, scrambled their dialects, wondered Conig's scouts. The slant-eyed easterners had merely stared or murmured, amused, to each other when the sickly-pale scouts and scribes puzzled over the foreigners' covered women who surprisingly had no faces! Perhaps these were demons, succubis?

When Congicad's tax collectors had returned the Turkman nomads had vanished before the customary land-fee could be collected. Which was a bad omen. They'd left only a hodge-podge of smoking hearths and scattered debris to show their passing. Under no condition would foreigners be allowed to cross these lands without permission. Worse, they'd possessed swift steppe horses and cold steel, and looked remarkably adept on their steeds. Once more, it seemed the meddling Scolots had spread their stolen technology to where it oughtn't be.

It seemed the young warrior Conig (Mike?) had suffered some rather nasty concussion, his head hurting something fantastic as he tried to mount the shiny black gelding lacking saddle or stirrup. After two failures the bronzed giant finally mounted the small but powerful pony, startled to find his forehead was bleeding from a gash from hairline to eyebrow.

How many troops had survived the treacherous Turkman attack? Conan (contraction of *Conighad[n]*) vaguely remembered an ambush in some scraggly, forested mountain pass at nightfall, the reek of blood and screams which rent the eerie montane silence. Much like the Scythians' ambush which'd annihilated Conan's legionaries several moons previous, a fiasco which he alone had escaped after tricking a guardsman's besotted wife, then bashing the hapless husband's head in with a rock. A glimpse of boulders and debris tumbling down on his soldiers from above flashed across Conan's — Mike's? — fevered mind. They'd fought bravely and tirelessly against the Turkman marauders whose numbers seemed inexhaustible, armed with their composite, Asiatic horn bow and deadly iron, plus wooden javelins. The newly-proclaimed *Ymheradur's* moss troopers had been searching for days for these rascally elusive newcomers, only seeking to enforce the Holy Mother's land dues owed Her. This would allow the foreigners to reside on the militarily and technologically dominant Taurians' domains without further restriction until moving on. By the laws of these lands refusal of payment could bring banishment and/or destruction. To the Emperor and his not-so-loyal, overburdened subjects this seemed only fair, for they'd resided on this sacred soil since time immemorial.

Their swooning war leader allowed his steed to carry him westward toward the titanic, drystone hillfort many leagues distant which loomed on the midday horizon now like a natural green plateau, a semi-inhabited township often seeming like a Mesopotamian metropolis on bustling market days when craftsman and bondsman alike crowded its cobbled streets. Conan barely found strength enough to grasp the bridle or hug the overburdened steed's belly with his muscular legs. Sudden nausea and light-headedness had come upon Conan without warning. His great sword, now sheathed, bumped lethargically against his spine.

Come sundown he'd proved fortunate to have been

intercepted by one of his own troops whom had survived the cowardly Turkic assault, leading their swordmaster-at-arms toward the High King – now Emperor's – generous seat of power high up on its 1200-foot basalt outcrop of volcanic rock. Conan was barely aware of the majestic ferns growing on sparse patches of soil atop the mount, bleary-eyed and delirious as his fat-bellied pony trotted its way inexorably up the steep crag. Escarpments had been cunningly dug to ward off marauding Scolots adventurers who might try to negotiate its steep, palisaded ditches which would impale their horses should they proceed to attempt an assault, lured by rumours of untold amounts of treasure and slaves to be had. They would come by the thousands Conan knew from bitter experience, entire migrations of tall, nude, red-haired or blonde savages who foolishly fought the mail-armored Cimmerian mercenaries naked, as if their admiration of the male physique and brazen show of prowess during the heat of battle would impress the mighty *Combrogos:* the confederation Thirteen. Even their daunting weapons and untold numbers would not hold the field against King Cong's fearsome longbow infantry, armored battalions, and numerous cavalry blessed with the even deadlier, composite horn bow.

The chief *Derwin*, or High Priest, embraced his wounded son as Conan slid drowsily from his horse, the old man's cheeks sunken and pale, himself looking like death warmed over as his firstborn brusquely pushed away well-meaning women and squires. The arch-Druid's clothing was sparse but magnificent; bright white toga, leather sandals, gold headband and hammered gold torc of the finest craftsmanship around his scrawny, turkeyish neck. The old man's gnarled hands seemed somehow pitiful and shameful to his hardened son's gray-blue eyes, his father's eyes. Conan had chosen the life of a warrior, captain of the Emperor's mercenary guard, forsaking the ways of magick. The old wizard was bent now, a crony, although he'd once been as tall as Conig, though never as brawny nor warlike as his progeny. Seven other children had been born to the revered arch-Druid (unlike the Scotti's shamans who were celibate, and often shamelessly homosexual, their wise-women as well). The Taurians, or Daurians (Dorians, according to which dialect, of which there were many), had achieved a finely balanced and respected druid-hood over the millenia, had inherited all divine knowledge of wizardry, necromancy, and astral calculations for stone maneuverings from their god-like ancestors.

The young warrior looked at the old shaman with all the haughtiness and self-assurance that he could muster, instantly assuring the gathering spectators, his many kinsmen, that he, the *Scolot Slayer!*, was unhurt and undaunted. Conan tersely explained of his warband's ambush by the Turkman nomads, foreigners whom he vowed in fearful descriptions that he would torture and murder. His compatriots had already heard of the renegade band's brazen and foolhardy ambush on their High King's 21st legion, an outrage which would bring the unwelcome migrants fire and slaughter.

He met the foreign princess in the usurper-emperor's gilded audience hall: a sparkling, gold throne chamber of wood and faience beads, emeralds and quartzite embedded in its timbers, the plaster walls a-riot with frolicking dolphins and Mediterranean flora. Decorative bison horns and skulls upon the walls would someday be pointed out by honest but mistaken scholars as evidence of male-dominated "bull worship"!

Human skulls adorned the walls.

"Who be the foreigner," Conan demanded without preamble, not bothering to hide the scorn in his voice which he felt for all outlanders. Even the Emperor couldn't help but be shocked, the effete, middle-aged widower sternly rebuking his senior war-general for all to hear. Conan stared with appreciation at the comely young wench with the well-toned physique. She had the look of an Amazon. She glared back with frosty, beryl-green eyes, her color up and obviously discomfited by *Twysog* Conan's disrespectful, disdaining remark. The princess was indeed an Amazon, a *Sarmatian*, discovered Conan to his surprise, those hilarious warrior-women of eastern lore. The dark, alluring, coif-headed princess sat staring with obvious ill-will as the King lectured his brash, too-long-of-a-leash commander. Conan, all of twenty, disgruntledly had no idea what the ruckus was about. Was the stunning wench *not* a stranger?

Afterwards, while savoring his drink, the feisty Sarmatii princess had confronted the young, reckless field-marshal at his trestle table, spewing barb after barb of spiteful female rancor like a wild, Caucasian mountain lion. Conig had stared, silent but frosty as an overturned Minoan temple statue. He'd not deserved this tirade, quite nonplussed at this beautiful, shapely, "goodwill" ambassador's uninvited opinions of Conan's honour and manhood. Nor could he understand why this bitch, attired in a demure saffron silk gown (in the Greek style), held her hand on her dagger's hilt. Did she think he might challenge her to battle? It had never even crossed his mind to apologize.

Days later she'd dared belittle him of his training techniques on the jousting grounds where Conan's young, inexperienced fledgling archers practiced their marksmanship, boasting aloud of her nation's prowess at sword and staff, battleaxe and pike, horn-bow and lance. Even the Sarmatians' women were superior combatants,

Amazons all, taunted the Princess Felissa for the umpteenth time to Conan annoyingly while he instructed his archers. (Her interference was intolerable.) He found it difficult to concentrate on his marksmanship, hard to ignore her, for the curvaceous, brazen heiress had substituted silken robes of state for hard-riding warrior's clothes, twisted-braid gold neck torc, arm bracelets, Royal Purple satin cape and richly carved, iron sword; her rich, wild, chestnut-brown hair billowing in the wind. Her tight soldiers' clothes accentuated the high-spirited debutante's bodacious curves even more; Conigcad (better known as *Conan*) was sure many pairs of ravishing eyes were upon her. He tried to avoid her, which Felissa made *exceedingly* difficult.

When he'd rounded on her she'd drawn her broadsword (of superlative craftsmanship, but considerably smaller than a man's), grinning, beckoning Conan into mock battle. Dozens of pairs of eyes had settled upon them. At the moment he'd wanted to cleave the wench in two, even more so when she laughingly promised to spare his life should he be defeated – and of course he would be defeated!

However she'd failed to realize how powerful and uncannily agile the huge war-leader could be: although well aware that among Taurian and enemy alike, no man had ever bested Conan in hand-to-hand, mortal combat.

Furthermore, it was considered scandalous here for women to take up arms, for, unlike the hard-pressed Sarmatians east of the Caspian Sea, they had not had such long, antagonistic contact with Asiatic settlers; the Sarms had been forced out of necessity to learn how to ride and fight while their menfolk were at war, often with the new inhabitants of Greece, or with Iranian fireworshippers, and Huns in Siberia.

The audacious Sarmatian princess had proven herself surprisingly strong and agile for a woman, like a highly flexible ashwood sapling; slender of girth, but amazingly resilient and uncannily knowledgeable of the martial arts of the East. (Only once, however, had she succeeded in kicking Conan the Mighty in the groin, her windmilling sword antics and flailing drop-kicks unable to impress the enormous, mail-clad master-at-arms.) After a time she'd ceased trying to match Conan's brute strength and absorbing his battering blows, dancing nimbly away from his deadly swing. Neither shield nor dagger were on their persons.

They'd fought from late afternoon to sunset, when a mighty blow as if from a sledgehammer wrenched Felissa's sword from her benumbed hands: she would not beg for mercy, however, not even when Conan rakishly held his swordpoint to her breast and ordered the foreign hellcat to strip! She merely, bravely pushed away his broadsword with her hand. For that the great Cimmerian war-general flung the subdued woman challenger to the earth, tossed Melissa her sword, sheathed his own monstrous blade and strolled away, laughing, toward the bejewelled palace; thereby leaving Felissa Headcrusher, soon to be Queen of the Amazons, as the only living mortal to challenge him to combat and survive unmaimed. She'd spat at him.

He'd learned only later that she'd killed fifteen Scythians and twelve Mongols single-handedly in a heroic, camp-saving battle frenzy two months previous.

Melissa, however, had fallen madly in love (if, at times, wildly irrational) with the High King's cocky field commander, baiting him time after time in the Dorians' council chambers, yet constantly seeking out the muscle-bound, sullen Cimmerian like a trainer learning to befriend a bear. Conan ignored Melissa's barbs, or smiled infuriatingly, smugly at her when she'd often wanted to fling her dagger at him across the council hall. She always sought to outdo the finery of his jewellery, his torcs, arm bands, horned helmets, ceremonial weapons. Often Felissa would point out Conigcad's past failures in matters of leadership, publicly questioning his competence and moral standing (of which he was beyond reproach). The wildly jealous wench even went so far as to suggest at one war-session that, being that this 'boy' leader was as yet unbetrothed, perhaps the gracious *Járll* was unfit for high office, as he was obviously a virgin, not a man. However, the emperor's harrying and proposal that Felissa herself ought to provide Conan with sexual favours soon put an end to her efforts to depose Conan 'the Destroyer' (and a scowl of high color on her pretty face). Needless to say, she often intercepted the mercenary captain's cold, intimidating stare, reading in his iceberg eyes many unfortunate events which could befall her. Certainly she'd made him squirm in discomfiture at the regal assemblies.

Otherwise he generally pretended she wasn't there, looking right through her or ignoring her words in mess-halls, banquets, or other communal gatherings. Sometimes he even managed to bump into her without acknowledging her existence, skirting around the high-born, Amazonian princess as if she were a mere statue.

Until one day she'd cornered him behind the brewhouse and barracks, seizing him and kissing Conan passionately. He stared coldly at her, unresponsive, yet disturbed deep down inside, the drop-dead-gorgeous, bodacious, loquacious wench's lean but muscular arms wrapped, vice-like, around Conig's neck. He'd wanted desperately to tell her that he found her unattractive, that she was the ugliest and most disgusting harlot he'd ever had the misfortune of laying eyes on. When he had, stoically, told her of this, the sexy heiress only smiled invitingly and fluttered her sensuous, smoky eyes, unconvinced, resisting Conan's attempts to dislodge her bare arms.

He was not a good liar, Melissa informed him.

"You want to make love to me, don't you?," murmured Felissa coyly, smiling lopsidedly, becomingly, her dimples showing. Her great, sensuous eyes shone like fresh-cut emeralds. Cat's eyes. She kissed him again, this time scandalously sticking her tongue into his mouth. Unbeknown to her, Conan was no virgin, having discreetly practiced what lewd 20th-century AIDS sufferers would coin 'safe sex.' Various coy country maidens had received Conan's favour. (Within the royal city, however, he'd recently had the great misfortune of having picked the shortest straw – due to considerable inbreeding, the ruling elite had decreed that seven of Conan's clan be disbarred from mating with the court's royal denizens. Doubtless, being of outlander origin, Conan and his Cimmerian kin had been short-listed.) Felissa, too, had been discreet, and somewhat more liberal with her own liaisons in her Caucasian homeland. Several warriors of high repute had rashly proposed marriage, only to be ruthlessly spurned in her quest for power. It was not their "right" to propose, rather the reverse. They, however, renowned warriors all, held no grudge against the fairer sex.

Conan ravished her in the alley.

****

Mike awoke in the morning feeling groggy and totally burnt-out. Jodi lay sleeping in the crook of his arm, snoring softly, her mouth open. Her head lay on his hairy chest, hair all a-frizzle.

He remembered smidgins of the dream, a wildly fantastic and frighteningly real past-life recall, Mike was convinced. The idea scared him. He'd begun to think of himself as a crusader, a loose cannon, one-man death machine, a rural superhero doing battle with the world's monstrous but all too human Mafia legions. A lone Crimestopper, who shoots first, asks questions later. Defender of the Faith (what faith?). Faster than a speeding locomotive…It's a bird, it's a plane, no it's…SuperMike!

SuperMike. Yeah, right. Super dead, you'll be, too, Aurora berated himself. Jackass. Faster than a speeding dodo bird. *Who the hell do you think you are*, toting an Uzi about the farm like a robot patrol.

Who do I have to be?

All these child molesters, sex deviants, fags, rapists, serial killers and bigots running amok in the world, being paid to sit in prison, or writing bestseller autobiographies and making a million for their families; indeed, if everybody thought like him there'd be no crime, no criminals, no spineless, innocent victims publicly complaining of their abuse at some deviant's hands…What this world needs is more martyrs, Mike thought to himself.   He recalled the barbarian hussy, in his dream, telling him that in her country rape was unheard of, because their women were too hot-headed and deadly to be taken alive: and if one were, the perpetrator's existence on earth would be short, for she'd kill him in the end, or else her kin or friends would, even if it meant sparking off a clan war. Among the so-called Sarmatians, or Alans (ancestors of the Hellenes), it was a custom for a young girl not to marry until she'd killed her first man in battle! Considering this, Mike thought the Indo-Europeans and other darkie, woman-hater cultures had brought calamity upon themselves for their submissive attitudes. All this eclectic and bizarre information he'd gleaned from some Greek dude named Herodotus who'd lived over two thousand years ago; Mike had read these profound accounts in a far-out book by Time-Life called "The First Horsemen."

Mike had no sympathy for these victimized whiners.

He believed the Jews had brought near extinction on themselves during the Holocaust, for, come on, how many had actually tried to assassinate that loony-tune Hitler? Mike secretly believed that the Bible – which they themselves had created! – had nearly caused the Jews' extermination. And Stalin? What about his (supposed) purges in the '30s of millions of Russians? It seemed extreme cowardice was merely the opposite side of the coin as mass murder; nobody could accuse insane terrorist organizations like the IRA and certain Muslim sects, Jihadists, of at least not achieving some of their agendas; it seemed to Aurora that if you could pull off a suicide bomb-attack against U.S. army barracks in Lebanon then you should be able to knock off a few dictators or Presidents, such as Abe Lincoln or J.F. Kennedy. Perhaps the world was just plain insane.

The world needed guts.

No guts, no glory.

He dressed quickly, feeling bitter, knowing that if any fucker ever tried to harm his woman he'd chase him across the whole effin' world, torture the bastard publicly on NBC news live from coast to coast. They could put him in prison for life, pay for his lodging and he could sit and read books in a high-security prison like all those other 'effers, or they could give him the electric chair, he didn't care…

The more he thought about it, the more his anger seemed to devour him from within like a monster which'd begun chewing its way out of his stomach like in the movie *Alien*.

Brilliant, autumn sunlight shining through the bedroom window, however, soon chased Mike Aurora's morbid, inner self-rantings away, restoring his zest for life. Jodi rolled over in bed; groaning as Mike stood gazing out of an old-fashioned, sash window at the acreage's awe-inspiring fall colors as he zipped up his pants. Saffron drifts of quaking aspen leaves surrounded the old homestead; other piles of leaves consisting of sapling birch, aspen, tamarack needles, maple, balsam poplar, adding a delightful splash of motley brown, red, orange, yellow. Tall grasses around the dilapidated house were also turning autumn-yellow. Fall flowers had replaced spring and summer's wild flora.

But Mike rubbed his eyes in disbelief when it seemed the old, crimson, Massey-Ferguson tractor mired in the garden had crept several feet closer to the house during the night.

Nonsense.

Yet he could scarcely deny the large rectangle of stunted, withered vegetation and bare, black, oily earth exactly matching the somehow sinister tractor's profile.

I'll just pretend it's not there, Mike told himself.

He didn't point out the moved relic to Jodi as she stretched and slowly dressed.

The old man was up to his tricks again.

Or somebody.

Downstairs all was normal. He and Jo ate breakfast, deep in conversation, as was often the case, for Jodi was a chirper in the morning, a real early bird. Mike's watch showed 7:20 a.m.

Today he planned to rig-up an expensive video-monitoring system and four security cameras (all stolen property, of course), his last hurrah, a daft but plausible way of monitoring the farm's four most dangerous, but visible, spots; entrance, driveway, and the three sheds. (The inescapable fact that neither he nor Jodi could watch the TV-like screen all day seemed only a minor flaw in Mike's calculations at the time.) And he was only kidding himself if he thought his battery-based system could handle the extra load, Jodi reminded him. He certainly couldn't run his gasoline power-plant twenty-four hours a day. He'd taken to waking and studying the grounds from a window four times a night anyway. Perhaps he was being overly paranoid. He figured the chances of more good ol' boys showing up at the farm was about 40/60, in his favor. The province was not a crime hot-spot, Mike considered, especially not the peaceful, rural, Lakeland district.

Mike was, however, worried about police.

He'd had only a few daytime visitors this past summer, one a travelling salesman who looked lost (and who, had he known, came this close to staying so), the others some kids selling raffle tickets. Had they known his awkward predicament, they would've considered themselves lucky not to have been riddled with the wacko's bullets from his kitchen window! The travelling saleman pushing Hoover vacuum cleaners had given Aurora a real scare, driving into the yard at seven in the morning in a shiny, metallic-blue '92 Cadillac Seville.

Mike spent the day wiring infra-red surveillance cameras to a monitor upstairs in his room. Andersen clearly thought him loony tunes. She'd told him this to his face this morning, only to receive Aurora's infuriating, uncompromising smile. Sometimes he could be so stupid, she thought morosely as she scrubbed the kitchen sink, peering out the window at him standing near those accursed sheds toying with one of the robotic, white surveillance cameras. The video screen would show four separate locations, he'd explained. Still, the idea was dumb.

She felt trapped, desperately wanting to be free of the farm's tense, oppressive atmosphere, but no amount of cajoling, threats, or begging could induce Mike to move elsewhere. Jodi knew if she left him she'd be signing his death warrant. But if she stayed she could offer no real protection. Why, she'd never fired a gun in her life!

Jodi broke down and began to cry, feeling wretched and helpless, feeling doomed, as she leaned pitifully on the sink's formica countertop.

TWELVE.

Jodi Andersen dreamt of hell.

Rather, her own version of what hell on earth would be like, a never-ending vista of rolling flames, billowing, roiling clouds of thick, black smoke choking the skies and a deafening din of metal on metal, like ringing anvils being struck across the plains. The earth was afire.

Rather, the Queen witnessing her own people's scorched-earth policy as well as her enemies' travesties. Thatched roofs of half-timbered shanties burnt easily; only empty, stone shells would remain of the Sarmatians' hovels. In this year 1142 B.C., well before the triumphant, traitorous rise of the empire-building Groegs and Lladins, the united Cimmerian/Sarmatian empire was falling in the east to the new and improved Asiatic hordes. A treacherous alliance of barbarous infiltrators had, if not united, then tacitly agreed to cut the Gordian Knot, spilling over the endless desert steppes of Afghanistan and into the difficult, semi-glacial, Caucasus massifs.

Amongst them were Mongols, Huns, Goidels, Georgians, Albanians, Parthians, Basques, Ossetians, Slavs, Armenians, and Romany, all led in the vanguard by the scheming, ever-rapacious *Gelonae*. Malaysia had proven too hot for the pale-skinned, red-haired, kilted barbarians; the orientals' women offered no sport (the thrill of the chase), their petty, shaman chieftains overthrown and enslaved; the West's proud confederacies were much more of a challenge, their womenfolk (potential slaves) stouter of heart and more independent-minded. Furthermore, literal mountains of gold and entire nations of swine and chattel were known to exist beyond the Red Mountains – the Caucasus Alps (as they were known in the Ancient Language). The scythe-outfitted, chariot-riding Scolots and Goidels, related septs speaking similar tongues, also had much in common with their distant progenitors, including a large number of common root-words and some customs as well which the *Ghaidhéltachd* cherished (call it a misguided home-coming reunion). Due to their endless sojourn in the Dark Hinterlands of the Unclean Ones in southern India, Burma, Pakistan, Indonesia, and western Mongolia, the Scytti, from racial abhorrence of the enslaved natives, had begun to drastically inbreed to perpetrate their beloved, pale traits and occasional strains of blond hair. It wasn't unusual for brother to marry sister, grandfather his granddaughter, uncle his niece. However, much of the damage had been done aeons ago, when, out of sheer bloody-mindedness, the *Prydain* had married into the Australoid cannibal savages' patriarchal lineage, thereby irreversibly altering their own unique language and age-old traditions.

Queen Felissa, clad for battle, watched the foreign horde come streaming through the valley like beetles, careening along on their rocking, racing chariots outfitted with scythes in their spokes. She watched from her drystone palace ramparts, stern-faced, but confident. Her nation, the Scotti would find, would not be bowled over so easy. Let them try and storm her imperial palace.   Let them. A deadly maze of slate juggernauts awaited them. Her doughty warriors would rain rocks down upon their heads. Then a volley of deadly arrows to feed the sacred ravens with the enemies' corpses. The barbarians may pillage the countryside, but eventually would be forced to retreat come winter.

Lady Felissa whirled about just in time to parry a Turkman's sabre, kicking the surprised Asiatic in the groin then chopping off the brute's turbaned head with a fierce slash of her razor-sharp broadsword. Down in the cobbled courtyard, several intruders were now being savagely engaged by Sarmatian swordsmen.

Felissa steered herself away from the slowly-leaning corpse's jetstream of blood spewing from its severed neck; a gaping head lay gazing up at her glassily, astonished, from the wallwalk. She kicked the gruesome cadaver from the battlements, scowling, watching her victim plummet five hundred feet to the thinly-forested valley below.

Machines of death up on the armoury's roof were catapulting boulders and naptha onto the now-fleeing invaders, chasing the Kazakhs and Scolots down the embankment while longbow infantry unleashed a hailstorm of arrows onto the enemies' tightly massed ranks. Screams of pain and agony rang out across the plains.

The barbarian Queen smiled grimly as the discoordinated marauders retreated in panicky disarray, pursued by Melissa's beloved husband Conan's horsemen down the outcrop's intimidatingly steep slope of briars and bracken.

The Queen screamed his name aloud when the barbarian interlopers turned on Conan's cavalry, surprisingly and swiftly capturing his cohort and spiriting them away into the enemy camp's innumerable masses.

****

Jodi woke in a sweat. Trembling, disoriented, she gasped aloud, gulping hard, sitting bolt-upright in bed. The room was dark; a merest glimmer of moonlight radiating through the bedroom window. Mike had yet to complete his surveillance monitor's hookup, so it, too, stood blank on a dresser, unseen.   The room felt cold.

Mike lay beside her, undisturbed, on his belly, snoring lightly.

She lay back, breathing easier, relaxing. Her queen-size bed felt warm and comfortable under a mountain of blankets. A Little Trees, grape-scented air freshener helped mask the room's stale, musty air.

Jodi nestled against Mike's shoulder, feeling horny, for they hadn't made love for over two days. She kissed his neck, wishing he'd wake up. How ironic, she thought to herself introspectively, that for over twenty years she'd lived quite content without men, without 'hot' romance. Ever since the age of thirteen, she'd liked boys, but had never done "it." Unlike her girlfriends.

Mike groaned, feeling Jodi's hands go about his waist, caressing from behind. She kissed his ear lovingly, rubbing his chest, wishing he'd do likewise. Smiling secretly, Mike played dead, hoping she'd cease and let him sleep. However when her dainty hand slipped into his underwear, caressing, cupping, he knew he'd had enough. Yet he resisted, enjoying this almost exclusively female game of playing hard to get.

She rolled him over and kissed him urgently, moaning as she climbed on top, mounting him for the ride of her life, finally climaxing and abating, lying, sated, beside him, drowsy with love. And slept.

****

Down in the basement Mike Aurora unexpectedly found what he'd been searching for.

He rummaged through boxes of disused newspapers and fliers, the eerie, gloomy, cement basement dank and clammy as a tomb. Mike felt a soul-numbing chill as he cradled the black booklet in his hands, and it wasn't merely from this big basement's chilly atmosphere. For here, before his very eyes, illuminated by kerosene lamp, were figures, diagrams, charts. And it all became horrifically clear to him, alone down here, how the old man's diabolical little black book of past misdeeds unfolded, like a juvenile TV episode or some of the trashier novels he had read, the plot so impossible it deserved to be deleted from the script. Yet so horribly plausible. So stupid and arrogantly sure of himself his lecherous old uncle had been, as if by writing down his sick fantasies he would ensure his own untouchability and immortality. For, surely, these were just a demented, dirty old man's depraved fantasies. Weren't they??

Aurora stumbled up the basement's terrifying steps feeling sick, feeling mortified, vowing for the present not to let on to his girlfriend upstairs what he'd read in the damning diary of his uncle's. He felt killing angry, for why would anybody entertain such blasphemous death wishes?

He smiled robotically at the copper-haired woman whom he'd been co-habiting with for over three months. Jodi followed him with perplexed, curious eyes as he stepped dazedly into the foyer, recovering some composure.

"Mike, you look pasty," remarked Jodi with a wince, as if he were Count Dracula, *Vlad Tsepesh* shambling up from his crypt and out from his dirt-packed coffin after a centuries' long slumber. He hadn't had a decent night's sleep in days, and looked it. "Is anything wrong, hon?" She smiled uncertainly.

"No," lied Mike with a discreet shudder, "nothing's amiss. Just damned cold down there. No sepulchre or coffins, ha, ha..."

Jodi nodded, returning to her dishwashing.

Mike trotted outdoors, jogging lethargically toward the

derelict sheds. The air was frigid this morning. November snow had yet to fall, although the crisp, frosty ground beneath his plodding sneakers felt hard and unyielding. Brittle autumn twigs and myriad, motley-coloured birch, aspen, poplar, maple leaves crunched cracklingly underfoot. Aurora breathed deep of the refreshingly cold air, almost choking on the sub-zero ozone as if it were smog.   Crisp, yellowy grass swished past his legs.

He halted at the nearest outbuilding, catching his breath, for it was a brisk 100-meter dash to the hulking sheds, all looking too derelict and disused to possibly hold hundreds of thousands of dollars' worth of pirated warehouse goods. (Which, at this point, was still an assumption.) Aurora speculated the buildings were thirty years old, at least. One looked like it were a hundred. Mike exhaled aloud, far from out of shape but no thousand-yard sprinter, for sure. He leaned askew like a sickly, dying tree.

And suddenly felt a pistol barrel put to his head.

"Let's go for a walk, shall we, friend?" A nasal, older man's voice came from behind. "Into the forest. Move it!"

Two middle-aged men, one in grey suit and purple, polka-dot tie, the other dressed casual, but flashily, and both in their late forties Mike guessed, gripped his arms, steering Aurora toward the bushes. Jodi wouldn't see from her vantage point at the kitchen window Mike realized with a sickening lurch of his stomach. Smart cookie. He'd neglected to wear his shoulder-holster – although in this case it would've been of little use anyhow. They had the drop on him. One of the accosters, a mustachioed, long haired rogue, hippie-type, patted Mike's legs and chest for signs of weapons. "Keep moving, pretty boy," snapped the dark, East Indian (?) intruder gruffly. Both men were short, shorter than he, Mike realized, and wiry. He reacted lightning-quick, crying out and jerking his head sideways suggestively.

"Get 'em, John!"

His assailants' heads spun simultaneously. Mike slammed a foot against the East Indian/Pakistani's knee brutally, while driving his big fist into the other's midsection, temporarily disabling him. Aurora threw all caution to the wind, regardless of the pale, balding thug's silencer aimed at his neck. *The pistol's safety had been on!* He seized the taller, surprised Paki's wrist (which clutched a revolver loosely in its grip), twisting powerfully, enraged, then pirouetting and flipping the astonished, braided-haired interloper over his broad back with a Judo move he'd learned in high-school wrestling competitions.

Aurora blocked whitey's left arm, surprised he hadn't yet been shot, defending himself from the hunched-over attacker's puny, ineffective, fisted blow.

Mike rocketed upward, catapulting his knee into his foe's chin with such impact that he felt the man's skull tilt backward with an ominous *"crack"* of his spinal cord, the collision of his knee with his vanquished opponent's chin causing Aurora's entire body to vibrate sickeningly, his teeth chattering.

The Paki vaulted onto Mike's back like a wildcat, pistol dropped somewhere amongst the overgrown, concealing brushwood. The entire action had taken only a few seconds, one man lying unconscious on the ground, the other two now wrestling savagely in a choking, strangling, life-and-death grappling struggle.

Mike snarled angrily, whipping his assailant from his back like a rag, his plaid shirt ripping from shoulder to shoulder in the stranger's grip.

Blinded with a red rage, Aurora seized a lengthy trunk of brushwood and proceeded to club the cringing criminal to death.

It was only Andersen's ineffective, wailing restraints which kept Mike from dashing open the beaten man's bashed, bloodied skull into a watermelony pulp.

THIRTEEN

"My God, you've killed them."

Andersen stared at Mike as if he were a raving lunatic. She knelt beside the battered Pakistani (Aurora assumed he was Paki, from the man's accent), not surprised that he had bludgeoned him to death, for she knew Mike had an unhealthy, racist attitude towards Third World people. Jodi discovered to her horror that the other fellow's neck had been broken, how, she had no idea, no idea how Mike, strong as he was, had overcome and killed these two trespassers. It looked to her as if the unfortunate, older male had been pile-driven from above with his neck over a rock. His neck was cocked at a crazy angle.

She stood up shakily, feeling nauseated, her knees like Jello. Mike stood a few feet away, panting hard, his merciless blue eyes flashing dangerously, fists clenched around a bloodied spruce shaft.

The farm seemed suddenly quiet. Skylarks ceased their

banter, as if bowing their heads in a funereal moment's silence. The pristine sky was a pure, radiant, azure blue, but the wintry sun held no warmth.

"How did you come upon them?" queried Jo, trying to sound conversational.

It was a long time before Mike spoke.

"By one of the sheds. They each had a revolver."

Jodi glanced around, puzzled, sighting no weapons in the short, frosted grass beside the outbuilding. She inwardly questioned Mike's sanity.

They explored the farm's grounds together and in silence, finally discovering a white Dodge Maxi-van parked not far down the road.

Jodi left Mike to dispose of it the best he could.

And to bury the men.

****

"How can you fiddle with those stupid bikes when you should be canning the spinach," Jodi bitched to Mike as he dismantled a dirt bike's carb. He'd bought a half-dozen packages of the stuff that morning in town, hoping to supplement his winter larders.

He glanced up, his butt freezing, sitting in the cold early-winter sun beside the largest of the sheds. A cardboard box sat beside him holding the carburetor's components, ready to be carried back to the house where the real fun would begin. The weather was unusually mild; no snow had fallen, yet. A yellow, plastic-looking YZ 250 two-stroke Yamaha stood leaning on its kickstand to Mike's right. It was a grotesquely tall, lean, mean-looking machine (though not as menacing as the huge KX 450 Kawasaki inside the barn-like building). No road lights. A racer. Kid's plaything.

"Get off my case, will ya, woman?" He turned back to his work.

Jodi's eyes flashed. She kicked him in the thigh. "Somebody's gotta be on your case, you big oaf! At the very least, help me with the canning!"

Mike grinned; he enjoyed seeing his girlfriend's colour rise. For all of her urbane sensibilities, Jodi was still a cowgirl at heart. And, yeah, he supposed he had been slacking these past few days.

Mike leapt up playfully, seizing Andersen by the arm as she dodged away, shrieking, wrestling her to the cold, hard ground. He was only play-acting, laughing at Jo's discomfort and fear, though unwittingly hurting her.

"Okay, now, let's see, what did you call me? Oaf, wasn't it?"

Jodi grimaced gamely, her wrists pinned to the chilly earth.

"Say uncle, or I'll spank you. Or maybe you'd like that?"

Jodi laughed, despite herself, struggling in vain while Mike straddled her ample chest. Her short, burgundy winter jacket was getting muddy, serving only to anger her more. She bucked desperately, unable to dislodge this man, this oaf!, who weighed over sixty pounds heavier than she. Mike only looked solemn and determined.

He leaned forward, suddenly gripping her neck with both meaty hands, kissing her lips hard. Jodi automatically resisted him, digging her long fingers into Aurora's flesh with claw-like fingernails.

Mike, chuckling, rolled off of her, suddenly wincing in pain.

"Bastard," muttered Jodi. "Get the hell off me, you jerk." She gave him a shove.

Mike got up slowly, rubbing his collarbone with a hurt expression.

"You scratched me, you bitch."

"Oh, poor Mikey, 'widdle Josi scratched 'u, didn't she? You've got a booboo, have you?" She inspected his neck with a giggle, becoming serious then remorseful as she studied the extent of his injuries; her long, scarlet, oval fingernails had gouged him deep for an inch-long gash.

"Sorry," she murmured with an embarrassed laugh, blushing. "Come on, baby, I'll rub some ointment on you."

Mike grabbed her and kissed her fervently, then released her.

And told her he loved her.

And if uncle Joe had his way, it would be the last time he ever would.

****

Grimly Aurora read aloud the smuggled diary found that fateful day when he'd been intercepted by whom he took to be ruthless smugglers. Jodi sat listening in silence, uneasy, fumbling nervously with some embroidery she'd been knitting. She sat at his feet like an obedient dog, staring up at him as he spoke. Mike sat in uncle Joe's rocking chair in the living room describing grisly murder fantasies (or were they?) without relish. It was blackest night outside, the mundane room illumined by candlelight. His Briggs & Stratton generator was out of gas. (As was often the case.) Mike's wind turbine's magneto had inexplicably burnt out, proving to have been, unfortunately, too good to be true.

This had occurred only two days ago, November 22.

In essence, what Mike was describing were child abductions.

Slayings.

But were they confessions? wondered Jodi with growing horror. Her stomach felt queasy.

Six men, Mike seemed to be saying, were involved. Kidnapping and spiriting away various children from different provinces over a twenty-year span. Runaways, orphans, Gypsies. They'd used the farm as some sort of rendezvous. Clearly Mike's uncle had been dangerously psychotic, thought Jodi to herself. His own seeming confessions proved this.

What was more, the "diary" pinpointed the locations of several unmarked graves, most shocking being the arrows and crude diagrams suggesting four burials interred at Nimchattan's old, abandoned manor house (!) four miles east of Mike's farm. *Oh, Slap me silly, Sydney!* Aurora felt a tight knot of fear in his gut, his logical mind rebelling at the diary's far-fetched, horrible intimations. A cold, winter wind whistled eerily about the corners of the house, hurling gusting snow at Mike's abode, a home he'd inherited but had come not to relish too much. Already a foot of snow carpeted the prairie ground; winter was here to stay.

Should further, bizarre events take place Mike and Jodi

would be snowed-in and at the old bastard's mercy; without electricity, Aurora stood not a chance in hell of starting either his or Jodi's vehicle in these ⁻25°C temperatures. (He did have the generator to fall back on, however, and several days worth of gasoline.) A raging prairie blizzard was in full spate.   The big, antique range radiated heat at full force, but the old farmhouse still felt cold. Chilling draughts ghosted through its dark rooms. Most fearsome of all would be a reenactment of the deceased's uncanny antics which Jo and Mike had witnessed on October 31. Hallowe'en, of all nights to tempt Satan, when the depraved old man had begun early that evening to flicker lights on and off, then interfering with the stereophonic equipment, including Mike's unplugged guitar which had been left on the floor for a brief moment. Not noisy, this, but disturbing. Mike was sure it was the old man's shade, ghost, poltergeist, whatever the hell you call it that had ruined his wind generator, melting the brushes inside the intricate machine's water-tight aluminum casing. That night, for the very first time since Aurora's arrival in the spring, he and Jodi (having fended off hurled crockery and other assorted debris) had fled in her Datsun, spending the night in a motel in nearby Spiritwood.   Having observed the Disincarnate's aborted materialization attempt in the foyer (a blaze of disorienting colours), Mike and Jodi had

had enough. That evening, threats had proved useless.

Ghosts just wanna have fun.

Now it was seven minutes to midnight, and Mike and Jodi were VERY apprehensive.

Holding the old man's diary in his hand, Mike fretted, "Were they safe"? Just what sort of supernatural powers were he and Jodi dealing with. Were their lives in jeopardy?

Could a ghost kill, if provoked?

Mike often found that Satanic heavy metal music seemed to appease his uncle's spirit.

Which boded ill for him, if the Powers of Darkness be involved.

Perhaps, just perhaps, he would refrain from playing such soul-lifting ditties as Mercyful Fate's "Black Funeral", or Slayer's "Antichrist" from now on, inside the house. Maybe Anne Murray instead. Who knew what he might be calling up here?

Maybe I should borrow one of Jodi's George Michaels albums to get rid of the fiend?, thought Mike to himself with a wicked smile.

The grandfather clock struck midnight; a cuckoo emerging from its wooden cranny.

Mercifully, nothing happened.

Confusing and disjointed as the old man's leather-bound, slim black book was (in human skin!, it purported), Mike and Jodi began to unravel some of its mysteries. Involved in dozens of break-and-enter cases throughout Saskatchewan, the province's ex-police commissioner's irascible eldest son, Derry Kravchuk, a now forty-seven-year-old con-man serving 15/20 years in Saskatoon Penitentiary (since 1987). A convicted pedophile. North Battleford constabulary had been trying for years to determine the whereabouts of the now-retired police commissioner's spoilt son's cache of stolen warehouse goods. (Many suspected the series of robberies of having been insider jobs.)   Twice in 1970 and once in 1976 the professional burglar, kleptomaniac, and child rapist had been tried in court but had, in '70, both times, been acquitted, first on circumstantial evidence, the second because of a bungled police investigation. However in '78 Kravchuk had been charged again, this time nailed with confidence racketeering and thirteen counts of possession of stolen property. The charges stuck, and he'd served five years in Regina on a nine-year prison term, let out early on parole for good behaviour but rearrested some years later on charges of buggery.

Since 1982 Kravchuk, having met Joe Aurora on a hunting expedition in northern Sask., around Smoothstone Lake north of La Ronge with some other like-minded buddies, had joined forces with the then fifty-six-year-old oldtimer and his disreputable associates (former Chicago hoodlums!) to organize a small-time smuggling ring. Mike's rogue of an uncle had had a criminal record as long as his arm (funny nobody'd mentioned this to me?, thought Mike), and had been a rum-runner for years selling illicit booze to Native communities in northern Manitoba, Saskatchewan, and later the Yukon.

It was suspected that Kravchuk's father, a well-to-do real estate agent, former police commissioner and now M.P. for Assinaboyne had pulled a few strings, greased a few palms, made a few bribes, to keep his retread son in easy living. The bum (Derry, that is) had never worked a day in his life according to Joe Aurora's suspect diary.

He'd been a typical welfare bum, according to uncle Joe, deadbeat dad, abusive and manipulative; known from police records to have stalked his ex-wife; for years the worthless piece of shit had collected fat Social Assistance cheques with the help of a doctor buddy who'd passed on bogus info to said department about his patient's "injured shoulder."

Sixty-five B&E's had been perpetrated by Derry and company on private residences. Two unsolved museum robberies in Regina and Swift Current. Fourteen warehouse heists had been bamboozled, an unprecedented series of unsolved crimes. Obviously, somebody had been pulling strings. Police, politicians, the whole gambit.

Nobody other than Kravchuk – who, horribly, was doing time for double murder – had been imprisoned for any length of time. As for old man Aurora, he'd been a sex predator (!) and petty thief for over thirty, sordid years, never once imprisoned for more than five, ironically.

An incredible series of unsolved crimes – from petty thievery to major B&E's, warehouse hold-ups in the dead of night to old uncle Joe's alleged child abductions and torture.

Furthermore, Mike ascertained that he, himself (!), had *killed five of the seven, original men involved in uncle Joe's now defunct crime ring!*

The bad news was that twenty-eight others had somehow become entangled in the operation since 1985. Four (mobsters, if he understood correctly) resided in California now; six in Manitoba; one in Montana; one in the N.W.T.; two were in jail for wife battery. God knew where the others were.

A Moosejaw address indicated that a cement business, Tyrone's Cement, was somehow involved; Joe's little black book had provided few clues to the meaning of this cryptical, scribbled slip of paper.

Time to get answers.

But how? Blackmail? Intimidation? Or was it still too late to go to the cops?

Even on self-defense, Aurora was looking at many

years' imprisonment for having opened fire on the housebreakers unprovoked, his motto, be Quick, or be Dead.

But the statements about murdered children and numerous others, Mike couldn't ignore. No names, mind you, but the damning diary seemed pretty graphic. If this was all a lark, he conjectured, then old Joe must've had one hell of a sick imagination or sense of humour. As howling, blizzard winds hounded the former log cabin Mike's skin crawled with the memory of the human hand he swore he'd dug up, and not dreamt. Often, one had the tendency to imagine something so realistic one could see it in one's mind's eye, although it hadn't ever really happened as imagined, Aurora surmised.   He also had the eerie sensation just now that someone was watching him from behind. Jodi gave a start as Mike swung around bodily in his rocking chair.

At the head of the banisters stood old man Aurora, speckled with grave mold, his baggy, old-fashioned, khaki trousers and scarlet cardigan glowing a sinister, pallid yellow in the stairs' gloom, his gnarled, flesh-peeling, skeletal hand settled on a bulbous balustrade, fingers drumming nervously. The abomination leered at Mike and winked, thumbs up, then vanished, fading to black.

"What you lookin' at?"

Mike swivelled his head at Jodi's voice like an

assembly-line robot, too stunned for expression. All was dark upstairs. He'd never before seen his uncle, only a glimpse, once, of a face in flames, and was momentarily taken aback. Jodi's voice had surprised him, for clearly she'd not seen 'it'. The old man wore dull-coloured, dungaree-type trousers with suspenders, thread-bare wool cardigan, and oversize, worn-out work boots. He'd had no teeth. Sinister gray eyes. All in all, save for the sickly grey, mildew-splotched, decaying flesh, the old man had appeared quite real, quite solid. And bald as a snooker ball.

"I just saw my uncle's ghost."

Jodi stared, eyes a-goggle, up at the stairs, seeing nothing, for there had never been anything to see. At least nothing corporeal. Her face turned ashen.   For Mike, she understood, this was the first instance – no – there'd been one other – two others – only a face, one in the woodstove's glass viewing plate, another as a hairy, half-human, spider/octopus abomination on the stairwell – that he'd seen his notorious, dead uncle. Dead, that is, in the flesh.

Mike and Jodi climbed the stairs warily, eyes darting all over the place,   crawling into bed with alacrity. Downstairs, a big block of well-seasoned spruce crackled and spat nostalgically in the cast-iron woodstove well over fifty years old, giving the old house a pungent, sprucy smell of cones and melting resin. Upstairs (where warmth rising from below took the chill off the night air), the peculiar but comforting smell of wood heat from a well-maintained chimney lulled Aurora into a relaxed, semi-sleep state.   He'd sawn and chopped this winter's wood supply himself, cutting the plentiful bottomland timber with a huge, Husquvarna power saw (also contraband) and stacking it in a small shed beside the house.

The two rolled over and went to sleep.

FOURTEEN

Jodi and Mike were reunited in the spirit world.

The lovers (a.k.a Conigcat and Melissa) were formally betrothed at the sacred altar of *Lughnása*, or *Lludh*, joined in matrimony by the High Wizard of Caledonia (a land someday to be called Greece). Conan had been daringly rescued by a crack squad of Melissa's retainers from the Gauls' iron grip. The plaid-kilted barbarians (who, ludicrously, often fought naked for sport!) had planned to sacrifice their giant captive at the upcoming festival of Lammas Night in late July. However, the warrior Queen had had the gall to raid the *Ghaédheltachd's* territory in south Poland, surprising the Goidels' drunken garrison in the north of that cantred who'd been unprepared for a nighttime attack by an apparently defeated, enslaved, degraded, and demoralized subject people. 'Twas often that when the *Prydani* seemed vanquished they would rise up in rebellion, setting off a new chain of explosive, and deadly, confrontations. Although the Scolots had spread their dominion throughout western Europe, subjugating numerous easily defeated, and divided, tribes, or *trefs*, numerically they were not a threat. Great weapons of war had they in plenty, but so had many competing nations. Only in *Eire* were the Scotsmen's authority all encompassing, for the uninvited barbarians had, through a series of treacherous usurpings and marriage alliances, eroded the primitive and superstitious natives of that emerald isle, that Sceptered Isle, which they had intermarried with to an irreversible extent, rearranging customs. Only in the western isles, where the indigenous Fomorians had built the magnificent, ingenious, concentric, drystone palisaded enclosures had the *Cimbri* retained some independence. However, in future legends of the criminally insane *Tuátha de Danaan* (Irish), the Fomorians would be represented as evil, man-eating ogres, hags, leprechauns, which of course was nothing even close to the truth. Even long after the *Prydain* were cruelly and treacherously exterminated the Fomorians (Cruíthi) would be vilified as such, though their only crime lay in defending themselves (rather viciously). In millenniums to come these people, sold out by themselves, would be destroyed by their own blundering, unwitting descendants who, by searching myopically for their own glorious and enigmatic ancestors would trample the *Cymry* asunder like blind sows searching for their crushed piglets.

Now, inside the opulent dolphin-frescoed, Brittonic-Minoan palace of Gnossos, island of Crete, land of the Four Tribes (the *Parisi*), just off the coast of Mediterranean Greece, Conan and Melissa made a pact to crush the alien intruders irreversibly, swearing blood and fire against the numerous, ungodly human trash – the Scythians and Phoenicians – who had washed up on Europa's shores in formidable *currághs* and Egyptian/Phoenician vessels to defile these sacred lands.

"Dethrone the evil Prince's velvet-gloved, iron hands of sin," droned the balding High Priest of Wicca, a lisping, almost whispering old wizard standing barefoot in white toga and gold torc. He paused meaningfully. *"Wheel the Wyvern in."*

Four mail-clad guardsmen trundled into the palace's sumptuously painted throne-hall a small, earthenware dragon.

Rather it was a clever likeness of some unknown, prehistoric beast, of the kind unearthed in fossilized alluvial silts or seen embedded in limestone cliffs, a gilded, winged, red, green, and azure terra-cotta figurine, approximately two feet high by four feet long, wheeled in on cast-iron rollers. Not only was the sinister, spitting, saurian/serpent the people's idol and flagmast, it was their Protector and progenitor.

Tomorrow, a momentous battle on Crete's shores

would be fought against an unholy, multinational host of Egyptians, Chaldeans, Babylonians, Assyrians, Phoenicians, Hurrians, Armenians, Hittites, Chechnians, Achaeans, Kazakhs, Persians, Turkmen, Gauls, and Scythians (Tocharians). Against them an equally powerful coalition of *Groegs* (Cruíthi), Caledonians, Minoans, Cretans, Etruscans, Parisians, Mycenaens and numerous other continental, pan-Celtic divisions of scythed charioteers and archer-infantry plus the whole of the Minoan fleet, the Sea Peoples of antiquity. Little did the islanders realize that the incoming waves of Sea Pirates onto Crete's rocky shores had been greatly underestimated by Her astrologers and certainly more formidable than any Minoan could've believed. Not only the might of sacred Egypt, but of Phoenicia, cruel Assyria, and the Scolot hinterlands of Russia's steppes. However, Conan's army was also the largest ever mustered in Cambric domains, although the defection of Canaan and Phoenicia, Aramaic subject states under the tyrannical control of kings Midas of Troy and Gygges of Lydia had been an astonishing, and disturbing, revelation to Conigcad's informants overseas, just three moons previous.

Unknown to the boastful *Parisi*, upon the morrow the islanders would be no more.

Mike awoke at dawn, rolling over against Jodi Dawn Andersen's naked shoulder. She slept peacefully. He lay with his eyes closed, warm under a heavy layer of blankets. The bedroom felt miserably cold. Last night's howling, blizzard-blowing winds had finally abated. For now. However, three feet of snow lay on the ground like an undulating layer of frozen, desert dunes. Above him a skylark tapped at Mike's window, then flew off playfully into the bushes.

Aurora remembered the Cretans being massacred in last evening's nightmare with a sleepy shock. Though much of the gory details were beginning to recede, he recalled that some on this doomed, Achaean archipelago were of Sanskrit and Aramaic origin, who had intermarried (*by force*) with the Parisian natives and then subsequently, treacherously, risen to high office in the labrynthian palace of Knossos. Afterwards, there had been a terrific eruption of Mt. Thera, destroying the newly arrived inhabitants and covering the venerable isle with lava flows – twice, in one century. A mad narrator in Mike's dream had told of future events, like an Afterword in some ancient Greek chronicle. Within a generation a cataclysm would destroy much of the island known as Atlantis; obliterating its famous ports and forcing the Egyptian and Phoenician lords of that sacred isle to sail to mainland Greece, where they spawned a new (diabolical) language and culture, the classical Hellenic civilization of the Dorians, while displacing the indigenous Helots – the Children of the Sea – and isolating the patrilineal, warlike Spartans, former Celts, to the southern island of Sparta. Those 'sophisticated' islanders were called *Déarg Gall* or *Scotti* in their own language and worshipped *Dághda* (the Good God), father of the gods. A little voice in Aurora's head told him that to verify this, all one need do is isolate Hellenic words starting with *"P"* – the big five – who, why, when, where, what – by separating the initial consonant to reveal the proto, or pre-Indo-European, root. (Later offshoots would replace it with the orient's 'Q' sound, a phoneme ubiquitous to Central Asia, prehistoric America, and the Near East .) The 'P' was often a relic compound of 'ap', meaning 'of', as in 'Apollo'; (other syllables being allophones, interchangeable according to inflection and declension — s for h, gw for f, m for b, yada, yada, yada).

Poppycock.

Mike knew nothing, really, about languages; nor how they formed.

He did however remember Melissa being sacrificed on a Druidic altar somewhere in Brittany. Carnac, he was certain. The priest of Shaitan had cut out Felissa's (Jodi's) still beating heart.

When finally freed of his bonds, Conig, or Conan, the Barbarian, the Invincible, as he would later be known in twentieth-century comic strips (also known as *Conan, the Destroyer*), had turned Gaulish Eurasia into a charnel house, *Twysog* Conan ap Merddyn's forces massacring the foreign marauders by the thousands, burning their crops, enslaving women and children, destroying the Phoenicians' temples of harlotry in Tyre, demolishing Nineveh, overthrowing Babylon, harrying Egypt, and annihilating the Scythians' steppe domains.

His heroic descendants would travesty Greece, Rome, Carthaginian outposts in Spain, Sicily, Anatolia, Abyssinia and Oman, and would harass the Goidels' client, Grecian city-states along the Black and Caspian seas, raiding throughout continental Europe, and invading Ireland.

Mike's Timex read eight o'clock. It was still dark outside, cold, and decidedly unpleasant. He stretched in bed, then quickly dressed, glancing uneasily up at the video monitor which was now up and running. All four images showed idyllic winterscapes on the monitor screen, undisturbed by any living thing. Outdoor lights, the new, Noma™ power-miser LED type, shone ineffectually into the wintry morning scenery, casting weak shadows on wind-sculpted snow. (He guessed his battery bank was all but depleted by now.) Should anyone trespass onto the property the video monitor would beep loudly (due to tripped infra-red sensors outside). He hoped. Mike had awoken three times last night to spy the snowbound vista. He'd barely slept a wink. The state-of-the-art cameras had built-in sensors which would detect any large, moving object trespassing onto the farm. But he knew this tranquility couldn't last. Twice in the last forty-eight hours Aurora had been petrified by false alarms which turned out to be moose or coyotes.

He patted Jo's shoulder, telling her not to get up. She murmured assent.   It was starting to snow again, Mike noticed. He stared down at her slumbering, angelic face, feeling suddenly as though somebody had walked over his grave, a feeling of impending catastrophy, dejá-vu, precognition.   As if one day soon he or she could be slain. Who could they turn to? Mike had no relatives that he knew of. Jodi's family – he couldn't turn to them either. But to go to prison – no. That wasn't Mike's way. He experienced a surge of love and regret as he gazed upon her, then left the room, carefully treading down the stairs. He carried a pistol tucked into its shoulder-holster, like Clint Eastwood taking on the criminal underworld. Except he wasn't as brave nor as savvy as Eastwood's movie personas. Aurora wasn't sure whether he was being brave or monumentally stupid. He raised a hand, feeling day-old stubble on his chin. Recently he'd grown a full-blown, handlebar mustache, a soup-strainer like his Celtic ancestors (he wasn't Celtic). Mike Aurora, save for a plain, black T-shirt and faded blue jeans and sneakers, looked like a barbarian.

He was a barbarian.

He ate breakfast alone, having started a fire in the imposing woodstove which now reeled off heat and the nauseating reek of creosote. He'd been burning unseasoned wood, these last few days; Mike knew he should get up on the roof and clean the ancient brick chimney before it became a fire hazard: he'd heard of too many houses having gone up in flames due to neglect. Outside, his pale gray Impala was buried under a fine coating of thick, icing sugar snow. Time to get outside and do some shoveling, he guessed. His station wagon's distinctive, rectangular headlights poked out oddly from the mantle of snow as Aurora gazed out of the kitchen window. Afterwards he listened to some metal ("Speed Metal Concerto," a headbangin' instrumental, courtesy of Yngwie J. Malmsteen), careful not to take his eye off the sash window. He had the whole front yard in view. The back door was bolted.

Of course, he knew that even a four-wheel-drive vehicle would have difficulty getting into the yard, today. A snowmobile, perhaps, could.

He wasn't overly concerned: he had a special arrangement with the local slow-plough operator, an acquaintance of his.

Jodi came bounding down the stairs, lingeringly kissed Mike's cheek from behind then made herself breakfast. It was 9:30 a.m. The sky was foggy and overcast, a blizzard blowing snow against swaying trees, obscuring the view of yard and buildings.

It was Saturday, a Long Weekend holiday; they wouldn't be going anywhere for a couple of days (the municipal snow-plough was expected today).

Mike scanned the farmyard with his Buschnell 8 x 40 binoculars, studying its crested knolls and snow-bound buildings for signs of life, animal or otherwise. (Not than anyone would be foolish enough to be out there, freezing their ass off, on a day like this, he thought.) A jackrabbit leap-frogged over the terrain, paused, then dashed into a hidey-hole beneath an outbuilding. Mike spotted a small, long-eared owl perched watchfully on an aspen limb, tucked unobtrusively behind a spruce bough. Strangely enough, Aurora loved Saskatchewan winters, adored winter scenery with its gothic, rustic, hoar-frosted vistas. The old barnyard, especially, provided picturesque, rural views of faded clapboard buildings, galvanized, rust-streaked steel roofs, leaning, collapsing ruins, wood-shingled lean-tos, derelict farm machinery which hadn't experienced use in God knew how many years. It was all like an old-fashioned, western ghost town (no shit) in miniature. Come to think of it, Mike liked all seasons, though winter, early spring, and late autumn provided uniquely spellbinding, cryptic scenery.

Summers, however, were almost unbearable, due to the prairies' scorching heat. And forest fires made the air hard to breathe.

Jodi ate Honeycomb cereal for breakfast, washed down with orange juice. Mike usually bought more nutritious cereals, Harvest Crunch or the like, but last week the Leoville grocery store he patronized had had a disappointing dirth of selection. Andersen listened with minor surprise to the innocuous music playing on his CD deck, a rather tame hard rock/metal band which even she recognized; a Canadian trio called Rush, who's music Jodi liked, as did many of her peers. She had to refrain from rushing into the living room and congratulating him, lest he frown and change the music to something heavier. Some of Mike's tapes scared her – wild, demonic, death metal, whose lyrics and overall attitude gave her the creeps. Jodi wished he would switch to pop. Something sane like *Wham!,* or *Boy George,* two of her early, teen favourites.

Aurora was a die-hard Sabbath sloth.

Since his wind charger had gone on the fritz, Mike'd switched to using "D" batteries in his big ghetto blaster or CD player when the generator (he had stored-up plenty of gasoline for the winter) wasn't running.

He spent two hours at his word processor, typing up a storm with his weird book, which, quite frankly, Jodi thought made no sense at all. Sure, it was only a first draft, but it wasn't very plausible, was it? Though to give him credit, Mike's grammar and vocabulary were sound, his typing not bad. Not good, mind you, but not quite horrendous either. Of course Jodi was no horror addict, but she had read with not much interest the few chapters he'd given her to peruse. Vampires in New York. How dumb. And done to death. She, of course, nice girl that she was, had told him it was just fine.

Jodi baked cookies while Mike swore at his manuscript. She'd been layed-off from her job two weeks ago, after a disastrous fire gutted part of the restaurant she worked at one evening.

As she mixed the cookie batter, someone pinched her on the rear.

Andersen spun around, certain Mike had crept up from behind. Her cheeks flushed red.

Mike sat in his deceased uncle's rocking chair fifteen feet away absorbed in a Canadian publishers' directory, foot across his knee. Jodi flung an eraser at him. He glanced up uncomprehendingly.

"What's that for?"

Jodi squinted unbelievingly, rubbing her butt. "Don't pinch! That hurt."

Mike sat expressionless, then frowned, wriggling his fingers, looking like Jack Torrence in the movie *"The Shining"*, thought Jo disgustedly. "I didn't," he countered weakly.

"Did so."

"Did not."

"Did so."

Mike shrugged, then returned to his book.

A pair of lewd, icy hands clasped Jodi's breasts from behind.

She fought hard against the unseen, iron grip, crying out. Mike dashed into the kitchen, uttering a threat, whereupon the poltergeist ceased its vile antics. However moments later it began to ring a tiny bell, a dainty, white, china ornament which sat on the countertop. Jodi seized the object and halted its tinkling ring-a-ding-ding.

The malicious entity had begun to take Mike's threats with a grain of salt.

The rest of the day the invisible presence continued sporadically to ring pans, dishes, move items almost imperceptibly, making a general nuisance of itself.

Worst of all, a bottle of chili had somehow had its contents dumped into Jo's chili-con-carné she'd been diligently preparing for supper.   She broke into tears, allowing Mike to throw together a taco salad instead. (All the while, pots and pans pealed throughout the kitchen, until Mike yelled *"Shut the fuck up!"*) Mealtime had been fraught with minor disturbances, calling for constant vigilance. Furthermore, the unseen, bothersome hands continued to occasionally brush against Andersen suggestively.

'It' tried to crawl into bed with them upstairs that night.

Mike bodily tossed the malevolent being from the bed, hearing it snicker as it shuffled off into the darkness.

It left a stink of opened graves under the covers.

For the next few days the unholy poltergeist, stone-throwing Incarnate, increased its frenzied antics with disturbing frequency.

On December 7, 1994, Jodi Dawn Andersen left Mike and his loony house of doom.

FIFTEEN

Mike moped about the house for days, too despondent to do anything. Jodi's departure had come out of the blue. One day she'd announced calmly that she was leaving.

"Where are you going?" Mike had asked, astonished.

"Back to my folks' house for a few days until I can find an apartment," she explained tersely, without tears. Jodi had swept her hair back from her forehead. "Look, Mike, whenever you're ready to move away from here you'll know where to reach me. Until then, it's been nice knowing you, but, see ya."

She'd slipped away so quickly, not even bothering to pack anything but her suitcase, that he hadn't been able to dissuade her or physically keep her from driving off. He had shovelled the driveway the previous week, so Andersen's departure had been facilitated by good, hard-packed snow. (A buddy of his who worked for the local R.M. had ploughed a path some days ago through Aurora's badly drifted field; bending the rules a bit, because it wasn't a school route.) Mike hadn't chased after her, thinking she'd be back in a few days.

He'd been wrong.

Two weeks passed, and still she hadn't come back. When he'd dialed her folks' number from a payphone in Leoville her mother informed Mike coldly that Jodi had gotten herself an apartment in faraway Shell Lake, of all places. What about her job, her furniture, he'd queried incredulously. Clearly Jodi's mommy had heard her little girl's most convincing cock-and-bull story about big bad Mike's cruel treatment of her. Mrs. Andersen had hung up on him.

To entertain himself, and to break the lull which had pervaded his life, Mike Aurora one day in early April trekked down the grid road during a warm spell, shovel in hand, toward old Nimchattan's place (which he had heard was rumoured to be soon used as a granary). It was an absurdly warm, early afternoon of the 13th, Friday, of all days to tempt Satan, when Aurora, whistling, set off for the old farmhouse four miles distant. Spring was well on its way, causing great rivulets of runoff beside the road; making fields impassable, so much so, that at times Mike could scarcely tell the wind-waked ripplings of a sinkhole from the many small lakes amongst the hilly district. He was merely humouring his darker inclinations and hadn't an iota of belief (well, okay, some) that there really were bodies buried on the old, disused farm grounds. Besides, he'd discovered several glaring flaws in his mad uncle's story which clearly and unequivocally proved the spurious diary's statements to be bogus. Concrete facts which also proved the old bastard a pathological liar. A slushy layer of sticky snow, just a few patches remaining, impeded his progress down the muddy driveway opposite the meadow and lone field of his property, and then onto the disused, country road. Gravel crunched irksomely, noisily under Mike's rubber boots as he walked amidst eerie springtime silence, an unnaturally echoing silence, he thought.   He felt like a complete fool, a skulking, shovel-bearing criminal rambling down the lonely stretch of road bounded by resinous poplar.   He fully intended to flee into the bushes should a vehicle approach. Mike's hearing was excellent, would detect any automobile approaching from behind on a macabrely still day such as this. He even fancied he could incorporate today's experience into his frightfully bogged-down novel some way.

He arrived at the abandoned farmyard at 3:22 in the afternoon, wishing he'd brought his car, although he needed the exercise. Christ, it would be dark soon, Mike cursed. He really didn't believe he could penetrate the frozen topsoil. Crows squawked arguingly high up in the treetops. In his jacket pocket was a small flashlight in case the grisly task took longer than expected (and, alas, it would). The journey had already taken far longer than he anticipated. Only once had Aurora had to dash fearfully into the roadside bushes when an old, green jeep rumbled past.

And now here he was, alone, in this shaded, somehow-creepy farmyard hemmed in by spruce trees. Straight out of some Hallowe'en cartoon. He felt a chill whiz up his spine as he contemplated the funereal task. *I'm not a bloody caretaker, what is this?*, Mike scolded himself. Aurora had to admit it, he was afraid. The derelict manor seemed just the place where a stalker might live, incognito, and bury his victims' bodies. *Yeeeee.* Mike wanted to go home. Right now. But still he was intrigued.

He pulled out his uncle's diary, turning to a tattered page seventeen, making sure he wasn't being watched. Hunky dorey. A tall spruce grove stood between Mike and the prosperous-looking Nimchattan farm across the road. Ironically, he had so little time to dig, for in another three hours, four at most, heh, heh, it'd be dark. *Mommy!* he cried out in his head. Why don't I just go back and forget about the whole thing? Mike scolded himself. Fortunately, he'd brought fresh *"D"* batteries for his flashlight as well as a spare pair in his jacket pocket. Sucker for punishment. He wouldn't consider doing this at all had the last few weeks not been unusually warm, with the occasional snow flurry to break the lull. Spring, it seemed, had arrived early. Back at the farm Mike had been able to stick a garden spade into the semi-frozen ground. For what that was worth. He only intended to dig one spot anyway.

Just a meter or so.

He chose a spot near the great, hipped-roof farmhouse indicated by the diary. In front of an ancient Ford Comet lay the so-called grave, purported the diagram.

A coal black, burnt-out automobile chassis minus engine, windshield, and axles stood up on lichened cement blocks. Rusted fenders and body made the relic look grossly sinister.

Not what he wanted to see.

Not a good start, Mike thought to himself. He'd rather he were off on a wild goose chase. Obviously uncle Joe had been here, then. The auto frame sat half-buried beneath last fall's dried shrubbery.

On the mucky ground, numerous mossy bricks and chunks of cement lay strewn before the defunct Comet. The site was located on the west side of the old, neglected, vandalized house. Gigantic spruce boughs thoroughly blocked the view from the road except for one, significant gap in the foliage. However, the gap was tiny, and screened with wintry brushwood. Aurora vowed he'd use his flashlight sparingly. The day was clear as could be, and a full moon scheduled.

A slight depression at the spot made Mike's skin crawl.

He found the earth harder than he'd anticipated, his spade balking at the task.

The Ford's spooky, blank headlights, devoid of glass, seemed to watch him with an eerie personality of its own. Its rear-end fins reminded him of his uncle's alleged murder-sprees during the era of greased hair, motorbikes, and bobbysocks. The wrecked '60s-era automobile's intact grill looked murderously menacing. Mike found it hard to ignore the diabolical relic's omnipresent stare. Its grill and bumper seemed to grin skeletally with tarnished chrome.

By eight o'clock it had been dark for over an hour. As predicted, a full moon hung high in the eastern sky.

Mike had dug two, three, four feet down and found nothing.

His face was a beaming ray of relief and undisguised pleasure when, up to his shoulders, almost five feet down in that cold, cold earth nearly as hard as permafrost, he'd found zilch.

Disgustedly he realized he'd been had.

Aurora leaned tiredly, satisfied, on his spade's long handle, murmuring gratefully to himself and sweating profusely, despite having removed his black, polyester-cotton jacket. He wore only a checked red flannel shirt now. He was sure the temperature was well above zero, a miracle for this time of year. Yet Mike felt almost entombed down here in this five-foot-deep hole, as if some malign being, lurking above, might step out from the shadows and darkness to whack him over the head and bury him alive. The macabre image made his scalp prickle.

Well, finished. *Whoopty doo!* He reached up for his coat at the hole's edge opposite the huge mound of irksomely backsliding dirt, ready to leave, smiling like a child and feeling like a moron. Old uncle Joe, what a clown. Such a senile, warped old kook. Shoulda' been offed years go. He must've been totally loopy, if not downright dangerous.

Mike leapt up, grabbing his flashlight from the rim of his amateurishly excavated, rectangular hole, ready to shovel the pungent, brown soil back into the "grave." Heh, heh. Wild goose chase, more like.

Just to be doubly certain, smiling, Mike stuck his spade into the hole one last time.

And hit something hard.

His smile faltered.

His shovel brought up a human femur.

SIXTEEN

"Eeeeeeeeeee!" Mike's mind screamed to itself.

He brought up a thigh bone, grotesquely small, ivory white.   Twirling it around and around in his hands as if he didn't recognize it. Mike unearthed a dainty, skeletal hand of definitely primate, and therefore, presumably human, origin. And then a skull. Damn, damn, damn, he should've quite while he was ahead! Bury the goddamn thing and get the hell out of here!, he told himself.

He did.

And he went back home and slept like the dead.

Mid-week he received a letter in his mailbox from Jo, imploring Mike to put the farm up for sale, destroy the sheds' contents and move away, move-in with her in her small Shell Lake apartment until the farm was sold. She'd gotten herself a job at a local grocery-mart downtown and was now earning a decent income.   Mike could get by for a while on his inheritance money, couldn't he?, she queried.   The letter had been frank and conciliatory, and the more Mike considered her advice, reading Jo's superb handwriting over and over again back at the farm, the more he found that Jodi's reasoning made more sense than his own.

Except for the bodies.

He arranged to meet her in a restaurant in Shell Lake on a blizzardy afternoon in late April.

"So, how are you," probed Jodi quietly as she sipped her cup of steaming hot coffee. The café was empty save for two waitresses loafing about, waiting for G.S.T.-hounded customers to enter the lower-class bar and grill.

"Not bad," Mike replied, fidgeting. "I've been worse."

Andersen nodded. "I'll bet you have," she murmured under her breath. God, he missed her, Mike thought to himself. He felt trapped inside himself, like a tiny, plastic, voiceless jack-in-a-box. Aurora felt numb, cold inside, as if he were trapped under ice, unable to express emotions to anyone, his only sympathetic ear his typewriter. Jodi looked especially lovely today; face flushed from the cold, porcelain cheeks shiny and rosy as a china doll's. Her hair, as usual, had been freshly washed and given a chic new perm though cut shorter than usual. It barely reached her shoulders now. Jodi still looked great. Her lipstick was blood-red and attractive as sin. She wore a fashionable turquoise turtleneck and iridescent, green slacks.

"What are you going to do about the farm, Mike?" enquired Jo casually, eyes downcast while stirring her coffee. Mike's own tasted tepid and strangely like menthol. He hated strong, bitter coffee. Aurora paused, staring vacantly out the window into the restaurant's crowded, snowbound parking lot.

"Don't know," Mike said listlessly.

Jodi refrained from comment.   She put a hand on his and squeezed.

"I missed you," she said embarrassedly.

"I think I'll do something drastic with the stuff in those sheds."   He lowered his voice, then cleared his throat. "Got any ideas how to dispose of it?"

Jodi looked stumped.

"I think I'll burn it," Mike remarked. Of course he realized this would not deter his dear, dead uncle a whit.

(In fact, dear, *sweet* old uncle Joe would be *somewhat* put out.)

"All of it?"

"Yeah," replied Mike, laughing to himself. "I hate to do it. And there's no telling what could happen afterwards."

"You should sell the damned farm, Mike," Jodi remarked with a sinking feeling of despair.

"Hon, I've got as much chance selling a farm here in Saskatchewan right now as I would if I were to buy real-estate in Beverley Hills for ten bucks. Nobody's buying land these days. Ten years ago, sure, but not now. The effin' place doesn't even have hydro or telephone lines." Mike touched his forehead suggestively, riled.

Jodi inclined her head, responding personally to his anger. Her big eyes flashed.

"I won't go back," she murmured defensively. "You don't know what it's like, having that pervert uncle of yours touching you all over! It's your problem, now, not mine."

She started to rise, hot-tempered, ready to leave. An approaching waitress eyed them quizzically as she brought them their order.

"Sit down," Mike insisted, snatching Jo's patchwork-patterned leather purse. She obeyed, sniffing haughtily, nose in the air.

An oriental waitress brought their burgers and chicken nuggets, then scurried away.

They ate in silence, appreciating this rare, restaurant meal. Neither of them ate out much. Mike spurted a huge dollop of ketchup onto his cheeseburger paddy, a scrumptious quarter-pounder. "Mm, mthis is mgood," he mumbled with a mouthful of cheeseburger.

Jodi remained distant.

"I've invited an exorcist from an Anglican diocese in Saskatoon to cleanse the house," Mike said out of the blue. "If he can. Unfortunately, my faith in this sort of thing ain't too deep. For one, I'm an athiest, and I don't want anybody snooping about the place, lookin' for clues."

Jo's exquisite, beryl-green eyes lit up with a glimmer of hope.

"That's a good idea," she remarked.

"In the meantime, I wanna start getting rid of some of that stolen merchandise," Mike said softly, "at least get it away from the farm. As well as that jeep and Mercedes. Oh, and the Dodge van." Mike paused. "Care to give me a hand?"

Andersen glanced down into her coffee dregs for a long moment before responding.

She glanced up, studying Aurora's odd blue eyes as she rubbed her cheek thoughtfully with an index finger.

"Sure."

Half an hour later they drove to Jodi's apartment and made love.

****

The minister wandered about Mike's seemingly ordinary farmhouse looking puzzled. He was a small, balding, Polish immigrant dressed in immaculate tweeds. He reminded Aurora of a couple of thugs he'd offed. What, no bell, book, or candle? Mike thought peevishly. He'd expected a Bible-thumping, dog-collared, black-garbed patriarch. The little man with thick glasses looked to be in his fifties.

"Do you believe in Jesus Christ, Mr. Aurora?" asked the Anglican chaplain.

"Sure," Mike lied.

"But you're not a regular church-goer, are you, Mr. Aurora?" queried the Canadianized Pole with his funny, broken accent.

"No," replied Mike, eyeing the menacing shadows obliquely. "I'm kinda' non-denominational."

"I do hope you're not a Jehovah's Witness," remarked the plain-clothes priest, his thick Polish accent difficult to understand. "If you are, I shall have to leave."

Mike frowned, amused.   What was this guy, a nut?

"No, I'm not," he said with a mirthless chuckle. "I'm a Baptist – or at least my folks were." That too was a lie.

The elderly chaplain halted at the foot of the stairs.

"I sense Satanism in this house," remarked the dapper priest suddenly, "or something akin. Tell me, Michael – may I call you Michael? – tell me, have you ever dabbled in Satanism, witchcraft, the occult?" The irritating Pole turned his watery, pale blue eyes on Mike.

"Nope." Mike had hidden all of his tapes, paperbacks, posters.

"I see."

The minister of Christ snapped open an attaché case cradled in the crook of his left arm, removing – you guessed it – bell, Bible, and candle, plus incense.

The minister lit the candle, some myrrh inside a silver incense-holder, and proceeded to read aloud a few lines from his tattered Bible.

Immediately, the unholy assault began.

Objects began whizzing frenziedly past the old chaplain's ducking head, smashing into the walls with stunning impact and a deafening din of metal and glass colliding in mid-air. The unbearable crashing, tinkling noise of glass shattering assailed the now-animated living room and adjoining kitchen. Shrieking psalms, the crouching priest scuttled behind Mike's massive wood heater, clutching his silver cross with reverence as he chanted Holy scripture from his cloth-covered black Bible. He'd dropped his candle.

"In the name of God, I command thee to flee, unclean spirit," wailed the chaplain in mounting desperation, sobbing in terror, *"the power of Christ compels you! The power of Christ compels you!!"*

Mike dashed outside, cringing as he listened with disbelief to the farmhouse's cacophony. Springtime had arrived weeks earlier, endowing the homestead with a dazzling array of blossoms and unfurling leaves. From inside Mike Aurora's haunted abode the Anglican minister's exhortations rose to an excited fever-pitch, hurling prayers at the enraged, disincarnate entity with terrified, panicked, repeated frequency. Aurora cursed himself for leaving the fool priest alone in the infuriated household, turning to rush back inside and order the entity to desist.

As he reached the verandah's steps the chaplain began to shriek in mindless terror.

And when Mike entered his now silent house of horrors, he realized the priest was nowhere to be found.

The chaplain had vanished.

****

Where was the priest? Mike kept asking himself over and over again. He sat in Jo's favourite, cushioned armchair; a plush, tatty, silvery thing which had obviously seen better days. The armchair was ridiculously small, barely bigger than a rocking chair.

But the smell of Jodi's perfume permeating the flower-patterned rocker quieted Mike's unease and made him feel he'd had something worth living for. The initial draft of his horror novel Aurora had completed yesterday afternoon. He thought it extraordinarily dumb. No choice but to revise and, inevitably, rewrite. *(Oh, god.)* Outside, driving sleet was assailing his haunted house.

Aurora hadn't a clue where the Polish priest had disappeared to. Had the kook been frightened off (leaving his car??), or slain and dragged away somewhere?

Or spirited away into the Other Side?

Mike hadn't seen Jodi for almost four weeks. Four days ago the Anglican chaplain – Mr. Waszowski, wasn't it? – had vanished into thin air, leaving only his faded Bible, little silver bell, incense burner, attaché case, and black candle which had almost set the living room afire. And his damning car.

However, the diabolical entity which controlled the house and had been subsequently growing in strength and making its presence felt at all hours of the day seemed absent. No longer could Mike sense the crazy old man's presence within lengthening shadows. Had the malevolent being, having taken the priest like a spider accepting a silk-wrapped gift from its mate, decided to vacate the premises? And taken the poor bastard where? To do what with?

And when would it return?

Dimly, Mike suspected the alien creature which inhabited his domicile was only a clever clone of his uncle, an illusion perpetrated by some extraterrestrial monstrosity. (Or, perhaps, he'd been reading too many H.P. Lovecraft stories over the years.)

He wished he had a telephone. He wanted to call Jo, beg her to drive down to the farm. Even the sound of her voice on the receiver would be enough. Worse, since Mike's tiff with his so-called "friends", he'd had associations with no one. His were the kind of neighbours who might drop by only if you'd died and begun to stink so badly they could smell you from the road. Knowing these stuck-up farmers around here, perhaps not even then. Mennonites, most of them (well, I guess that excuses them, doesn't it?, he thought). Nobody save a few high-school kids selling raffle tickets had dropped by.   He'd come to hate his neighbours. Hicks. Pot-bellied, red-faced farmers. Anglo-Saxon swine.   His enemies.   Mike wanted to persecute them somehow.

Fortunately he'd procured a year-old German shepherd from a private sale over a month ago to keep him company. The (usually) playful little bitch lay beside his chair, snoozing. Mike had noticed a private ad in the local paper, Western Producer. He also had a half-wild cat Jodi had brought several months previous; the poor thing now spent most of its days up in a tree, hounded by Aurora's mutt which he had paid a hundred bucks for. The hound was lazy, but loveable, a marble chocolate-gray colour.   The kitten was a calico.

Mike ventured outside, into the late May sleet which now looked to be turning into hail. He wore a dark green bomber jacket, which Jodi had given him for his birthday. His rubber boots clogged-up with mud as he stalked toward the corrals. To Aurora's left the garden, which had been freshly dug recently, was now muck. *Baaaaaing* goats sighted him from their derelict enclosure and ran toward the flimsy railings in anticipation of a snack, perhaps a piece of paper or his hair if nothing else. The startled nannies watched him with curiosity, for it was not milking time, and if it was not milking time then it must be...*play time*.

Four baby goats, recently born, began hopping about in the straw, a couple of them bucking like broncos. One was pure white, the others brown or sable. (One of them began to suck on Mike's finger thinking it was a bottle.) The two nannies, big mommas, reared up on the fence to nuzzle Mike's wet face. He shied away, disliking their awful breath. He still found their cross-slit eyes a bit unnerving. Mike rubbed their bare, flat heads and smooth muzzles, laughing. He handed each a fistful of alfalfa to munch   on,   gluttonous   all.   Even   Satan,   the never-to-be-trusted billy caged in a separate stall who would butt you in the rear if you weren't careful. Mike seized his great horns as he entered the billy goat's small enclosure, for the rambunctious beast always assumed he wanted to butt heads with him! The two tiny bucks and twin does were still of suckling age. One was pulling greedily at his mother's teat.

His German shepherd, Shelly, followed him eagerly, tagging along at his heels as Aurora meandered along the moss-dotted railings. Much of the ancient corral would soon be in need of serious mending.

Mike pondered the unmarked grave he'd found at old Nimchattan house. He'd been studying human anatomy in numerous medical texts, and felt certain the bones discovered were those of a child, the femur an upper section of thigh bone. Nor had Mike any idea what to do about it now that he'd unearthed the bizarre, unsuspected grave-site. By rights he should inform the police, for some poor parent must be grieving somewhere over this missing waif. Who had it been? A local child?

Or a runaway as uncle Joe's diary suggested?

Describing uncle Joe and his two buddies' rape and torture of the little ten-year-old from Wainwright?

Aurora stopped dead in his tracks, suddenly recalling an isolated passage in his mad uncle's diary graphically and horribly describing a child's murder which, although not indicating her burial, seemed to suggest a local occurrence.

Mike's dog whined and scratched at his pant leg, as if begging attention.

The German shepherd clutched a human thigh bone in its mouth, grinning happily.

Mike frowned, eyes widening.

As if sensing his intention, the half-grown mutt ran away playfully as Mike reached for the bone. He chased after her, tracking the hairy bitch into the forest, following a well-trodden, familiar trail.

One of the graves had been exhumed.

Mike looked around, wild-eyed, sensing trouble. Yet not a leaf stirred in the ultra-humid, deciduous woodlot. It had stopped hailing.

He yanked out his .357 Magnum from its shoulder holster, head swivelling as he searched for an intruder. No police cordons had been set up around the six-foot-deep hole. Not that any investigation would be conducted without their visiting him first.

The forest grave was empty.

But it stunk something unimaginable. Or something did. His German shepherd eyed him quizzically beside a big birch tree. Shelly had dropped the bone at her feet. Aurora sniffed the pungent forest air, following the source of the noisome stench and almost gagged.

Sticking out from behind the birch bole hung a man's stiffened arm.

Aurora nearly puked when he rounded the tree, gun poised for firing, and confronted his old nemesis's maggot-crawling, skeletal, widely grinning face. Much of the skin had been eaten away by rodents or insects. The fully-clothed cadaver had been thoroughly defleshed, showing only occasional patches of almost-year-old, rotting flaps of greenish muscle tendons or gnawed lumps of fatty tissue. Severely dessicated, the thing smelt to high heaven. Mike's guts lurched uncontrollably. The stiff's hair, full of dirt, crawled with beetles. Its jaw gaped unnaturally wide, as if the hinges had decayed away. Viscous goo oozed from its punctured abdominal cavity. Red ants scrambled throughout the corpse's cranium and black eyesockets.

Who the devil had unearthed this thing? Mike asked himself. "Was it you, Shelly?" he demanded, his voice echoing eerily in the forest's Stygian gloom. The dog just gazed at him stupidly, head tilted. Her tongue lolled; she'd been *eating* the damned thing! Of course the dog hadn't unearthed it, stupid, Mike scolded himself. The grave had been three by six deep, he'd measured it thoroughly.

I see.

So the old man was hanging around after all. Aurora

peered at the grisly cadaver, verifying the stiff's identity, assuring himself that it was no Anglican priest.   Or a dummy.   He thought the thing a pretty good likeness of those seen in horror movies like "Creepshow."

Mike returned calmly to the house and proceeded to gather some dry kindling and brushwood from his woodshed.   He meant to build a funeral pyre in the woods, what he should have done long ago.

****

"Why don't you want to leave the farm?" asked Jodi as she leaned against Mike's chest. Northwest of the province they'd drove, planning on a week of fishing at Turtle Lake.   They'd spent two days already casting reels from the lake-dock before abandoning that route. They had caught nothing. Tomorrow they planned to rent a motorboat for the day.

They had driven some eighty kilometers just to sit in Mike's parked '77 Impala station wagon this early June mid-afternoon, reminiscing over past experiences.   Both had discovered an astounding variety of wilderness scenery along the roadsides, putting into question Mike's designation of this part of the province as "prairie." It was really part of the heavily-forested Canadian Shield region bristling with lakes, sloughs, and what seemed to be dying or dead forests along the open roads. Most, in fact, were large tracts of tamarack shedding their needles each year which turned yellow, looking like great stands of dead, denuded spruce mixed among the muskeg bog, stricken with some beetle or caterpillar infestation. Some were infested with larva, but not all. Mike could recall a few years back when hairy, gray army-worms had covered the whole Lakeland region like a disgusting, wriggling, invading horde of caterpillars which you couldn't avoid stepping on or running over, literally dropping from the trees. Things had improved considerably since then, the views particularly enchanting this summer. Mike and Jodi had even seen a big black bear ambling alongside the road to Spruce Lake.

In Jodi's palm sat a pale green orchid of uncertain strain, which she'd found near a slough. Neither she nor Mike were aware it was a rare bog orchid, which brought a heavy fine for picking this U.N.-registered, endangered species.

Mike's Impala sat parked on the shoulder of a disused logging road six miles or so east of Turtle Lake, the isolated, sprawling recreational mecca of innumerable southerners and vacationers, not to mention Americans, those weirdly dressed globetrotters who look lost wherever they go.   It was a fun lake to camp out at, which Jodi and Mike had been doing for three days now. They were using her brother Mark's tent-trailer which had a tiny, propane heater inside.   They cooked outdoors at a secluded, lakeside campsite that seemed well worth the parking fee.

"Why don't I want to leave the farm."   Mike pondered this.   "Because I'm an egghead and I want what is in those sheds, and I wanna keep the farm to pass onto my children."

Jodi deftly steered around the subject of children. She had no wish to be a mother yet.   Not until her financial problems and love-life were clarified.

The two sipped their cans of Sprite, sharing a bag of tacos sitting betwixt them.   Jodi glanced at her gold wristwatch which indicated 11:00 in the morning.   Time for dinner back at their campsite, which today would consist of roasted wieners, marshmallows, and leftover potato salad.   Then off into the wilderness to search out blueberries and mushrooms – big, orange, aspen or birch boletes.

They spied a pair of mule deer crossing the road before Mike started his   car and maneuvered the boat-like station wagon through a tight 180 degree half-circle, then backing up and cruising away.   Rain was forecast, the sky glowering leadenly.   Sharp ruts made the service road treacherous. Soon big, fat rain drops which smelt like – you guessed it – acid rain, splattered onto the vehicle's bug-smeared windshield.   Mike steered quickly around a small garden snake slithering across the road then deftly braked momentarily to avoid smucking an oriole flitting across the car's grill.   The station wagon rolled along smoothly and quietly once on the blacktop; before that, they had had to put up with its tires occasionally making whining noises as it straddled hard, shallow ruts.   A disused railway ran parallel to the route; a rather somber reminder of days when one could simply catch the rails and head for parts unknown, seeking employment, during the Depression era.   Spruce trees abounded.   Surprisingly few potholes marred the disused road's surface (although *washboard* would be a good way to describe it, remarked Jo).

Back at their idyllic campsite, Jodi and Mike prepared dinner under the camper's awning as relentless rains poured down violently from Black Sabbath-inspired skies. A loud crack of thunder, followed by others, deafened momentarily whilst shaking the ground.   Swollen storm clouds spread a shimmering blue-gray pall over Turtle Lake.   A fork of lightning somewhere in the west speared down into the lake's frothing waters.   A stiff wind had arisen, breaking the silence before a storm. Whitecaps swelled and tumbled onto the rocky shore, for a heavy nor'wester had begun fifteen minutes ago to assault the region, being a thorough nuisance as Andersen and Aurora coped with roasting their frankfurters under an extended tarpaulin. Mike was glad they weren't out on the lake today.

Both were soaked to the gills.

By midday Mike and Jodi had been banished to their tent-camper, for a real howler of a storm raged out on the lake, hurling five-foot whitecaps at its shores and lashing the camper with a maniacal onslaught of torrential, monsoon-like rains. *So much for today's blueberry jaunt,* thought Jo and Mike privately as they sat inside playing chess by candlelight. Earlier that afternoon they'd ventured out, bringing back a sizeable haul of birch boletes (half of which, unfortunately, were riddled with worms) and getting soaked for their pains. Now each had a blanket wrapped around themselves along with a fresh change of warm, dry clothes. The camper, however, leaked badly in the corners, necessitating a thorough mop-up every fifteen minutes. The tiny nylon and fibreglass camper/tent shook and trembled fragilely on its wheels. They could hear breakers slamming onto the rocky shore outside, through a screen of trees on a small bluff overlooking the frothing lake.

They shared a bottle of Tequila and grenadine to warm their innards; discussing their predicament, and at times, arguing over what was clearly a hopeless situation: a veritable siege of hostile human interference, as well as unseen malevolent forces possibly even more deadly than the criminal elements already involved.

That night, in bed together, Aurora dreamt of ancient Greece.

****

He'd woke up sweating, having witnessed all sorts of unimaginable brutalities and vile behaviour that should never have been witnessed by mortal man. Horrific child sacrifices by both the Keltoi and Spartans (proto-Greeks) to appease the gods Baal and Marduk, which would also be adopted by invading Phoenicians to feed their diabolical idol with daily offerings of baby girls to flames. Mike had also beheld depraved Bacchanalian cults of necrophilia and bestiality commited by those who owed their allegiance to Apollo, Bacchus, Mars, Aphrodite, Dionysus, and Zeus, who Conan's tribe had referred to as the Liars, those who worshipped Sa'an, the false God of Light which had been introduced by the Goidels and later Assyrians.   In his dreamworld Mike was forced to watch ritual sex between children and men, little boys especially, or immolated at yearly fire festivals to the gods Lugh and Belinus.   Or little girls married off to old cronies who were literally walking bags of bones! In turn, he'd witnessed the *Prydanis'* own condemnation of their vanquished enemies to flames; in his dream they'd set Athens (their one-time former capital) afire, looting, pillaging.   That particular sept had been known as the *Alans.* Their Thor-winged helmets set the great empire-builders a'tremble, harrying (this time incarnated as the *Peleset,* or *Parisi*) incestuous Egypt, hounding Her pharoahs, Fathers, from the Lower to the Upper Kingdoms, installing puppet regimes of Aramaic origin, and later, Circassians of Georgian descent upon Egypt's sacred throne.   The red-haired "barbarians" surged forth from the steppes and from the seas in their large, skin-covered coracles or dragon-prowed longboats of clinker-build, only one of many opportunistic Sea Peoples taking advantage of the corrupt, stagnating city-states of the Near East. (Known by their Cimmerian neighbours as "incestuous fire worshippers.")   Their attacks had been uncoordinated, and few, if any, mutually planned.   However, for each foray into foreign domains there were ten of Goidelic inception into their own, and while the menfolk were away at war against their neighbours the *Pretanis'* martially trained women and children were often besieged by opportunistic Achaeans, Armenians, Georgians, Parthians, or any number of their own tribes whom had intermarried and forged mutual alliances with the slant-eyed interlopers. Thus, confusing the issue, they'd come to be called Sarmatians, Amazons, Cimmerians, Aryans, Vandals, Wends, Germans; Alans, Huns, Scythians, Teutons; Parthians, Cimbri, Umbrians, Thracians, Illyrians, Vulcans, Bulgars, Belgians; Bohemians, Britons, Dacians, Gauls, Scots, Caledonians, all who'd come (supposedly) to worship the great Mother Goddess *Wicca,* Lady of the Northwinds, and her warlike, Bright consort, Belinus.

In the West, since 2700 B.C., many foiled attempts at conquest and colonization had been made by the *Fíne Gaél*, in the future designated as Beaker Folk, Urnfield Culture, Battleaxe Ware, Hallstatt, and La Tène.   One man, Conigcad mab Euain, would dispute such wholly false representations of these "invading" cultures whose evolving wares and grave rituals were in fact his own!

On Europe's southern peninsula (someday to be known as Italy), a bold, treacherous elite of superstition-riddled oppressors had extended their influence into that of the waning, stagnating Etruscan city-states. (Later to be dubbed "Scots" by their Germanic and Roman enemies.)

They came to be called Romans, the Rom, or Latins, half-descended from low caste Gypsies whom had migrated westward in search of easy loot. They had not found it; rather, slavery. The Romany had come as an isolated, impoverished tribe from the Indus valley of India, though their origins lay in the south of that wretched sub-continent.

Then Greece under Alexander the Great had arisen, backed largely by subject Gaulish and Cimmerian mercenaries from Macedonia and northern Greece who did all the heavy fighting while the Greek phalanxes took the glory, spreading their puny pseudo-Semitic lingo across the known world in, really, what were isolated, urban city-states wholly dependent on the goodwill of the natives who controlled the trade of tin, salt, iron ore, gold, etc. The Hellenes would be subjugated in turn by their rapt pupils, the *civitates* of Rome.

The Romans, following the path of their pedophile Grecian forefathers, used Gaulish and Germanic muscle to gain their own ends, eventually dispossessing their very models, the Etruscans, and later still played an unwitting role in a predestined Judaic plot to seize the world by sacrificing the Israelites' precious martyr, Jesus Christ, a harmless if somewhat dotty guru claiming to be the Saviour, Son of God, although really an indoctrinated scapegoat threatening the Roman Emperor. Hail to

Caesar.

And then the mighty, glorious Franks, Northmen, and a rabidly anti-Roman driving force of Cimbrian Vikings from Jutland invaded and toppled imperial Rome's corrupt empire, slaying Her citizens and freeing the slave-class – which made up ninety percent of its population. The Saxons, in turn, unpaid, disgruntled freebooters whose legionary bribes had been slow to materialize took to the seas, invading an unprotected Scandinavia, Britain, and continental Europe while a crippling famine and pestilence raged. Jesus Christ's leapfrog onto the world's spiritual throne had been preordained, the Germanicized Northmen, inbred Celts, converted Latinos and Orthodox Greeks, pagan Slavs, and the unfortunate, alliance-riddled, Romanized, Celtisized and Germanisized Britons ready for conversion to Satan's church... Christianity.

All this was to come however, witnessed by Mike Aurora in his dream-state through a seer's greenish crystal ball. The future of the world depended on Conan's ability to change the course of history, to forestall humankind's slow but inexorable devolution into quasi-humans. Through gradual stages of flawed evolution *homo sapiens* had degenerated into separate races, sub-species, if you will; Mongol to the east, Negroid to the south, Australoid to the southeast,

Indo-European to the northeast, all of which would eventually spread their hybrid races like squids' tentacles across the globe with calamitous, inbred, degenerate results and reverting to a primitive illogic in a world where apes seemed smarter.

Evilution.

Michael John Aurora, a.k.a Conigcad (Conan) mab Euain ab Sian ben Ewairt o' Sioned, Borealis, Lord of the Northwinds, sat in his worn and tattered war gear gazing concentratingly into the ancient seer's spherical, mystic time machine, deliberating over the druid's momentous predictions.   Should the old wizard decree Conan's destiny, ought he to accept this crony's prophecy or ignore it?   The thin-lipped, mutt-faced priest breathed shallowly, wheezing, leaning with concentration over the gold-mounted crystal ball roughly the size of a human head.   Several trophy skulls holding dripping candles, craniums sheared off above the forehead, lit the grotesque hovel.   Cong, ex-king of Scythia (Scotia), warrior-bard, and Keeper of the Seven Keys shook a rattle to the beat of ceremonial music played outside his venerated abode.   The dark night was oppressive, windy and cold as any one might experience here in the wastelands of southern Scandinavia, a land of brooding moors, dark fjells, and lonely fjords.   A sinister wind moaned across the snow-laden Danish plains – a light frosting for December – flitting through the cob-built hovel's drafty door-frame like vengeful wraiths. The small, whitewashed, straw-and-dung building lacked apertures of any kind.

The shaman (once known as the dreaded *King Cong* of Dalmatia) announced that Conig must leave his aged, earthly body, venture forth into the ether to confront the unholy magicians who now desecrated his country and bring back the Spring Queen, Melissa mer Holilyn fer Leia, without whose rejuvenating powers the earth could not continue. A new and deadly horde of ocean-borne slavers from Poland's Baltic Sea region threatened the Cimbris' expansive domains. Conan must sweeten the air now defiled and rescue his Queen from hellfire's damnation and the prospect of oblivion, or an eternity in limbo. The *Deutchelanders* must be destroyed, or all was lost. Without the Lady Mother there could be no return of spring for the northerners, no dykes to hold back the sea in the Netherlands and no escaping the encroaching icefields beyond the sacred Faeroese islands. (Iceland, land of the Frost Giants.) And no escaping or resisting the depredations of the Northmen. Lord Conan must return his departed Queen to her earthly paradise and lay her troubled soul to rest or the Cimmerian confederacy was doomed. It had been thirty-seven years since the Druids of the Others had sacrificed the northmens' Queen of the Woods. Now, Conan, an old, embittered man, a warrior-king who would be the last of his line if what the aged sorcerer had said was true, sat listening to his confidante's bewailing entreaties to save the world. For the blind, crippled wizard had seen the earth's distant demise in a dream, the monstrous machines of destruction that would denude its surface of vegetation, snipping off its Holy trees with metal claws, polluting the skies, bringing nuclear devastation to all and ultimately reducing noble man into the vicious savages of primeval Asia, Africa, Micronesia, and the New World yet to be. Nevermore to be heard the sweet, lilting speech of the Cimbri in the mouths of babes, powerlessly witness to the degenerates' ritual slashings and bloodlettings and senseless circumcision and purification rites. Mankind's future depended on Conan's success, lest they degenerate and decay like dead Egypt's depraved progeny.

Unfortunately, Conan must leave his earthly cares behind, say goodbye to seventy-two years of passion and – *aye* – pain, nevermore to gaze upon his numerous offspring and growing grandchildren with stern, patriarchal pride. Never to taste the sweet tang of fall-ripe apples, or to sail the waves and feel the salty sea-spray at the tiller of a proto-Viking longboat which rode those northern oceans like a great sea serpent.

Fatigued, the aged Sea King left the magi's cob-built hovel with tears in his eyes, right leg limping noticeably from an ancient thigh wound.   The sea dog's white hair billowed out with the harassing north wind, resembling a mop of wool streaming from his balding scalp.   He walked tall, champion over a thousand foes, grim-faced and sour toward his *llys*, allowing the boreal winds to carry his sobs across the moors and neither fearing nor caring whether someone would hear.   For him, his life was over, his spouse of twenty-eight years, Heolwen, dead, his sons squabbling over which of them should rule in his stead and what tactics to use to crush the Teutonic menace.   He had expected another twenty-five years of life, as promised him by the Holy circle.   How unfair and callous the Fates had been to push him into a future whose very family structure had been eroded and degraded.   An urbane society whom he could neither imagine nor relate to.   And to live for a time as – what? A slave?   Or as a mole in the dawn patrol?

Inside his private chambers, Conan prepared the draught which would hasten his demise and plummet him into a shadow world of undetermined frights and Leviathan struggles.   A world of goblins and trolls! Hel awaited.   His clan – his nation – would not understand, would find their Führer dead on a wooden floor tomorrow morn from this capsule of yew berries, mistletoe and minute traces of strychnine which he held in his palsied, gnarled hand.   He heard a rustling in the corner as he popped the concoction into his mouth.

Is that you...Melissa?

****

Michael John Aurora spaded the ground methodically, creating a huge pile of pungent, black earth behind Nimchattan's old farmhouse.   It was a sunny day; he was alone, screened by a heavy thicket of spruce, jack pine, and one gnarled, twisted oak which looked for all the world as if it had died.   A wall of rose briar and Saskatoon bushes obscured the view from the road. *God, I'm gonna get caught here yet,* thought Mike to himself. He dug unhindered, boldly excavating the grounds while quite aware that at any time someone from the adjacent, working farm across the road could wander onto the property.   Fluffy, white clouds lingered in the west.   A patch of blueberries surrounded Mike's spot of bare earth. It was two in the afternoon and he'd dug three feet down already, having started two hours ago. Joe's diary had indicated this spot behind the collapsed greenhouse-addition at the rear of the looming, hip-roofed, Edwardian-era manor house. Somebody well-to-do must have owned the place once, Mike surmised. It was bigger than the average prairie manse by far, he thought, habitually referring to it as "the Mansion." It wasn't really, though, just a big house. Asphalt roof tiles were peeling and flapping in the wind as Aurora excavated the lonely site. Riotous shrubbery and tall swordgrass overran the rear of the ancient demesne. Tall, broken-glass window frames looked down on the self-conscious, irreverent human violating the glorified pseudo-mansion's back yard. Undaunted, the trespasser worked till six, sweating heavily in the hot, midsummer weather, having no idea what to say should he be found here. However Mike had a full view from behind the house of the only entrance to the rustic farmyard . The sprucy smell of tree resin and oozing sap wafted across the backyard. An odor of hot, decaying timber lingered on the shimmering air.

The digging proved surprisingly easy. Nevertheless, Aurora took his time, stopping for regular breaks, a cup of coffee from his thermos, a snackbar for the munchies. Luckily the ground was devoid of rocks or he could never have made the progress he'd had.

Yet he felt watched.

Uneasy.

He unearthed an old pocket watch of possible value. When the midday sun disappeared for a time behind the gray-lined, pillowy clouds Mike felt a chill of superstitious fear, feeling like some character out of a horror movie set. He thought of vampires slumbering in boxes of dirt in the manse's basement. The only things missing to match Bram Stoker's bestseller were the castellated parapets, sub-alpine trees, and wild Transylvanian peaks, though Aurora thought the place creepier than any gothic ruin he'd ever seen: A modern-day Carfax abbey cast in a prairie setting. Maybe it was the dark hue of its siding, but this dwelling looked as if it were a thousand years old; it could've been transplanted from Olde England for all he knew. He expected denizens from Night of the Living Dead to shamble out from behind the wreckage. Such were the thoughts of Mike Aurora, 24, as he dug down to an undertaker's depth.

The sun was setting. He hated being stuck down here in this pit, bent over, vulnerable, in this musty-smelling hole. A screaming red-tailed hawk hovered high above the manor's rooftop, *"peeeewing"* its curiosity or perhaps displeasure at Mike's desecration of private property.   So far he'd found one bone which may or may not have been human.   But screw all else.   Maybe the bones had been removed.   Moved elsewhere.

He continued to dig and found nada.   At six and a half feet, Mike, exhausted, gave up and filled in the oblong hole.   He glanced at his Swiss watch and found it was near midnight when he'd finally finished.   His flashlight was almost dead.   Time to get the hell outta here, Mike considered, in no mood for a midnight confrontation with the undead.   *They're back, and ready to party,* he recalled cynically from some recent horror movie – Return of the Living Dead.   His skin crawled, just the same.   Mike Aurora had a George Romero personality and was quite surprised he hadn't scared himself to death.

A rising midnight wind whooshed down through the treetops, swaying the blackish brutes' boughs under a three-quarter-full moon harassed by wispy *aurora borealis.*   A spooky, whispering moan seemed to emanate from the forlorn, old house as if in answer to some demonic reaper seeking out its prey.   Mike, shivering, shuddering, was glad he was leaving now. He was amazed he hadn't witnessed further psychic *anomalies* here since he and Jodi's encounter with the – what? – sheets?   Maybe it takes two to tango. Whatever revenants resided here seemed to be in a catatonic slumber.   Had he seen anything, anything at all, Mike was certain, he would've fled long ago.   Even more surprising was that he and Jodi had witnessed the bizarre manifestation in broad daylight.   Worse yet, chased like children by blobbish, glowing 'sheets'. Maybe they'd been kids in sheets after all?

Yet as Mike struggled into his bomber jacket he watched with growing horror a gradual luminescence of coloured lights, what looked like fireflies, shining phosphorescently from the manor's windows like lanterns.   He seized his shovel and fled, only once stopping to look back over his shoulder from the driveway where his car sat discreetly parked.

A multitude of leering, devilish faces peered back at him from mawing windows, teeth spiky and deadly looking.

****

Back of his house in a thicket of slough and marsh, Mike Aurora torched each vehicle one at a time, then with the aid of a come-along pushed each sorry relic into the burbling, bubbling pond while ravens pestered and cawed from their macabre roosts. The tranquility of the site was disturbed forever by this crime, something local kids would relate with scary stories around late-night campfires, for time immemorial, brooded Mike as he operated his primitive winch. Jodi stood at his side, watching the white, Dodge van disappear into the great pond's muck, exhaling a sigh of relief when its rooftop vanished beneath the water's surface. It had been pushed downhill, over a bank, sluicing into the murky depths after a nail-biting wait and finally sinking beneath the black morass with a burbling sound of resignation. Aurora had plumbed the slough's mucky surface one day with a long pole in a small dinghy. The backwater was remarkably deep; well over fifteen feet in places, including its reed-choked perimeter.

She and Mike had been busy for over a week slashing and chopping away at willows and saplings crowding the old clearing leading to the marshes, to facilitate the automobiles' passage. So far they'd sunk two already without much mishap, although the Mercedes had momentarily snagged on some underwater debris. Beavers had made a mess of the north end of the slough.

One could just as easily refer to it as a lake if it weren't for the swamp-like flora, reflected Aurora, chin resting on his shovel-wielding, gloved hands. The entire episode more than a little resembled Norman Bates' solution in Hitchcock's classic "Psycho." With a good hand-winch (and ten metres of heavy chain) Aurora had eased the vehicles into the pond, working from a tree across the cluttered marsh. He felt like an utter criminal doing it too.

Three down, one to go.

Four days later, the Joe entity invaded Mike's environs once more, having taken a blessed two months' absence. The spook was furious at Aurora's destruction of evidence, growing in ferocity daily, a feat incapable of sustaining before its abduction of the Polish chaplain, Waszowski. Jodi had been absent, so hadn't witnessed the murderous psychic phenomena as it hurled crockery about, ripped typed pages apart and generally wreaked havoc. Aurora, naïvely, had believed the old man's ghost had been appeased by its abduction of the hapless Saskatonian deacon.

Time to lay the old bastard to rest.

June 27, Jo and Mike arranged a covert meeting with a member of an obscure witchcraft sect; an acquaintance whom Jo had known for years, since way back in high school. Mrs. Kate Grandison, a thirtyish, ash-blonde, married woman with three children and a reputation to protect, had reluctantly agreed to meet with them at a coffee shop in Weyburn.

She sat across from them, nervously pleating a napkin while her seven-year-old son Jeffrey squirmed restlessly beside her. Mike explained the situation to her without elaboration, sober-faced, leaving out certain details best left unsaid. The woman had short, cute, bobbed hair and pale blue, almost turquoise eyes on an attractive if unexceptional face which betrayed her unease at being here. Her clothes suggested upper middle-class, possibly bourgeoise, although she was in fact the rural wife of a well-known Weyburn neurologist. Mrs. Grandison, Jodi had explained, was a parapsychologist and member of a secretive sect called Wicca. Mike certainly had heard that name before, although unable to clarify the cult's beliefs (which he thought were a hokey cross between Irish and aboriginal creeds), a much-maligned circle of modern-day witches which he believed dated back to the Middle Ages. However, the name, Grandison, rang a bell for him, because he'd read an article in a local paper last Hallowe'en or thereabouts about her activities as a ghost hunter, of all things. She was a card-carrying member of the Toronto branch of the American Society for Psychic Research. She spoke a fair bit of Druids and ancient religion (picking up Jo's cue), and how her cult had been persecuted during the later Middle Ages.   Kate, as she preferred to be called (herself a professor of psychology), was clearly uncomfortable about talking to a total stranger about her beliefs.   She had an Inquisition mentality, as if expecting Papists or Puritans to burst into the café and apprehend her and her child.   Yet she seemed quite sincere about what she believed in.

The four of them sat at a small aluminum table surrounded by strangers, for the coffee shop was packed. When Kate (one clearly paranoid individual), inquired about and heard of Mike's dreams her curiosity was perked.   She grilled him at length about the names and events which he'd managed to recall.   Jodi and Mike drank Cappuccinos while the seemingly neurotic woman sipped herbal tea.   Her dark-headed son nursed a strawberry milkshake while devouring a cheeseburger. The midsummer's day was mercilessly hot, muggy; everyone sweated despite the party-coloured roadside café's fans whirling overhead.   Outside, the parking lot was crammed tight with cars bouncing miniature suns off of their hoods.

Kate wrinkled her small nose, still debating whether to visit the farm let alone take up Mike and Jodi's case. She sensed there was something they were not telling her. Her guts quivered with foreboding, clearly telling her to leave the case alone.   She couldn't be sure whether these two were on the up and up or a couple of complete loonies.   They looked deceptively normal.   But then they all did!   She hadn't known Jo well in high school during the eighties, had been the waif's senior by four years.   Nor would her husband Matt take kindly to her seeing a pair of good-looking lovers such as these, a wildly jealous man who seemed to think her cult rituals centered on Bacchanalian orgies with strangers.

Furthermore, she had no idea what the two wanted of her.   Theirs was a clear case of poltergeist display, the kind she tended to avoid at all costs.   Kate wasn't a shaman or exorcist who could banish a naughty spirit with some abracadabra mumbo jumbo, no matter what the papers claimed.   She wasn't even a high priestess of her local circle, which consisted of thirteen dedicated professionals and blue-collar workers.   Only the local magi knew the ancient texts needed for recital to lay a troublesome ghost to rest and send it on to the Other Side, a paradise of lush greenery and perpetual sunlight.   Kate suspected the two credulous, shiftless characters scarcely comprehended the religious faith and tenets of Wicca, the egalitarian Mother Goddess druidism of *Ma Gog* (she became quite hot under the collar when Mike righteously informed her that the Gaulish druids were polygynous apes, or shameless homosexuals, their women chattel, barter, as attested by Roman accounts – who the hell was he to say?), Diana, Hecate, Isis and Bridgit just a sampling of Her many guises.   Of course She had a consort too, said Kate, equal in status, though ever mysterious and mischievous as a child (as was She from time to time).   His name was Diágh, she pontificated, Lluddifer, Belinus, Baal, Beelzebub, Krishna, Lugh, Gránnos, Lucifer, Daghda, Tlwydda, Teutates, Yahweh, Mars, Ares, Apollo, Moloch, Allah, Hercules, Hermes (yada, yada, yada), and many others in sundry different languages and badly distorted creeds.   She and He were dozens of deities with various roles, and He and She were One.

Uh-hm, another nutter for sure thought Mike as he listened to Mrs. Grandison's harangue.

Mike and Jodi held hands under the table, nodding, perplexed, but scarcely able to understand Kate's ramblings.   Quite frankly her cult's rituals sounded stupid and meaningless and one couldn't help understand why Christians had persecuted them so and still did in any way they knew how to get away with.   Yet Mike felt that some of their tenets held more truth for him than any religion he'd heard yet, but realized also that their reverence of a feminine principle would put the cult beyond the pale with patriarchal, world cultures.   Also he mistrusted anything too closely allied to the names of

Lucifer and Saturn.

"Do you worship Satan?" asked Mike foolishly out of the blue.   Jodi kicked him in the shin.

The somewhat overweight, yet attractive, middle-aged woman stared coldly for a moment, then started to rise. "I can see where your sympathies lie, perhaps I should leave."

"No, no," Mike uttered hurriedly, apologetically, eyeing the flustered Mrs. Grandison with mysterious, cobalt-blue eyes, "you don't understand, you see it's just that I happen to listen to heavy metal, and wondered where you stand in relation to Him." (Jeez, I sound like some HM devil's disciple myself, Mike berated himself.)

Mrs. Grandison blushed with embarrassment, settling down into the couch-like café seat once more.   She took a sip of her strawberry-flavoured tea, glancing about nervously before answering.

"I believe," said Mrs. Grandison, leaning forward furtively, "as do many of my fellow initiates, that Lucifer was once noble but he was confused and tainted by more primitive societies who began to practice the most barbaric and horrific rituals in his name, as was written by the Greeks and Romans about the Gauls who were monsters, believe me. European witchcraft represented the extinguished faith of continental and British circles of druids, you see, not that of the Gaulish druids nor of the

Scythians, who, as you know, were anyway eradicated by the Romans. Our own cult, who built Stonehenge, Avebury, and the like, however, had, for political reasons, been targeted by the Romans and wrongly painted with the same brush to stem Celtic resistance and to gain access to the enormous slave and mineral wealth of the north. And that the Gaels provided Julius Caesar and his despicable ilk with just the damning propaganda that he wanted to hear, and that the Gauls were our enemies and Caesar's none-too-numerous allies. So they branded us Gauls too."

Mrs. Grandison sat back, smiling smugly, certain of her guru's divine truth thought Mike as he raised an eyebrow. Her tale intrigued him just the same, echoing his own conviction, for he'd come to associate the semi-mythical druids with all that he'd grown to admire: a fanatical hatred of world religions and a fervent death wish against urbane society.

Jodi grasped his sleeve and urged him to tell Kate of the weird cross-lingual experience they'd shared the night they first met.

Mike, reluctantly, explained of his momentary lapse into an alien tongue while Mrs. Grandison's eyes narrowed with half-suppressed disbelief. Then she laughed in scorn.

"Tell me, then," demanded Mike aggressively, "what

lingo does your little   cult speak during your rituals?"

The pink-faced, amused woman smiled perplexedly. "Why, English, what else?"

"No secret language?" Jo interjected.

Kate's smile faltered.   Her eyes became frosty and aloof.   "That's a secret even I'm not at liberty to discuss," she answered falteringly, still sipping then finally draining her tea.

"Why not?" demanded Aurora.   He liked seeing her on the hot seat.

"Our prayer speech, you mean?"   Kate stammered, suppressing a cough.   She meant to deflect the subject, but Aurora's incredulous, challenging tone had touched a nerve.   "Because we still fear the Church!" she hissed.

"You've got nothing to fear from us, we're athiests," Mike remarked with a toothy, self-satisfied grin.   Jodi glared at him and said "Speak for yourself."

Mrs. Grandison considered this for a long, tense moment.

"I don't speak it except for one or two passages," admitted Kate at last, "but the Communion speech uttered by our coven master and his consort is rumoured to be *Cumbrian*, an early dialect of Old Welsh, possibly an even older and more complex version, a close relative of Breton and extinct Cornish and nowadays called insular Brythonic. A very difficult and archaic language."

Then Mike uttered a sentence which left Kate and Jodi flabbergasted. Kate recovered from her discomposure and accepted a saucer of cherry pie from an approaching waitress.

"Where did you learn Welsh?" queried Kate nonchalantly as she took a bite of her pie.

"I didn't," Mike responded.

"I admit I've been reading a book on Welsh grammar," began Mike with a halting laugh, "but by no means have I learned to speak or understand it. I tell you, with no bullshit, that I have no idea how I learned to speak it. But over the past few months I've begun to transform into someone else..."

Kate was intrigued but mystified. Who were these people anyway? Even Jodi seemed changed from what Kate remembered of her from grade school. Aurora's soul transmigration, if this was a genuine case of spirit possession, seemed a fascinating and ground-breaking study to suggest to the Canadian branch of the A.S.P.R. which documented paranormal activity around the world. She knew a fellow parapsychologist in Winnepeg who might be willing to study and compare Mr. Aurora's bizarre claims from a psychology viewpoint if Mike consented.

"I am very interested in your case," responded Kate at last, wiping her lips with a napkin. Her son Jeffrey had finished his meal and was becoming restless. "I would have to speak with the coven leader before any cleansing rituals or laying on of hands could take place. Ridding a residence of demonic revenants can be an *extremely* dangerous, and emotionally draining, experience. I've only once before been involved with a coven exorcism."

Mike sighed. "What's your fee," he asked resignedly.

"We have no fee," replied Mrs. Grandison, "all we ask is that our names and methods remain anonymous. We have no financial affiliations with the general public whatsoever, and would prefer to keep it that way. As you probably know, communal covens are small and, of course, completely confidential."

Mike nodded his appreciation.

"I think I like your religion already," said he with a slowly spreading grin. Kate responded in kind, suddenly envying Jodi Andersen's barbarously handsome boyfriend and wondered what kind of sex-life they had. Her own husband was a fortyish, unromantic boor.

Kate glanced at her watch, then ended the meeting, saying she had to be at the local school to pick up her eight-year-old daughter Samantha at 3:00 o'clock to take the kid to piano lessons. However, Mrs. Grandison, beaming, promised to visit Mike's farm after shaking hands with them both and exchanging addresses, phone numbers, and directions as she slung her mahogany brown purse over her shoulder.   She made an appointment for Saturday, July 18.

＊＊＊＊＊＊＊＊＊＊＊＊＊＊＊＊＊＊＊＊＊＊＊＊＊＊＊＊

Mike had a sinking feeling when he saw the blue-and-white police cruiser in his yard as he and Jodi pulled into the drive.   In fact his belly hit rock bottom and for a moment he couldn't breathe.

"Oh, my God," murmured Jodi with a gasp.

Mike regained his composure, still feeling queasy but taking command.

"Don't say nothing," he advised. "You don't know anything about what went on. You're just my girlfriend come down for the weekend. So stay calm. They're not gonna search the place unless they have a warrant."

Jodi felt like bolting.   Or vomiting.   Or both.

A tall, crew-cut, graying constable strolled about the police car, hat-less, whistling, while his partner sat inside and swung around to eye Mike's approaching Impala.

Each had the typical, close-cropped, police-academy haircut beneath their high caps. The loitering officer outside the patrol car stood expectantly, bright yellow stripes down the sides of his black trousers shining glaringly as hot sun-rays radiated from clear blue skies. His mustache, matching his dirty-gray hair, was short and neatly trimmed. He had lips like Mick Jagger. His darkish partner inside the cruiser had a huge beak of a nose and beady eyes, and was ugly as sin. Mike thought he looked Semitic, not his favourite race. He, too, exited the police cruiser as Mike and Jodi did likewise.

Mike fought to remain cool as he approached the cruiser, its radio crackling noisily as it fed a steady stream of dispatch information, making him feel uneasier by the second.

The graying cop – officer Michaelson – drew out his pen and a notepad upon introducing himself and the even taller Saudi-looking constable Sawedi who'd joined them, then began questioning Mike about a certain Anglican minister whom had last been known to visit the farm as indicated by the missing Pole's diocese schedule-log. Constable Michaelson raised an eyebrow but said nothing when Aurora informed him of the chaplain's intention to hold an exorcism (?) in the old farmhouse. And yes, the brief ceremony had gone just fine (no, actually, officer, he was spirited away by a malevolent poltergeist, haven't seen him since), and the little chaplain had left around 2:30 in the afternoon.   Yes, he drove a newish, metallic-gray Ford Esprit.   Haunted by a poltergeist, you say?   But no police investigation about the alleged rappings, groans, and door opening and closings witnessed and heard at all hours.   No soundings or measurements taken to ascertain whether an intruder or merely pranksters were using secret hidey-holes or passages?   Very unusual story.   (This guy's an obvious nut.)

Somehow Mike kept his grip on the situation, though he sensed the two police officers didn't believe a word of his story and even wondered if they had wandered about the farm while he was absent, peeking into windows and checking for signs of a late-model Ford Esprit hatchback of a deceased (?) Polish chaplain.   The thought of the two constables stumbling onto the numerous graves in the woods almost made Aurora break into a cold sweat. Jodi remained silent, looking guileless, only responding when one of the P.C.'s directed certain queries at her. Fortunately, Mike thought, the house and derelict outbuildings were securely locked, but Christ, what about the oblique presence of surveillance cameras?   Explain that one.   Although Mike had gone to great pains to conceal the slowly-panning white cameras (which only operated at night) he was certain that close scrutiny of the trees and foliage would locate the give-away sentinels. Or maybe the Gestapo had ventured behind the flintstone/clapboard former cabin and followed the wide swath through the underbrush, which came out onto a swamp. Perhaps they had taken note of the tire tracks leading into the morass, or the burn marks in the grass.

If the officers had, they kept their counsel to themselves.

Inside the house Mike could hear his German shepherd yiping and scratching frantically. The damned mutt must've got accidentally locked-in this morning when he and Jo had left for Weyburn, which was one bloody long drive. Mike anticipated dog crap all over the place. It had certainly occurred to him, many a time, that the malignant entities which haunted the old farmhouse might harm the dog or spirit Shelley away into never-never land.

"Mind if we look around a bit?" asked the ruddy-faced, mustachioed elder constable, sergeant Michaelson, closely scrutinizing Mike's body language for signs of fear.

"No, not at all," said Mike, fervently praying the obscurely situated clearing back of the house would not be discovered.

Mike and Jodi disappeared into the house, almost

panicking as the policemen meandered off toward the corrals, conversing loudly as they inspected Aurora's inquisitive Toggenbergs, Nubians, and their offspring. Obviously theirs was only a preliminary investigation, Mike reassured himself, for the constables hadn't flashed the search warrant he'd so dreaded.   Much of the stash had been dragged back into the bushes, like so much refuse; bikes, hardware, cartons of this and that left underneath great swaths of plastic – now, only a fraction of the farm's horrible booty remained in the outbuildings. Had he been a little less cunning he might've been certain of the officers discovery of the farm's stash of stolen goods and the wide clearing leading to the marsh. However, ever on the ball, Mike had erased all visible signs of old tire treads within the yard and done his utmost to camouflage those leading to the swampy wetlands behind his house.   He'd piled boughs and branches and a large mass of old brushwood across the clearing's entrance, as well as standing up felled trees and propping them against others over the trail to make it look natural and untouched.   This would only be a temporary measure; effective only until their leaves dried up and fell away.   Unfortunately he realized that experienced eyes would likely uncover the ruse.

All he could do was watch, and wait.

He had one thing going for him, however; behind his

uncle'se house, the thistles, nettles, and thorn thickets were crawling all over the place, which had originally been a pig pen. A recent heavy rain had turned the fenced area into a quagmire, fence posts leaning drunkenly, as if mired in a small lagoon. It would take brave men, indeed, to venture into that muck, which would easily be up to one's ankles. When he and Jo had disposed of the incriminating evidence the open corral enclosure had been parched and dry, its surface webbed with tiny cracks this spring. Let the two R.C.M.P. bozos walk into the swampy muck.

After half an hour of idle wanderings, the uniformed R.C.M.P returned, exchanging a few words with Mike at his doorstep, then left. Aurora closed the door on them, then let out a huge sigh of relief.

****

Immediately upon entering his house Mrs. Grandison felt an overwhelming surge of psychic power accumulating around the rustic homestead. Although no adept (to her knowledge, anyway) Kate sensed a mildly senile "something" hovering just on the edge of her subconscience. She was well aware that Aurora was a hard-core heavy metal nutbar, something she meant to discourage him from, for she felt it may have a bearing on the alleged poltergeist's mischievous personality, maybe even triggering the haunting. She knew that many heavy metal rock idols (Ozzy Osbourne, Blackie Lawless, yada, yada, yada) dabbled in Satanism and black magic, and infiltrated their records with backward messages which worked on the subconscious alter-ego. Kate knew that many gospel albums had been implicated as well. A glance around Mike's living room told her that he was a serious degenerate who virtually thrived on occult material and dark subjects. He had one *very* strange poster of some hideous, insectile, alien monstrosity up on his wall, as well as many cheese-cake, half-naked, nubile models in suggestive poses. She felt uneasy around such people and tended to avoid them, although her sect seemed to draw them like magnets. Scattered around his living room were trashy, paperback horror novels and sexy pin-ups of half-nude hussies in silky lingerie which revealed a breast, thigh, or shoulder suggestively enough to make her blush. Kate felt wildly jealous over such models' beauty and lack of inhibition. Mike was an aspiring writer, he'd told her. Another would be, could be, should be, holier-than-thou, goofy messenger of – what? A glance at Aurora's open cassette case gave her a disturbing tally of popular modern hard rock from grunge to thrash – shockingly demented names like Megadeth, Judas Priest, Slayer, Black Sabbath, W.A.S.P., Grim Reaper, Twisted Sister, Iron Maiden, the like. All notorious devil worshippers. Kate wanted to leave.

Then the vision hit her.

It slammed into her head like a wrecking ball, demolishing Mrs. Grandison's concrete barrier of psychic protection she'd built to counter such haunted locales. Her coven had drawn a circle of protection last night for her security. But the horrific vision which flashed across her mind for a brief moment devastated Kate, forcing her to slump down into a chair. The grisly flashback had occurred near the stairs.

Kate sagged into a chair in the tiled kitchen, gasping for breath and holding her forehead as if having suddenly incurred a splitting headache. Mike and Jodi exchanged worried glances, for neither had expected Mrs. Grandison to react so violently and so quickly to the homestead's gloomy atmosphere and had been told by her that she was neither experienced medium nor fully-qualified doctor of parapsychology; rather, an apprentice.

Kate regained her breath, glancing frightfully around the nearby living room and scullery.

"I just witnessed a murder re-enacted in your living room," blurted Kate, looking up at Mike with frightened, sincere blue eyes. "A – a multiple murder – four men with balaclavas over their heads. I-I-I saw a spurt of machine-gun fire from somewhere to the right of that clock over there; though the house was too dark to make out the murderer's face. It happened some time ago, I believe, before your arrival." (The thought never occurred to her that it had been Mike pulling the trigger, or that it had happened fairly recently!)   However, the dark-room-like- image which had flashed across her brain like a video replay, devoid of sound, had given Kate a horrendous, eyeblink glimpse of blood-spattered walls and a stitchwork pattern of bullet-ridden, jerking bodies in living colour.

Mrs. Grandison questioned Mike at length about the house's history, his uncle and forebears, but found his reticence and lack of knowledge of the dwelling's past baffling and more than a trifle disturbing.   The way he exchanged glances with his tongue-in-cheek girlfriend suggested to Kate that there was something being withheld from her.

Just out of curiosity, Kate suggested she stay overnight, try to contact the unfortunate revenant and lay his or her spirit to rest.   (Yeah, right!)   She had some brief experience with channeling on paper, said Kate, had witnessed in her fledgling witchcraft seminary professional and world-renowned exorcists and amateur ghost hunters displaying their skills for the credulous and not-so-credulous.   She herself could testify to some very baffling phenomena, which reinforced her belief in the Hereafter.

Mike and Jodi seemed to dislike the idea of Kate staying the night at his uncle's house, as if expecting some bogey might carry her off to some Shadow Zone. Had anyone been harmed here during Mike's stay? she asked.   No.   (Absolutely not: Why, old uncle Joe wouldn't hurt a hair on a child's head!)   Then surely the house was safe; after all, it wasn't some battlemented Tudor-era mansion literally oozing evil from its fabric, was it?, no castellated hall with statuary tumbling from its parapets, she reasoned.   To be honest, explained Mrs. Grandison, from the outside, the old farmhouse seemed quite charming and harmless-looking.   It was only once inside that one felt its oppressive atmosphere of menace. She explained (almost convincing herself) that whatever images or noises heard were merely 'recordings' of past miseries on the cosmic ether, not reality, nothing to be afraid of unless one let one's mind be influenced by malign forces. Mike, taciturn as ever, hadn't even apprised her of the manic goings-on when his pals were down last summer, nor of the Polish deacon's abduction by an extra-dimensional entity only weeks previous. Aurora seemed to resent her saying that his choice of music was somehow unhealthy, that it could influence whatever powers infested the house.   For all they knew the place might've been built on some ancient Indian burial ground.

Haya, haya, haya, haya...

Although badly shaken, Kate was more determined than ever to see this thing through, for without doubt, she had just experienced genuine, occult phenomena, a rare case of precognition from some past tragedy.   Yet she was baffled as to why Aurora's abode lacked electricity, the basic amenities of life (he didn't seem to be a pauper), especially since she'd noticed, earlier, his amazing wind turbine high above the steep, peaked rooftop and the perplexing fact that Jodi and Mike used candles and kerosene lamps on dark, overcast days such as this. Such conditions were playing right into the demon's hands.   A sudden cloudburst sent a clattering of rain down overhead.   When Kate remarked on this, Mike chuckled and told her his generator magneto had burnt out, and that in the meantime he was utilizing a tiny, battery-operated AC inverter for small appliances, stereo, TV, the like, as well as a combustion-engine generator which was a real gas guzzler, believe-a-me you. Lighting was far too much drain for a cheap, transistorized, 600-watt power source, he informed her. Mike was still waiting for the company he'd purchased the little wind turbine from to send him the parts, for its warranty had (typically) expired ten days before the magneto had fused itself from some unknown cause or mechanical flaw.

They sat the remainder of the afternoon away drinking coffee, deep in conversation, skies looking darker by the hour. A heavy midsummer's rainstorm was forecast, and storm warnings broadcast over the radio earlier. Aurora didn't have TV reception although he was seriously considering getting ahold of a large VHF antenna. (He nearly mentioned he had a stolen satellite dish which he wanted to install, but hadn't a rat's inkling how, before catching himself.) The subject turned to Mike's eccentric, deceased uncle Joe, who seemed to prefer living in the Dark Ages, Kate remarked. Mike, tight lipped, agreed. Straying away from the touchy subject of his uncle Joe, Aurora steered the conversation deftly toward his nearly finished first novel, a tale of contemporary horror and intrigue. Oh, no, not another overworked vampire theme, Kate thought to herself.

With an almost fatherly pride, Mike showed her a daunting pile of rejection letters from numerous small presses and multi-national publishing giants alike, as if unaware that his trashy novel would almost certainly never be published.   Didn't he know that only university professors, reporters, gays and feminists were being published these days?   Oh, and grammar teachers.   No wonder contemporary fiction was so boring, pontificated Mike.   One needed to rub shoulders with editors or the wealthy to launch a first novel nowadays.   Yup, it was a dog-eat-dog, corporate sharks' world, acknowledged Mike, and by God if he were in power he'd depopulate it utterly. Seriously. Kate sensed a strong streak of anti-Semitism or at the very least fascism in Aurora's demented philosophy. He confessed to having been reading Macchiaveli's *"Prince."*   Jodi, whom Kate had struck up a friendship with only recently though having known her for years, presented to the world a kindly, dreamy eyed, conservative personality.

However Kate realized that Mike Aurora had a definite obsession with prehistory, a subject he had only taken to recently.   Why was this?, she probed.   He and Mrs. G. shared an almost parallel and fanatical zeal for druidism and anti-Christian dogma.   Soon drinks were being poured, their blood warmed by a shot of whiskey, a six-pack of beer.   Aurora loved nothing better than a glowering, cloudy afternoon of Jew-bashing, especially ridiculing or condemning the Old Testament, blaming their pacifism for the Holocaust and their Judeo-Christian disciples and prophets, even Jesus Christ himself, for the centuries of rabid anti-Semitism.   Wasn't it their own breakaway sect, the *Essenes*, that started the pogroms against Jews?   Kate found Mike's racist theories really too much.   Although despising Christianity and all its imitators, she understood Aurora's philosophy to be extremely dangerous, for he proudly and jokingly referred to himself as the Antichrist after a couple of beers.   If ever such a man got into world power there'd be a pogrom the likes of which the world had never seen. He'd make Hitler seem like someone you'd wanna have for your grandpa, Kate surmised privately. His creed was aimed at others, rather than Jews. Not, like mad Adolf Hitler, of Jewish-descended agnostics, but of Muslims, aborigines, modern Indo-Europeans of the old mentality, rapists, serial killers, gays, stalkers, molesters, and all those who refused to adhere to Mike's New World Order. Or nearly everyone.   Even Jodi spoke up to ridicule Aurora's insane master plan, for if he had his way, why, there'd be no one left.   He spoke of eliminating entire cultures with chemical weapons and repopulating the planet with a race of Caucasian supermen, of nuking the Middle East, if necessary.   It became quite apparent to Mrs. Grandison that Mike was quite unbalanced.   In his own way he was just as arrogant as any Old World male chauvinist, even advocating extermination of all gay men. Why only gay men, countered Andersen peevishly, why not lesbians, children, Jews, monkeys.   The answer, replied Mike sagely (in his opinion), was that bisexuality was, and still is, prevalent in all male-dominated primitive societies such as the Greco-Romans, not to mention India and Mesopotamia, or Africa and Siberia. He argued with a smug, righteous smile that only a relatively taboo-free society could initiate new technology – a race of god-like men like the ancient Britons or Sarmatians (madness settling in, thought Kate wearily), although reluctantly admitting that he couldn't prove any of this.   He was a wacko, quipped Andersen playfully, irrating him, trying to corrupt them with his nutty ideas!   Aurora was too self-confident and self-righteous to be taken aback, only grinning unabashedly.

But Kate had begun to look at him with awe: What a scary politician he'd make!

She had never heard anyone express her own muddled thoughts as he did.

Around five o'clock Mike began supper, something else Kate thought unusual for his generation, for most she'd met lazed around the house watching TV while wifey cooked supper, or else were bachelor slobs.   Mike Aurora was neither, it seemed, though certainly no Mr. Clean, at least not by her standards.   She'd learned that he and Jo no longer lived together and about the awful details of Jodi's sexual harassment while the poltergeist was present. The invisible intruder would pinch, bite, and try to join her in the outdoor shower. She'd found this too much. Kate, in turn, withdrew an impressive portfolio of photos and newspaper articles or notes from prestigious psychic journals from her attaché case, detailing genuine spirit manifestations around the globe, a thoroughly professional woman with short, ninetyish hair and diamond earrings. Mike appreciated the fact that she didn't evangelise, or try to convert them in any way. Unlike Jehovah's Witnesses nutbars and some other fanatical organizations, the followers of Wicca don't go door to door explaining their mission to sway the world to Jesus, or the guru Oombo Boombo, or whoever, a definite handicap to the druidism movement if it wanted to take over the world, remarked Kate frankly. Even today they were still blatantly prejudiced against by government and targeted by evangelical Christian sects, such as the Pentecosts, Presbyterians, J. Witnesses, Baptists, etc., all who labelled the Old Religion as Satan's disciples. (All of which would be consigned to the flames of an electric funeral pyre if Mike's ilk had their way, he pointed out, as vengeance for the Holocaust, child molestations, and womens' rights abuses suffered since time immemorial.) He would be the Redeemer, if fate willed it. He candidly, shockingly remarked, his back to them while standing at the cupboard, that he'd love to become known as the Impaler, the Stalin of his time.

The trio ate supper in silence, anticipating a grisly Otherworldly confrontation come nightfall. Jodi had assisted her ex preparing beef curry and rice along with boiled California white potatoes, beets, and salad. Kate told them of her career as a parapsychologist under the tutorship of a Dr. Greg Schumaeker of Regina university after the dishes were placed in the sink. She'd been involved with a team of scientists and hand-picked laymen responsible for unmasking (literally) and debunking two well-known mediums and spirit photographers from the States.

Kate then unfolded a baroque-looking ouija board from her deep purple attaché case, explaining the weird alphabet-inscribed board's function and purpose. Mike eyed the thing dubiously, unsure whether he wanted a doctor of parapsychology poking into the place's ether, discovering the terrible secret of the sheds which it harboured and the multiple murders he'd unwittingly commited. If ever Kate Grandison found out, he was certain she would run screaming to the police. No one – *no one* – must find out about uncle Joe and his smuggler buddies. Only Jodi knew of the bodies buried at old Nimchattan house – one of the factors influencing her decision to leave. Mike might tip the police off concerning the alleged child murders commited at the Nimchattan dwelling (though in no way incriminating those folks, who, as far as Mike knew, were oblivious of Joe's deeds), he didn't know.

When it grew dark, Mike became nervous. What an incredible risk he was taking by inviting this nosy parapsychologist-in-training out to the farm, for surely uncle Joe would find it easy to spirit this attractive, married woman away to God knows where. (He hadn't even ascertained what the devilish old spook had done with the Polish chaplain.) Certainly these last five days the demented entity had been unusually quiet, no longer hurling crockery about, or opening and closing windows, nor thumping on the walls and ceiling. Threats had long since ceased to hold the Disincarnate at bay. Twice Mike had had horrifying wrestling bouts with his unseen antagonist. Over a year ago, he would've laughed you out of the house had such an occurrence been suggested possible. Only thrice had Aurora witnessed genuine, visual manifestations of his uncle's restless shade.

Around nine-thirty he lit the remaining candles and gas lamps (the generator, again, was out of fuel), crossing his fingers furtively and fervently praying the house's horde of spooks might behave themselves, tonight. A moaning wind *"w-h-o-o-o-s-h-e-d"* around the living-room window while a pattering of sudden rain tapped on the roof's shingles. The derelict farmhouse's roof timbers groaned and creaked overhead like an unseaworthy Spanish galleon, buffeted by a bullyingly increasing north wind. Kate and Jodi settled themselves nervously into armchairs, quietly anticipating a circle of hands which Mrs. Grandison had earlier suggested. A séance. How corny, thought Mike as he secured his unfinished manuscript inside a small, white safe with combination lock. The blunt-cornered safe sat on the hardwood floor opposite Kate, Jodi, and Mike's stereo stand.

They sat uneasily in a bluish circle of candlelight, holding hands on the cool, bare, hardwood floor. Two other sources of light had been doused, or where in the process of being so. Buxom, bikini-clad women stared down unnervingly from pin-ups on the walls. Kate was surprised Aurora didn't have a pentagram painted on his wall. Ahead of her a lone, log-cabin-style wall (a remnant of the original building), unpainted and unadorned, confronted Kate's view with its rough, mud-filled ugliness. Chinks had eons ago been plastered with sphagnum moss and mud now crumbly and dry. She found it odd that he hadn't bothered to plaster-over or panel the eyesore. Beyond that, Mike explained, lay the root cellar. The other sections had been paneled recently with an inexpensive plywood veneer, and then painted. The dark walls gleamed seductively in gaslight with their stunning, coyly smiling, lip-licking pin-up girls which Jodi so hated.

Kate said a short prayer to her archaic Goddess, then summoned the former log cabin's deceased inhabitant/inhabitants to make their presence known. Wind whooshed about eerily outside. Then a heavy metal pounding of thunder shook the rain-sodden night, giving Mrs. G. a momentary scare. Jodi sat wide-eyed and silent. Mike looked mildly pleased, not at all perturbed by the sudden crack of thunder overhead reverberating like Thor hammering at his heavenly anvil. Taran the Thunderer, Celtic god of the underworld, was abroad this night, Mike reflected aloud. Such thoughts brought to mind the ancient Dorians worshipping the storm god in their drystone towers, brochs, in the Caucasus mountains and in Sicily (the famous and ever-mysterious *nuraghi)*. He expected Zeus or Apollo to make a token appearance inside his stuffy, overly warm, Lysol-scented living room, clutching their white togas at the shoulder and demanding who hath summoned. Oops, wrong number, Zeus.

Instead what they received was a foggy emanation materializing before the shocked trio, a nightmarish, shifting rainbow of luminescent, steam-like vapors of Otherworldly light.

Alarmingly the two red candles and lone gas lamp faded to a wan, sickly blue, as if having had their light, their very essence, sucked away.   Jodi slumped into a sudden, comatose slouch.   Kate's head lolled drunkenly from shoulder to shoulder.   She appeared to be in deep trance.   Mike stared about wildly, unable to remove his hand from Kate Grandison's rigid grip.   Jodi's had slipped from his left hand, icy cold and clammy to the touch.   The unearthly room had waned to a frightening, unholy dimness surrounded by oscillating colors reminding him of certain Star Trek reruns he'd seen on television.   A phosphorescent, deep blue of metallic hue radiated sickeningly from the flashing entity taking shape before the petrified-with-fear Aurora.   A dancing, dazzling assemblage of weird flickerings of almost stage-light brilliance gradually lit up the room like a TV screen's artificial glow.   Mike, speechless, watched helplessly as the astonishing apparition took form.

A dark, curvaceous, seemingly confused woman clad in barbaric leathers slowly coalesced from the twinkling, steam-like fog, glancing about bewilderedly at the strange modish paraphernalia of 20th-century existence. A grimacing face, streaked with warpaint, stared about with dismay and horror at Mike's bizarre living-room décor.   The Valkyrie (???) gaped in bafflement at the blown-up images of half-naked women on the walls.   A monstrous proto-Viking broadsword was strapped to her back.   Puzzled, the radiantly beautiful warrioress turned, almost floating, as she surveyed the room with newborn eyes.

"Why hath thou summoned me?" she demanded angrily.   Her voice sounded as if it were filtered through a distance-enhancing, echoing, voice synthesizer.   Mike, terrified, heard her words but understood little of the archaic Old Brythonic dialect.   The phantom pointed a long, slender, accusatory finger at him, repeating her frustrated demand.

"What is this astral plane you call home," enquired the shimmering visitation, her silky voice very far away. *"Why am I here? Why do you gaze at me so, lolling about there like marionettes? Answer me, underlings!"*

The spectre wielded its sword threateningly, advancing in a haze of mist and ice-cold vapor.   Inside the farmhouse, the temperature had plummeted several degrees.   Mike couldn't move, could only gape as the revenant drew its colossal broadsword from its back and aimed its cold steel at his throat.   He felt its solid iron touch his cold-sweating skin, almost burning with its hellish coldness as he flinched away.   Daringly he pushed away Felissa's (?) broad hacking weapon with his free hand.   It felt astoundingly sharp and real.

"Where are my children," called Melissa, her far-away

voice rising in despair and confusion. Her watery gray eyes gazed about the room searchingly, seeing nothing familiar, neither palace walls, ceremonial drinking skulls, nor glowing braziers. *"Conigcad! My husband, where are you?"* The frightening warrior-queen began to sob, then screamed aloud. *"Conig!!!!"*

"I'm here," answered Mike soothingly, sounding foolish in his inadequate English. The ghost screamed again, wailing beseechingly in her alien language. It seemed nobody had told her she was dead.

A howling, frigid wind lashed Aurora's face as a swirling cyclone struck up in the ground floor room, scattering debris about and buffeting the four walls like slapping hands. Felissa Headcrusher began to fade away into a cloak of suddenly warm steam, her plaintive voice receding into the ether.

Only to be instantly replaced by something infinitely more hideous; a searching, dancing quintet of octopus feelers, tentacles, protruding from an oozing blob of what Mike assumed to be ectoplasm! Five, now eight, realistic, gigantic tentacles with deadly, gnawing suckers appeared and groped about the room, slithering toward the three cross-legged participants arrayed out on the floor, one of which who was now awake and scrambling shriekingly for cover. Kate Grandison remained in a comatose state as the slimy, horrible, oozing thing – it was a giant squid Mike suddenly realized! – groped about her clothes and ankles. A prehistoric squid presumably, not to be found in any extant biology text, Mike realized. *Jesus, the thing must be over fifty feet long*, he postulated in a manic, frantic state. A gagging stench of brackish sea water and smelly marine life permeated the sopping-wet living room which was being inundated by saltwater and ocean spray. It was a clever hoax, Mike rationalized, but realistic. Too realistic! Gnawing, python-tightening, surrealism. Somehow his uncle's disembodied spirit, his reanimated persona, or whatever the good-goddamn you wanted to call it, had simulated this mock marine freakshow from hell with startling clarity, right down to the olfactory and visual and tactile senses. It wasn't real.

Sure the Christ felt real.

Rushing into the kitchen, he seized a butcher-knife and cleaver and began hacking futilely at the disincarnate blob's rubbery, sucking tentacles, dismayed as, for each one he lopped off, another grew onto the red-oozing stump to take its place! The slippery monster's tentacles (an octopus, not a squid, he now realized to his growing horror), each as big around as a tree trunk, had dragged the unwitting medium four feet across the room toward its deadly embrace and champing, beak-like mouth. Jodi, instead of screaming hysterically, grabbed a meat cleaver from Mike's hands and started chopping and slashing at the greedy underwater denizen which'd somehow found its way through space and time into Mike's living room. (He'd regretfully stashed his M16 assault-rifle, revolver, Uzi, and other weapons upstairs upon Mrs. Grandison's arrival.) Eight gigantic arms sought diabolically to entangle themselves around Mike and Jo's legs and waist as the two desperados battled the unholy Leviathan, dashing out of harm's way while slashing viciously at the big, lumpish aggressor. Devilfish. Considering the colossal strength of those tentacles, the heroic defenders were faring remarkably well, having sliced off all but two, swollen appendages which jerked Kate toward it in a merciless tug-of-war. Its feelers, fortunately, took some time to rejuvenate to battle its puny, human opponents. A reeking lake of blood covered the floor.

Three feet away from the thing's horrific mouth Mike sawed off the remaining tentacle as the gigantic, lumbering, silent beast from the Underworld sought to devour the entranced Mrs. Grandison while Jodi screamed at her to wake up. Sticky, sickeningly realistic blood sopped onto the three bewildered victims' clothes, painting their fabric a gaudy, disgusting, gleaming scarlet red. Disarmed, disabled, the seemingly grinning hell-beast slothed about its quivering, enormous, defenseless body.

Suddenly there was nothing and Aurora was plunging his butcher knife into a decayed, punky, log-built wall. From behind him he heard Jodi sob in horror and relief. And a gruff, demonic voice overhead.

"You're only living on borrowed time, so defend...fend...fend...fend...fend..."

The demented, Satanic voice trailed off into oblivion like a record player abruptly unplugged.

The kerosene gas lamp, miraculously still upright, flickered back to life.

Mike's living room floor was once again spotless and dry, defying all metaphysical laws.   No blood on their clothes or on their weapons.   Mrs. Grandison stared about in bewilderment.   Remarkably unhurt.   Aurora looked like a mad slasher standing there beside the staircase with his butcher knife raised.   His wild-haired shadow cast a demented, outstretched visage upon the rustic, former log cabin's wall.

A   veritable deluge of rain outside poured down upon the house, creating huge mud puddles in the darkened farmyard.   Mike put his gleaming, unbloodied butcher knife down and helped Jo move the emotionally drained medium into a bouncy beanbag chair.   Kate lolled about on the low vinyl chair, eyes droopy and her body numb with cold and fatigue.   She had no inkling of what had just happened.   No signs of the monumental struggle were apparent in the well-lit, candle- and gas-fumed room.   Nor had she any particular message to report from the Other Side, although her intentions had been to do just that.   Kate wanted very much to communicate with the recent dead, something she'd never done. Aurora brought her a glass of water to sip before settling on his haunches beside his pasty-looking girlfriend.

"What happened?" asked Kate puzzledly.

"You summoned up something from the Netherworld," replied Mike with frosty blue eyes, tapping his fingers listlessly on his haunches.   "A demon."

"A…"

"A demon," Mike emphasized.   He stood up, describing the monster's dimensions.   "It was about yea high, had eight squid-like tentacles – with suckers – and two tiny, protruding red eyes and had the strength of ten men. Quite frankly, you're lucky to be alive, Mrs. Grandison. The thing looked for all the world like a giant, thirty- to fifty-foot, deep-water octopus, Mrs. G.   No, for all the world it _was_ a giant, ocean octopus."

Kate seemed content to leave it at that, giving a noticeable shudder as she glanced around the room with newborn eyes.   A fiend from hell had been here.   She thankfully hadn't experienced the pungent smell of seaweed, saltwater, blood, and fishy marine life which normally inhabited the darkest ocean depths. Whatever powers infested this house must have tremendous influence on people's minds thought Kate, not only to leave her in a state of temporary, catatonic shock but also introducing tactile hallucinations to one's mind.

Then Mike told her and Jo of the first bizarre manifestation they'd missed, a nightmarish prehistoric, Bronze Age, or Dark Ages' visage of some pre-Celtic goddess or possibly an authentic warrior queen whom had drawn her mighty Germanic broadsword and had even attempted to communicate with him in her strange, forgotten language whose makeup seemed quite unintelligible. She'd been an exceptionally tall woman he explained, lean but muscular, dressed in tanned leathers, with long, untamed, rich brown hair flowing wildly from her shoulders; she had full, sensuous lips and a rather long, sharply pointed nose and a square jaw ending in a dainty little chin. Except for the green eyes, she looked a lot like Jo (and one of the most beautiful, lusty women he'd ever laid eyes on). He suggested the name Melissa, one which had occurred frequently in his dreams.

Kate jotted down details of Jodi and Mike's bizarre experience, noting sensory as well as audile sensations during the alleged manifestations as she scribbled in her crimson notepad with an expensive, ball-point pen. Jodi sat in a flower-embroidered, beige rocker twisting her hands nervously, face ashen. Large shadows showed beneath her big, heavily mascaraed eyes (which now looked pale green in candlelight, to Mike's unease). Aurora stood motionless beside the recently repaired staircase, hand on a bulbous balustrade.

"And nothing else occurred?" asked Kate. "No messages, statements of any kind?"

"None."

Kate pondered this for some length, perplexed and mystified over these seemingly random, spontaneous recurrences of paranormal phenomena, many which seemed to defy common logic. Aurora had said something about the woman, Melissa, calling for her children: How did he explain being able to partially understand, yet not entirely, an ancient language extinct for over three millenium, one which he doggedly insisted was over *three hundred thousand* years old! The full story here was missing; why should a cranky old man return to torment a nephew he'd never met? Was the farm situated on an ancient Indian burial ground or some other localized high-energy hot spot, as Mike suggested earlier? A system of ley lines? Had genuine murders actually happened here and could she prove it?

Outside it continued to rain cats and dogs. A heavy gust of westerly wind slammed into the old farmhouse, causing the living-room window to momentarily rattle. A berserk wind-chime out on the verandah tinkled spookily. The three red candles were burning low in their silver candlesticks, atop a dresser.

Candles flickered, curtains shimmered; Mike's home had a noticeable and uncomfortably cool draft.

A deafening explosion of thunder boomed across pitch-black skies like cannon, receding slowly with a malcontent grumble towards the east. Halo-like ball lightning momentarily lit up the night sky in the distance on a flashing horizon. The storm showed little sign of abating. Then, surprisingly, and to Mike's dismay, big hailstones began assailing the shingled roof, promising certain ruin for his struggling garden plants. The hail grew to the size of golf balls, lasting for about ten minutes before petering out. Mike swore like a sailor who'd just been put in the brig.

Everyone, awed by this majestic show of brute force nature was displaying, remained silent.

And listened.

Tic-toc, tic-toc, tic-toc…

The antique grandfather clock stopped.

They listened expectantly, unnerved, waiting for something monumental to happen. Kate noted a dramatic drop in temperature inside the house in her notepad. The rain squall had stopped.

One by one the candles were snuffed out as if by some invisible agency, as if someone had blown them out. Only the dimly burning, bronze-hued kerosene lamp remained alight.

"Is there a Presence here?" Kate asked aloud, her authoritative voice sounding oddly loud in that tomb-like silence.

Only dead silence answered her query.

Mike Aurora lit a match, watching, dismayed, as it quickly faded to a wan blue, then disappeared. His spot over by the staircase seemed especially swamped in shadow. The single gas lamp failed to illuminate the inky stairwell's glossy, hardwood banisters. Mike remembered with an uncomfortable, goose-bump shudder that this very spot he was standing was where two of he and Jo's attackers had been gunned down, peppered with machine-gun fire that fateful night. He had mowed them down with such deadly vindictiveness that afterwards he'd been shocked and sickened by his own murderous, hidden impulses. Those men had had families, friends, girlfriends or wives obviously who would grieve for and wonder what had happened to the four masked men, even if they had been led astray by organized crime (and, if uncle Joe's diary wasn't pulling his leg, had been accessories and/or accomplices to numerous child abductions, rape, and murder). Aurora had looked up the men's addresses, noted the names and phone-numbers of the victims' associates.

A little girl appeared at Mike's side.

She gazed up at him with quizzical, colorless eyes, seeming to radiate a yellowish-orange glow all along her body.   Her hair was long, black and curly, her little flower-patterned, indigo dress wrinkled and faded.

"Please, sir, I need to find my way home," the tiny waif pleaded with expectant eyes. "Can you help me?"

Mrs. Grandison gasped aloud and rose to her feet, stepping cautiously toward the lost child.   Jo soundlessly vacated her armchair and moved almost protectively to Mike's side, gazing down upon the little girl with astonishment and fear.

"Hello, little girl," Kate murmured unalarmingly. "Are you lost? Can't you find the Light?"

"I'm lookin' for me mummy and daddy," replied the little imp crabbishly, rubbing her big eyes as if crying. The radiant being spoke with a pronounced Cockney accent, perhaps a London dialect, Mike surmised.

"Where's home, kid?" enquired Mike soothingly.   He towered over her like some Viking frost giant.

The little waif turned and pointed.   "That way," said she. "I live with me mummy and daddy and grampa in Sask-a-toon but I got lost and some men took me away and did bad things to me and left me, and now I can't find my brothers and sisters no more and would you help me find my way home?"

Mrs. Grandison looked up at Mike and Jodi with astonishment.

"What's your name, sweetheart?" Kate asked coaxingly.

"Melissa."

■■
Melissa??

This house seemed to be some strange, occult magnet for lost souls, a type of "Bermuda Triangle" of the dead thought Jodi Andersen to herself.   Clearly no one spirit agency had supreme control over the place, apparently crossing into its ether like pilgrims travelling down a long tunnel and entering through a revolving door.

"What's your last name, hon?"

"Can't remember."

"Do you know where you are right now? Do you know where your parents are?" inquired Kate gently.

"No."

"Do you live alone here?"

"No."   The tiny apparition paused.   "The two bad men who took me away live here."

"Can you tell me their names?" prodded Kate sweetly.

"Ronald and Derek. I don't know their last names. I

don't like them. I hide so they can't find me." Melissa peered about as if seeing the house for the first time.

"Why don't you like them?" persisted Kate.

Melissa hesitated, then glanced from face to face. "Because they hurt me and touched me body. They're mean and nasty and I don't want to talk about it anymore. I'm gonna go now, bye."

The oddly colorless little ghost began to fade before the adults' eyes, suddenly blinking out of sight and leaving the frigid room in total darkness, for, by then, even the lone gas lamp had died.

Immediately the tall, kerosene lantern fluttered to life. Before the apparition's disappearance Kate had reached out to touch the lost little girl's face and been disturbingly surprised when her fingers passed through the spectre's pale visage. Kate's hand now throbbed with icy numbness extending all the way up her elbow.

The trio spent the rest of the night in vain anticipating further paranormal activity.

****

Jodi, Kate, and Mike sat at the kitchen table the next evening in front of an ouija board, a bizarre-looking alphabet board with a moveable pointer on rollers that each participant was to lay hands on (a real hands-on experience, thought Mike grimly).   A single, blue candle lit the dining room.   There was a bloated full moon outside, an auspicious time for a séance, said Kate. She'd timed her arrival with the month's augurs.   A sepulchral, ululating loons' chorus from nearby (where two drowned vehicles lay sunken in a lagoon) raised the hackles on each sitter's neck.   The séance was about to begin.

A spooky, boreal owl's hooting was carried across the trees on a breezy north wind.   Aurora felt more alive at this moment than any he'd ever felt, alert to every pin-drop noise, his every awareness faculty on red alert for queer phenomena.   He'd had his belly-full of ghostly happenings this past year and a half.   He wanted an end to it.   His nanny goats brayed naggingly out in their corrals.   A ceaseless "ribbit, ribbit" chant of frogs' speech escaped from the muskeg-like marshes behind the ancient Saskatchewanian farmhouse.   Let the ceremonies begin.

Kate Grandison uttered a witchy prayer before starting the macabre session.   Then she addressed the house's unseen, numerous   inhabitants loudly, requesting their presence without a whole lot of frills and mumbo-jumbo. Neither Jodi nor Mike had experienced, first-hand, an event such as this before.   Parapsychologist/psychiatrist Kate Grandison had explained the entire process to them.

Whatever personalities manifested themselves through the planchette, warned Kate, they mustn't under any circumstances open their mind to the malevolent spirit beings. The farm had experienced trouble she now realized, and likely some tragedy. If only she knew, reflected Mike. Best she not. He was afraid some disgruntled spook might inform her of Mike's damning role in the affair. At stake were his life as well as Jodi and Kate's, the farm, and all the accumulated stolen property at his disposal. *They're mine!,* Mike told himself. *All the powers of Hell shan't take them from me.*

Lo and behold the pointer began to move, steered either by some unseen presence, or by one of the sitter's subconscience.

Hi, my name is Joe.

Joe Aurora. I raped the little girl Melissa, remember Mike?

Yeah. Yeah. Me and my buddies. You don't wanna know their names, no. Hey Mike, by the way, you better get the ——————— off my land, boy, 'cause I'll kill you. I'll kill you, I'll kill you, I'll kill you, I'll kill you. Nice tits, Jodi.

What is your purpose here, Joe? Why do you remain?

Why not? Got nothing better to do.

Have you any pertinent messages for us, Joe?

Hell, no.   I just wanna bug the hell outta ya.   Mike and Julie especially.

Why do you wish to remain here, Joe.

Pause.

To tell that ——————Mike to get the ———————— off my property before he has himself an accident.

Why?

No answer.

Why, Joe?

No answer.

Are you tormented here, Joe?

Let's just say my soul's burning in hell, lady.   By the way, what the —————'s it to ya?

Michael wants you to leave this place, Joe.

Ha, ha.   Michael is a liar, lady.   He needs me.   He's shot up too many people who've tried to interfere, you know what I mean?

What do you mean?

Christ, you're dense.

Oh – gotta go, dudes.   The royal bitch herself is a-comin'.

Long pause.

Hello, Mike.

Pause.

Hello.   Who's this?

Pause.

Melissa Headcrusher, queen of the Amazons and Sarmatian, Cimmerian, and Vandal Federation and Lord of Circassia.   Conigcat, are you there?   Which of you mortals are my husband's vessel?   Why must I communicate in this dumb language you call English?   'Tis not a speech that I recognize.   Why must we speak backwards?

Backwards?

Yes, backwards!   For example, why must you say "a black pencil" rather than "a pencil black".   It is not rational.

What age are you from, Melissa?

That's Felissa.   What do you mean what age am I from?   What other age is there?

Pause.

The year is 1995, Melissa.

Pause.

Really?   You're kidding, no?

No.   Why do you remain, Melissa?   Have you a message or an errand?

I – I don't know.   However, I do dream.   About that sweet little girl, Mel – Oh, my God, that was me!   That dirty old man!!!   I'll flay him alive with mine own sword when I get loose, I'll roast his flesh, impale him while he lay slowly dying, nail his hands and feet to an oak tree!   I will watch him die a protracted death, suffering, keeping him alive with smelling salts and myrrh!   May Gwoden and Tharan be my witness, may the gods of wrath be at my side!   I swear it shall be done, old man!   Suffer the crucifixion he deserves, when I shall drink his blood as he lay dying!   Oh, yea, and then shall I partake of his flesh to strengthen mine body and soul as in the days of yore!   Thy ravens shall feed upon him, mighty Crom!   Thoran the Thunderer, carry him off on wings of ash to Hel.   For you, this I shall do.

Can you do that, Melissa?

Pause.

No.

Do you know where you are Melissa?

Hades.

Which is?

The Netherlands.   The Shadow Zone.   Twilight Zone.   Purgadair.   Land of Redemption and Eternal Challenges.   The Hall of the Slain, where the warrior-folk eat, drink, and be merry.   Land of Eternal Youth, Crom's domains for those of valour.   Valhalla, where the Valkyries, the warriors of Gwydion, carry the fallen after battle.   But not dead; only awaiting rebirth.

Why do you search for your husband, Melissa?

That's Felissa!

Pause.

To be freed from the Frost Giant's eternal grasp.   I be held by the Gauls' magician Dían Cecht in the land of frost, you know, and only await my faithful Death Lord, Conan, to free me from the evil Fir Bolgs' fifth dimension.

I have to depart now, the Celestial Carpenter calls my name.   *Os gwêlwch 'n dda, iach ti chi!*

Pause.

You fuckers!

Who did this to me?!   Was it you, you sanctimonious little prick!?   Big man, big man, shootin' us in the back with a god-damned assault rifle.   You think you can get away with this, huh?   One tough hombre, big E.   Yo' ass gonna sit in the slammer for 10 to 15, believe a' me you, believe a' me you, boy.   Can't remember your goddamn name but I will, and when I do, mister, I is gonna dismantle you.

Who is speaking, please?

Jake.   Big Jake Cravshaw.   I work – *worked* – at C&S Building Supplies in Regina until one of you peckerheads blew me away.   I won't rest until my murderer is six feet under, let me tell you.

Are you alone, Jake?

Nah.   There's five or six other blokes and some misplaced kids here.

Where are you, Jake?

Right here.   On the table.   Say, what the hell is that goofy game you're playin', anyway?   Some new-fangled board game?   A, B, C, D,….

You do realize that you're dead, don't you, Jake?

Pause.

Ah, jeez, I guess so.   Don't seem like it, ho, ho!   The old man, you know, he ain't got no idea.   Used to be a fine old guy, but he's lost it now.   Don't recognize me at all.   Yep.   By the way, I didn't have nuthin' to do with those kids' deaths.   Tragic thing, Christ.   Derek and Ronald and the old fart they did it.

Who's in control where you are, Jake?

The old man.   Joe.   It's his place, he does all the circus antics.   We don't have no control at all, we just get dragged along.   Like puppets with a hand up our ass.

You don't have any power at all?

Nah.   If I did I'd bust through that board and beat the shit outta ya.   The old man allows us – except for that barbarian lady, she got her own switchboard – to communicate with yous.   Cat Lady, she's the only broad in this haunt who can scare the bejesus out of old Aurora. You see the size of that lady's sword?   She is one good-lookin', Judo-expert mama, I tell ya.

Do you believe in God, Jake?

You betcha.   Believe in God as much as I believe the moon is made of green cheese.   What are you stupid, lady?

What is life like on the Other Side, Mr. Cravshaw? (Jodi asking.)

Dark.

Nothing else?

Pause.

Cramped.

Cramped?

Yeah.   Stuffed inside this house's timbers and fixtures like a cat in a sardine-can.   Uncomfortable as hell. Can hardly move.   Know what I mean?   You know, I haven't talked to anyone in ages, not since one of you blew me away with that Uzi.

Can't you see the Light, Jake?   (Mrs. Grandison.)

Pause.

What light?

The Light which will set you free.   Float to it, Jake. That is your salvation.

Pause.

Jeez, you must be a fruitcake.   There ain't no light here.

Why are you trapped here, Cravshaw?   (Mike.)

You gettin' lippy with me, boy?   Well, I'll tell you, Butthole Surfer, I'm here 'cause the old carpenter, some druid named Dan Cet, cast a spell hundreds of years ago and arranged for this place to become possessed.   Or so the warrior-babe, Melissa, says.   Other than that I have no idea, except that Joe seems to be Dan Cet somehow, don't ask me why.

We'd like you and your friends to leave this place, Jake.   Would you tell Joe that for us?

Sure.   Won't do any good though.   It's up to King Kong and Dan Cet to settle in single combat.   Which one of you is Kong by the way?

No answer.

I am.   (Mike.)

Whose "I"?

Mike Aurora.   I own this farm now.

Pause.

The hell you do.   Joe owns the farm.   You musta shot me.

No answer.

It was you who shot me, wasn't it?

No answer.

****

Thunder once again rumbled ominously across the western sky, promising more rain amid gusts of prairie wind.   Only moments ago the séance had ended when Dían Cecht, a nightmarish Gaelic god created from men's imaginations stormed out into the night.   Balor had blasphemed Mrs. Grandison's religious convictions, the one-eyed, invisible deity desperately trying to sway the fledgling medium's allegiance away from the Great Mother. Balor (or *Baal* to Near Easterners), had attempted ceaselessly to convince them that homosexuality and causeless warfare were alright, that women were mere chattel to be won, sold, and debauched, or traded and sacrificed (along with babies!) to Dághda, Creator of the Universe. But the gods had no power.

Mike, Jodi, and Kate had learned however that Joe Aurora had been senile for the last five years of his miserable life, and that the old codger had taken to demonism like a weasel to a chicken coop. The deceased crony had dabbled for years in black magic, Satanism, and necrophiliac sex-acts with the dead. What dead?, Mrs. Grandison had asked. The unseen antagonist had only jiggled the pointer, as if laughing.

That's for me to know and you to find out, spelled uncle Joe.

All the more eerie as midsummer thunder grumbled threateningly from a distance amidst a silence before the storm. All was quiet now save for the sneaky noise of mice gnawing up in the rafters. There'd been an inexplicable population explosion this summer of the pesky rodents. Nothing Aurora had tried this year (including a cat, which spent most of her time up in a tree) had had its desired effect.   Rats were another problem.

Kate Grandison was more than a little horrified. She'd carefully written down everything the malcontent entities had spelled out on the planchette. (A different device, employing a pencil on rollers, which wrote out the discontented spooks' answers, or complaints.)   The old demon, Baphomet (a.ka. Joe Aurora), had gleefully confided to them that he and his "friends" had partaken in terrible sex acts with children and corpses, had drawn circles after midnight and had summoned the Evil One. Even in this liberal nineties's generation, Kate found Joe Aurora's horrific tales of ritual murders too much to take. How much of the revenant's ramblings were true and not mere tall tales, she wondered (poltergeists were notoriously unreliable when giving testimony, causing many in the parapsychology profession to believe these to be the subconscious 'telekinetic' doings of children or disturbed adults).   Had Satanism been practiced here? Had pedophilia been going on in the region way back in the 50's and 60's at the peak of Joe's life?

More disturbing were the oblique hints Joe and his disembodied friends scattered here and there of his nephew's role in the haunting.   Hadn't Jake Cravshaw (one very disturbed individual) mentioned Aurora shooting him in the back with a submachine gun?   Had he meant old Joe, or Mike, Kate wondered.   If so, who was telling the truth, Mike Aurora or this razzed poltergeist?   And was she in any immediate danger?

The small clock above the propane range showed fifteen minutes to one.   Jodi Andersen yawned sleepily, suggesting they turn in for the night.   There was little chance of old Joe making further nuisance of himself, for the Disincarnate had angrily informed them that he was growing tired of their questioning and that he'd drained his resources earlier and that hadn't they enjoyed his impersonation as a giant sea squid? (Octopus, dumb ass, Mike had retorted.) No, they hadn't, Jodi had snapped bitterly.

Mike dragged out a spare cot for Mrs. Grandison to sleep on, then prepared the bed upstairs for he and Jo, for they didn't dare leave one another alone after what had happened tonight.   Jodi had left behind one of her folding cots as well as much of her furnishings at the farm.   They would sleep upstairs, in the same room. No way could Mike risk losing Kate (or Jodi, for that matter) to some unknown ethosphere.   Obviously uncle Joe felt less antagonistic toward a modern-day witch than he had toward the missing priest.

Or so Mike thought.

Their beds ready, they slept (or tried to).

While uncle Joe looked on.

****

When Mike awoke, the house was in a shambles.

He woke up alone, bewildered.   Neither Kate nor Jodi were in the room.   The place looked like it had been hit by an earthquake.   How had he slept through all this, thought Mike uneasily as he lay in bed, in a daze, surrounded by debris as diverse as kitchen garbage and leaf litter.   He was virtually laying under a layer of last autumn's half-decomposed compost!

Quickly dressing, he rushed downstairs, and, seeing (but not believing) the extent of the havoc which had been wreaked, raced into the kitchen, noting aghast the carnage which had ripped shelves literally from the walls, overturned table and chairs, and smashed his crockery all over the room.   It was like a whirlwind inside the building had struck.   Cupboard doors hung crookedly on their hinges, as if wrested open by some monstrous agency.   Nothing had been left unturned.   Only the propane range had been left standing upright and undamaged, and that only because it was still connected to the gas lines. The living room had been turned topsy-turvy. All his tapes, CD's, books, papers, knick-knacks had been tossed about by some tantrum-throwing, lunatic, disembodied poltergeist who happened to be Mike's dead uncle.

What had happened to Jodi and Kate?

Papers crunched underfoot as Mike wandered, in a daze, back into the parlour. Had they both vanished into some other realm?, thought Mike in a trembling, cold-sweat panic. As he gazed around, a timid knock came from the door. He stepped gingerly over broken glass strewn about the paint-smeared foyer, reaching for the door leading out to the verandah. Why they'd fled while the indoor assault was happening and why he had slept through it Mike hadn't a clue.

He jerked open the door, smiling abashedly.

A towering, decomposing cadaver which tainted the kitchen's air with the fetid, god-awful stench of decay stood before him, dressed in suit and tie. Tweed suit, and tacky, calico tie. Slack-jawed, vacant-eyed, the massive, moth-eaten corpse slouched top-heavily out on the sunlit verandah, its bony-knuckled fist raised lethargically after the knocking. A wide-mawing, skeletal, chin-and-throat grin literally set Mike's hair on end. For a moment he stood petrified. Empty, black eyesockets stared back unseeingly at the young would-be author who stood yammeringly mute inside the messy foyer. The monstrous, leaning corpse, ribs protruding through its meat-decaying, worm-wriggling, shirt-rotted chest and abdomen, stood there silently, grim, and motionless.

Mike slammed the door and turned the lock.

Out on the western-style verandah a tremendous crash indicated the undead ghoul's inexorable, sudden collapse onto the balustrades, its ebbing life spent, whatever evil power controlling it fleeing the exhumed, quickly disintegrating body. It stunk like nothing Aurora had ever had the great misfortune of encountering – the only exception being the last gross, cadaverous relic which Shelly (or somebody) had dug up on Mike's farm.

Uncle Joe's pranks.

Mike raced upstairs for the security of his mechanical death rattler, his purloined AK47 assault rifle.

Outside, there was no sign of the gruesome, once well-dressed cadaver. Somehow, the unholy-smelling mass of rotting meat and splintering, year-old bones had picked itself up and hauled itself off to God knows where. (Or something had.) The ghastly odor of putrifescense still hung about the air. Mike, half gagging, explored the smashed deck's environs thoroughly, noting the busted row of bulbous balustrades where a possibly 200-lb. human corpse had fallen to the crumpled grass below.   No longer had Mike certainty of his much-vaunted assault rifle when he considered how the resurrected corpse had vanished so suddenly; only moments after he'd run upstairs for the weapon.   How to kill that which was already dead?

Aurora raced around the corner of the house, assault rifle in hand, searching high and low for his horrendous visitor from the woods.   Bright, early morning sunlight filtered warmly through the branches of black-mottled, ghost white aspen, peeling paper birch, some of which were mere saplings dotted about the unkept farmyard. He jammed a clip of ammo into the weapon's stock, oblivious of the threat of being seen in broad daylight traipsing about the farm toting an illegal assault rifle. Jodi Andersen and Kate Grandison were nowhere in sight. Had the hulking, undead marauder frightened them off? Or – worse – had the nightmarish (possibly cannibalistic?), exhumed abomination done away with them somehow?   Mike wasn't at all certain that he was not still dreaming.   He shook his head, trying to reorient himself in this hideous montage of reality on this balmy, Monday morning.   Certainly by no known law of nature could he perceive how the long-buried, nine-month-old corpse had been exhumed from its secure, woodland grave.

He checked the barn, calling the women's names. His overloud, bravado voice boomed back unnervingly inside the new-looking, cruck-ceilinged barn, ricocheting off the sheets of galvanized steel overhead. Giant rafters looming above looked big enough to hide an entire refugee family. No one hid behind the rotten hay bales, or the giant, round alfalfa mounds which were slowly disintegrating into mossy, moldy, shapeless heaps. The rank odor of rotted straw and alfalfa mingled in the air in the form of nostril-tickling dust particles.

Where in the world could they have gone?

Nobody stirred near the outbuildings, either. Aurora raised his voice to a bullish roar, anticipating the ladies' crashing arrival through raspberry bushes or spruce like an elk stag uttering his mating call.

No answer.

A flock of mallards however exploded from the nearby swamplands, startled by Mike's sudden tumult. It scared the shit out of him. Starlings flew up in raucous protest. A thin veil of sapling birch, aspen, spruce, and Jack pine screened the bottomlands partially from view, an often dry slough in spots which Mike had sometimes traversed without getting his boots wet. The heady fragrance of rose blossom and wildflowers lingered in the musky air amidst nearby cattail and well-aged manure.

He half-expected to encounter the unbearable stink of a year-old dead man who could at any moment come shambling along with slavering jaws and bloodied, bony-knuckled, desiccated hands.

He found the fully-clothed, ghastly, immobile Hell-fiend sprawled on its back, staring gruesomely up at the bright blue morning skies back of an empty, galvanized-steel grain silo opposite Mike's farmhouse two hundred yards distant.   A gigantic swarm of horseflies alighted on the horrific mass of tattered, moth-eaten cloth and decomposing bone, flesh, and exposed innards. Maggots crawled from the nightmarish carcass's mummified eyesockets, nostrils, and gaping mouth.   Mike felt his guts retch, perilously close to woofing his morning's cookies.   Much of the cadaver's skin, muscles, and tendons had long since been eaten away by beetles and grubs.   How long had this gross thing been exposed to the air, Mike wondered.   He kept his assault rifle trained cautiously on the still corpse lest it leap up from its comfy bed of rotted bedding straw.

The emaciated body lay there spread-eagled on a low mound, just a clothed sack of bone and cartilage, a skeleton really, which looked to Mike's mortified eyes more hideous than any late-night feature creature he'd ever seen.   And he'd seen plenty.   More ghastly and diabolically real than any which had ever walked the

B-grade horror movies Hollywood had been grinding out since the '50s ('90's horror "classics" were so ludicrously stupid they didn't count to Mike as serious horror flicks). He stood there with his AK47 trained on the horrible salesman of death with a mixture of revulsion and fascination.   What spark of dark powers which drove that grave-denizen to lurch out from its woodland hole, still resided within the empty-craniumed, emotionless husk, this visage from hell?   Had uncle Joe, exhausted from his titanic feat of exhuming the body, then driving the stinking bone-bag across the farmyard like a puppet-master controlling a marionette, succumbed to defeat, or did the cantankerous old man's spirit still cunningly inhabit this sorry-looking, skin-and-bones stickman?

Mike prodded the stiffened cadaver with his foot to make certain it wouldn't rise again, then methodically began piling together dry straw and twigs onto the rank carcass for a makeshift *auto-de-fé*.   He would hold a funeral pyre right here beside this steel grain silo, burn the horrible thing before it became re-animated again. He must do so quick before Jodi and Kate return (if they return) and ask difficult questions.   Kate Grandison, Mike guessed, was still unaware at this point of the walking dead man's origin.   Let it remain that way.

He'd tell her it was his uncle Joe, back from the dead

to reclaim his property.

No sign of the ladies yet.   Dousing the gruesome creepshow host with a liberal shot of diesel fuel, he set the speedily-contrived pyre alight with a match, watching with grim satisfaction as the tinder and straw burst into flame with a *whoosh* and a horrendous, stinking gust of acrid, pungent smoke having its genesis in mold and death.   The bulky, decomposing carcass smelt like nothing Mike had ever encountered (sizzling as it burned like a rotten pork chop) nor wished to encounter again. It lacked the sweet aroma of roasting, fresh meat.   He prayed to whatever archaic gods manipulated the universe not to allow the putrifying, flame-engulfed corpse to jerk itself from its manure pile and inadequate pyre.

Half hour later all that remained were a motley assortment of large bones, cinders, and ash.

"Jodi?!"   Mike perambulated around the farm, calling out his missing guests' names in quickly rising apprehension.   To hell with the machine-gun he toted in his hands.   Better to be interrogated about the weapon than caught by surprise and dead.   He was, out here in his front yard he thought with alacrity, readily visible from the driveway.   "Kate?!! Where are you two? It's alright now, the thing is gone. Burnt. You can come out now."

No answer.

He was just about to return to the house and search through the smashed crockery and overturned furniture when the two terrified women crashed through the underbrush concealing the swamp behind Mike's cunningly aloof, but sentient, farmhouse.

Jodi began to babble aloud, tears streaming down her face as she dashed toward her solo, armed daylight patrol, a one-man killing machine who circuited his homestead daily with a concealed pistol. She leapt into Mike's arms, relieved, her slender body wracked with sobs as she kissed his ears and cheeks. Mike stood embarrassedly in front of the stolid, ashen, but calm Mrs. Grandison whose purple afghan had been torn by numerous thorns and hawthorn. The middle-aged woman bent over, gasping, and exhausted.

"Where is it, where is it?!" Jodi demanded, on the verge of hysteria. Mrs. Grandison gazed at Mike's automatic assault-rifle with a perplexed, uneasy, speculative look. Was this guy who he claimed he was? What had she and Jodi seen but a walking corpse without soul, animated by some unholy magician. Surely an assault weapon was futile against the diabolical forces at work on the farm! Aurora would be well advised to unload the place as quick as he could or at best lease it out to somebody. Perhaps it was he who was drawing the unwelcome presences.

"There's an effin' *walking* corpse on the farm!" wailed Jodi. "Oh god, Mike, it was horrible, it had no eyes, hardly any flesh left but still it came on, lurching grossly and kinda' bow-legged and stiffly and slow after we fled outside after the house started shaking and it started chasing us across the yard but…"

"I know, I know, babe," murmured Mike soothingly. "It's dead now. Finished. Caput. I set fire to it behind the Rosco."

Kate straightened up.   "The Ros…?"

"The steel silo," Mike indicated. "The one with the red logo stenciled across the top. I found the corpse atop of a low mound of bedding-straw looking rather tuckered. I burnt 'em as he lay there; don't ask me who it was 'cause I don't know, and I don't want to know, either."

Jodi wiped her tears away, feeling absolutely foolish and apologizing for it.

They trudged back to the granary in silence, around the back of a squat, round, steel grain bin.

The bones and cinders were gone.

Mike stared agape at the spot.   He distinctly recalled leaving his bitch, Shelly, cowering under his bed. Where had the bones gone?

Only a black pile of ashes and scorch marks indicated the site.

Aurora scratched his head puzzledly as Kate and Jodi looked on, mystified.

Suddenly opposite of them inside the garden enclosure, old uncle Joe's dilapidated '56 Massey roared to life, chugging coughingly as it idled, unmanned, mired at the edge of the garden. Jodi, Mike, and Kate stared mesmerized at the blue-gray puffs of smoke emanating from the iron horse's smokestack.

They bolted toward the house when the faded, red iron monstrosity lurched from its sinkhole of mud, creeping horribly towards them with a ghastly chug-a-chug-chug and its diesel breath stinking up the yard. Not a living thing sat at the wheel, its blank head-lamps looking like evil, extraterrestrial bug eyes over a menacingly grinning, tarnished metal grill.

Wisely, Mike yelled *"To the house!"*, spurring the three toward Aurora's diabolical abode which perhaps would be no safer than outdoors. Joe's ancient, rusted tractor was clipping along across the garden at a stately five m.p.h, smashing and grinding its way through the soil and pummeling the vegetables in the ground into pulp. The little tractor crashed through an aged, wooden barricade on its inexorable, onwards advance. Mike, Kate, and Jodi had reached the deck with plenty of time to spare, looking back in horror at the terrifying iron monster creeping toward his house.

"Get down!" yelled Mike.   The two did so immediately, not questioning as Aurora aimed his lethal weapon at the self-controlled leviathan crossing the gravel drive and turning suddenly toward the house.

He rattled off a lengthy burst of machine-gun fire at the advancing, diesel-belching monstrosity, bullets ricocheting dangerously off the mechanical beast's grill. The Massey Ferguson chugged forward unfazed.   Kate and Jodi screamed hysterically down on the deck, covering their ears during the assault rifle's short, staccato bursts of deafening white noise.

"Into the house!"   Mike hustled his now-incoherent guests into his home, slamming and locking the door when the first bone-jarring thud shook the building to its foundations.

The maniacal, unholy farm implement had rammed Mike's verandah.

Suddenly the machine's cacophony ceased.   The spent tractor sat below the verandah looking innocent and harmless, parked skewed out on the unkept lawn.   Its faded, crimson paint gleamed brightly under noonday sunshine.   Kate peered out the kitchen window at Mike's unholily unleashed tractor, the same tractor which two months previous had failed to start, even after priming, when he had wanted to move the corroding derelict into uncle Joe's barn.   A faint haze of diesel-smoke drifted bluish and rank over the farm's pastoral environs. The mechanical, lumbering titan had crushed most of Mike's garden produce with its enormous back wheels, leaving sizeable trenches in the black soil. The Massey's popping, oily, misfiring engine had ceased its menacing chug-chug-chug only moments ago.

Tentatively Aurora opened the door, peeking out to see if his abominable uncle's tractor be truly dispossessed. The ancient, overpowering smell of farmyard grease and decade-old, caked oil drifted across Mike's shabby, half-mown lawn and toward the house. The machine's oily engine ticked loudly approximately twenty feet from where Mike stood, awestruck. Across the untidy farmyard, a pair of yellow-bellied sapsuckers hammered noisily on an old, dead poplar. It was a wholly idyllic, and ironic, sight, the derelict tractor, woodpeckers on a tree, aspen, birch, spruce, hay meadow, flocking starlings, and rufous-sided towhees something which ought to be painted on nostalgic calendars, reflected Mike.

Cautiously he inspected the dormant tractor, satisfying himself that the murderous giant had been rendered harmless (but by whom – or what?). He thanked his lucky stars that none of the three vehicles sitting in his yard had been rammed by that unmanned, rampaging contraption. It was then that Mike seriously considered abandoning the farm; he knew he couldn't stand up to this.

Kate Grandison stepped off the verandah, horrified at the day's events, as well as last night's. Jodi stayed inside, hugging Mike's German shepherd as if calming the petrified beast, which'd sensed their terror. It had been a rough morning for Shelly too. The mongrel seemed to sense paranormal manifestations minutes before any mortal. From the corral Andersen could hear Mike's goats *baaing* plaintively. She wanted to leave immediately. Jodi knew nothing about the Anglican chaplain's disappearance, except for what little Mike had told her, and found it horrifying that a man could vanish into thin air in broad daylight; she thought it best that all three leave before someone really got hurt! She believed his insistence on remaining at this accursed farm bordering on insanity, a mere testament to the man's monumental stubbornness. His pig-headedness. Her love for this avenger-cum-super hero she found all the more exasperating and he wasn't making it any easier; Jo reflected that she ought to have suffered the pain and severed her relationship with this soon-to-be felon months ago. Mike was dragging her down into an abyss of grief.

"Mike, I'm leaving," she announced suddenly. "You two can play ghostbuster all day if you want, I don't care, but I am not going to be a victim to some psychophobic, megalomaniac kick of yours. This place is cursed, and I want no part of this charade. 'Bye."   She snatched up her purse from the cluttered, broken-tile floor.

"Wait, Jo," intruded Kate, laying a pacifying hand on the striding, younger woman's sleeve.   "Mike?"

"Yeah?"

"Is there someplace we can talk this over? The three of us? I'm intrigued with this case but I have to be candid," she said, wiping her nose with a Kleenex, "this place scares the hell out of me! I'd like to present it to the Canadian Parapsychological Research Institute."   She paused breathlessly.   "I think we have a genuine poltergeist infestation here. Is there someplace we could go. Someplace safe."

Mike hesitated for a long moment before replying. He really didn't want this snoopy stranger, this white witch, ghost sleuth, digging into his uncle's sordid past nor he and Jodi's recent criminal involvement.   He meant to refuse, but Jo cut him off mid-sentence.

"We can go to my place," she offered. "It's only a single room suite, but it's safe, at least."

"Mike?"

He hesitated.   "Sure."

"Shall we?" said Kate, leading the way down the verandah's trash-littered steps.

****

"Pour me another cup of tea, will you, Mike?"

Jodi sat with her legs crossed on a begonia-spotted sofa inside her apartment, beside Kate, shapely legs sheathed in inviting, rainbow hued, leotard-like pants with cool ring chains around her perfect waist and a style which Mike could only sum up as imitation spandex. She wore a   black leather jacket with red cuffs and a sexy, silken, magenta halter-top beneath.   On her feet were high-heeled, toe-pinching black leather boots. Like most young women, Mike surmised, Jodi dressed for style, not for comfort.   She'd changed out of her more rugged, rural clothes into suburban attire.   Aurora stood inside Jo's tiny kitchen fetching sugar and cream; his mind wandering.   The others sat on a large couch discussing the weekend's harrowing events.

Mike stepped into the living room carrying a tray laden with a glass teapot, cream, and sugar.   He deposited the sterling silver tray (a family heirloom) onto a coffee-table then slumped down beside Jo and gave her a reassuring, one-armed hug to which she responded with a long, lingering kiss. Mrs. Grandison squirmed, for she'd not experienced such romance with her frosty husband for eons. She felt like excusing herself as Aurora caressed Jodi's jacketed shoulder then brazenly caressed her thigh.

"Isn't he a bear," remarked Jodi when Mike released her. Kate smiled, blushing and wishing she were somewhere else, feeling her neck and face flush hotly. She'd been carrying on an affair with an uninspiring local dentist in Weyburn for over six months.

"Mike, can I ask you a question?" inquired Kate.

"Sure. Shoot."

"Why do you stay at the farm. It's haunted by *extra-ordinary* occult emanations and hallucinatory tactile manifestations, so why stay? Why not leave, move in here with Jo?"

"Vandals," responded Mike coolly, never missing a beat. "Can't trust anybody these days, least of all young punks."

"My boyfriend is an extraordinarly stubborn man; he's overly self-centered, obsessed with independence, and claims he needs silence to write his stupid book," interrupted Jo sweetly. She looked at Mike, eyebrow arched, as if goading him into a confrontation.

He just smiled and said, "If the shoe fits, wear it."

"Have you considered offering it up for sale?" queried

Kate.

Mike shook his head. "Nope. Got more chance selling A-bombs in Saskatchewan than farmland at decent prices, right now."

Jodi got up and went into the kitchen, returning with a plate of cookies.

The three of them talked intermittently, puzzled, attempting to assemble the missing pieces to Mike's bizarre story. Firstly, no motive for the haunting. Secondly, no corroboratory evidence to back up the entity/entities' claims. Mike remained silent on crucial remarks, not daring to risk telling Kate the entire story. He had lied, covered his own tracks, committed murder. How could he confess such to a mere stranger? Jodi silently prayed he would tell all.

Afterwards Mike had driven home alone, deep in thought as he passed through Spiritwood, a thriving community illuminating the night from many miles away with a dazzling collection of colored lights, street lamps, house lights. It was a typical, prairie town. Kate Grandison had left Jo's place three hours before he, needing to get back to her family in Weyburn. She'd told her husband she would be visiting her older sister Clara in Meadow Lake. Mike and Jo, who'd been sending each other signals of sexual frustration all evening, had fallen into each other's arms the moment

Kate closed the apartment door behind her.   They had made passionate love in Jodi's bedroom, kissing heatedly, exchanging positions until midnight.   It had been almost two weeks since they'd last coupled.   A much needed release from the weekend's horrors, the two had melted into one another like old, high school flames.

After their languorous, lingering lovemaking, Mike had dressed.   He'd told Andersen he needed to be alone for a while, time to think, clear his head.   Jodi had to go to work in the morning anyway, after the end of a long-weekend holiday.   She'd understood, or so he believed.   But in fact she thought his excuses tawdry and irresponsible.   Hadn't he had long enough to think things over?   Typical man, balking at a free place to stay for the night.   Headstrong as a god-damned donkey. She'd known no one else and had no plans in the foreseeable future of doing so.   Now Mike drove at a brisk speed beyond the outskirts of Spiritwood as he passed through the sleepy little town and out into blackest night.   He was thankful old uncle Joe wasn't a travelling companion.   He wouldn't relish the old man's disembodied presence here in the car.   Or was the demented spook watching him from the back seat?

Mike peered into the rear-view mirror, sighting only the distant, glowing lights as they receded from view. He felt a chill down his spine.

He <u>was</u> alone, wasn't he?

He slid a tape (Fastway, *Trick or Treat*) into the car's cassette player, headbanging and singing along, mindlessly losing himself in the primal, barbaric beat of his depraved music.

Fondly Aurora reminisced on Jodi's sexual finésse, cursing himself now for leaving her warm, naked embrace at this wee hour of the morning. Why hadn't he stayed. Why was he driving the one-and-a-half-hour trip from Shell Lake at this time of night, was he nuts? Was he suddenly developing a brain tumor, for Chrissakes? He enjoyed performing cunnilingus on her, as much as she enjoyed giving him head. He imagined himself behind her now, screwing her (agonizingly slow), as she liked it, until the ravishing bombshell screamed in delight. Any day could be his last for lovin' her. Mike fully expected the police to take him away at any time. He was screwed, just as sure as God made green apples. Up the proverbial creek without a god-damned paddle, man. Ten to fifteen sentence (modest estimate), doin' time with a sick bunch of queers in prison, those gang-bangers of recent inmates. By god, by god, Mike promised himself, if he were in power he'd impale these sickos slowly and exhibit them on cities' outskirts as a warning to others. He'd never been molested as a child, but he knew other kids who had been. Foster kids like him.   Yes, indeed, ought to torture those effin' homos publicly till they die.   Hey, I'm not depraved.   No sir.

But he wasn't going to prison.   Oh, no, no, no…

Mike arrived home around three-thirty in the morning. He was disgusted with himself, wracked with exhaustion; tormenting himself for having left the comfort and familiar scent of Jodi's bed.   He had to admit it, though, he was worried about the farm, leaving it alone for such a stretch, his dog, cat, farm animals left with a maniac, stone-throwing poltergeist.   He was tired and listless, depressed, feeling down on himself, down on life.   He thought of committing suicide.   But Sir Conan wouldn't do that, would he, no sir, he'd fight till the end, victory or death.   Fight till death.   But Mike Aurora certainly was no Bronze Ages' warrior-bard, had no idea how he would get through all this mess.   He sat in his parked car, head on the steering wheel as he considered what to do next. The station-wagon sat quiet, engine shut off and ticking sonorously.   He was sleepy.   Mike switched on his headlights, scanning the witchy-looking farmhouse. Recently he'd repaired his wind charger, and his sorry-looking verandah was now illumined with a 12-watt bulb.   No other light lit the house.   A stiff, cool, freshening wind, hinting at rain, blew in the rat-trap homestead's vicinity.   He still paranoidly feared a break-in while he was away or, worse, a death-visit from a smuggling syndicate.   The clapboard farmhouse's interior was a shambles, he knew.   Uncle Joe's doing. Mike realized that in order to go to bed upstairs he would have to plough through broken dishes and various refuse. What else had occurred since he'd been gone?   Had the mischievous bogey tore his bedroom apart?   What about his tapes, stereo, CD's, novels, mags?

Mike got out of the car, stretched, then stalked grumpily towards the faded blue-green farmhouse while giving the crazily parked tractor a wide berth.   Psycho tractor, new movie.   Metal-man meets the boogeyman. Lilac curtains screened the darkened kitchen window. Had he noticed one twitch?

Hallucination.

Inside the foyer, Mike got a disconcerting surprise.

What the hell?

Someone – or more correctly, *something* – had spotlessly tidied up his house. (!)

"Uncle Joe!" Mike shouted. "I'm going to set fire to the outbuildings. You don't mind, do you?"

A low moan from upstairs gave Mike the shivers.   He held his flashlight, aiming it toward the stairs.   Shelly the Dog came bounding with a bark from the living room, momentarily giving him a heart-stopping scare.   For the dozenth time this month his stupid mutt had mysteriously gotten into the house, although her kennel was outside.

"How are you, mutt," inquired Mike, rubbing the dark-brown German shepherd's furry collar.   He'd first named the pup Debby, but found she responded to "Shelley" or "Mutt" better.   Mike observed that the dog seemed oblivious to uncle Joe's nefarious presence, most of the time; maybe she had discovered a way to tune the old rascal out (though the disembodied crank gave Mike the heebie jeebies all of the time!).   Also over the months that the big, half-grown German shepherd was probably safe here, alone.   Apparently uncle Joe had a soft spot for dogs.   If for nothing else.

He traversed the ground floor in mild exasperation. He had psyched himself up for the titanic chore of cleaning the house.   Again.   The powers of Satan were at work here.   Literally.   No use trying to reason with the old codger upstairs, might as well accept this boon. You know what they say, thought Mike, never look a gift horse in the mouth.   But he found it difficult to imagine the scene as uncle Joe's invisible powers of darkness reconstructed smashed glass, tidied up, and swept the floors.   In fact, Mike found it quite impossible to imagine.

Maybe I should just turn around and drive back to Jodi's, Mike said to himself.

"Uncle Joe! I order – I order! – you to depart this house and go wherever the hell dead people go when

they die. You 'yere me? Leave this place now, or I's gonna light those sheds and all that remains within with a big, fat bonfire right…goddamn…now."

"What's the problem, Michael?"

The deep, gruff, elderly voice shocked him more than he cared to admit.   He hadn't expected to be answered. Aurora hesitated, before speaking again.

"This is not your house anymore, old man, so leave. You're dead, remember? And I'm not! You don't belong here. You've been dead for three years, uncle Joe. Time you left, time you move on out, time you mosied on over to the Other Side, know what I mean? Why you want to hang around here? Aren't you wanted someplace else?"

A depraved, gratingly-mocking devil's laughter floated down from upstairs.

Mike shook his head and bravely headed upstairs.   He could almost feel the old man retreating before his noisy advance.   Having bested the bogle in physical combat once, Mike felt little fear, knew his dead uncle to be a craven coward.   Child slayer.   He knew Joe's type, had beat up plenty bullies in his day.   Mike daily wracked his brain searching for a way to silence the spectral visitant for all time.   He strode upward with gas lamp in hand; yet leery of the dark.   (One never knew what shiver-me-timbers, creepy thing uncle Joe might throw at you.)   He'd not rigged-up proper lighting on the landing upstairs.

Aurora quickly undressed then climbed into bed.

****

■■■

He took the Yamaha moto-cross for a spin across the rolling pastures next morning. The long-shanked, fibreglass machine boasted plenty power, ripping up the track with its wide, knobbly rear tire.   YZ125, 1978 model, faded yellow, like nothing Mike had ever owned. He'd had a Honda 75cc mini-bike as a kid in Belbutte. Aurora thrilled to the machine's loud, bleating roar as the big bike raced over grassy hillsides and through knee-high alfalfa on the meadow.

Until he hit a big rock and wiped out, hurting his knee.

Tentatively, Mike drove the off-road machine back to Warehouse #2, as he called it.   Lucky he hadn't banged his unhelmeted noggin on a rock out there in the fields. The stench of two-cycle exhaust fumes was nostalgic to him.   He'd always wanted a big bruiser like this as a kid. His foster parents had been too cheap.   (Though they'd been loaded.)

Afterwards Mike, awestruck, rolled one of the

Kawasaki ATVs out of the shed and coaxed it into running, the only quad he'd been able to start so far. Bright green, it ran like a top. Here was a big boy's toy he could really enjoy, roaring about the fields with the added security of four wheels. It even had reverse! Handy. 250 cc's of pleasing plastic power beneath his thighs (but disguising an iron horse). He wished Jodi were here. She'd loved the numerous rides on some of the stolen, inherited motorcycles. Mike wasn't worried some yokel might spy him from the road. What did they know of his financial status?

Who cared what they think.

Did they ever stop by to invite him for supper? Hobknob? Nope. And Aurora preferred it that way. He was too good for the fat cat farmers and their gossipy wives who lived hereabouts. He often heard their mega tractors, bailers, combines, and other expensive farm contraptions out in the nearby fields, or saw them trundling down the gravel road, chewing it up with their mighty tires. Ass holes. (Mennonites, most of them, of the most extreme Fundamentalist mindset - many refusing to drive a vehicle, preferring their horse and buggy.) He still recognized a few of them, privileged punks he'd went to school with for a couple of years before being transferred to Prince Albert like a piece of human commodities' market, and he occasionally met their red-faced, moribund progeny who had treated him like shit (ah, fond memories of hockey tournaments and school outings!).   Once he had been seen riding the old Harley recently down a gravel side-road by a crew of redneck jellybellies having their lunch-break beside a huge, fire-engine red combine parked alongside a saskatoon-berry-bush-festooned roadside verge.   One of the peckerheads gave him the finger.   He'd felt good, cool, speeding along on his derelict low-rider with shades on and his long, straight hair streaming out like a biker's. He adored the big Sportster (wishing it were a softtail, though) with its high-rise handlebars, long front forks and neat, twin-cylinder engine and badly tarnished, chrome, oil-filter cover.   Not to mention the giant headlamp in front.   What a cool dude he was riding that deadly hog.

Aurora stood admiring the bikes, arranged all neatly in rows, like a motorbike dealer appraising his inventory. Today, Mike figured, would be a good day to wheel these suckers out into back of beyond with all the other stolen crap of uncle Joe's.   Inside this enormous, garage-like wooden building he felt safe, certain of a quick hiding place should some brave ****** come strolling up toward the granaries.   He wore a pistol beneath his plaid-checked, red/green flannel shirt at all times.   Or most times.   And ready to take on all comers.

Mike strolled away casually from the musty building, carefully checking the padlocks on the other two. Monstrously high, prairie quack grass grew unchecked around the outbuildings. The ancient-looking sheds stood some four hundred feet away from the house in a meadow of their own brimming with Canada violet and rare lady's slipper crawling with fat yellow/black honey bees. Aurora thought about acquiring a set of used bee hives from somewhere. He would love to produce his own honey.

The date was 1 July, Canada Day. He had little to celebrate except for his continued freedom. Mike glanced at his expensive, quartz, Swiss watch (stolen) then strode back toward the distant farmhouse pondering why the senile old man (or whoever) had built the incongruous-looking farm implements' sheds so far away. The dilapidated outbuildings held no machinery of use to the farm, ironically.

For two weeks he'd neither seen nor heard a peep from the demented being infesting his house. And for several months hadn't encountered anymore hoodlums come to claim their contraband (not to mention a score to settle with him). Five of the hoods had been done away with so far. How many more were there? It was strange the R.C.M.P. hadn't been gallavanting around locally asking questions. Only once had Mike seen a cruiser on the grid road way out here in the back of nowhere. Aurora's police record was spotless, only one speeding ticket to his infamy. He'd long since ceased monitoring the video screen. It had been a foolish pandering to his nuttiness anyway to set the damned thing up. Mike had disconnected and removed the surveillance cameras. He had a hard enough time keeping up with his 12-volt energy demands, as it was. If yer' gonna die, might as well die with yo' boots on, boy, he figured.

He found the house's verandah cool and nostalgic-smelling, of old, decaying, sun-heated lumber, fresh paint on the window frames, and of course the ubiquitous herbs hung up to dry in a corner. He had begun to repaint some of the balustrade, but hadn't finished it. Dill, rosemary, sage, basil, oregano (the remnants of last fall still hanging there) dangled crisp and deliciously spicy at summer's height, a natural potpourri or air-freshener. Much of the hodge-podge, ex-cabin, farmhouse's exterior as well as interior were in desperate need of a fresh coat of paint. The big shack was flaking off its last, faded layer like a snake sloughing its skin.

Mike thought about contacting Mrs. Grandison, and arranging some sort of witchcraft ceremony to try to exorcise the house of its revenants. Kate remarked how her coven leader, a Mr. J. Ovelich, might consider ridding the harmless-looking though antiquated farmhouse of its "troubles", merely memory imprints (walking corpses notwithstanding) according to Kate. Okay. Only the coven master, she'd informed him, was authorized to attempt such a dangerous procedure. Mike wondered if he could somehow arrange for some hack to write about his haunting someday when he's out of jail, or maybe even make a movie of it like the Amityville Horror story. With him as the star wacko, of course.

Or maybe he'd even write it himself while in the slammer.

It was when he turned on the radio one morning that Mike heard of the mysterious spate of disappearances which seemed to be occurring in the region between Shellbrook and North Battleford. Six men so far, including a minister, had been noted missing, none local but known to have been seen in Leoville, Old Battleford, Shell Lake, Turtleford, and tiny Medstead. Mike's heart jumped three storeys. He turned up the volume as he listened to the details, which, by all accounts, seemed to be the most exciting thing to have happened since the start of WWII around here.

The net was closing.

Three vehicles missing, two rentals from major rental agencies, Hertz and Avis. The whole district was on red alert (Aurora could almost hear the klaxons sounding), abuzz with gossip and innuendo. Strangers roaming the communities were being questioned. Whispers of incomers practicing secret Satanic rituals like in the Martinsville affair. Church authorities on the warpath. A serial killer on the loose. Tire treads being examined by forensics experts in Shellbrook and Leoville. Whoa!

When the police search the farm the shit will hit the fan, thought Mike with the jitters.

Time to take an extended vacation to Hawaii.

Or China.

****

■■

Never one to shy away from grisly, macabre trouble, Aurora found himself on the 21st digging for a third body on Nimchattans' property, some distance from the empty, silent, vandalized manor. It stared back vacuously at him with gaping windows. It was a bright, moonlit night. Jodi and Kate stood beside the excavation, shivering in their jackets as a brisk, north wind blew across the wild -strawberry-blessed farmyard. Surprisingly (and bloody fortunate too, thought Mike), no dogs barked from the nearby hog-farm across the road. Kate found that unusual. She stood with her hands in her jeans' back pockets, worried. Mike was nuts. His story too hard to believe. Mass-murders in the community. Jodi had shown her the diary Aurora claimed had been written by his dear, dead uncle. He'd told her none of his involvement with the seven (or was it eight?, he'd lost count) missing persons who were now common gossip. An array of bright lights across the road made the TV-lit Nimchattan ranch-house look like an ocean liner on a murky, gray-black ocean.

A silvery, crescent moon hung from the night sky. Myriad twinkling stars lit the black heavens.

Aurora dug three feet down, then stopped for a breather. He found the digging tough going. Rocks and roots were everywhere. Hard-packed clay, clinging, chickweed mantles of vegetation, thistles and tough prairie quack grass made the excavation maddeningly slow. He had chosen a spot nearest the trees, far from the eerie, derelict, hipped-roof manor house which seemed to watch them with black, soulless eyes. It was an odd assortment of small, unpretentious windows high above and gothic, church-style window frames below, sadly vandalized over the passing years. A spacious, gaping, maw-like doorway faced the three jittery trespassers like a toothless mouth. Through it a small portico of sorts led into the sorry edifice. Kate and Jo stood sipping coffee, silent as detached mourners. Both felt sacrilegious and superstitious as crones as they stood there watching Mike excavate an oblong, grave-sized hole.   Their skin crawled.   He had shown them a shakily drawn diagram in Joe Aurora's senile hand.   The farmyard, according to it, was a virtual mass graveyard!

Black hulks of machinery sat in shifting shadows. The three trespassers stood in partial, moonlit darkness, the two women drinking creamy Sanka coffee from white mugs.   Kate had brought along a thermos.   Aurora laboured, shirtless, in the pungent-smelling hole.   A grave, purportedly.   The obnoxious odor of red elderberry, a shrub not native to the province, evidently, wafted across the cryptic yard.   Or was it a skunk just passing through, thought Kate?

Five-and-a-half feet down, Mike heard an angry shout from some roadside shrubs.

Mike leapt nimbly out of the unfinished grave, tossing away his shovel and reaching for his jacket.

A bulky, overweight, looming youth tackled Mike from behind, anything but what he had expected!   He yelled for the scampering women to flee.

Clearly Mike's opponent was no Kung Fu fighter, ungainly attempting to pin the wily Aurora to the earth but instead being lifted bodily through the air by a deft heave of his powerful thigh muscles, landing the attacker in a nearby brush pile.   In fact he was rather youngish, not so much overweight as big-boned, Mike realized as he met his youthful adversary in a renewed head-on charge. In faint moonlight he could easily discern the youth's unfamiliar face. But what of himself? He grappled furiously with his foe, outwitting the bib -overall-dressed country bumpkin and repeatedly slamming a big fist into the unfortunate's face. The miscreant hadn't even asked what we were doing here!, thought Mike to himself. Cool as a cucumber, he sucker-punched his surprised, mysterious opponent, obviously a Nimchattan boy whose head rocked back with each carefully aimed uppercut.

The two wrestled furiously as Kate and Jodi watched from a distance, mortified, unsure what to do, cringing in the protective shelter of the homestead's spruce trees. The solitary stranger had chased Mike across the rocky yard a mere eyeblink after being felled with a right-hook whollop to the chin which would've stunned a horse. Anticipating his determined assailant's baffling, resumed chase, Mike spun around, meeting the farm boy's tackle (he was a farm boy?) with an infuriated snarl, wrapping a meaty arm around the potbellied bohunk's neck. Now the two grown combatants scuffled viciously beside the looming, two-storey manor house. Pushed backward towards the denuded, tar-papered wall, Aurora seized the younger man's platinum blonde hair and pummeled his face like a bullying NHL hockey player/enforcer beating up his less-wily opponent as the refs watched.

Mike tripped the tall youngster (whom he guessed was about twenty or so) to the ground with a bone-jarring crash, straddling the redneck's chest as the vanquished attacker's head hit a chunk of cement hard, dazing him.

Aurora, seizing his shovel, fled toward the shrubbery.

****

For several days Mike awaited either the farm boy's appearance or that of the police. He had the sneaking suspicion the youth was in on uncle Joe's dastardly scenario somehow, though in what way he couldn't specify. Had the big, strapping, 18-20-year-old recognized him, he wondered? Mike couldn't see how he couldn't have recognized him. He was something of a recluse, but for his next-door-neighbour not to have identified him bordered on the sublimely ridiculous.

Mike, Jodi, and Kate hadn't managed to unearth any more graves.

Meanwhile Jo had been complaining of nightmares: having witnessed warfare with barbarians through

Melissa's eyes, horrified by the brutality and gore experienced by the tall, lithe, but courageous warrior-Queen of Caledonia. Somewhere in the misty Caucasus massif, too, Jodi had seen nomadic invaders vanquished to the last man, woman, and child, crucified or decapitated in blood-soaked fits of vengeance. It was a blood-drenched vendetta. First a Circassian and then an Armenian people had been subjugated and forced to pay tribute, eventually vaulting themselves (with the help of hired mercenaries) onto the ancient throne of what would become Čätäl Hüyük in Anatolia and reshaping the moribund, pan-Cimmerian empire of Hatti, the *Chatti*, or Getae, of Austria (the Hittites, whom had defeated Babylon, then Egypt, successively, though, ironically, no one people but a loose confederation of mercenary Free Companies). The sheer, mindless violence which the bloodthirsty Sarmatian queen instigated was mortifying, although the enemies of Chaltea had perpetrated worse on the peaceful north-folk of Asia's steppes, and on Felissa's clansmen in the Ukraine. Jodi, trapped flailingly within this nightmare dreamland, watched helplessly as dying men had their entrails examined for omens. Witchery, wickedness, abounded all the lands (in the guise of sinister cults), prophets and shamans on one side or the other burnt alive or tortured, sorcerers and devils, saith many.

In the hot, arid land of Canaan, a series of military setbacks suffered at the hands of marauding Shemites put the Chaldean inheritance in jeopardy, a priestly and aristocratic class of proto-Celts – the Samaritans – amongst the preeminent Phoenician-Akkadian population. Meanwhile the peaceful mountain tribes of Assyria, confused with and tainted by the Canaanites' sick, depraved rituals of bestiality, incest, bisexuality, and endemic infanticide were wrongly indicted by the colonizing Judaic zealots and massacred under cloak of night – an act of cowards, the maidens taken as concubines by the pot-calling-the-kettle-black Israelites who now occupied the Sarmaritans' lands.   But the Chaldeans' wrath would soon be monstrous; with Philistine mercenaries, an Akkadian king, Nebuchednezzar, would thrash the fighting spirit out of these Aramaic camel raiders and horse thieves, enslaving the "righteous" zealots till the fall of Babylon to the Assyrians.

To the even-more mysterious East, tribesmen dwelling on Siberia's southern steppes were being overrun and assimilated by loosely-allied Inuit, Mongol, Na Déne (not necessarily in that order), Kazakh, Ugric and Goidelic freebooters, their customs and dialects adopted, reshaped, reversed to suit others' needs, until some day in the long-distant future some Soviet archaeologist would unearth one of the natives' Kurgan mounds and discover a blue-woad-tattooed Caucasian male with animal motifs etched on his frozen body; like his consort, eviscerated and mummified so some Russian ethnologist could identify these freeze-dried wretches and their sacrificed horses and attendants as Scythians.

(What they'd found, in fact, were Ossetic-Iranian nomads who had made the steppes their home as far east as the northern border of China after a millennium-long diaspora from their Farsi homeland in India.)

Kate Grandison had been perplexed and deeply disturbed by Mike and Jodi's revelations. The two seemed to be genuine cases of reincarnation. Unlike the Hindustani religion of idols and demi-gods, a nation of superstitious fools thought Kate, her much-maligned cult, Wicca, believed in transmigration of souls but not Karma, which she knew to be an Aryan-Indian caste system meant to keep the poor and the dark in subjection. A country of fraudulent gurus, shamans (Latin "shaman", "simulator.").

She'd made inquiries into the farm's history at local libraries, newspaper printers, provincial historians. Saskatchewan history seemed, for the most part, devoid of the type of lurid murders and other, sordid occurrences which had bedeviled older provinces like Alberta, Quebec, B.C., Ontario, Newfoundland. A few unexplained disappearances however had occurred in the Lakeland district in the fifties.   It was these Kate found disturbing. Ten children and sixteen teenagers had vanished between 1951 and 1966, mostly runaways, or orphans, or Gypsies, or Cree Indians.   None, to this day, had ever been found.

Kate surmised the farm had been a psychic depot of atrocious happenings: one of the most "happening" places in North America.

On the way home she thought about Mike's case and its implications.   Over the weekend (staying nights at a hotel in nearby Glaslyn) Grandison had explored the old farmhouse for signs of possible fraud, trapdoors, secret passages, anything.   But found nothing.   Zilch.   Her training as a psychologist (whilst training for a doctorate of parapsychology at the University of Regina) had taught her all the myriad phony tricks and equipment numerous hucksters used; among them tape-recordings, trick mirrors, gauze, "ectoplasmic" jelly.   Missing, however, was the motive here for a sham haunting.

The summer night was overcast and dark.   Kate drove along in her '95 Cutlass, her mind in the shadow zone. The sedan's halogen high-beams barely pierced the dark night as it sped homeward, and a fog was starting to rise. Clouds obscured the stars and moon, threatening rain. The grid road from Mike's farm, branching off from a T between Leoville and Spiritwood, boxed in by trees on both sides, was rough and potholed (as if scarcely used) and made driving difficult because of a heavy layer of gravel. Her low-slung, expensive, gray-brown sedan jolted with each sinkhole. Along the roadside, gigantic Jack pine offered convenient perches for nocturnal, yellow-eyed, long-eared owls.

The iridescent glow of eerie, avian orbs caused Mrs. Grandison's heart to catch in her throat until realizing they were the night-vision scannings of statuesque birds of prey.

Kate felt a chill down her spine as she swung the big, luxury, Cutlass Supreme onto the highway toward Spiritwood, where she would spend the night before resuming her journey to Weyburn the next morning. She glanced nervously up into her rearview mirror, momentarily imagining having glimpsed a grizzled face there. A second, terrified glance reassured her there was nothing.

A pair of icy, unseen hands seized the steering wheel, struggling with Kate's grasp as it forced the vehicle off the road.

■■ ı

****

One, two, three, four, five, six, seven, eight…

Mike Aurora, mantled in darkness, counted off silently the strides. The diagram had indicated eight paces into the forest, as if anticipating someone's sleuthing for bodies, or daring him perhaps to delve into the mystery. Beyond the old-growth spruce stood grim, quiet, Nimchattan house, scene (purportedly) of horrific murders. It was a ghastly dark night; too dark to be out doing this, reflected Mike, never knowing when someone might reach out and grab you. He understood the terrible risk he was taking after his last confrontation with whoever was guarding the place, whether a Nimchattan good ol' boy or some other ruffian. He was alone. As usual. The broken-down homestead stood a considerable distance away.

He just had to know how many bodies were buried here. Behind a screen of venerable, old trees Mike felt safer doing his skullduggery than out in the open where he'd be vulnerable to ambush like a nesting prairie chicken. He had his revolver with him. For six weeks he had waited for the farmer's son (who else could it have been?) whom he'd beaten up to visit him for a reckoning, maybe with a couple of friends for backup. Inexplicably, no one had showed up. Had the fellow been seriously injured, he wondered? Or, more insidiously, part of the unholy ring of smugglers, kidnappers, rapists? Aurora had left the bohunk dazed but conscious, that he knew.

However the 'gravesite' had been filled in and laden with grass, leaves, and boughs of pine.

Before turning himself into the police Mike needed to know what exactly had happened during those dark years in the fifties and sixties. He could imagine a relic '50s Ford pick-up truck cruising the streets of local towns, scanning for teenagers out after curfew. Mike, fearful of the big youth's return yet obsessed with his mission, felt crushed between compulsions like a crab stuck between a rock and a hard place. He knew full well that the stranger might be waiting nights, weeks even, watching so as to apprehend the mysterious, badgerish, excavating culprit.

Mike heard of Kate Grandison's near-fatal accident out on the highway toward Spiritwood. He'd learned of it shockingly from an acquaintance of his in nearby Medstead whom he'd gone to school with for almost two semesters and who now was a burn-out dope dealer, ex-fireman, and former boyfriend of Jo's who wanted in on the action. (Her action, that is.) The woman had broken both her back, and her leg, in the ghastly car crash, fortunate indeed that a local roadside household had witnessed Kate's collision with a power pole and telephoned an ambulance quickly.   The white witch almost certainly would've died in the collision.   Mike and Jodi had gone to visit Kate at Spiritwood's general hospital and been told her harrowing story about the invisible hands steering her car off the road.   Kate had been in traction, but conscious and reasonably well considering the circumstances.   She'd insisted the nurse allow Mike and Jodi into her hospital room.

Aurora had been watching the abandoned farmyard since that afternoon.   He'd spied no one about, though work was in progress across the road, likely building repairs of some kind.   The old acreage stood a fair distance across the gravel road from its owners' working silage and pig farm – a noisome-smelling place – so his spading of earth oughtn't be heard, he'd thought at the time.   But after a few inches Mike had lost nerve and retreated into the underbrush like a common criminal, waiting instead for the dark blanket of night to fall.   He figured it was certain they didn't own a dog; if they did, it was a miserable guard dog.   Mike had driven his station wagon and parked it some ways down the road in a well-concealed trail to make a quick getaway should he be discovered skulking about, shovel in hand, on the farmer's mossy, stony, prime real-estate.

An owl's hoot gave Mike a start as he stood there in the darkness under huge trees.   He wanted to go home.

He had better things to do, surely, than spending his nights digging for bones in an abandoned farmyard. What was he, a nutcase? Admittedly, he relished the danger, and the challenge. He liked risk. Mike could get his head blown off tonight, though.

This time he found nothing.

Several hours wasted of back-breaking labour, scrounging about in the dirt in pitch darkness, feeling for bones. He'd found only gargantuan roots, pebbles, stones. And a half-corroded tailpipe. Now his back ached. Six-and-a-half feet down he'd calculated, and had hit only sand. Mike had widened the pit in the slim hope of finding the target.

He found it much easier to refill the graves than to dig them. Aurora worked in darkness, fumbling about like a mole. He kept an eye out for approaching trouble, shambling amidst the leafy security of trees, nervous as hell as he spied the brown, two-tone, lit-up ranch house across the road; every once in a while he'd catch a glimpse of someone passing an uncurtained window backlit by flickering, blue television radiance – most likely the local evening news. A fine mist of rain drifted down from black, midnight skies, overcast and humid. Only occasionally had Mike flicked on his muffled flashlight to see where or what he was digging. The delightfully nostalgic aroma of dark green, leathery aspen leaves or a variant of such (known as *balsam poplar* he alerted himself) whose leaf resin reminded him of pine, brought back fond recollections of his none-too-exciting childhood.

Aurora filled the musty hole in, covered it with leaf litter, then meandered cautiously across the unlit farmyard/lumberyard toward the old, hip-roofed farmhouse. He took thrill in exploring (and, sometimes, vandalizing) abandoned old buildings, although he'd not set foot inside the sorry relic since he and Jo had been chased away by those inexplicable, blobbish, white things from up in the attic. Ghosts, he could hardly believe it. Should be used to such improbabilities by now. Ought to become a professional ghost hunter, thought Mike. As a kid he'd even kept, packed in a briefcase, all the accoutrements of a modern-day ghostbuster. That, too, had not panned out.

He climbed a short, simple flight of red-brick steps and entered the old Nimchattan house's exotic, baroque foyer, his flashlight muffled with a silk sock. Awed by the manor's weird, antiquated grandeur, he strolled about, on tiptoe, not afraid of spooks anymore. The worst they could do was chase him, right? No fear of the Nimchattans sighting his yellow-blue beam, for the structure's windows were facing the opposite direction. Most of them were boarded up. Into the derelict, empty living room Mike crept, eyes and ears on the alert for anything unusual.   Anything at all.   The ancient, tomb-like manor echoed resoundingly with Aurora's movements unnervingly.

He climbed up onto a solid bay window to relieve himself out its gaping frame, peering down into a jungle of overgrowth.   A faint, westerly breeze stirred the leaves of poplar and elder-bush.   Mike held onto the sturdy red cedar window frame in case he should fall the ten feet or so through shrubbery and broken glass.   The unbidden thought of somebody (or something) creeping up from behind and giving him a shove out of the high, three-sided window pricked Aurora's not-overly-superstitious conscience.

Immediately Mike felt a vicious shove between his shoulder-blades, the only thing saving him from a nasty three-metre plummet the fact that   one arm still braced the empty window frame.   He fought against the icy, unholy pressure trying to diabolically push him out the window.   With both hands he strove against the relentless pressure exerted against his back as he hung onto the bay window's frame with all his might until, suddenly, the distinctively human *yet not human* presence vanished as quickly as it had come.   Mike hadn't even heard the trickster's footsteps creep up from behind, nor its retreat.

He ran from the old house and never looked back.

****

He met the Grand Sorcerer in his dreams for the final, monumental combat.

Conan met the magician's sword with a mighty parry of his own, pushing the magi back toward the serpent's lair. A gargantuan, anaconda-size, python the size of a house awaited the battle's outcome with silver slit-eyes, coiling mesmerizingly about inside its iron cage in a cave within the Hall of the Mountain King. Awaiting its morsel of human flesh. As an oversized boa-constrictor, its scales glittering with a green-gold zigzag pattern, the serpent would naturally squeeze the life out of its prey before devouring him whole, swallowing the struggling morsel slowly. With a reverberating clang of cold steel the Cimmerian launched another ringing fusillade of blows at the magician's hell-forged steel, flexing his enormous, bronzed thews with the strength of tensile, cast iron from the finest ironmaster's smithy. Conan's foe was withered and old, beyond human reckoning in fact; a streaming, white-haired crony with the body of a leper.

Yet he fought with the strength of ten men.

With sorcery the seer summoned the dark powers of Hel, the old man's uncanny, blue, blind eyes possessed of a reddish, sparkling fire. A fire not of this world. He'd been blind, but now he fought with demon's eyes. The war god Tyr, Jupiter, Duw, Theos, Yawah, Allah amongst many names, the Usurper, eventual destroyer of all that is good dwelled within the withered, reanimated crony's dead body. Conan had killed him earlier in the evening with a lance thrust from his horse. Milleniums ago he, the priest Dían Cecht, had sacrificed Melissa. Now her consort's reincarnated soul fought in the pumped-up flesh of a distant descendant, battling the perverted powers of evil which threatened to flood the world with a deluge of evil intentions.

The prophets had spoken, aeons ago, of the war god's son-to-be, Krishna, who would come to the world as a messenger of good, a Saviour, Iesu Christ, the master of lies and Bright Deceiver. He whose minions would corrupt the world for two thousand years and more.

Conan the shepherd's son had been chosen from amongst many to do battle with the Leviathan, and to slay the unholy serpent, Set, depraved idol of a thousand nations – if he could. If not then all must fail. And Conan, Crom's dark champion against Light, King Conan to all and sundry, had never tasted failure in a thousand campaigns ten-fold. Today, he must not fail, victory or death, because, consigned to the flames would be his nation, while a new, diabolical, ethnically inferior race of sub-humans called Latinos, Germans, Slavs, Anglo-Saxons, Gaels, Romanians, Hungarians, Finns, and Basques would inherit the earth and pollute the Holy Mother unto death with their evil deeds. They were actually a new species-to-be, a clever clone, a look-alike falsely dubbed Homo Sapiens Sapiens who would become a cross between thinking man and still-extant, walking, cannibalistic, brutish man-like ape (archaic Homo sapiens – you know who you are). But less noble than a carnivorous dinosaur: Known as *Cultosaurus Erectus* (Allosaurus on two legs, wearing a top-hat and wellies). And all men represented in those distant days-to-be would be of his ilk. Aborigine, Caucasian, civilized, savage.

At the twelfth hour, the fates had miraculously weakened the horrible monster dwelling within old Tzi Shi's wizened, corrupted body. Conan, naked but for a loincloth in a hall of flames, battled the necromancer, who wore a black robe with silver stars mercilessly, batting at the mad priest with a magic sword of bronze.

Until the sword broke.

****

The shepherd-king dashed his broken, enamelled sword hilt at the Incarnate's ugly, leering face.

His spiral-incised, gilded weapon nonetheless slammed into the old man's slavering jaw, its jagged yet razor-sharp alloy embedding itself in the wizard's purulent head with the goring impact of a bull's horn.   Tzi Shi gaped in agonized surprise, gripping the fantastic gold pommel with gnarled, tattooed hands and squealing like a swine being butchered.   The evil enchanter sunk unto his knees, only inches from the frenzied, coiling, monstrous serpent's cage.   The old magician's eyes began to dim, then glaze over.   Victorious, Conan seized his vanquished foe's mighty, steel broadsword and decapitated the dying immortal, holding up the horned devil's blood-dripping head in smug triumph.   He, a mere peasant's son, now High King of Vanaheim, had won.   He, Conan the Destroyer, had defeated the world-to-be's unholy powers arrayed against him, the merchant axis alliance of Athens, Berlin, Rome, New York, London, Moskva, Babylon, Carthage, Ur, Mexico, Teotihuacan, Beijing, New Delhi, Brussels, Paris, and all other defilers of his sacred earth.   Great nations had been vanquished this day, entire language affiliations canceled as if from a computer screen.   English, Latin, Amerindian, Chinese, Greek, Africaan, Slavonic, Germanic,

Hindustani and a countless host of other imposters had painlessly ceased to exist, as if silently and lethally poisoned by a new and deadly chemical weapon attacking man's central nervous system, released in cities across the globe with an innocent-looking fog.   All this Conan, son of Lucifer, had attained this day.   A new subspecies of humans would be summoned to colonize the earth, plundering silent, forlorn metropolises around the globe; a new speech, one never villified with the innocent blood of millions, sent to reprogram obedient survivors.   A dialect not heard in regions for thousands of years, a proto-language, to the expectant, traitorous folk to their own nation's creed as yet undifferentiated. For the immediate future, the only worry would be how to quickly dispose of the millions of dead of the human race's filth which had polluted his planet in Conan's absence and enslaved themselves.   All this Conan ab Lucifer had bequeathed to the survivors of the Holy War, the War of Light, truly a war to end wars.

The triumphant empire-destroyer held up the dead magi's long sword with both hands over his head in thanks, an irascible, self-confident grin on his lips; praising and adulating the approaching Earth Goddess and her Consort, great Beli, the Wind Lord who walks the earth as an invisible but palpable presence, a giant, a Cyclops.   Parabolus, His alternative name.   Cong glanced toward the beast coiling in its lair.   The Guy was hungry.   Smirking, lit by a smoking dozen of torches upon the hall's blackened, sooty walls, Conan seized his decapitated foe and pushed the stiffening, bloodied body within reach of the serpent's lair.   Ywah slithered slowly toward the proffered feast, coiling around the dead wizard's feet and dragging the Pope, His own vanquished champion, between the open portal as Conan stood grasping the three-inch, ensorcelled bars of steel of a towering gate, the monster drawing its booty inside a malodorous snake's pit toward the gigantic constrictor's looping coils.

Conan had plenty of time now to consider how to destroy the distracted serpent.

"God bless you," whispered the tittering walls.

****

Mike awoke with a startled gasp.

He lay in bed on the second floor, sweating, trembling. The recent images of charred, desolate, urban sprawl replayed in his mind; a world of dark chaos, endless putrifaction and death, heaped masses of bodies to be burned. Gas chambers. Concentration camps. Epidemics. Vignettes of horror, played out in the 22nd century.

Chemical and nuclear warfare the lethal offspring of his infernal, fertile dreamscape. He could scarcely recall his earlier, nonsense nightmare set in some Bronze-Age cornucopia teeming with dragons, giants, anaconda-size serpents, wizards, trolls, seers, goddesses, gods and evil messiahs who had come to destroy the world, not save it. Mike was confused. And then the second nightmare had come along, describing a holocaust world of Aryan supremacy, genocide, a world gone woefully wrong. The apocalyptic date of 2026 sprung to mind, a year of sneak-attacks by a newly formed nation which had utilized chemical warfare and, finally, a Star Wars technology to jam their enemies' signals and obliterate countless major cities with a kind of nerve gas. Worse yet, the cunning perpetrators had seemed despite all of this a noble, democratic culture of Welsh-speaking militants (!) colonizing the Western hemisphere, preaching a dual-sided-coin doctrine of egalitarianism, peace, fire and sword, plunder and genocide. Fallen were the mighty U.S.A., capitalist Russia, Britain, France, Italy, among others, left to ruins and decimated in a righteous but *unholy* war, a holocaust instigated by modern-day witchcraft sects, the descendants of persecuted sorcerers burnt at the stake in the Middle Ages.

DNA warfare, broadcast over radio before-hand,

allowing the aggressors' sympathetic but ultimately powerless allies (themselves the victims of militia-dominated regimes controlled by ultra-religious riflemen's associations) time to evacuate their homes, for the impending cloud would leave untold numbers dead on the streets of towns, villages, hamlets, communes. The formerly-democratic Western nations had succumbed to a religious revival of neo-Mormonism, in any case, since the fraudulent elections of 1999, 2005, 2010, and 2020, leaving the tiny, newly independent Cambric state once known as the British principality of *Wales,* other than Canada, the only free countries in the entire northern hemisphere! In Mike's ghastly, surrealistic nightmare the wretches had gathered at various check-points, declaring their brotherhood with the newly-forged invaders, separating the chaff from the wheat, while frauds were systematically obliterated in fiendish gas chambers. The usurpers' novel, deadly weapon had wiped out entire nations within hours, leaving the surrounding wildlife untouched. Most of the world's teeming metropolises had been forever silenced, forbidden entry except by men and women wearing decontamination suits in order to plunder the murdered inhabitants' cornucopia of goods. Brain scanners instantly detected the cowardly survivors' motives, intentions, way of life. For the crime of enslavement of one another, for the multitudes of animal species since ancient times made forever extinct because of sheer avarice, for horrific gender and race discrimination, for pacifism and allowing murderous criminals the elixir of life, uncountable millions were eradicated at the push of a button. Christianity, Judaism, Islam, Shintoism, Buddhism, Hindu and a score of primitive religions worldwide had one day ceased to exist save for a small band of terrified guerrillas hiding out in the world's mountains and tropical jungles, vowing revenge. Hunted by helicopters, heat scanners, spies.

Horrible.

Aurora lay in bed for over an hour, unable to return to sleep. It was still dark outside. The mare had taken him, on this night, for a wild ride indeed!

He sat up, switching on his battery-operated nightlight. Opened a dresser drawer, extracting a sheath of papers, clippings, invoice statements. Mike held them gingerly in his hands, peering blearily at the scrawled figures. He had found them only yesterday morning behind his bedroom wall by accident, idly peeking in through a loose seam of unpainted plywood.

Here were invoices from three or four Regina warehouses and one in Winnipeg. Just exactly why old uncle Joe had hid them here, almost as if for somebody to find, Mike had no idea. Quantity stats made up the bulk of the pink, blue, and white invoice sheets and carbon papers. Four warehouses had been the target of heists way back in the seventies. Mike had yet to make head or tail out of the information. Somebody, apparently, had master-minded a nighttime series of burglaries with authentic-looking semi-trailer transports, and unloaded the contraband at this most unlikely of places. He found it hard to imagine three eighteen-wheelers rolling down the Ranger-junction grid road and then over the field trail leading to his uncle's acreage. However the names of several individuals on the onion-papery invoices seemed to suggest a high-ranking company official or executive's connivance. He could imagine three big semis with freshly-painted company logos and corporate headmen flashing phony authorization papers to unwitting guards.

Aurora got up, wandered about the house till sunrise. A gorgeous, sunny day had been forecast. Good day for some weeding in the garden (or what was left of it) then some writing later on. Mike was well into the fifth revision of "Return of the Vampire…1993" and quite satisfied with improvements made so far. He'd been writing inconsequential short stories for some ten years, but only brief sorties, never novel length. They'd been shit. His cool, childhood chums had thought him a kook, but often laughed at or been grossed-out by Mike's horror stories.   Ghostly yarns, psycho thrillers, monster trilogies making up the bulk of his amateurish, earlier writing.   He generally wrote with a pen then revised several times with a typewriter.   Already Mike reckoned he'd spent over $200 in writing materials this past year. He knew one guy, a real berk, who'd spent over two thousand dollars alone on postage over the last nine years, one Eric Jobeson, whose quaint historical toilet paper had been rejected so fast and so unanimously by Canadian, British, and American publishers that Aurora thought it a wonder the weirdo hadn't flung himself from a bridge. Eric, this minor acquaintance of his (a loser if ever he saw one), had so far written a novel set in 13th-century France, a flop horror nobody'd liked about a punk-rock band in Siberia, and a gruesome gut-turner chronicling Vlad Tepes' horrific impalement spates in 15th-century Transylvania which even had the gall to present Dracula as a Dacian-Celt hero, champion of the peasant.   What a dude.   Jobeson had let him read an unfinished manuscript one time in P.A. and Aurora had thought it a load of hooey.   Mike would've liked to have read the guy's other work, but Eric lived in Yellowknife now, although he'd once been in the same class as he in Prince Albert elementary school, but had since moved.   Only occasionally did Jobeson visit his old high-school chums in central Sask.

A beautiful day unfolded as forecast. Mike ate a hearty breakfast of No Name granola cereal and apple juice then headed outdoors for a couple hours' gruelling slog in the garden, then some clean-up chores around the yard. He'd gotten out early, having finished breakfast and washing-up by eight. A pristine, deep blue midsummer sky devoid of clouds arched overhead. Land of eternal skies, as prairie dwellers fondly referred to it. Flies buzzed maddeningly around ancient-smelling farm dwellings. Green-throated hummingbirds flitted from flower to flower, poking their long probiscuses into anthers for the delectable nectar. Two sprawling apple trees (whose spring blossoms only a couple of months ago had freshened the air) stood inside Mike's mangled garden, laden with half-ripe fruit.

A dull green Chev van rumbled into the yard, having traversed the thistle-overgrown and thickly-nettled trail alongside Aurora's alfalfa meadow, having crept up so suddenly Mike was surprised he hadn't heard its noisy, muffler-less engine before then.

Three men jumped out and opened fire with semi-automatic rifles.

Mike barely had time to leap behind a massive pile of bedding straw. He'd been hit; his left calf muscle had taken a slug below the back of the knee, piercing a leg bone. Groaning aloud, in excruciating pain, Mike clawed and wriggled his way out of the field of fire. Another attacker leapt from the back of the van waving what looked to be a Kalashnikov assault-rifle. Four dead-serious men in balaclavas were now advancing from different vantage points with rifles at waist-height; he could hear them charging but could see naught but a searing red pain through blurred vision. The pain of his leg-wound had suddenly increased. Hissing through his teeth and ignoring as best he could the unbearable, burning sensation of a bullet-wound, Mike clawed at the revolver beneath his clumsy T-shirt, sweating feverishly.

Ten feet away and advancing, the masked men scattered when Mike Aurora flung his arm over the great dung-heap and opened fire erratically. None of the blue-jeaned intruders were hit, but Mike's wrist, bucked by the .45's barking explosions, felt broken. He'd fired three shots blindly, way off the mark.

A series of deafening, high-pitched gunshots sounding like a Civil War battalion's fusillade responded to his gunfire. It was shootout at the O.K. Corral for sure, thought Mike, except he had no clan gang to back him up. He cringed when their bullets whizzed overhead or slammed into the bulky dung heap. He was pinioned between the corrals and a wide-open garden area, his left leg shattered. He was a dead man. Hunted, no longer the hunter.

Two of the armed rogues had taken cover, waiting for Mike to pop his head up over a dung-heap the size of a small house.   Two others had dashed into the farmhouse, a fourth man having leapt late from the back of the battered van, dashing upstairs toward Mike's room overlooking his front yard – a convenient sniper vantage from his open bedroom window.   He could see they'd have a clear shot at him from there.   It was plain they didn't care a rat's ass who they killed; an entire family could have been holed up here for all they knew.   Mike waited fatalistically for the end.   All of his folly had come down to this shootout.   Alone.   Outnumbered. Injured.   He raised the pistol and put its barrel in his mouth.

Just then the soft purr of another vehicle's entry into the quaint, suddenly-quiet farmyard momentarily stilled Mike's hand.   There came a short, puzzled cry of warning and then an explosion of high-powered rifle fire.

Heedlessly Mike stuck his head over the top of the pile, having crawled laboriously to its shitty crest.

Andersen's little red '77 Datsun swerved off of the drive, pelted with a noisy barrage of gunfire.   Great craters imploded into the defenseless car's metal body as Jodi's hatchback veered onto the grass.   Three of the men had ran out into the open for a better shot.   Mike caught a glimpse of Jo's terrified expression just above her steering wheel.

She swerved her Datsun toward one of the hapless gunmen who'd gotten a little too close.   Mike raised his revolver to shoot, his hand trembling uncontrollably. Fifteen feet away or so the aggressor facing Jodi's hatchback raised his rifle, aimed at her windscreen, and pulled the trigger.

The windshield imploded with a horrendous collapse of thousands of tinkling chunks of safety glass.   The racing Datsun kept coming, tires spitting gravel, bumping into the fleeing marksman and catapulting him over its hood.   He flip-flopped over the hatchback's other side, finally landing on the drive with a broken back.

"Aim for the friggin' gas tank!" someone yelled.

Mike let off a volley of gunfire as the four, remaining gunmen aimed at Jo's car sitting inert, skewed sideways across the unkept lawn.   One of them, the dude with the bulky machine-gun, ducked around a corner of the house, another scurried in a crouch across the grass toward Jodi's car.

Mike sighted nobody now inside the dull red four-door.

He jammed another round of ammo into his .45's revolving chamber and recklessly opened fire again, emptying all six chambers with another round waiting in the palm of his hand.   The looming house's western-style verandah splintered with each booming crack of gunfire.

The ruffian with the Kalashnikov returned fire with a deadly salvo of high-impact machine gun bullets whizzing by Mike's head in excess of six hundred rounds per minute, a short burst of only a few seconds' duration.

Jodi poked a tiny handgun out the passenger window and fired once, surprising and slightly wounding a creeping assailant as he rose up into view only five feet away from her small import's flattened, front left tire. The swarthy, Mohawk-haired attacker (last from the van, and unmasked) clapped a meaty hand over his left arm, grimacing wide-eyed with gritted teeth as he retreated, cursing, towards a decaying stack of lumber nearby, diving for cover; still clutching his high-powered rifle.

Another fusillade ripped over the noonday breeze as the three remaining thugs aimed for Andersen's car, one targeting Jodi in the front seat, another her scarlet Datsun's gas tank.

Both missed their targets.

Aurora launched yet another futile series of shots, fighting gunfire with gunfire, preferring to die with a fight just like the gunslingers of old. Someone fired a volley of rifle shots from an upstairs window, missing him entirely, swiveling a carbine in Mike's direction who was either punch drunk or had never fired a weapon before.

Aurora shot him between the eyes, and sat up, marvelling at his marksmanship...

Andersen surprised Mike by opening fire from her Datsun's smashed windscreen while the hatchback was being riddled with semi-automatic gun fire; her pea-shooter no match perhaps for the .306 carbines and what not but nonetheless a dangerous factor. Where the hell had she gotten that dinky thing, Mike wondered? (She had emphatically refused a Colt .38 handgun that he had offered her last year.) He felt a surge of misplaced pride as he slid bullets into his revolver's magazine, then fired again. He wore an ammo belt, heavy and uncomfortable around his waist, but the ultimate in hyper-preparedness; a bulky giveaway along with his pistol, but not so noticeable when wearing an oversized T-shirt, sweater, or flannel shirt as he often did. Just like the criminal he was.

Mike heard a loud cry from the verandah. One of the skulking besiegers now scurried along its recently-varnished balustrade with a dragging right leg. Good shot, Jo!, Mike marveled. He trained his .45 Magnum at the old lumber pile, waiting for the other, temporarily disabled assailant to reappear. The granite-jawed offender stayed out of sight behind the ancient stack. Mike kept one eye on his flaking, A-frame, storm-gray farmhouse lest one of the trespassers (like, say, the dude with the big Tommy gun) skirt around and sneak up on him from behind.

One of the men lost nerve and ran pell-mell for the antiquated, olive-green van nearby, jumping up into the driver's seat before Mike could get a good bead on him. The madly fleeing trespasser (the one with the Kalashnikov, ironically) ducked down and cranked the groaning, oily-smelling van's engine to life.   It sat only meters away from the house steps, facing the ripped-up verandah with its weathered, antique wagon wheel and years' old moose-rack for decoration.

Another rascal fled stumblingly for the van, chickening out, then another.   No license plates were discernible on the ageing, run-down vehicle.   Mike fired a trio of shots, then allowed the intruders to jump into the Chev Maxi-Van through its back doors, two wounded chumps with injured arm or wounded leg, the last pulled into the van now on the move as it wheeled about and did a donut on Mike's gravel driveway, spitting pebbles as it roared off toward the meadow.   Mike rang off a volley of shots at the retreating vehicle's rear end, punching great holes in it.

Then around a corner, and it was gone.

Aurora collapsed atop the looming dung heap, smiling with relief, head on his arm as he marveled at today's bizarre stroke of luck.   Obviously he'd been dealing with no big-time crime syndicate here; no Russian gangsters or Taiwanese hoods.   They couldn't even take out a lone gunman.   No Mafia hit-men would've turned tail so fast, he was sure.   The rank odor of manure, fresh and ancient alike, had never smelled so good, so indicative of life's joys taken for granted.

Jodi came running from her car, waving her tiny, snub-nose pistol in her hand as she dashed toward Mike's bulwark, calling his name hopefully; her voice rising to near-hysteria.

She found him near the top of the manure pile, sweat-stained, shit-smeared and bloodied; in agony, but in great spirits.   Jo knelt in her nylons on the mostly rotted, earthy-smelling bedding straw, much of which had been there before his uncle's demise, hugging Mike as he rolled over and embraced her young, supple body.

■■

SEVENTEEN.

Uncle Joe's spirit had disappeared.

No bumps in the night, moans, groans, or clanking chains as was the old man's wont.   Jo and Mike sensed it immediately inside the house.   The change.   Gone was the cloying atmosphere of doom inside the early twentieth-century, former log cabin, converted farmhouse. Mike had told the doctors he'd been wounded in a hunting accident.   Four months had elapsed since the shootout with the five, nameless strangers.   Another grave had been arranged for the slain one left behind.

Mike had turned himself in to the police in August of '96.

And awaited his Retribution.

EPILOGUE:

"Political observers are horrified at the irresistible charisma and dogmatic left-wing fascist connections of Llywelyn Morgan, a.k.a Michael John Aurora, the rising, up-and-coming candidate for Prime Minister whose supporters openly boast of an Aryan New World Order at this weekend's long-awaited debate in Ottawa. Morgan's new and totally unanticipated party's leapfrog in the opinion polls has put his Commune Alliance Party way ahead in the latest polls, according to Reid Statistics' Bureau. Morgan, the fifty-five-year-old candidate and well-known, bestselling author of twenty-six novels, biographies, various non-fiction and controversial ethnological and anthropological works, has captured the hearts of Canada's disgruntled middle-class majority with his Ten-Point program dedicated to eradicating crime and putting environmental agendas once more on the nation's conscience. Even more controversial, Morgan's unabashed

Welsh nationalism and racist rhetoric has inflamed the hearts of millions here in this country, promising to repatriate literally *millions* of hectares of farmland and to reinstate capital punishment for numerous, serious crimes. Already, Human Rights' organizations have launched marches protesting Morgan's proposed torture laws for sexual assault and other gender-related offenses across major cities in Canada, unanimously condemning the Commune Alliance Party's stand against homosexuality, organised religion, and lap-dancing. However, political forecasters predict a Morgan sweep in the election at the end of this month due to a skyrocketing child-molestation epidemic sweeping this country since Prime Minister Cretién's same-sex adoption policies thirty years previous. No question, Morgan possesses an uncanny ability to stir the masses into a frenzied fervour, rather frighteningly reminiscent of Adolf Hitler's diatribes in those dark ages of World War Two and leading up to that sordid holocaust. Jewish militants in Toronto have also condemned Morgan's assertion that the Judeo-Christian legacy caused widespread environmental and gender stereotypes and abuse since the fall of decadent Rome to what Morgan, as a professional historian ostracized by mainstream academia, contends was a highly civilized and liberating pan-Celtic, not Germanic, army which destroyed a corrupt Roman slave-state. Ironically,

Amerindian nations across the country have applauded Morgan's diatribes against the very European descendants whose ancestors nearly wiped out the bison herds of North America and relegated the aborigines into reservations with only the very poorest lands for sustenance. He also has advanced the preposterous idea that ancient Europeans were the *first* to settle the New World, citing the contentious finds of skeletal human remains of acknowledged Caucasoids in Washington state over thirty years ago. Clearly, Bob, this surprising Commune Alliance Party has captured the imaginations of ordinary Canadians across the land and inflamed its opponents."

"Yes, Derek, I would agree. However, many of Llywelyn Morgan's opponents have concentrated on some of his party's more ludicrous election promises such as mandatory martial arts' training courses for children in elementary school, and have aimed derision at Morgan's proposed official language status of Welsh with English, Cree, and French, pointing out quite rightly that very few people in this country have actually learnt to speak Brythonic, as he has, even though the rest of the Commonwealth has already given it official status. No doubt Mr. Morgan, himself, has been almost single-handedly responsible for resurrecting this ancient language, having cracked the Cretan Linear A, C, and D hieroglyphic and alphabetical stone tablets on the island of Crete, off the coast of mainland Greece, several years back and humiliating the world's scholarly community by identifying the pre-Hellenic civilized and, apparently, peaceful, Minoan society's speech as an early Welsh or Breton dialect, which flies directly in the face of twenty-first-century scholars and those previous who had portrayed ancient European culture as a savage, Celtic race without any civilized refinements, even so far as to say that they lacked the bow and arrow, a contention that Morgan claims was *indeed* true for the Goidelic or "Q" Celtic-speaking Gauls who fought naked and on foot with slingshots. Even so, some academics are still reluctant to accept Mr. Morgan's controversial decipherings of the Cretan Linear tablets, choosing rather to vilify his character and pointing out his rather rabid Welsh nationalism. Certainly much of Greek and Roman history, if what Mr. Morgan says is true, will have to be rewritten."

"Yes, that's correct, Bob, and undoubtedly the so-called Democratic Commune Alliance Party, or CAP (no relation to Communism, incidentally), has had to play down their candidate's murder-trial and subsequent acquittal some thirty years ago which had the entire nation's rivetted attention. But back then the young would-be author's name had been Mike Aurora, a Canadian citizen who later changed his name and went on to become one of the world's premier linguists and most respected anthropologists. Here we have a gracefully ageing, handsome, fiftyish, erudite celebrity in this election, running for office in one of the G7, (fourth-rated), countries and promising practically the sun and the moon to get a vote. I don't know about you, Bob Cole, but I find this know-it-all upstart chillingly reminiscent of a Genghis Khan or Stalin."

"I agree – ah, here come the candidates now, Mr. Morgan and his wife Jo, Liberal candidate John Perry of New Brunswick, NDP candidate Sue Every, Reform Party candidate Preston Manning Jr., and current Prime Minister and Progressive Conservative leader Bud Weiser up to the podium. Let's give them a hand, folks –"

■■ ı

<u>About the Author</u>

Albert A. Ernst, fifty six, hails from Glaslyn, Saskatchewan, Canada, and has studied, as a hobby, over thirty Indo-European and non-Aryan languages as diverse as Mandarin, Japanese, Hungarian, Gaelic, French, German, Romanian, and Welsh. He has also lived on Vancouver Island, off-grid, for sixteen years. Mr. Ernst spent the summer of '92 touring various ancient sites in England, from medieval castle ruins to stately homes, hillforts, and megalithic monuments. Formerly employed with L&M Wood Products, Sask., as a trim-saw operator (14 years), he is now semi-retired to work on further writing projects. Operating a hybrid 1.1 kw solar/wind array, producing his own power, Albert's hobbies include gardening, playing guitar, reading, writing, exploring abandoned farmhouses on motorcycle, and listening to heavy metal music! (Up the Irons!)

His other books include "VLAD DRACULA: THE

IMPALER" (a novel of historical horror), published by Austin Macauley Publishers, 2024, and a recent re-release of same (via Ingramspark, KDP, Draft2Digital, etc.), an updated version published in March 2025. Go Check it Out!!!!!!

www.ingramcontent.com/pod-product-compliance
Lightning Source LLC
Chambersburg PA
CBHW020638120726
47906CB00001B/25